# DREAM

## CATWALK SERIES - BOOK ONE

### S. Q. ORPIN

ISBN-13: 978-1-7329732-1-3



Published by Wild Hibiscus Press

PO Box 1761 Lafayette CA 94549

Cover created by Fresh Design

*Dream is dedicated to my parents, for encouraging my creativity and making the dream seem possible.*

# THE CATWALK SERIES

The Catwalk series was inspired by the exciting but perilous world of modeling in Los Angeles. Dream was motivated by an accident that redefined the life of the author's model-niece, Sterling. Wanting to give a voice to additional characters and in response to a 'What next?' storyline Catwalk expanded to a five-part series. The stories encompass a deep examination of characters struggling to find meaning in life and love.

The books are written from multiple viewpoints allowing the reader to explore the diverse characters, while delving into the deep, and sometimes dark, human existence and tumultuous relationships. The series contains adult situations and language, including sex, trauma, and violence.

**DREAM** introduces the cast of characters and the relationship developing between Casi and Kyle. It layers the superficial world of modeling with the lifestyle of a small-town man, creating challenges and pitfalls. **HOPE** continues as reality and conflict consume the couple and supporting character storylines develop. **TRUST** explores the emotional rollercoaster of love, career, loss, and coming to terms with the past. **SEEK** reveals secrets and back story helping the characters move forward as emotional scars are healed. **LOVE** is the final book in the series, which spans five years, achieving triumph and finding meaning in life and love. The series primarily focuses on the main characters of Casi and Kyle, but supporting characters are intricately woven throughout the five books.

*Dare to Dream, Hope, Trust, Seek, and most of all, Love.*

.

1

———

# BACKSTAGE

"Three minutes, girls!" belted the overbearing Mary Anderson, more lovingly referred to as Mother Mary, by the models of Beyond Modeling Agency. A dark-skinned, plump woman, of indeterminate age, suspected to be in her fifties, she bustled around the show preparing them for the catwalk. As an independent manager, Mary was part counselor, part friend, and part general. Fussing about their appearance or scolding them for their tardiness, Mary kept herself busy fixing hems, plucking stray hairs, and concealing bruises or bad decisions. Perpetually immaculate and professional, with her rounded figure fitted into designer clothing, and the ease of a woman comfortable in her skin. With the efficiency of a drill sergeant and the tenderness of a mother, Mary consistently produced a bobby pin or tissue, ready to wipe a tear or redirect a negative attitude.

A dozen years earlier, a fresh-faced and shaky-kneed Casi Roberts stumbled down the catwalk in poorly fitted six-inch heels. As a vigilant protector of young women, Mary intervened, preserving Casi's innocence as she stiffly posed for a cheeky photographer with intentions beyond capturing the latest fashion with his Nikon. With stars in their eyes, new arrivals assumed they became celebrities as they attended after-parties and clicked with the 'crew' which frequented the newest nightclubs and celebrity affairs. They posted detailed accounts on Facebook and Instagram, as if the 'likes' verified their success.

After a trip to the Cayman Islands on a yacht partying with celebrities, Casi had been crushed when Mary informed her she couldn't attend future events. Pictures posted online featuring a popular actor with his yacht full of attentive groupies, contained a background with an underage Casi, topless, drink in hand. No one else cared about the individual girls, seeing them as colorful wallpaper for the celebrity. But Mary refused to let her be categorized as 'model ass', as a blogger tagged the bevy of beauties. It was difficult at first to turn down the invitations, but Casi soon realized the promoters were paid to fill an order for a certain type of girl. She recognized the benefits of being on the fringes and enjoying the perks of the celebrity scene, without the unwanted attention. She remembered Mary cupping her face, saying, "Baby Girl, you're better than this. Don't let them use you as a mattress. They won't remember your name in the morning. You'll be put out to pasture with the other hopefuls long before your time should have been up."

Casi cringed at the recollection of Mary's stern warning about her career being on the precipice between success and failure, and the constant reminder about aging out of the business. Pushing the thoughts from her mind, she wriggled into a skin-tight, spandex mini-dress, adorned with chains and an obscure, abstract animal pattern. The catwalk didn't intimidate her; she could prance down it blindfolded and not miss a beat. The runway brought comfort, predictable and superficial, with no real consequence. Overly made-up and masked to mirror the nineteen mannequins parading behind her, Casi liked the anonymity of the job. Life outside of work seemed to be the challenge.

From the time Casi turned seventeen, she had been 'handled' by her overbearing stage mother, Sonya, and any agent who took a slight interest in her until outgrowing their 'image'. At her 7th agency in twelve years, Casi lost count of the places she'd lived, never settling long enough to call anywhere home. A natural beauty from Burnaby, Canada, blessed with fine, classic features, and large hazel eyes. Discovered on Kitsilano beach, Canada; a head-turner in a floral bikini, honey blonde hair swinging past her sun-kissed shoulders. At the time, her name was Cassidy, but the first agency insisted 'Casi' sounded edgier. At a casting call, Cassidy discovered she had been downsized by three letters, thanks to her mother's meddling. She had gotten used to the name, grown into it, in fact. The most frustrating part was correcting people when they only saw it written and pronounced it as Casey, and the continual struggle of teaching them to pronounce it with a short A.

Within a year of relocating to Los Angeles, Casi moved to her first model apartment. As an only child, it was a huge shock to find herself in two-bedroom condo housing twelve women. Each room featured several sets of bunk beds and two single beds. The women came from Europe, Asia, South America, and the United States. Each one eager to make it in the industry, but few got booked for significant jobs and went home in debt, dreams shattered. Sometimes Casi loved the living situation, making new friends and pretending to have sisters. It was fun to share outfits and makeup as they got ready for a night out, stepping over suitcases heaped on the floor. They gossiped and laughed the night away, having to mega-dose on caffeine to appear somewhat less comatose the next day. Other times, it became claustrophobic. Too many bodies, too many clothes on multiple surfaces, and a bathroom strewn with hair products and makeup. Brutal fights ensued, with hair pulling and fingernails flying. Not anything like the sexy catfights in a poorly written B movie, with pillows and hair tossing; these brawls usually left the victims dismissed from castings because of scratched faces and clumps of hair missing.

Casi double-checked her breast tape and took her place behind the curtain. The designer introduced her spring line, and her bold choice for the season, gray. "Shocking!" Casi turned to make eye contact with the girl behind her. Not surprisingly, every single girl had her head down, trapped in the iridescent glow of cell phones. Like dominoes, each person began taking selfies, hash tagging their posts, #model, #the-smell-of-success, #glamor-girl, and #chillin' backstage. Casi considered herself a pro with all forms of social media and frequently posted to keep socially relevant. She crafted an image of the sexy party girl controlling the situation. Avoiding the stereotypical drunk girl posts, with smudged makeup, tripping down the stairs like an amateur.

Her true self had become magnificently masked, and it was difficult to locate her. With a perfectly scripted, superficial life, Casi was the envy of her peers. Movie-star handsome, Alix Grey, the charismatic street artist turned famous graphic designer to the 'in' crowd, was a catch. If you didn't own a painting, bag, or t-shirt with one of Alix's designs, you weren't considered celebrity-chic. Although admiring his struggle to rise above his addiction, and a two-year stint in jail, to become one of the leading celebrities in the art world, Casi had an underlying boredom. She deemed the lovemaking adequate, predictable in its intensity and regularity. But other than being a trinket on his arm, she questioned if she mattered to him at all.

Mary's firm hand on Casi's lower back snapped her out of the fog. Time to perform. Swinging her long, lean legs and placing one foot in front of the other simulating walking on a tightrope, she fell into the comfortable pace of the stage. Shoulders slumped, eyes glazed, and a look of disinterest completed the model image. One, two, three, swing long brown hair over her shoulder. Four, five, six, turn to the left. Seven, eight, nine, end of the stage, broken doll pose for three seconds. Thumb in waistband and turn. With the swagger of a rock star, she completed the runway, ready to be primped, fluffed, and stuffed for the next run of designs. Breaking protocol on her way back, she glanced out at the meager crowd below. The blank-faced attendees tended to their phones or chatted with a neighbor, disinterested in the parade of half-dressed women on the runway. The designer, Elizabeth Manson, grappled with a disappointing year, having one flop after another. More knock-off than standout, her designs were a poor interpretation of trendy. The media raked her over the coals for her vapid model selection, weak color choice, and conventional style. Elizabeth Manson, was on her way down in the industry, making it painful to watch. Designers struggled to stay current in an industry obsessed with youth, beauty, and shock value. With the wave of reality celebrities, agencies scrambled to find a balance between the way things had been, and the lightning speed of sensationalism.

Casi smoothed her hand over her sleek, waist-length, espresso brown hair as the artist reapplied stage makeup. The heavy black eyeliner, creating the quintessential 'smoky eye,' overpowered her hazel eyes and gentle features. Encased in a black and gray leather dress with too many zippers, and six-inch, open-toed boots, she waited her turn behind the curtain and watched a girl strutting the runway; head held high, haughtily pissed off at the world, owning the stage. *Why can't I act like her?* Although confident in her abilities, especially in front of a camera, turning thirty filled her with a gnawing, disjointed ache. As she confidently strutted on the stage, the model ahead started to wobble around a turn. Casi winced, anticipating the disaster. Trying to recover from the misstep, the girl leaned right, balancing on one heel. The bored audience found a sudden interest in the impending disaster, cameras at the ready. Suddenly on her knees, breasts launched from their tape, and one ill-fitted stiletto dangling from her foot, the red-faced figure staggered to regain her composure. Casi sidestepped the train wreck with practiced ease, familiar with fallen deities.

At the end of the show, Casi rolled her hair in a tight bun on top of her head and slipped on her standard uniform of black leggings, and an Alix Grey designed oversized sweatshirt. She scrubbed off most of her makeup and headed toward the door.

"Casi, wanna hit the clubs with us? We have red carpet treatment with our crew at Tension. It'll be hella dope." Hanging out with models and a random, wannabe promoter at yet another new club was of little interest to her. There was no appeal to getting drunk on someone else's dime while you seat-danced to the music, and pretended to be the coolest girl in town, snapping selfies to prove it. Casi was a club regular, not needing a promoter to get in the VIP section. Dressing scantily and losing herself in the music while dancing the night away sipping champagne was her escape. But she wasn't inspired to do it next to eager, star-struck hopefuls, barely pushing eighteen. Underage girls were hustled through the back door, while bouncers were paid off as the promoters ensured the pretty ensemble they were the chosen few in a world of excess and instant celebrities.

"Thanks, but not tonight, Alix has an opening," Casi lied. They gazed at her with admiration. It was obvious the eager fans would take her spot as Alix Grey's girlfriend in a second. She also realized they tried on a regular basis.

Casi clicked on her Uber app and arranged a pickup, checking emails on her phone while she waited. A message from her father, Jack, telling her about his plans to change the menu at his restaurant to feature dark draft beers, suggesting a visit to try them. She smiled at his attempt to connect, despite her dismissal of him after he remarried. Several messages from her agency about bookings. One from her mother about needing money, with a lengthy explanation. She sighed and opened her banking app to transfer funds, having grown dispassionate about her mother's constant financial crisis.

The car arrived, and Casi climbed in the backseat, pulling her knees to her chest, and resting the phone on one thigh. Continuing to check emails and update Facebook with selfies from the fashion show, she lost herself in an alternate universe. An hour later, they pulled up to her address on Fountain Avenue, and she got out, still distracted by her phone. After the driver left, she realized her lack of engagement and acknowledged she floated through life in a haze and admonished herself for not being more present.

Casi trudged up the concrete steps of her apartment building. Despite being extremely fit, a result from her intense hiking workouts, a mysterious weight on her shoulders made it difficult to breathe. She removed her hair tie and unrolled the bun, concerned it restricted the flow of blood to her brain. Yanking open the solid glass doors to the lobby, she nodded to the doorman slumped behind the faded wooden desk. The previously spectacular 1920s mansion in old Hollywood had been converted to twelve apartments, showing its age with worn, faded wallpaper and threadbare carpets. The proximity to Sunset Boulevard and the main attractions made it a desirable address.

"Be careful around the wires, Miss.," the doorman warned. Casi couldn't recall his name. In his early forties, thinning hair, and nondescript, she rarely spoke to him in the past two years. Construction on the apartments was also a numbingly normal occurrence in her daily life. She walked by a partially open door and glanced in, expecting to see generic dark maple cabinets, black granite, and stainless appliances; the standard fare for the newly wealthy. Noticing the doorman settling back into a nap, she eased the door open to snoop inside. She was surprised to discover light pecan cabinetry, appearing to be hand-crafted. The workmanship was exquisite, even to the untrained eye, and she reached out to touch the creamy, smooth cabinet face.

"Can I help you?" a deep, husky voice asked.

"Sorry, I..." Casi started, but couldn't finish, mesmerized by sapphire eyes. She assessed the tall, lean frame, chestnut brown hair, tanned skin, and piercing blue eyes, rimmed with dark lashes. His handsome face, with a chiseled jaw, held her attention before traveling to his wide shoulders, tapering to a trim body, fitted with a t-shirt, revealing part of a tattoo on a well-toned arm. Her eyes continued their journey to a muscular stomach, taut under the thin material. Lingering over his slim hips, accented by a low-slung, leather tool belt, her skin prickled with arousal. The smell of the wood, mixed with the slight waft of cologne, made her weak in the knees. She had a sudden urge to know this man, intimately. To taste his mouth on hers and feel his strong, calloused hands caressing her.

"Casi, what're you doing?" Her happy bubble burst, hearing Alix's slightly nasal voice.

"I...uh." The stunted utterance made her seem medicated or demented. A crimson blush washed over her face as she attempted to back out of the doorway gracefully. Stealing a final glance of the mystery man she caught a smile in his eyes acknowledging he wanted her just as much as she instantly desired to be with him.

# 2

# THE KISS

Casi slumbered restlessly. She dreamed of the mystery man and the desire in his deep blue eyes. The connection was intoxicating and drew her to him immediately. She understood it was unlikely she would see him again when he completed the remodel. After endless hours of tossing and turning, she rolled to her side in the king-sized bed, cursing Alix's choice of satin sheets. She could never get comfortable, too hot or too cold, and a perpetual sensation of sliding to the floor.

Alix decorated the apartment to his unique specifications. Stark white walls with a white carpet, and mid-century modern furniture, featuring neutral shades, chrome, and glass. It was not a welcoming home, but he enjoyed the way the scant interior showcased his work. Most of his paintings were very large, well over six feet. The giant canvases with the bright acrylic paint loomed over the meager furnishings. Secretly, she despised his earlier paintings. She perceived them as commercial and shallow, made to appear edgy with the drips of paint and unfinished body parts of the skeleton-faced subjects. He presented himself the same way, haughty and bored with life, unable to tolerate the crush of the paparazzi. Casi was amused how, in reality, his agent called the press ahead of time to let them know where he would be. She gave him kudos for being a superior actor, always appearing annoyed by the attention, and pulling his signature leather jacket to half cover his face, yet revealing enough of his sharp jaw to be recognized in every tabloid. She was often with him, one of his fingers attached to hers in a casual, yet primitive sign of his ownership of her.

Casi had met Alix over four years ago, at a nightclub he co-owned, on an evening out with friends from her model apartment to celebrate her 25th birthday. An uneasiness enveloped her, worried about her age in the modeling industry. Not as tall as an average model, at five-seven, her dazzling hazel eyes and classically beautiful face landed her bookings in magazines and print ads. She typically didn't get runway work due to her height, but the designers sometimes chose her for their newer designs because of her comfortable, practiced gait on the runway, and ability to make the most ridiculous outfit, chic and stylish. Her mainstay was lingerie and swimsuit shoots, showcasing scandalous creations with her curvy, yet lean figure.

She wore her typical attire of black leather pants, spike heels, and a barely-there charcoal sheer top without a bra to the club. Her hair at the time had been the popular Auburn, which accented her eyes and creamy skin. Trying to maintain a size two was a challenge with her larger breasts and hips, and she usually avoided sweets. That night she had downed two pieces of birthday cake, which had been a surprise from her roommate. The sugar from the cake and champagne, mixed with the Red Bull in the car, made her queasy.

Alix sauntered in, self-assured in his well-worn, tapered, black skinny jeans, white graphic t-shirt, and leather jacket, oozing confidence and sexuality. She recognized him from the gossip columns, often featured with a model or actress, lounging on a yacht or a dramatic location such as Africa, looking sultry in every one of his adrenaline pumping activities. Shorter than most of the women he dated, but his dark, chiseled features, and well-defined body adorned with tattoos, gave him a Greek-god quality. He hadn't noticed her since there were too many mirrors to distract him en route to his private lounge. She contemplated he might be a challenge, estimating he had been with every woman in Hollywood. Casi considered being his newest conquest might be the change she needed in her life to help define her career, or at least make her the 'It girl', for the moment. She acknowledged a life with him would be written for her; scripted and superficial with minimal effort on her part. She walked up and gave him a seductive smile, showcasing her perfect white teeth and full lips. Alix visually undressed her, making it clear what his intentions were for her body, then extended a hand and pulled her on his lap. When she pressed her mouth to his, her immediate future was secure. The hint of tequila and tobacco set her skin on fire, and she noted she was headed down a road of passion and unpredictability, frightening her to the core.

Casi stretched in bed, focusing on the clock as the minutes ticked away to the early morning light. Alix's smooth hand slid over her side, gently caressing her thigh and coaxing her toward him. He skimmed over her hip bone, gliding past her ribs, resting momentarily on her breast, delicately brushing her nipple. She often sensed he evaluated her weight before they made love. He seemed to enjoy the fragility of her bones protruding; the skin taut as it stretched across her frame. Familiar and predictable, she usually found comfort in their bedroom activities. He could easily get her aroused, and she no longer needed to impress him. Four years had found them in a comfortable rhythm of busy working days, and nights out on the town. The sex originally was heated and exciting, monumental in its intensity, but gave way to less frequent and casual sessions, which filled their needs.

At thirty-eight, Alix worked hard at maintaining his body and looked better than most men half his age. Casi was attracted to him for what he offered physically, but more for the role he allowed her to have in his life. He took care of their finances and made the social plans. Rarely did she go out with friends on her own, or plan anything outside of their relationship. He pressured her to stay rail thin and remain in position two steps behind him. She was secure with the role, blasé expression, and an original Alix Grey outfit displayed on her fragile frame. As a walking canvas for him, she knew she could not let herself forget how fortunate she was. Sonya adored him, and he always played to her favor, loving the adulation. When Casi had cried to her about his first affair, her mother scolded her for being petty. Casi became efficient at minding her behavior and adjusting her attitude.

Alix breathed on top of her and she went through the motions of sex. She became antsy, and his touch felt alien and intrusive. She faked an orgasm, and thankfully he finished quickly. She swept away the covers and went to the bathroom. She stared at herself in the mirror through the foggy glass, shaky and foreign in her body. Again, the belief of an incurable illness and impending death came upon her and she started to cry. The steaming tears melted into her skin, waking up her senses and burning through the numbness. Alix walked in the bathroom and she pretended to wash her face. He lifted the toilet seat and started to pee, discussing the agenda for the evening. She giggled at the ridiculousness of the situation, and he scowled at her and shook his head.

$3500 for blood work, urine tests, x-rays, an MRI, and examination all revealed Casi was a healthy twenty-nine-year-old woman, much to her dismay. She hoped they would find a tumor in her brain to explain her disjointed emotions over the past months. *What would she have done if they told her she had three months to live and needed to get her affairs in order? Would she slip out of this life as quietly as she lived it? Would anyone notice she was gone? Would anyone take her Facebook account down or would she perpetually be immortalized as the sexy girl dancing at the club?* The thoughts gave her a chill as she walked inside her apartment building, stopping to pick up her mail from the row of boxes on the wall.

She glanced at her blurry image in the tarnished brass, tucking a stray hair behind her ear, tired of the neutral brown. Casi peered at her outfit; black yoga pants and a crop top, with a black crocheted baggy sweater, lightly skimming her body. She tried to remember when she had last worn jeans. Her best friend, Dylan, constantly chastised her for her lack of fashion sense, stating she dressed like a fat girl, clad in leggings and oversized shirts. She hated the way her bones stuck out in pants, making her legs appear as sticks beneath her wider hips. She preferred to downplay her breasts, aware they were too noticeable on her small ribs. Dylan liked when she primped for the nightclubs, accenting her assets in skimpy clothes and wearing her hair down, instead of what he dubbed 'the bun head'. She untwisted the bun, letting it cascade in a wave down her back, almost reaching her waist. She had a sudden urge to cut her hair off and do something drastic and extreme.

She walked past the apartment being remodeled, and the twang of country music caught her attention. The upbeat rhythm mixed with the heady scent of freshly cut wood, and the desire to be part of the moment overcame her. Casi opened the door and strode confidently to the lean, muscular man, measuring a piece of wood on his makeshift workbench. He glanced up and gave her a half-smile, almost as if he had been expecting her. A smile touched her lips as she came within inches of him. Without thinking, she placed her hand to his strong jaw and brought his lips to meet her own. Bewilderment crossed his face, but he let her take the lead. His lips were firm and inviting, and the sensation awakened every cell in her body. She switched her brain off and pressed her chest against his, commanding the moment. He wrapped his arms around her, and she felt breathless and tingly. She kissed him passionately, exploring him with her tongue. She caressed the smoothness of his skin, wanting so much more. He embraced her tightly, sliding his hands over her back.

Coming to her senses, she jumped away and covered her face with her hands and he scanned her quizzically. Since first seeing him, she often fantasized about kissing him, imagining how he would taste and the warmth of his mouth on hers. Having acted on the impulse was another matter entirely. Whatever confidence she lacked in her career and personal relationships, from a young age it became obvious she could mesmerize a man with a smile. In the four years she had been with Alix, she never detoured beyond the heavy flirting stage. She realized her actions were impulsive and considered the ramifications of her betrayal. *Would Alix forgive her if he found out?* He'd had numerous affairs, which he didn't classify as cheating given his belief of being one with the universe and allowing your body to guide you, and some other love and light bull crap.

Casi turned and bolted for the door, tripping over the extension cords clumsily as she exited. "Miss. are you alright?" The doorman questioned as she fought to regain her balance.

"Um, ya, fine," she mumbled, pushing the elevator button a dozen times. She escaped into the enclosure and glimpsed the handsome man in the doorway of the apartment watching her with confusion. She sank to the floor as the doors closed, her face ablaze, and prayed Alix was still out.

Unfortunately, he was in the apartment and smiled at her as she came in. She burst into tears, humiliated by her actions. She ran past him and locked herself in the bathroom and fell to her knees and wailed like a lost child. Alix pounded on the door, but she yelled for him to go away in a broken voice. Twenty minutes later she pulled herself together, took three Ibuprofen to calm her raging headache, and splashed water on her face. She came to the living room where Alix sprawled on the white velvet chaise checking proofs of his latest work. He put down the pages and reached out. "Babe, what's going on? You've been a zombie for weeks and now you're running around crying like a lunatic?"

Casi let herself be drawn into his warm embrace, and wished the seat was wider to accommodate them both, as she held an awkward crouching position. She gave Alix credit for being perceptive. Although generally, and unapologetically self-involved, he always treated her tenderly, and let her express herself freely. "I'm lost," she cried.

"Babe, I know thirty seems intense. We've been together a while, but I've always been upfront and honest; I'm a solo dude and I don't do commitment. Whatever your friends are filling your head with, our journey doesn't include marriage and babies." Casi tried not to laugh. *Bless his little heart; he was making this about himself as usual.* The other models did lecture her continually about getting pregnant by a celebrity or sports figure to secure her future, but she lacked the desire to have children, especially for 'locking down' a man.

There was a knock at the door before she could explain, and Alix slipped from under her to answer. Two uniformed police officers greeted him, glancing past Alix. "We were informed by the doorman, Ray Dawson, there may have been an incident." The sturdy female nodded to Casi.

Alix turned, connecting her earlier behavior to what they were saying. She cast her eyes to the velvet seat, picking at imaginary fuzz, trying not to cry as she whispered, "Um, no, no, everything's fine."

The female officer crouched beside her and gave her a compassionate smile. "Mam, if you need to make a statement I can talk with you privately."

Casi raised her eyes, capturing her stare. "It was only a misunderstanding; nothing happened."

She read her pained look and the blush in her cheeks correctly. "Alright, we'll let Mr. Dawson know there's nothing to worry about and inform Kyle Jensen to keep focused on his carpentry work, so there are no more *misunderstandings*."

The male officer explained to Alix how Casi had stumbled out of the downstairs apartment, dazed and confused, and there was concern something happened to her.

*Damn it*, Casi thought, as she watched them leave. *Why did the doorman choose today to be suddenly awake?*

Alix raised an eyebrow. "Do we need to talk, Babe?"

*What do I say? I blindsided a guy by randomly kissing him, and just now found out his name is Kyle Jensen... Wow, what a divine name!* Casi cursed her ADD thoughts. "You were right, I'm having a hard time approaching thirty." She stood and gave him a kiss on the cheek. "Thanks for being supportive, I'll be ok."

As they got into the elevator, the male officer asked, "What the heck was that all about? Do you think the carpenter threatened her? He didn't seem the type."

Officer Mandy pushed the elevator button. "No, everything is fine." She recalled the sexy woodworker they had spoken to and thought, *I suspect the only threat was a passion awakened in a woman who has been 'handled' by too many people for far too long.*

**3**

———

# DESIRE

"*L*ick your lips," the photographer coaxed in a sultry voice, panting slightly. Casi complied, curving her shoulder to enhance her cleavage. "Closer together, girls," he breathed. She edged toward the freckled girl beside her who reeked of body odor and cigarettes. Roll shoulders and suck in stomach, butt up, hair back, bedroom eyes. Casi followed every command like a trained poodle and threw in a few of her signature moves. Lingerie modeling was her best money maker. Confident and sexy no matter how itchy or tiny the material, she possessed a natural sexiness and easily sold the most hideous of creations.

Adorned with a bejeweled thong and bra set, barely keeping her parts private, Casi seduced the camera. She preferred cotton bikini panties in her real life, never having been a fan of butt floss. She wondered if the freckled girl cuddling with her showered recently as another waft of body order came her way. Casi considered it to be highly unprofessional to show up to a job without making sure you were plucked, waxed, and scrubbed to perfection. Knowing she would be provided with about three inches of material, and canoodling with a gaggle of girls, Casi took extra care to ensure she was body perfect. Of course, she had imagined the touch of Kyle's hands as she showered. She wished she could tame her mind, which seemed to be living in an alternate reality to the rest of her.

Freckle-girl over-arched her back and brought the girl-on-girl pyramid to a crashing end. Screams, cursing, and pushing ensued while the assistant tried to untangle the tumble of limbs and lace. The photographer stormed away in disgust, ranting into his phone in an eastern European language. "Ten-minute break girls," the assistant called, scratching her head, trying to figure out how to reset the scene to please the photographer with the inflated ego.

Casi had three more editorials that week, two more for lingerie, and a swimsuit layout in Malibu. Scrapes and bruises were unacceptable, and she checked herself for damage. Again, came the panic of the dreaded thirty creeping up on her. *How long could she pull off these shoots?* She assessed she was in better shape than any of the other girls, some more than ten years younger. She mentally thanked Mary for being so strict with her in the past about proper sleep and eating habits. Most of these girls existed on Red Bull, cigarettes, and late night parties. No makeup or Photoshop completely covered the puffy eyes, and mottled skin, obtained from bad choices. Mary had always warned them that the fastest track to being a former model turned retail sales girl was poor asset management. The assets being their faces and bodies.

She managed to stay focused for the rest of the day, losing herself in the surreal world of the bright lights and whirring and clicking of the digital camera. She pictured Kyle watching as she reclined on the bed, breasts barely covered. She stroked her hand over her taut stomach toward her satin panties, teasing as she slid a finger beneath the trim and bit her lip. She was careful not to lose herself in the fantasy for too long, aware of arousing the photographer instead of Kyle.

After the shoot, Casi hurried into her black yoga pants and a sports bra, slipping on a blue, plaid, flannel shirt. Alix loathed the outfit and told her she looked like a hobo. The shirt originally belonged to her high school boyfriend, Joey, who lovingly wrapped it around her their last night at the beach before she left for LA. At the time, she vowed to be back each summer and thought she and Joey would be together forever. Now she wore the threadbare keepsake when life overwhelmed her. A connection to her roots and a type of security blanket; as if the pale blue material had the power to shield her. One year turned into five, and Joey married her best friend, Dawn. She sometimes longed for the predictability of a mundane lifestyle. She often wondered if her life was any better than theirs. She hobnobbed with celebrities at glamorous events and lived in a chic apartment, but the beach was well over an hour away on the best traffic day, and she never found the time to enjoy it. What she missed the most were the carefree times hanging out with friends at the beach or someone's basement, laughing so hard, your sides hurt for days. Friends were what she lacked. She had a mentor, a boyfriend, and the people in her 'crew', but only Dylan related to her genuine self. Sometimes silly, scared, kind, and emotional. The real Casi was tucked deep inside, afraid to make an appearance in this superficial world.

Casi did her best at avoiding Kyle, keeping her head down as she passed the apartment he worked in, pretending to be engrossed in her phone. Alix hadn't asked her about what had happened that day, and she tried to act upbeat around him, avoiding additional questions. When they made love, she fantasized about Kyle, bringing herself to a new level of sexual pleasure Alix reveled in.

Ray, the doorman who did have a name, peered at her quizzically now as his eyes hovered over her, watching her walk past the apartment being remodeled. She felt cheap and prayed he would go back to not doing his job.

Casi entered the elevator, glued to her phone, and hit the button for the third floor. A scoff emanated from another passenger and she turned toward the glaring, ocean-blue eyes of Kyle. The blood drained from her face and she suspected she might faint. He was delicious in faded jeans, with his tool belt accenting his hips, highlighting the area where she tried to avoid looking. His ocean blue t-shirt, featuring a brewery logo, hugged his body with an unintended definition. He evaluated her intensely for a full minute and then extended his hand. "Hi, I'm Kyle. I'm on a job here for another few weeks." A blush rose up her cheeks and an intense urge to cry overcame her. His hand was offered in jest, and she feared his touch would make her lose control, again. She focused on the buttons on the panel, wishing she had taken the stairs. She swallowed loudly and tried to catch her breath and slow her heart rate, keeping her eyes on her phone. He took another dig and stepped back. "I'm sorry, Miss., am I standing too close? I wouldn't want you to be threatened. I'm installing new cabinet faces on the roof bar. Next time I'll take the stairs."

Casi stuttered, "T-The roof is above the top floor?" She wished she could suck back the words that made her sound like a simpleton. *Way to represent the model industry, dumb ass,* she scolded herself.

"That's usually where they keep them." Kyle mocked her obvious discomfort. Finally, they reached her floor, and she stepped out, then hesitated. He leaned forward and pushed the door-close button, indicating he wanted nothing to do with her.

She hastened to her apartment and called out to Alix. No answer. She checked the computer where he listed his engagements. He was doing an installation of one of his paintings in a new gallery downtown. The media would be there, and it would be quite a party. She glanced at the clock; six o'clock now, and if she hurried she might get there before the actual installation happened. Casi walked to the bedroom and caught a glimpse of herself in the full-length mirror and groaned, "Damn it!" She focused so hard on trying to avoid Kyle, she forgot she looked like crap.

Dylan, who was also her hairdresser, had been at the shoot with his partner, Roy, doing the makeup. Dylan gave her a heavily teased hairdo, using a gallon of product, and Roy had been liberal with the eyeshadow. Although she adored him, she hated how he always hurried to leave, and she needed to unravel the mess he created in her hair. Once, when she pleaded with him for help, he quipped, "Honey, I do the do, but I don't undo."

She turned on the shower and shed her clothes, stepping gingerly into the scalding stream. The water stung her skin, but released the stress of the day as she washed away a multitude of products. She was pleased with editorials like today. Despite the minor tumble, it had been smooth and uneventful. She lost herself, listening to the music they chose specifically for her, seeing how she responded. The beginning prep could be tedious, with people all around, doing hair, applying products, and tugging her into outfits. Modesty went out the window when you were a model. No part was off limits to tape, waxing, tugging, and rearranging. She regularly found her breasts being squeezed into tiny tops, or 'fluffed' up to sell more lingerie. Her face became a playground for dramatic makeup, and her hair had been dyed, bleached, permed, and teased into ridiculous styles. She liked it best when the team consisted of Dylan and Roy, but especially only Dylan. He was better than a therapist; the closest person in LA she shared her secrets and fears with. He would talk about the ups and downs of his relationship with Roy, and she discussed her boredom with Alix. Unlike Mary, who had always been more of a mentor, and God knows more of a mother than Sonya. Casi knew Mary always wanted the best for her, which made it difficult to share her true emotions of insecurity and self-doubt. Mary had enough to worry about, aware Casi was starting to age out of the business, and the time would come to make some decisions about her career.

She worked the shampoo through her tangled strands and used the excess to scrub her face, another habit which irritated Alix. He designated products for each body part and never broke his routine. For fun, she would rearrange his carefully placed bottles in the shower to irritate him. She found it hilarious how annoyed he would get as she pretended it was an accident. He chastised her for not paying attention to detail, claiming this to be her major downfall in life. The suds ran down her shoulders and over her breasts, which were large for her small frame, maintaining a C-cup bra size. As she enjoyed the warmth of the water and the pop of the suds stroking her, she decided what to wear to the party. Maybe her black halter dress, which hugged her body with the silky material. She would pull her hair into a tight twist at the nape of her neck, adding smoky eyes and a dash of crimson lips. She rinsed the grapefruit scented shampoo and applied conditioner. Her arm brushed against her breast, and she thought of Kyle's rough hands stroking the wood cabinets. She imagined his hands on her, filling her with desire.

She rinsed the conditioner and got out of the shower, giving her hair a quick towel dry. She applied face cream and slipped on white lace panties with a matching bra. She put on a faded blue mini-dress, applying light eyeliner, with mascara, and petal pink lipstick. Before she lost her nerve, she grabbed a bottle of Pinot Noir and two glasses. She took the stairs up to the rooftop garden, thankful the doorman never dragged his lazy bones up this far.

Kyle knelt beside the redwood bar, recently added to enhance the terrace for the residents. He had his iPod earbuds in, and she detected the faint throng of heavy metal music. He didn't hear her approach, and she took a minute to admire him as he leaned forward to secure a hinge. A smile crossed her lips as she strode over and plunked the bottle down. Having been caught unaware, he sat back on his heels, kneeling before her, slowly removing the earphones. He eyed her with distrust, his sea-blue eyes lingering over her bare legs in the short skirt. It appeared her actions confused him, and he was unsure what to make of the situation.

"Peace offering," she said, glad her words and tone were not that of a stunted third-grader.

She gave him a radiant smile, but he narrowed his eyes. "I'm unsure what game you're playing, but I'm not interested in your scam."

*Ouch, that was well deserved.* "I'm not sure what came over me the other day, and I apologize for what happened afterward. If you got to know me, you'd see I'm a much better person than that." She extended her hand confidently. "I'm Casi Roberts. I'm twenty-nine and a model since I was seventeen. I live in one of the third-floor apartments with my boyfriend, Alix Grey, a well-known artist. I should be at his reception, but I wanted to introduce myself properly."

A smile reached his eyes as he scanned her face. He rose and took her extended hand. "Hello, Casi Roberts. I'm Kyle Jensen, from Blackberry Falls, Washington. I'm thirty-three, and obviously, a custom woodworker. Do you come here often?" He gave a slight chuckle at his pickup line.

"Only when I need to apologize for my bad behavior. So pretty much every Tuesday," she joked back, shaking his hand, aroused by its strength and roughness.

He reached past her and the electricity between them burned all the way to her toes. "Nice selection. Do you have an opener?"

"Damn it! I'll be right back."

Kyle shook his head and sent a text to his brother. "The gorgeous woman who kissed me the other day, came to where I'm working and produced an expensive Pinot?"

Jake texted back, "She probably put a date-rape drug in it. Get out of there!"

Casi glimpsed her reflection in the mirror as she entered the apartment. "What the hell are you doing?" she asked the fresh-faced girl staring back at her. She was unclear what might happen, but for once she wanted to live in the moment.

She returned and handed him the wine opener. He kept his eyes on her as he filled the glasses. He took a sip. "I'm unsure what you're aiming for, but it's not the first time I've heard mention of a boyfriend. You're a beautiful woman, and I'd be lying if I said I didn't want to throw you down on the chaise and get to know you intimately. I have two weeks left, and then I'm headed home. I don't need the distraction of a spoiled model."

*Wow! This guy cuts to the chase.* Casi set down her glass and came toward him. "Two weeks?" She cocked her head as she ran her hand over his chest, and gazed into his deep, blue eyes, and smiled seductively.

Kyle put a firm hand on her hip and moved her back. "Little girl, you need to take your games elsewhere."

She again stepped forward. "I'm not a little girl, and I'm not playing." She kissed him assertively, tasting the wine as she parted his lips with her tongue. He hesitated and searched her eyes. He responded passionately and pulled her closer. He kissed her with intensity as he brushed his hands under the material and discovered the lacy panties.

She ran her hands over his t-shirt, feeling the definition of his chest muscles and toned abs, slipping her hands underneath to touch the heat of his skin. Casi liked to express herself sexually, an intimacy between lovers, but there was something different about Kyle. This sensation was foreign to her; the loss of control and a willingness to let her body take over. She moaned as he slid his hands toward her breasts, and she began to unbutton his jeans. He clasped his hand on top of hers, stopping her from proceeding. *What the hell? Was this a game for him now?*

Kyle backed up and refilled their glasses. She wasn't sure how to react to his apparent rejection. He turned back to face her and handed her the glass. The silence hung between them like a suffocating wall. "Is this what you want? A quickie on the roof? Then you go back to your boyfriend, and I pretend like nothing happened and return to my life in Washington?"

Casi realized she hadn't thought it through; this wasn't a movie, magically ending with happily ever after. It was real life, messy and awkward. "That's not what I want." She surprised herself with the statement. "I came to apologize for what happened, but somehow ended up in the same place. Although I'm sure the sex would be mind-blowing for fifteen minutes, you're right, we both have lives to return to."

"Fifteen minutes? You're seriously underestimating me."

She loved the way his eyes crinkled when he laughed. She kissed him on the cheek. "Goodbye, Kyle, I have an event to attend. I'll be seeing you around."

She straightened her back and walked to her apartment, feeling his eyes following her. As she closed the door, she realized she had been holding her breath. She entered the bedroom and changed to the black jersey halter dress. Black liner, red lips, chignon, and she swung out the door in ten minutes.

She strolled into the warehouse and pushed through the crowds of celebri-wannabes and took a glass of champagne, noting that mixing alcohol was not a wise choice. She saw Alix by the enormous graphic installed on the back wall of the warehouse-turned law offices. The street art made the firm seem edgy and hip, the exact image they were trying to portray to their celebrity clients. They based the pay scale on confidentiality and cover-ups, but their clientele afforded it.

Alix acted annoyed as she approached. Of course, he always appeared that way, haughty and irritated, dialed up by her perpetual lateness. She kissed him, aware of the cameras flashing. She purposely wore kitten heels to be eye level. She took a step back, gazing up at the giant piece. "Awesome!" She genuinely meant it. Alix possessed a wonderful talent. Underneath the street hype, he began to bare his soul in his new work, and she admired his ability to be raw and vulnerable. She witnessed the growth and transformation from a street graffiti-thug, who struggled with addiction to a man who blossomed into a truly talented artist. His early work portrayed mostly blocks of black and white, crudely drawn and stark. His latest work contained a depth of color and layers of drawings, which played off one another to create a masterpiece of chaos and peace interspersed. She gave him a soft smile. "You're super talented, Alix." She noticed his face radiate from the uncommon compliment.

It was increasingly obvious her relationship with Alix would end. Their time had been destined to be brief, but he helped her navigate through this insane world for the last four and a half years, and she was indebted to him for being her provider and lover. A weight lifted off her shoulders at the revelation. Taking another glass of champagne, she figured she would ride this wave to the shore.

**4**

———

## APPLES

Casi brushed her teeth and examined Alix as he showered. He was particular with his routine, using a myriad of products to achieve the desired effect. He glanced up as he toweled off. "Why are you hyper-focused on me? It's unnerving."

She laughed. "When do you leave for South Africa?"

"Ten days." His expression softened. "Are you doing the jealous thing where you nag me about the women there?"

"I thought it might be an appropriate time for me to move out and be on my own for a while."

"Babe, you don't need to play games. We're cool. I'll come back, but it'll be a few months."

"I'm serious, Alix. I care about you, but I'm in a holding pattern, and it's time for me to make a change."

He analyzed her in the mirror and put his chin on her shoulder. "Is this about marriage?"

She stroked the side of his face. "I don't want to be married, to you, or anyone else. I'm at the end of my career, and I need to redirect my attention to where I'm going next."

"Like a journey of spiritual awareness?"

"Exactly." She pretended to embrace the concept.

"So, we need to travel on separate planes for a while and see what enlightenment lies ahead?"

"You totally get me, Alix," she lied.

"I'm super chill when it comes to material stuff. Take anything you want for your new pad," he offered.

"Thanks for making this transition simple for me."

"Sure, Babe." He took her hand and led her to the bed. Casi went through the motions, being in tune with what he liked, so her mind didn't need to be present. She breathed heavily, faking an orgasm while she considered where she might enjoy living, and what she could afford for rent. "Babe, I suspect you weren't present there."

She moved toward him, putting her head on his chest. "I enjoyed it, but you're right, my mind was elsewhere."

He kissed her gently. "You're excited about your new life, but let's enjoy these last ten days and do all the rad shit we like to do together before I leave." She snuggled against him, realizing his tremendous support over the years, and appreciated they could end their romantic relationship, but remain friends.

❦

"I'll take you to Nobu tonight for dinner," Alix said as he left the next morning.

"I have a casting later, but I'll be home early." She was eager to call Dylan and tell him about her mature decision to strike out on her own.

Casi turned up her stereo and danced in a t-shirt and underwear as she scanned the apartment, deciding which items she might like in her new place. She wasn't attached to anything, she concluded with a shrug, thinking it might be an opportunity to buy things which were more meaningful. She had moved into Alix's with a suitcase full of clothes, two suitcases of shoes, and a box of shells and rocks she collected from beaches around the world. In the time she had lived there, her shoes had multiplied at an alarming rate.

She heard a knock at the door and wondered if it was Dylan coming to celebrate the news. "Hey." She smiled.

Kyle held two clean wine glasses. "I thought I'd return these. I wasn't sure what time you got up."

"You waited until you saw Alix leave?" Her smile expanded as he fidgeted on the landing.

"Something like that." He glanced past her to the living room. "I drank the rest of the wine." They stood in silence, considering what to say next.

"Do you want to come in?" she asked.

He studied her bare legs and exhaled. "Perhaps you could put on pants?"

Casi laughed and left the door open as she strolled toward the closet. Kyle took it as an invitation to enter, smiling as he watched her walk away. He surveyed the open concept condo, decorated primarily in white. He noted the matching glasses on a bar and reunited the pair from his hand. "Nice place," he said, as she came back out wearing shorts, still without shoes.

"It's comfortable," she said. He walked around, eyeing the unmade bed with satin sheets in disarray from a night of activity. He shook his head remembering how she had been all over him the night before, then run off to Alix's installation. "Do you want something to drink?" Casi asked, drawing his attention to the kitchen.

"Sure," he said, against his better judgment, sensing he should leave and be done with her. He frowned at the sleek kitchen without a coffeemaker, or anything implying cooking took place. Casi opened the fridge, staring at an assortment of bottled water, Red Bull, and vitamin water. One apple sat alone on a shelf. He peered in behind her. "Do you ever cook?"

She giggled and shrugged. "I make popcorn. The real kind, not the microwave type."

"Impressive," he teased, finding her charming, despite her apparent hopeless culinary skills. "Does Alix?"

"Not at all."

He looked her up and down. "Who feeds you?" he asked with the concern of a social service worker.

"You're hilarious! We eat out or order takeout. Do you cook?" she asked, witnessing how mortified he seemed.

"Yes, I do."

"Impressive," she mimicked, making him laugh.

"I take it you don't make coffee either?"

"I go to Coffee Bean down the street." Casi reached to the back behind nutritional drinks. She pulled out two cokes and handed one to Kyle, assuming he would prefer it to Alix's array of healthy beverages. "Secret stash."

"Excellent," he said, glad he didn't need to pretend to like the unorthodox drinks. "What's the story on the apple?"

"I found it at a produce stand the other day, and it appealed to me, so I bought it." She contemplated the lonely fruit. "It was expensive." She smiled at the sticker which read, Washington. "Hey, it's from your homeland!"

"Most apples are."

"Huh." She removed the sticker and washed it before slicing it directly on the granite counter, making him cringe. She arranged the pieces on a paper towel and sat, indicating a stool beside her. "Kyle Jensen, tell me all about your fascinating life in Washington."

He smiled, understanding she was being facetious. "Why don't you tell me about your exciting life here first," he challenged. "For instance, what do you do all day? Clean?"

Casi threw her head back and laughed. "Rosa does the cleaning," she said, and he rolled his eyes.

"Jesus Christ, you LA people are lazy."

She countered, "We're busy."

He peered at his watch. "What are your plans?"

"A casting at eleven," she said defensively.

"Shouldn't you be getting ready?"

"Only pants and shoes are required," she joked.

"You don't cook or clean," he paused. "Or work much. What else do you do all day?"

Casi scoffed, "Today is light. What do you do in a day?"

"When I'm at home, I'm up by seven, make coffee and feed my dog. I work for eight to ten hours at our wood shop."

"At your wood shop?"

Kyle clarified, "I own the business with my brother."

"Then what? Your wife is at home making dinner for you, with little kids running around?"

"Neither," he said bluntly. "I cook dinner, maybe put on a movie, or go to the bar to hang out with my friends for darts or pool. Mondays, friends come over for sports night."

"Do you live in an apartment?"

"No," he said, not elaborating.

"Are you homeless?"

"I own a house on a lake. I designed and built it myself."

"Really?" Her eyes widened with awe.

"Really." He inhaled, wishing she wasn't so breathtaking.

"Do you have pictures?" Casi slid her laptop toward him. "Are you on Facebook?"

He shook his head, considering it would be a mistake to be her friend in real life, but deadly online. "Yes, I am." She typed in his name, easily locating him, and sent him a friend request. He laughed as his phone beeped, and he surmised he had no choice but to accept as she smiled sweetly at him. She scrolled through his photos. He moved closer to her, not remembering what pictures he had posted. She squinted at an image and then at him. "My brother, Jake."

"Handsome. Same eyes as you. Older?"

"Almost three years," he confirmed. "My dog Colt," he said at the next photo of the brown, German short-haired dog.

"He's adorable. Girlfriend?" she asked, noting an attractive brunette sitting on the dock at a lake.

"Friend," he corrected, hoping there weren't more of Lauren. "My house." He pointed to a picture of friends gathered on a porch, barbecuing.

"She peered closely. "Awesome place." She scanned images of the lake, friends, dead animals, and fishing trips. She enlarged a picture of him without a shirt.

"Stop violating my privacy." He placed a hand over the screen to prevent a more thorough search.

She lifted his sleeve. "Stunning." She admired the tattoo of a Pacific Northwest depiction of a salmon.

"Ok, you've seen enough." He reached over and switched to her home page. Her relationship status linked her to Alix, and he tried not to acknowledge it.

"Alix is going to South Africa in nine days."

"And I'm leaving in twelve." She stared at him for a long minute, and he wondered what she was thinking. "Casi, I'm not sure what you want from me."

"I'm breaking up with Alix," she said quietly.

He put his hand on her arm. "Are you ok?" he asked, sensing a sadness about her decision.

She waved her hand around the condo. "I've always lived with someone. I want to be in my own place."

"You don't seem happy about it," he said with concern.

She surprised herself when a tear escaped down her face. She wiped it away. "I'm happy, but I'm anxious about my career. I'm turning thirty in a few months."

He reached over and touched her cheek, wiping away a new tear with his thumb. "It might be a good time to make some changes." She leaned against him, hugging him tightly. He was shocked at first and then pulled her closer. He loved the weight of her in his arms as if she belonged there.

"I should leave for my casting." She pulled away slowly.

"Do you need a ride?"

"Uber is easier." She clicked the app on her phone.

Kyle stood, taking their cans and trying to locate the recycling bin. "Do you pay someone to take your recycling?"

"I'll toss them on my way. It sounds abnormal, but Alix would freak out if he knew I was drinking regular coke. He's conscientious about my weight. Modeling is a tough business."

He shook his head. "I'll take care of them." He leaned in to kiss her tenderly. "I guess I'll see you around."

"Don't go back to Washington without saying goodbye to me."

"I won't," he promised. He picked up the cans and eyed Alix's schedule on the open laptop. In two days, he would be at another installation for the evening. He smiled at Casi and thought he might invite her to dinner, having enjoyed getting to know her better. As he walked to his truck, he called his brother.

"Are you on your way home?" Jake asked.

"Not yet, there are two more weeks on this job."

"Twelve days. Work faster, we miss you."

"How's Colt?" Kyle asked.

"Same as he was yesterday when you asked," Jake chuckled. "Did you visit that girl again?"

"I returned the wine glasses."

"And you left them on the doorstep like I told you to?"

"What would she say to her boyfriend if he found them?"

"She's a cheating little tramp?"

"She's moving out in a few weeks."

"Perfect. You'll be home, and she'll be footloose and fancy-free," Jake asserted. "You're playing with fire."

"There's something special about her," he murmured.

"She's super-sexy. But she has a boyfriend and lives in LA. Come home now, that's where you belong."

"I'm afraid I'll fall right back in a relationship with Lauren." He focused on Casi walking out of her building, in black leggings and sunglasses with an aura of a movie star.

"Would it be the worst thing in the world?" Jake probed. "You guys were a great couple."

"I guess." Kyle sighed at the vision of Casi climbing into an Uber. "I have two weeks to figure it out."

5

———

## LIFE'S A BEACH

*C*asi booked a swimsuit editorial in Malibu for the end of the week. Dylan offered to drive, and she readily accepted, looking forward to the road trip. His car was crappy and in need of new tires, and the air conditioner or heater never worked depending on the weather. Curling irons, hair dryers, and other hair paraphernalia needed to be moved from the seats. A free ride and spending time with Dylan, laughing and eating junk food, cinched the deal. Casi didn't own a car, finding the LA traffic insane, plus the nightmare of parking. She liked taking the train, taxi, or Uber, and walking was good exercise.

Since Kyle's visit, Casi stalked his Facebook page, snooping for clues about his life in Blackberry Falls. He didn't post often, mostly he'd been tagged in photos. She smiled when she located his 372 friends, compared to her almost 5000, then winced at the thought that he knew all those people, and he wasn't added by strangers. She made a mental note to start deleting people who didn't complement her life.

Mary gave her a lead on a cottage for rent in West Hollywood. Expensive at $1800 a month, but she could swing it. Sonya had been surprisingly helpful and supportive about the impending move and offered her latest 'boyfriend' to assist.

Casi finished packing her day bag and threw in Twizzlers and Ketchup chips sent in a package from her father. She anticipated the trip and the familiarity of the sand beneath her feet. March was the ideal temperature for her, and it would be nice to escape the smog and suffocating throng of people. The swimwear company rented a sprawling mansion on a cliff overlooking the ocean. It featured a private beach, accessed by what appeared to be a terrifyingly steep staircase. She assumed she would be posing amongst the large boulders, staggered along the waterfront. Only a few girls were scheduled for the layout which made her happy. She detested standing around waiting while some newbie tried to grasp how to appear sexy while attempting not to face-plant into the water. Casi surmised her childhood swimming in frigid water in the lakes of Canada gave her an advantage over the models from warmer climates.

Dylan, annoyingly early, as usual, honked his horn for her to come down. She thought about how her father would be appalled at the lack of chivalry. Of course, he didn't comprehend the difficulty of parking on Fountain Avenue. She rushed from the building and ran into Kyle coming up the front steps with coffee. She waved cheerfully and called back, "Off to Malibu for the day. Gotta work for a living." He watched her climb in the car as he sipped his latte.

"Who's the hottie?" Dylan asked, tipping his sunglasses to get a better view.

"Ew, just drive." Casi blushed as he pushed for details.

The trip was uneventful, backed up on Santa Monica, but only lightly congested on the Pacific Coast Highway. They finished the snacks in the first half hour and stopped for coffee and a bathroom break. Blue skies and a gorgeous day in the high '70's with a delicate breeze made the trip pleasant. She cranked the window down and let the air caress her face. "Ugh, you're going to destroy my hair!" Dylan chastised.

She studied his coiffed hair, crisp with product, rolled her eyes and put up the window. "Why do you care?" she asked, fully aware he didn't fetch his mail without his hair done, and a perfectly matched outfit.

"You never know who I'll meet today. My fortune teller said love is in the air." Dylan assessed her reaction. "Ok, Roy and I are on hiatus. He doesn't understand me. He's dull and possessive. I need sizzle; fireworks! It's a waste of my talents."

"TMI! Total over-share," she laughed hysterically and wiped the image of him in any talented sexual act from her mind.

"You're such a prude, that's what's wrong with you!"

"There's only one thing wrong with me? Besides, I kissed that man you drooled over. How's that for scandalous?"

"Good start. You're not getting any younger, and as your slightly older, and wiser bestie, my advice is to live it up. Sweetie, those boobs are heading to the South Pole, fast," Dylan laughed as she smacked him on the arm and tried to muss his hair.

"Hey, hey, don't mess with the merchandise, biatch!"

The shoot went amazingly well. Dylan styled loose, beach-babe hair, enhanced by the sea air. The swimsuits were sensational; metallics being in this year. As a bonus, they got to keep the suits they modeled, most priced well over $200.

Casi grimaced at the scrape of sand in every crevice and wished she could shower before driving home, but the rental ended at 4 o'clock. She stripped down and did a quick towel off, removing the breast tape which kept her nipples from making an appearance while frolicking in the waves. Her hair felt crispy and sticky, and she was anxious to hit the PCH and be home. Mid-week the traffic wouldn't be too bad coming from the coast, but as soon as they neared LA, it would be horrific. She pulled on her leggings, cursing the grit in her unmentionables. A scented bubble bath and a glass of wine would be a wonderful end to the day, she concluded, as she happily strolled through the expansive rooms trying to find Dylan. Everything had started to come together; the prospect of the new cottage and the life ahead made her ecstatic. Modeling jobs were constantly booking, and her day rate continued to increase.

She called throughout the building and detected giggling behind a door. It didn't take a rocket scientist to figure out what that stemmed from. "I'll wait for you by the car," she yelled. "I guess he found his passion," she said to herself, as she hiked up to the road. They parked on the inner curve of the mountainside above the house, since the incline of the driveway proved challenging for Dylan's manual transmission. The hill became extra strenuous on the way up, and her legs burned when she reached the top. She walked along the unpaved path to the car, wishing she took the keys. It appeared the back window might be partially down, which would allow her to reach in and pull up the lock and be able to relax in the car while she waited. She wondered if any snacks remained, as her stomach churned after eight hours of no food. She had a sudden sensation of flying, twisting madly in the air before she skidded to a stop while grazing over the uneven surface. *What just happened?* Thoughts raced through her mind, but everything became jumbled and fuzzy. A blur of a bright red sports car racing down the mountain road penetrated her fog. She tried to lift her head, but the pain tore up her spine and her legs were numb. She tasted the saltiness of blood and sensed the wetness of tears on her face, but she was shrouded in a cloud of uncertainty and confusion almost like a dream.

"Oh, my God, Casi!" she heard someone shriek. The warmth and coarseness of the gravel radiated through her and the vibration tingled along her spine as they ran toward her. Several voices above her sang out. "Don't move her, her back might be broken."

"Did you see the car?"

"I saw a red Lamborghini."

"I got a partial on the license plate."

"I can't believe they didn't stop."

"Is she going to die?" one of the models sobbed.

Dylan threw himself beside her, his face close to hers as his eyes welled. "Casi, Sweetie, oh my Darling Baby. Hold on, Honey, the ambulance is coming."

A bright flash sparkled before her eyes and she thought maybe an angel had come to escort her to heaven, then realized it was a camera. *Was someone taking pictures of her? Face down on the ground in a crumpled mess? Did she still have legs or had they been severed?* Hot, salty tears flowed down her nose and mixed with her blood in the gravel. She thought back to Kyle waving goodbye and all the possibilities life held minutes ago.

6

———

# DAMAGE

Casi floated through the beeping and pinging of machinery, mingling with the aroma of antiseptic and roses tickling her nose. Her face felt puffy, and her body was hot and cold at the same time. She tried to speak, but she seemed disconnected from her body. Panic started to rise in her throat and her heartbeat quickened. The pulse of a monitor kept pace with her anxiety, and she sensed warmth on her arm. "Casi? Can you hear me?" a lilted voice asked. She tried to open her eyelids, but the weight of them prevented her. "You're in the hospital. You were in an accident," the pleasant voice confirmed. Through mere slits, she detected a blurry form. Cold fingers pried her eyes open, and a light shone in. "I'm Dr. Amir. Are you able to speak?" Cocoa-colored hands flashed the light in her eyes, requesting her to follow.

She wanted Mary. She wanted the comfort of her strong arms, pulling her to her ample bosom, telling her everything was going to be fine.

"Casi," the sing-song voice came again. East Indian, registered in her mind. "Can you move your toes?"

*Thank God, I still have legs,* she thought. *But are they functional?* A vibration tingled from her feet and she groaned. Firm hands rotated

41

her left leg, and she screamed out from the pain radiating up her spine.

"Increase by 20 CC's," Dr. Amir directed. He came to her side and touched her shoulder. "A car struck you with great force. You have a bilateral fracture in your pelvis. From our preliminary tests, we don't anticipate it will require surgery, and most of your large motor function should be restored with physical therapy."

Casi wished the dryness in her mouth would go away so she could talk. She grunted in response, and the attendant came into view holding a plastic cup, cautiously securing it between her lips. The lukewarm water tasted stale, but she gulped it down, sucking madly at the straw to extract the liquid. "Careful, sip slowly." Casi choked, sputtering and coughing as the water dribbled down her chin. The nurse gently cleaned her face and moved the cup to the side table. Tears sprung from Casi's eyes involuntarily, stinging her over-sensitized skin. She was a snotty, blubbering mess, requiring other people to mop up her drool. Too many emotions raced through her mind. Every muscle in her body writhed in agony; a wave of nausea engulfed her, and her brain felt like a milk-soaked sponge. She slipped into a dream-like state, listening to voices speak in a language her mind could not comprehend.

A soft hand stroked her cheek, tender and loving. "Mary," she croaked as her eyes flew open.

"I'm here, Baby Girl," Mary comforted and took her hand.

The familiar touch made her feel safe and grounded. "Thanks for being here," Casi squeaked.

Mary shushed her, fixing sheets and untangling wires, the perpetual organizer. She smoothed Casi's hair as her own eyes filled with tears. "You gave me quite a scare, my Little Peanut," Mary said earnestly. It had been years since Mary called her the nickname. When she started mentoring Casi, she said, "You are just a little peanut in a big world of mixed nuts."

"Everything hurts," she sobbed.

"I know, Sweetie, just let the meds do their work. Don't fight it. They gave Dylan a valium. He was hysterical." She chuckled. "I called your dad. He'll be on the next flight out of Bellingham. Your mom will be here soon," Mary explained, rubbing Casi's cheek to calm her.

"Hey, Babe," the familiar nasal tone of Alix's voice came through her sleep. She groggily opened her eyes and attempted a smile. He gave her a kiss on the forehead, and she imagined her face must be badly damaged from the shock in his eyes.

"Alix, can you get me a mirror?" Casi asked. He hesitated, unsure if he should fulfill her request. She saw Mary shake her head 'no.' Fear rose in Casi's chest as she contemplated what remained of her face. Alix returned with a small compact, and Dr. Amir came to her side. She took a deep breath. "I'm ready." Vanity took hold as the desire to examine her face superseded the knowledge of whether her body functioned. She hoped the fire in her limbs indicated the ability of movement. Alix held the mirror above her face. Casi sucked in her breath at first glance. *Let's assess the damage.* Definite road rash on the left side stemming from her forehead and covering her eyelid, cheek, and chin. Her bottom lip swelled under a crusty scab, leading to a bloodshot eye, barely visible through the bloodied and abraded eyelid. Her nose luckily appeared straight, though severely cut and raw. Her right side featured a large scrape with a liquid hazel eye embedded in a greenish-yellow bruise, peering out like a jewel in a pool of sludge. "Damn, I'm fucked up!"

She slept through the rest of the day with the help of the medication administered intravenously. The pain subsided to a burning throb, giving respite from the sharp penetrating ache as it started to wear off.

"Got any to spare?" Casi opened her eyes to the grinning face of her mother. "What's a girl gotta do to get some of these premium drugs?" Sonya cooed, reading the label on the drip bag.

"Believe me, the price is too high," Casi squeaked.

"Don't fret, you'll be as good as new in a few weeks. We will find the bastard who did and sue him for every penny. Early retirement for you, my girl."

"Did the police catch the guy?" Casi tried to turn her head, but the spasm in her neck made it impossible.

"Not yet. But there are a lot of security cameras on those mansions in Malibu, and the police predict there will be a lead soon." Like most women her age, Casi carried a basic health insurance plan and didn't want to consider what this stint in the hospital would cost. She also feared the impact it would have on her career. Sonya moved around the room, arranging cards and bouquets while flirting with interns, keeping herself busy as Casi drifted off. It brought comfort to have her there. As strained as their relationship was, it made her less afraid.

Balloons and flowers flowed through the door, sporting tanned legs and leather loafers. "Baby!" Dylan rushed to the bed. "I was frantic! They sedated me!" He half-hugged her before he placed his arrangement in front of the others to make sure it took the starring role. Air kisses to Sonya and then he rushed to Casi's side, grasping her hand. "I'm taking full responsibility for this. My therapist agrees. Since I make poor choices in my personal relationships, I'm being punished."

Casi didn't see the correlation between his choices and her trauma, but guessed it made sense to him. "I don't blame you."

"It's ok, Honey; I can own this. I've made up with Roy and promised to make him more of a priority. I literally disintegrated when I got home! Did I tell you they gave me a sedative?" Casi wondered if he suffered brain trauma after witnessing her in a heap on the gravel. He rattled on about Roy, and things his therapist told him. She enjoyed the upbeat tenor of his voice and the warmth of him as he joined her on the bed.

Sonya departed for her yoga class and Dylan left soon after, making Casi feel isolated and anxious. She thought about pressing the call button but couldn't think of a valid reason. She tried to calm her mind and focus on her breathing when a tall figure walked through the door. She burst into tears. "Daddy!"

"Oh, Sweetheart, I'm here." Jack embraced his daughter cautiously, observing the wires and tubes attached to her. "You can come back and stay with us and we'll take care of you." Casi hadn't considered her needs after being released. The pain kept her very present in the moment. They chatted for a while about her work, his restaurant, Ava, and their garden. After a while, the nurse came in to give her dinner and said visiting hours were over. Jack shocked her when he announced he would be staying with Sonya. He laughed and said, "We're on decent terms, Honey. She's one crazy lady, but we're civil if we can lead separate lives."

It surprised her to be jealous. Although happy her parents called a truce to their fiery war, it made her feel left out. She believed she resided in the middle; they lived independently, but revolved around her like the sun. She giggled at the image and her father raised an eyebrow. "Painkillers," she lied.

Casi spent the next five days in bed with a therapeutic pillow below her lower back, and a donut-shaped foam ensuring her pelvis remained still. The catheter freaked her out as she saw the bag fill, but she recalled she was at the mercy of others. She received several sponge baths and was poked and prodded constantly. She reasoned her career as a model prepared her beautifully for being an invalid.

On the fifth day, Dr. Amir advised she must try walking. The bones should be set enough to support her with the help of a walker, and he wanted to ensure her muscles didn't get weak. They detached the catheter and IV, and Casi became terrified the pain would escalate, or she might pee on the floor. Despite having lost any humility, she was not willing to embarrass herself further. The nurse pulled back the sheet and the physical therapist, Juan, guided her legs to the side of the bed, lifting her to a sitting position. She listened intently, finding his accented voice calming, distracting her from the excruciating pain. An additional gown covered her bare backside as she eased her foot through a white garment. *No!* Casi wanted to cry, as the attendant adjusted the adult diaper. Juan put her hands on the front bar of the walker and secured a belt around her waist to steady her. Booties hugged her feet, and she cringed at the spectacle she must be. Juan eased her forward, and she tried to push her loathing of the situation to a minimum. She concentrated on sliding one bootied foot in front of the other, shuffling into the hallway.

"Wouldn't you be a sight on the runway?" Casi glanced up from the grimy, worn linoleum floor to observe a group of models, who must have come to visit her, or rather verify the validity of the rumors. Standing with cell phones in hand, smacking their gum, with mock concern plastered on their blank faces. Casi contemplated crawling the length of the short corridor and knocking them out.

"Don't you have clubs to be trolling?" Alix sneered as he positioned himself between the girls and Casi.

"Ya, like seriously, we just wanted to find out how she is doing. We're, like, uber-stoked to see you, like walking and stuff," said the ombre-haired girl in front. The other girls redirected their gaze to their phones, mortified to have been called out by Alix Grey. As they turned and walked away in unison, he gave them the two-handed, one-finger salute. *Dang, he could be cool!*

"Hi, Babe," he said as he kissed her. "Don't worry about those skanks, they aren't even on the B-list. Um, this is bad timing..." She suddenly remembered he needed to leave for South Africa. "They've pushed the deadline, but the club opening is bringing celebs from all over the world, and the installation has to be completed. I need to be there...but...are you going to be alright? I mean, like how we'd talked about us moving forward...separately?"

She watched him struggle, as she stood there battered and bruised, unable to walk without assistance. "Alix, go. Nothing has changed. This stupid accident isn't going to screw up the plans we've made."

"Babe, you don't need to move from the apartment, focus on healing." The realization there would be no cottage in her near future devastated her. Alix gave her another quick kiss, promising he would check in on her frequently. Casi knew as soon as he landed in South Africa and was surrounded by his art, the surf, and a bounty of beautiful women, she would be a distant memory. He swaggered down the hall in his black tapered jeans, turned up at the ankle, half-boots, and a black leather jacket. *So, this is how it ends,* she thought with a sigh.

7

———

# DISCOVERY

*C*asi pushed the disappointment of the lost cottage from her mind and focused on healing and putting her life back on track. Dr. Amir was thrilled with her progress, and Juan was scheduled to come to the apartment three days a week to continue her physical therapy. The police were following up on leads from several video cameras in the area, but an uneasiness gnawed at her, indicating she was a low priority. Her father offered to help cover the hospital bills, but it made her feel like a loser to have him take care of her debts when she was almost thirty. She reasoned it wouldn't be fair to accept his help when she kept him on the outskirts of her life.

Jack escorted her to the apartment after she insisted she would be fine and could take care of herself. She put on a brave face and pretended not to be in pain as she used crutches to make her way up the front stairs and down the hall. Her father shook his head as he walked slowly beside her, declaring he would not drop her off at the curb. They entered her apartment and he glanced around at the sparse furnishings. He took his time checking to make sure she had everything she needed, hugging her tenderly. He brushed a strand of her long hair from her face and his eyes welled. "I miss you, Sweetie."

She tried to smile, her lip stinging. "I miss you, too."

"Can I make you something to eat?" Jack ran his hand over her back and protruding ribs.

"Dad, I'm fine."

"Do you want me to stay here while you shower?"

Casi managed a laugh. "I'm fine. I only look like crap. Dylan will be here later, and I'll wait to take a shower," she said, sensing his displeasure to leave her alone.

The apartment welcomed her with familiar surroundings, away from the chaos. Alix had left for the airport early, and Sonya stocked the fridge with fruit and vegetables. She organized a stack of takeout menus by the phone, reminding Casi she still needed to be conscientious of her figure. Aside from an obvious dwindling of her medications, her mother seemed to be helpful.

Jack stepped from the elevator and nodded to a man with piercing blue eyes, hesitating by a doorway. He came forward and introduced himself, saying he knew Casi. He blushed as he mentioned her name, making Jack wonder at the nature of their relationship.

"How is she doing?" Kyle assumed the man was Casi's father by the familiar hazel eyes.

"She'll recover. I wish she would come home and stay with me, so I know she's ok," Jack said with regret.

"Where's home?"

"Bellingham, Washington."

"I'm from Blackberry Falls, Washington." Kyle explained his custom work, indicating the apartment behind him.

"Incredible!" Jack eyed the cabinets, walking closer to have a better view. "You do beautiful work."

"My brother and I have a business," Kyle stated.

Jack turned to face him. "How well do you know Casi?"

Kyle hesitated before answering, "I talked to her a few times." He glanced away with flushed cheeks.

"Maybe you should get better acquainted," Jack suggested. Kyle cocked his head, curious at what he was inferring. He offered Jack a scotch, telling him more about his business and his brother, as Jack told him about his restaurant and brewery. He chatted about his wife, Ava, and the heritage home they restored. Kyle listened intently, sensing a kinship and agreeing to come to the restaurant when he got home. "When do you head back?" Jack asked.

"Three days." Kyle assessed the nearly complete kitchen.

"It's a wet time of year. Too bad you can't pick up more work out this way and stay longer." Jack glanced at the boxes of tools and equipment.

"I'm not in a rush to leave." Kyle grinned.

Jack smiled, deciding to make a few calls as soon as he left. He stayed out of Casi's life for over a decade, but something about this man indicated he would be the ideal match for his daughter.

Sleep came and went throughout the next few nights, and Casi became restless. She ate most of the fruit, but the vegetables stumped her for what to do with them. She thumbed through the stacks of magazines from Mary. She soon burned out on napping and Facebook did not hold her attention. Stuck on level 676 of Candy Crush, she decided to take a time out before she became violent with her iPad. The apartment was too quiet, and strange grinding sounds came from the walls. She chastised herself for watching the horror film earlier. Her mind wandered back to her career and where she was headed. She knew she needed to be positive and an opportunity would present itself when the timing fit as the self-help book Dylan gave her claimed. For now, she needed more pain medication as the ache in her hip increased, becoming unbearable. "Damn, where did I leave the bottle?"

Juan had been there earlier, and they worked on her walking with a cane. The crutches hurt her armpits, but she liked how they stretched out her spine and took the pressure off her lower back. She contemplated taking a bath but didn't trust herself to be able to get in and out of the tub without doing serious harm to her fragile body. After fidgeting for another hour, she decided to get up and find her meds. She recalled they might be in the bathroom which was convenient because as she eased herself up she realized her bladder was very full. Her armpits ached from the physical therapy, and the trip seemed miles away. "One step at a time; focus," she repeated what Juan told her constantly.

She made it to the door, but as she crossed the threshold, one crutch snagged on the transition from carpet to tile. It escaped from under her right arm while she frantically tried to steady herself with her left crutch. Her legs weren't strong enough to support her, and she reached madly for the vanity in an attempt to avoid the impending fall. It turned out to be a poor choice, and she splayed out on the floor, sending the contents to the far corners of the room. "Motherfucker!" Casi cried out as she hit the floor, face first. She contemplated how to pull herself up and realized the situation was about to escalate. Her delicate, bruised bladder, still tender from the accident, couldn't handle the latest acrobatics. She cried as warmth leaked down her legs. Time halted as she sobbed, damp and defeated. As she remained on the floor in a heap, she thought she could hear the front door opening and steps coming toward her. "It's your imagination," she chanted to herself, but it sounded too real. Through the curtain of hair covering her face, she could see work boots, topped by denim. *No! Not him! Please make it a murderer instead. Who would be so repulsed by the sight of her, he would run back out.*

"Are you still alive?" Kyle asked calmly.

"No, I'm not. Please go away," she wailed.

"Pretty talkative for a corpse." He stepped past her, assessing the situation.

"I'll be dead of embarrassment soon enough. Please erase this image from your mind," Casi pleaded.

Kyle continued to the tub and turned on the water, adjusting the temperature. He took the bottles surrounding the ledge, sniffing each one, and settling on orange blossom to pour into the rushing stream. Casi could only see up to his knees, and it was an unusual perspective to be watching the scene from below. A piece of red material draped from the counter, indicating he removed his shirt. He knelt and slid his arms under her, scooping her from the floor as if she were a small child. He carried her across the room and cautiously lowered her feet into the foaming bath. He gently pulled her nightgown over her head while he supported her weight with his muscled arm. He smelled of cigars and scotch, and the warmth of his bare chest against her back put her at ease. Insecurity washed over her as she stood naked in front of a man she found incredibly attractive when she felt completely hideous. He read her mind as he smiled. "You don't have to be shy, it's not like I haven't checked out your modeling shots in your barely-there skivvies." She blushed at the thought of him going through her images, checking out her body in the privacy of his home. A little voyeuristic, even. It gave her a sense of pleasure to be thought of as sexy by him. The bubbles and warm water enveloped her body and the tension of the incident vaporized. He rolled up a towel and wedged it behind her shoulders to provide more support. "I'll be right back." Slight panic rose as she considered her vulnerability, unable to save herself if she slipped under the water. Before she could voice her concern, he returned carrying a large plastic cup. He filled it from the faucet as he knelt beside her. "Close your eyes," he commanded. He poured the warm water over her hair as he supported her neck. He lathered shampoo and worked the bubbles through her long strands. Casi peeked through her half-closed eyes to appreciate his bare chest, well-defined and muscled through hard work, rather than like the lumpy, steroid-using gym-rats around town. His sun-tanned skin radiated the glow of a man who often worked outdoors. She could see the tattoo on his right arm and tried to read the script on his ribs. "Eyes closed," he directed.

Rather than being embarrassed, she found the situation sensual and erotic. He rinsed her hair and massaged in conditioner with the aroma of grapefruit. *This is divine!* She leaned against his bicep and enjoyed the attention. "Wait, how did you get in here? How did you know I needed help?" Her eyes flew open.

He sat back on his heels and laughed. "Alix asked me to check in on you and gave me a key. He worried about you being alone but said you were too stubborn to have live-in help, and your mom would drive you crazy. He also mentioned you broke up. Actually, he said something more like, two existential beings traveling on alternate paths of enlightenment on their journeys."

"I told you we were breaking up." Casi frowned.

"True, but now it's official." He grinned. "Earlier I was on the roof checking out the stars, or searching for them through the smog," he corrected himself. "I heard screams, which I guessed was a movie."

"Thank God I wasn't watching porn." She giggled.

He laughed. "When I heard the crash and cursing and decided I should check to see if you were alright."

"My knight in shining armor," she teased.

"Want a razor?" he asked, killing the romance.

She pulled a bubbled leg up. "Oh my, that is quite furry." He handed her a razor and went about tidying as she shaved. He impressed her with his cleaning skills, and how he downplayed the urine-soaked nightgown. "Sorry," she mumbled.

He shrugged. "No problem, I have a dog."

"Rosa comes on Friday." She cringed. "Or maybe not anymore, since Alix is gone."

"I guess it's time for you to learn some domestic skills," Kyle teased.

She was unsure if she should laugh or cry, but decided his personality was natural and easy-going, putting her at ease. His toned, defined body aroused her, but her desire to impress him vanished and she relaxed and enjoyed his company.

Kyle came back with several items. "How about this?" He held up a pink lace negligee.

"I don't think so."

"This one?" He produced a skimpy black teddy.

"Are you having fun pawing through my drawers, Perv?"

"Then this should do," he stated, putting a flannel nightgown down. It seemed cozy and snuggly, and she tried to remember where it came from. "Ok, hang on." He reached in the water and released the plug. He turned on the faucet and rinsed her hair, letting the overflow cleanse her body. He took extra care to rinse her breasts, watching as the bubbles gave way to her supple skin and pink nipples. She turned to him and smiled at his eyes, reflecting an immense desire. She forgot about her aching, fractured pelvis, and bruised, scraped face. She savored the moment of this handsome man rinsing her body. He wrapped her in a towel and carried her to the vanity, as she leaned against it for support, and he patted her damp skin. "That's quite a scar," he said, touching the jagged cut, snaking from her lower back, zigzagging its way to her left hip.

"Oh." Casi investigated the scar for the first time. The area felt tender, but with her bruising and mobility issues, she hadn't noticed. She remembered the sear of the gravel tearing through her flesh and shuddered.

Kyle realized she wasn't aware of the scar. "Don't worry, it makes your perfect ass even more luscious," he said with a devilish grin. He blotted her hair dry and gave her body a final assessment before slipping the flannel gown over her head. "Do you have a hairdryer?" he asked, breaking the long silence.

"In the basket under there," she pointed.

"Jesus, that's a lot of equipment." He stepped back to survey the overflow of hair implements. She received a lot as freebies from jobs, or as hand-me-downs from perks Dylan got at hair shows. Glancing at the large basket, she realized it might be a good place to start paring down and organizing her new life. He brushed her long hair and blew it dry on a medium setting, taking extra care around her left temple and the significant cuts and bruises. "Interesting."

"Do I have a bald spot?" she joked, accepting another flaw.

"No, not bald. Blonde roots," he observed.

"Yup, I'm the one woman in LA who is naturally blonde, but dyes my hair to be a brunette. It has been platinum, jet black, auburn, flame red, even neon blue for one show, and many shades of brown, all in the name of fashion," she stated.

Kyle winked at her in the mirror. "I wondered when you were in the bathtub." She giggled, guessing his reference wasn't to her legs. "Blonde would make you even more captivating."

"You never know," she shrugged.

Casi examined her reflection as a whole rather than a piece at a time in a compact. He made her feel so sexy, she forgot about her injuries. Light bruising covered the left side and her eye was still swollen and blackened, although mostly clear of the broken blood vessels. The cut on her lip scabbed over and would not scar too badly, unlike the several long gashes near her hairline. She already inspected her body in the tub to discover remnants of bruises and abrasions. She reached for her pills, having forgotten her original mission. She struggled with the lid until Kyle leaned over and took it.

Kyle read the label and handed her a pill and a glass of water as he noted her dissecting her image. "Don't worry, you're still breathtakingly beautiful."

"Thanks," she sighed, and smoothed face cream over her tortured skin, avoiding the most damaged areas. She admired Kyle's body as he concentrated on drying her hair. Well-toned abs above faded jeans, revealing the top edge of his jockey boxer-briefs, giving promise to much more she would find pleasurable. She watched him maneuver the hairdryer, awkwardly, unfamiliar with this particular contraption but skilled with tools in general. She liked how one vein in his sculpted forearm pulsed as he maneuvered the brush.

"I figured you were used to being pampered like this." He met her gaze in the mirror.

She laughed at the comparison of Dylan doing her hair, which was never remotely sexy. Although he was a good-looking man, fit and well-coiffed. She only thought of him more as an extension of her own twisted personality. A buddy to laugh with and talk through your problems. He often tortured her hair, raking through knots and tangles with little regard for her tender scalp. "I wouldn't consider any part of my job as being pampered."

"Ok, Gimpy, you're done," he said, expertly winding the cord. The only tool to be put away correctly.

"You seem like you've done that a time or two."

"Not with one of these." He smoothed a hand through his short, wavy chestnut hair. "But a tool is a tool." He leaned toward her, and she prepared to be kissed. His face close to hers, one arm behind her back. His breath wafted over her face, the faint aroma of scotch and a wisp of cigar smoke on his skin. In one swift motion, he lifted her into his arms and carried her to the bed. "What's with these sheets?" He eyed the white satin. "They don't look comfortable."

"They're not," she replied. He pulled up the covers, tucking them around her in a caring way. "Will you join me?" she asked, trying not to sound too forward.

He inhaled and shook his head. "I have a policy of not sleeping in another man's bed. Plus, I need to get the wash going; some of us work in the morning."

She regarded the bedside clock. "Wow, it's 2:30!"

"What are these for?" he asked holding a stack of photos featuring Casi, he had found on the coffee table.

"Alix took those. He uses them for his paintings. They inspire him." She yawned and snuggled in the blankets.

Kyle glanced from the pictures of the half-nude, stretched-out girl, to the sharply lined abstracts hanging on the wall. "Sure, he does." He tucked a few photos in his shirt pocket.

"I thought you were headed home?" She sat up in alarm.

"It's the rainy time of the year, so I scheduled some custom work," he replied, realizing the correlation between the calls and Jack's departure.

"Do you like living in your house on the lake?"

"It's like paradise," he said with obvious contentment. "I'm from Elmvale, Washington, originally. It's a tiny town north of Bellingham. I moved to Blackberry Falls after college because of the beautiful lake, and its proximity to Seattle." He told her about his family and how he graduated from the University of Washington, with a degree in business.

"I'm from Burnaby, Canada. Do you know where that is?"

"Huh? East of Vancouver. I wasn't aware you were Canadian. Maybe there's hope for you yet."

She considered her Facebook page. Modeling pictures, selfies, and 'aren't we awesome' poses with her friends at nightclubs. It said she lived in Hollywood, making her question when it would be appropriate to change her relationship status linked to Alix. She told Kyle more about her life before modeling, drifting off, her voice sounding muffled in her head. She liked the comfort of him being in the apartment as she fell asleep. As she started dreaming of being on the beach, he kissed her on the forehead and whispered, "Sweet dreams." She wanted to reach out for him, but sleep immobilized her.

**8**

---

# PHOTOGRAPHS

$\mathcal{C}$asi woke to the sun shimmering through the window, casting a warm glow throughout the room. The clean laundry was folded on a chair. She checked the clock, surprised it was almost eleven. She spied a large Coffee Bean cup on the bedside table. Taking a sip of the vanilla latte, she wondered when Kyle set it there, sorry to have missed him. She glanced at the writing on the side, 'Good morning, Sunshine'.

Casi phoned Dylan and blurted, "I'm in love!"

"Of course, Sweetness. I'm fabulous!" he replied. She laughed and recounted the previous evening, giving significant detail to the shirt-less Kyle. "Wait, you peed on yourself and I'm supposed to find this erotic?"

"How are you stuck on one detail?" Casi wished she hadn't mentioned it.

"Proceed, I'm listening," he hummed.

She figured he was at his salon, wearing his headset. "Visit me later, I'll tell you more about it," she said, not wanting to cheapen the story. "Don't tell anyone about the pee thing, or I'll inform everyone what you were doing when the accident happened." She played on his assumed guilt, and the fact he and Roy were back together.

"You ruin all my fun," he sulked.

She hugged herself in the flannel nightgown and considered what to do with what remained of the day. She remembered Ava gave her the nightie for Christmas. At the time, she stuffed it into a drawer, sure she would never wear the prudish attire. Her step-mother tried hard over the years, sending gifts and always remembering special occasions. Her father sent packages containing her favorite snacks and little things she might like. The packages arrived when she needed them the most. The silly items and treats made her smile when the world pressured her with chaotic schedules and demands. She understood Ava had a lot to do with the care in putting it together and wished she could move past the deep-seated resentment of her step-mother.

Casi drank the latte and reached for her crutches. The bath had done wonders, plus the good night's rest. Although still in pain, it became manageable, and she took a couple of ibuprofen rather than the medication which made her brain foggy. She would hold on to the prescription in case the pain became stronger, or to use as bribery for her mother she noted with a mischievous grin.

After brushing her teeth and getting dressed, Casi decided to call her dad and update him on her condition. She made sure to be extra cheerful on the phone, and she heard the relief in his voice. Eyeing the large box of pictures she had spent days organizing, she considered the albums Ava made for her nieces and nephews. "Can you ask Ava where I can get one of those book things like she makes?"

"Sure, hold on, Hon," Jack said eagerly.

She sensed his pleasure at her interest in anything to do with her step-mother. Her father worshipped Ava. They were one of those annoyingly adorable couples who held hands when they went for walks and completed each other's sentences. Casi admitted Ava suited her dad, highlighting his best qualities, and being a true partner in the restaurant and brewery. "Hi, Sweetie, how are you doing?" Ava sounded genuinely concerned. Casi imagined the box on the way soon, full of thoughtful and useful things. "Dad says you want to get a scrapbook?"

Casi made a list of stores she suggested, and before she hung up, quickly said, "The nightgown you gave me at Christmas has come in handy, a perfect gift." She heard the tears in Ava's voice as she said goodbye.

❧

"Are you fucking kidding me?" Jake asked in response to Kyle telling him he would be staying longer.

"It is good money and I'm here already."

"It makes sense because you want to be there with that stupid woman," Jake accused.

"I told you about her accident, and she fell last night. What if I wasn't there to help her?"

"She can hire someone; you're not a nurse."

"I enjoy being around her, and I am sorry she's hurt."

"I talked to Lauren today," Jake interjected.

"What fascinating thing did she have to say?" Kyle sighed, tired of hearing how Lauren missed him and wanted him to come home and sort things out.

"Pretty much what she says every time."

"Just tell her I'm here for work," Kyle replied.

"You tell her," Jake insisted.

Kyle opened his Facebook page. Instead of a personal message, he updated his status to sound excited about opportunities in Los Angeles and the amazing weather. He ended with an undetermined estimate of when he would return.

Jake messaged him, "You should be ashamed of that chicken-shit post." Kyle responded with a smiley face.

Casi saw Kyle's post and gave it a thumbs up, commenting LA was happy to have him longer.

Jake rolled his eyes at her response. "If you're not back in two weeks, I'm moving into your house permanently, and changing your dog's name to Batman," Jake wrote.

59

Kyle laughed at the Facebook war, then scoffed when Lauren replied, "Washington misses you," with a sad face.

&a.

Casi made use of her healing time, doing her physical therapy with Juan, and sorting through the photos, putting them into a timeline of piles. The memories of her teenage years brought tears of laughter, recalling the antics they used to pull. She blasted her stereo as she sang and did her best to dance with the use of her cane. Kyle typically came by in the evenings, making her dinner or getting takeout. She looked forward to seeing him, disappointed if he had other plans. Sonya met Kyle one night as she left, taking her time to flirt and check him out. The next day she called and asked Casi more about him, questioning why he delivered her meals. Casi explained briefly how they met, leaving out most of the details. "He's down to earth, and he's been taking great care of me," she gushed.

"Darling, he's a workman! Lovely to have sex with, but don't get your hopes up for something more," Sonya said aghast.

"He owns his business and is a highly skilled craftsman." Casi added the last part based more on what she grasped from Kyle, rather than what she knew as fact.

"I'm sure in his small town, he's a big deal. But this is LA and you're a beautiful girl who should be searching for a wealthy husband before your looks start to fade," Sonya advised.

"Mother! I have no desire to be anyone's wife and I can take care of myself," Casi said defiantly.

"A romantic notion of the young and naïve, but you should be concerned about your long-term financial security. Have your little affair, but you know as well as I do, you will tire of his small-town charm."

Casi cringed. She was not one of those inept women desperate to be a trophy wife, residing at the coffee shop, perpetually in yoga pants. *Kyle is not an affair.* She wanted to yell but wasn't sure who she was defending. *Did she see this going somewhere, or did his masculinity and blue eyes mesmerize her? Would she tire of him as her mother predicted and feel trapped by the normalcy of a relationship? What did Kyle want?* He made his attraction to her clear, but was he the marriage and children type, and would he be ultimately crushed when he found out she wasn't? She pondered whether she was being fair to him, flirting like a school girl. *What did she know about love?* She had loved Joey as a seventeen-year-old girl would, but she adapted a more modern approach toward sexuality. Her mother was right, she did get bored with men quickly over it when they became needy or emotional. In fact, she lived with Alix for more than four years because of his lack of commitment and emotional detachment.

Casi reclined on the chaise, listening to the music, surrounded by her photographs. She considered Kyle and his caring manner that night, touching her intimately. Since then, he had been friendly, but his intentions were unclear. Maybe he was dating someone, and he checked on her out of kindness. It made her heart hurt, and she pushed it from her mind.

She let the afternoon sun wash over her as she relaxed, clad in a blue flannel shirt and Alix's black pajama pants. The sun warmed her and the memory of Kyle's physique, more so. She unbuttoned her top, skimming over her black lace bra, imagining Kyle fondling her breasts. She lifted her hips as she imagined the pleasure of his touch, before drifting off to a peaceful sleep.

9

———

**FALLING**

Casi opened her eyes to witness Kyle standing above her in the now darkened room. She stretched lazily and yawned, a smile still on her face from her earlier activities, and a vivid dream of him making love to her. "I picked up supper." He held up a bag of Chinese takeout in one hand and a six-pack in the other. "As a Canadian, I assumed you'd prefer beer with your Chinese. I noticed you're not taking your prescription, so your liver can handle a little alcohol."

"Aren't you observant," she mused as she lifted her foot toward him, letting her toes trail up the leg of his jeans.

"You have been doing your physical therapy," he said, not flinching as she continued her journey. "I also got you these." He produced a set of Egyptian cotton sheets. "Those satin things look uncomfortable as hell."

"After dinner activity?" she inquired.

Kyle blushed deeply, realizing the unintended sexual reference the new bedding would suggest. "I don't think so, Miss broken pelvis...." he trailed off, removing her foot before it could reach his crotch.

She laughed and stretched again. "Wait! What time is it? Crap..." She jumped to her feet.

Before he could put the bags down to catch her, she fell to her knees, sucking in her breath to calm the flaring pain. She bumped the coffee table and her photo stacks fluttered through the air. "What are you doing bouncing around?" Kyle reached for her in a panic.

"Ouch! I hoped a package would arrive. I must have dozed off after my physical therapy," she exhaled.

"Is that what you call it?" He raised an eyebrow as he observed her unbuttoned shirt and pants riding low on her hips.

"I got hot," she said absentmindedly.

"I bet you did." He grinned and produced a large box. "Is this what you were waiting for? Was that the source of moaning during your nap?"

"How long were you here?" She felt violated, although it had been his body she ravished in her fantasy.

"I only caught the tail end. You appeared satisfied; I didn't want to wake you." She ignored her flushed cheeks as she reached for it. She tried to tear through the tape to no avail and started to use her teeth. "Hold up there, Jaws." He shook his head and brought out a knife from his pocket, opening the edges and setting it on the table.

Casi eagerly sifted through the supplies, Ava included. She eased into a cross-legged position with a wince, not quite ready for the movement. She pulled out a large scrapbook, various scissors with different edges, fun stickers, two-sided tape, and several glue sticks. There were Twizzlers, Canadian candy bars, and a bag of Ketchup chips, much to her delight.

"You're like a little kid at Christmas," Kyle mused. He suggested they sit in the kitchen to eat, eyeing the coffee table littered with pictures. As she reached the counter, he teased, "I didn't know if you were aware this room existed."

"I occasionally get a glass of water," she giggled.

"There are a lot of vegetables in the fridge. What are your ideas for cooking them?" he asked with interest.

"I ate the carrots. I'm not sure about the other stuff."

Kyle shook his head, mentally planning a pasta primavera for the next evening. As they enjoyed pot stickers, cashew chicken, black bean prawns, and beef chow fun, Casi told him about the photos and how she organized them to create order in her life, frowning in dismay at the scattered piles. She wondered if his apparent contentment in life and easy manner stemmed from a sense of belonging in a community. She fed off the bustle of New York and LA, never standing out, but excited by the surrounding energy. It reminded her of the nightclubs and how she would dance freely on a table, if the mood struck her. No one cared, although a lot of the men tried to take her home. How would Kyle react if he saw her there? Would it turn him on, or would he run the minute she started her sultry dance?

"What are you dreaming about?" he asked.

"Dancing at the nightclub," she said honestly.

"Worried you won't be able to get up on those tables anymore?" he said, as she looked at him quizzically. "I may not post a lot on Facebook, but I've seen your club pics with your naughty dances."

"Naughty?"

"I guess it depends on whose lap you're doing them," he said with a smile. He cleared the containers and empty bottles and said over his shoulder, "Why don't you start on your album and I'll help you. I'd love to hear your stories." Casi sat back, satisfied at the impossibility of him dating another woman. She hobbled to the coffee table and pulled a cushion to sit on as she picked up the heap of photos and started sorting again. "I'll put your new sheets on, so when you pass out from your third beer, you won't slide out to the floor."

Casi regarded the open bottle on the table beside her, not realizing she opened another. She relaxed and considered the benefits for her to unwind. She watched as he expertly changed the sheets, smoothing the soft material over the king mattress and pulling the large duvet back. He slipped the pillow in a case and searched for the second one. "There's only one. Alix takes his with him when he travels. It's his security blanket," she informed him. He shook his head as he folded the second case and put it on the dresser.

He came toward her, so close she could smell his soapy cologne as he took a seat on the sofa, putting a leg on either side of her shoulders. She liked the familiarity, a gentle, yet suggestive stance. She melted into him, enjoying the pressure of his legs against her. He edged closer, whispering in her ear, "I guess we could...watch a movie," he finished, reaching past her for the remote control. "Up for another horror flick?" he laughed, scooting back. She hoped he would initiate an intimate embrace and frowned with disappointment at his withdrawal.

After an hour of organizing while they watched a horrible war movie, Casi jumped up and screamed. "Cramp, cramp!"

Kyle held her steady while she twisted. He arranged pillows for support and helped her sit beside him. "Almost like a lap dance," he joked.

"I do it much better than that," she stated proudly.

Kyle leaned back and surprised her by putting his arm around her shoulders, and she relaxed into him. The movie was violent, with explosions and a lot of fighting. Not her typical pick, but she could see he enjoyed it. After a while, he took her bottle and put it on the coffee table beside his. *Was he cutting her off?* He took her chin in his hand and tilted her face up to him. "Do you want to tell me about your dream?" He placed his lips to hers and kissed her so delicately, tingles danced down her spine. His intensity increased as he directed his hand to the small of her back and pressed his chest against hers. He parted her lips with his tongue, and she could taste the beer on his lips.

"It was about you." Casi smoothed her hand across his taut chest. Although she had kissed him before, this time was magical, sending fireworks through her body.

He swiftly removed his t-shirt with one hand. "What was I doing?" he asked, teasing her as he slowly undid her buttons.

She was glad she had taken the time to shower and shave her legs. Kyle liberated her from the flannel top and moved his mouth over her collarbone. "Definitely some of that." She shivered as he slid a thumb across her nipple. He needed no help to unclip her bra, and it joined their clothing on the floor. He shifted her toward the back of the sofa and perched himself on the edge, limiting the weight on her.

He hardened to her touch as she unzipped his jeans and rubbed the outline of his impressive manhood. She arched her back as he slipped his hand inside her pajama pants. "Make love to me." She reveled in the first wave of an orgasm as it began to build.

He let her finish before he pulled back. "I can't." He ran his fingers through his disheveled hair, waves curling at his neck. The light from the TV highlighted the slight lines of his face. He sat up, uncomfortable in his semi-erect state.

"Why not? What's wrong?" She braced herself for the revelation he was married.

He frowned at her in dismay. "You have a broken pelvis!"

In her lust, she forgot. "But it felt good. I'm sure if we're careful," she attempted, accepting she would throw caution to the wind if he was inside her.

"No," he said firmly. "We still have a month until you're healed enough for intercourse."

"Intercourse? Are you a Health-Ed teacher? Wait, did you Google my injury?" she gasped.

"I wanted to be safe; I didn't want to harm you. Speaking of safe, I don't have a condom with me. Maybe I should put those on the list?" he said with a wink.

She had only been with Alix in the last four years, and he was regimented about protection when he stepped out. She took the birth control pill and hadn't considered the complexities of having a new partner. She rubbed her hand across him. "There are other things we can do while we're waiting."

He chuckled and stopped her from unzipping his jeans again. "Slow down there, Tiger. Let's take this one step at a time. I only have so much restraint." She appeared wounded as she put her head in his lap, running her hand over the scar on his upper rib cage. "Boating accident years ago," he answered her implied question, pointing to additional marks on his arm, hairline, and behind his ear.

"You're still incredibly beautiful." She grinned in solidarity of their shared scars.

He ran his thumb over the red welt above her eyebrow, less

noticeable and starting to fade. He stroked the side of her face, tracing her bottom lip as he gazed into her eyes, trailing his hand down her collarbone and over her breast. He smoothed his palm across her stomach, still flat, but not as concave as a few weeks ago. "It's nice to see you filled out."

"Are you calling me fat?"

"No! Please tell me you're not one of those women who obsesses about her weight or throws up after a meal?"

"I'm in a tough business for body obsession. When I am anxious, I sometimes don't eat to gain control of my environment," she confessed. "I'm happiest at my present weight, but that's not acceptable for modeling."

"You're beautiful, Casi. Don't try to please anyone but yourself."

"What about my scars?" She doubted how the industry would receive her with the significant one across her hip.

"It adds depth to your beauty," he said, running his hand over her. The wound had mostly healed, still jagged against the smoothness of her skin, supple and perfect. The material from the couch aggravated it, making it a brighter red, and he was glad he hadn't taken it farther, even though it left him in agony.

She ran her finger over the script on his rib, *Dare to Dream, Hope, Trust, Seek, and most of all, Love*

"Lovely. Does it have a special meaning?"

He hesitated. "No, I saw it in a fortune cookie."

She noted the sadness dance across his eyes. "What about the fish?" she asked.

"It's a salmon. I'm a Pisces."

"A Pisces and a fisherman?"

"Have you been trolling my Facebook page?"

"Absolutely!" she confessed. "Tell me about your brother."

"He enjoys the outdoors and we have the business together," he stated evasively.

"Have you told him about me?"

"Get dressed and we can reorganize your scrapbook for you to finish tomorrow." He glanced at his watch.

She ran a finger over the band. "Tag Heuer, fancy."

"A graduation present from my parents. Both Jake and I have one," he confirmed.

"Oh, an educated man," she teased, wishing she completed her secondary education.

He smiled. "I always planned to have a business with my brother, but my parents insisted we get our degrees." He glanced away, making her uneasy about the true story.

"What are you omitting?"

He shrugged, aware his silence would only prompt more questions. "Jake got married as soon as he graduated. His girlfriend at the time was pregnant."

"Are they still together?"

"Yes, they have two kids now." He removed his hand from her breast. "Put your clothes back on." She rolled off and complied, sensing his brother might not be a fan of her.

They worked on the album for a few hours, as she told him about each picture, her friends, and where she grew up. She considered her teenage years and the plans she made. "Off in dreamland again?" Kyle asked, holding a photo out to her.

"Sorry, I tend to do that." She focused on the picture and smiled. "Joey. My first boyfriend," she said tenderly. "First, as in sexually. I had boyfriends before, of course."

"A pretty girl doesn't go un-kissed for long," he mocked.

"That's not what I meant!" She blushed.

"Wow, look at you." Kyle pointed to her in a bikini on the beach, golden blonde hair framing her smiling face as she stood with her arm around another girl, tanned and slender.

The image broke her heart, having lost contact with Katie. "Yup, can you believe it was almost fourteen years ago?"

"You look the same, but I prefer the blonde."

"You call me chunky, and now you're knocking my hair?"

"I did not comment negatively on your weight!"

Casi yawned, checking the clock. "Oh, my God, it's after one in the morning. Do you work tomorrow?"

"Every day," he said earnestly. "Perhaps I can start later and we can have breakfast?"

"I like breakfast," she said slowly.

He regarded the freshly made bed. "I could sleep here to make it easier?"

She knelt beside him and threw her arms around his neck. "Brilliant idea."

"I'll get a few things and be right back." Kyle texted Jake and added a smiley face. "I'm spending the night at her apartment tonight."

"I thought she was too maimed to have sex?" Jake replied.

"She is." Kyle laughed. "It's cool to spend time with her and I love kissing her."

"LA turned you gay." Jake wrote back.

Kyle returned within twenty minutes, small overnight bag in hand. Casi contemplated the awkwardness of the first time a guy spent the night and suggested she wash her face to allow him time to get settled. She pondered what she should wear to bed, if anything. She had taken to wearing a nightgown after her injury because of the frequent visitors to her apartment. Dylan slept over twice and insisted she keep her backside far away from him and well wrapped. He wore his skimpy underwear, which she called a banana hammock. She chose a semi-modest, shorty nightie and got in bed, while Kyle brushed his teeth. He came out in black jockey boxer briefs and joined her, wrapping her in his arms. Exactly how she anticipated.

"I sleep in the nude normally, but I didn't want you to try to take advantage of me while I'm unconscious." He grinned.

"I must confess I'm rusty with the rules on this whole sleepover thing. You don't have a wife pining away in Blackberry Falls, counting the days until you come home?"

He chuckled. "Only a brother and a dog. I miss my dog."

She bet old Jake missed his brother; all alone and no one to hang out with. Too bad she would keep Kyle for a while. She knew at some point he needed to leave; he had a home and business to return to.

For now, she planned on savoring the experience, pulling his arms tighter around her.

They slept well through the next few hours, never shifting away from each other. As the sun shone in, Kyle whispered he was getting up to take a shower. She watched him walk toward the bathroom, admiring the view. Long muscular legs, leading to a firm, rounded butt, tapering from his slender hips to wide shoulders, defined and muscular. He removed his jockey shorts and her eyes widened. Witnessing him fully nude was breathtaking. He smiled at her, aware of his masculinity. She threw back the covers and made her way to the bathroom, flinging off her nightie on the way. He stood with his back to her and she put her arms around him to steady herself. She slid her hands over his stomach, enjoying the definition of his taut anatomy. *Stupid pelvis*! She couldn't remember wanting a man this much. Every time she touched him, it sent electrical shocks through her body. He turned and pulled her closer, their bodies intertwined as the warm water caressed their backs. Kyle lathered her hair, letting the suds run over their bodies. His hands and mouth probed her, making her insane with desire. He drew one hand behind her lower back and the other between her legs. Starting at the base of her spine and radiating throughout her body, the wave intensified. Colorful explosions rocketed through her mind as her body vibrated with pleasure. She leaned into him and tried to steady her breathing as he kissed her neck and ran his hand over her hip. She opened her eyes, grounding herself from the mind-blowing experience.

Still unsteady and concerned about slipping on the soapy surface, Casi maneuvered to the stool as she smiled up at Kyle. He groaned when she lowered her mouth to him. He tensed slightly at her touch, making her curious about his relationship status and his hesitation to be with another woman. With experience and an eagerness to please him, she brought him to a speedy climax. His vulnerability in this situation made her powerful. He relaxed against the wall and waited to recover. "Aren't you full of surprises?" he breathed.

They toweled off, appreciating each other's body in the mirror. Everything seemed natural, as if they were destined to be together.

Kyle suggested he pick up bagels and coffee to eliminate the hassle of her going out with a cane. After he left, she dried her hair, assessing her reflection in the mirror. She was nervous at the realization of falling in love with him, yet unable to shake the premonition it would all end badly.

# 10

# BILLS AND PILLS

Casi mastered the cane and began adding daily walks up and down the stairs, holding the railing for support. Her lower back screamed in agony late in the evening, but she was determined to improve enough to have sex with Kyle. He slept over most nights, making her dinner or picking up takeout.

She had a renewed sense of doom. Mary told her it was because she sabotaged everything good in her life, which seemed harsh, but maybe true. Dylan was convinced Kyle hid a dark secret, but Casi believed Dylan watched too many Lifetime movies. Sonya became surprisingly supportive, with a slight undermining tone, making Casi question her real motives. She vowed to be happy and bask in the glow of new love. Alix would be home in another month, and she hoped to have found a new place by then.

She received a letter from the LAPD informing her they were following up on a lead about the driver of the car. She heard the gossip around town fingering the driver to be a drunken Brittany Rain, girlfriend of the rap star, DeShawn Matthews. His vehicle had been impounded until the investigation ended. Brittany slunk off to rehab for the fourth time.

Casi and Kyle fell into a comfortable pattern of kissing and cuddling, interspersed with heavy foreplay and mind-blowing oral sex. He never pushed for more, but she sensed a passion waiting to explode. She smiled thinking about him as she made her way down the last flight of stairs. She greeted the doorman, Ray, with whom she had become quite friendly. He loved to talk about cooking, and she looked forward to seeing him each day and discussing the latest recipe he tried. She sorted through a stack of mail from her box while she chatted to Ray about beef short ribs. He enthusiastically shared the technique of making a robust sauce featuring a hearty cabernet. "It sounds delicious. Next time bring a sample," she prompted.

As she slowly climbed the stairs, the LAPD logo on an envelope caught her eye. She stopped mid-stair and opened it, praying they found Brittany responsible. The letter was impersonal and stated the vehicle's release back to DeShawn, with no arrests being made at this time. "Are you kidding me?" she yelled. This translated to no money coming her way, and she had been counting on it to pay the growing stack of bills being sent daily. She ascended the rest of the stairs, aware the ache in her back kept pace with her mood. When she got back to the apartment, she called Dylan to get the name of a lawyer. A well-known celebrity attorney, Anthony Goldman was recognized for his antics in the courtroom. Anthony was a client of Dylan's, who often used the chair as a confessional, enacting the sacred hairdresser/client privilege. He gave her the number and told her Anthony agreed to a free consultation over the phone, as a favor. She didn't hesitate to call and left a message with his secretary.

The time had come to add up the invoices and see what she was facing. She converted her phone to a calculator and opened the mail she had been avoiding. Eight separate charges from the hospital with ridiculous fees for consultations, medications, blood tests, x-rays, MRI, and emergency services. Two for physical therapy, one for the ambulance, and several more for 'services'. As she totaled the sum, she felt like she might throw up. Even with the percentage her health insurance would cover, she would owe well over $30,000, wiping out the meager savings she squirreled away, and leaving her with a significant deficit. She went online to check her credit card balances, considering that as an option. She winced at the discovery that her shoe and handbag infatuation had nearly maxed out her cards. The pain from her back radiated through her chest, squeezing at her heart. She willed it away, not needing to incur more bills. "Damn it!" she hissed, hurling the papers in a tantrum. She buried her face in her hands and sobbed.

Several hours later, Anthony Goldman called her back. He had a slow pattern of speech, making him sound disinterested and lazy, but she had been told he was one of the sharpest lawyers in Hollywood. "Well...it's not ideal for you. I would say (long pause) DeShawn will most likely claim Miss Rain took the car without permission, and since they're not married, you would have to go after her. She drove on a suspended license and is doing 90 days in rehab. She doesn't have a job or money of her own (another annoyingly lengthy pause). The most you could hope to gain... is for her to do a few months in jail and the process would only increase your debt load, once you hire legal aid," he concluded.

"What about my medical expenses?" Casi cried.

"Honey, off the record....you can spend a fortune on an attorney to go after her, but this is Hollywood. Everyone is bankrupt, morally and financially," Anthony professed. She managed to thank him before she broke down in tears for the third time.

Over margaritas with Dylan, she wailed about her financial situation. He had choice words about the over-privileged Hollywood set. "You can make enough money with a couple of shoots. Maybe it's time to go back to work. I heard about a show this weekend at the Gallery on Rodeo." Apparently, he knew the makeup artist, who dated the photographer, who slept with the designer.

"Make the call," Casi insisted, fretting she was falling into a financial sinkhole.

⚜

When Kyle arrived that evening, she told him about the show. He expressed concern, but she showed him the pile of invoices and reiterated her conversation with the lawyer. "Casi, you're not ready," he pleaded.

"I understand the modeling world better than you. This is an opportunity for me to pay off this stupid debt." He frowned at her with a mixture of concern and distrust. She softened her voice. "Just one show. I need to get back out there and prove I can still keep up."

When Kyle left, he texted Jake. "Casi is in a shitload of debt because of the accident and is stressing out. Should I offer to help?"

"Don't be an idiot! She's a spoiled Hollywood brat and needs someone to run to her rescue," Jake accused.

"She's not ready to go back to work. I'm worried she'll make her injury worse if she isn't careful," Kyle claimed.

"She targeted you from the beginning as the sucker who'd pay for her lifestyle. Let her boyfriend offer."

"She didn't ask me for anything," Kyle asserted.

"There's a reason a gorgeous woman is after you. Cash!"

"Thanks for the confidence boost." Kyle fumed at his brother's depiction of the relationship. "She's not aware I have money, her mother refers to me as the workman."

"You understand what I mean. I'm sure she's trolled Facebook and seen your house and knows you own the business. Of course, now she's all messed up, you're the best she can do."

"You're an asshole!"

"Don't lend her anything! She's like what? Thirty? You owned your home, commercial building, and business by then. Time for her to pull her shit together," Jake scoffed.

Kyle considered his brother's words. He'd completed his degree at twenty-two and lived with Jake for two years to save money to buy the old stone dairy for the business. He moved to a makeshift apartment they constructed inside the building for a few more years until he bought his property on the lake and set up a trailer while he waited to afford his house. He paid cash for everything, never financing large purchases. He took every job he could find, filling in with construction to earn enough. By thirty, he had finished his house, and the business was thriving. He still lived well within his means, saving most of his money toward retirement. Jake was right to be concerned. This was Casi's issue, and he needed to let her deal with it.

When Casi walked through the backstage door of the Gallery, heads turned. She could see them whispering, verifying the truth of the rumors regarding her disfigurement. She was sure the pictures the girls took at the hospital made the rounds. She kept her head up and approached the wardrobe manager. Mary hovered nearby and gave her a nod. She understood Mary only came to support her, pretending to occupy herself with perusing the design layout.

The first outfit consisted of black satin mini-shorts, and a flamingo pink, sequin bra. Casi glared at the six-inch, silver, rhinestone-studded stilettos with regret, and popped a couple of ibuprofen. She pulled on the fishnet stockings over her thong and slid the shorts three-quarters of the way up before realizing an issue. The five weeks off, and carefree eating, packed on enough weight to put her up a size or two. She wiped the sweat from her brow as she tried to avoid the mocking looks from the rail-thin girls around her. Suddenly at her side, Mary, with swift hands, tugged the shorts up and over her curves, zipping them and giving her a pat on the bottom with a wink. The bra was stunning, lifting her swollen cleavage to Playboy envy. The luminous detail wrapped around her ribs as a sparkly accent to her curves. If she didn't sit, Casi was confident she could pull it off. One of the wardrobe assistants came to help. Squeezing her feet into tiny shoes was bad enough, but the height of the heel unsettled her gait, making her fear a perilous fall. Not only would it humiliate her further, but Dr. Amir cautioned her about straining her pelvis. The stilettos had metallic strapping which wound around her calves like snakes, hissing their venom through her raw nerves.

The music queued the start of the show, and Casi braced herself for the procession. She suspected there were bets on how far she would make it before disgracing herself. She gave a brave smile to Mary, and stepped through the curtains, following the rhythm of the pop tune encouraging party-goers to put their hands in the air. With each step, the impact of the metal tipped heels hitting the mirrored stage sent a vibration through her legs, exploding into her lower back. She tried to focus on the pinch of the too-small shoes on her toes, willing her blood to send the pain there instead. She zoned in on the music, transforming the stage into a club in her mind. She imagined she was back to her old self, dancing the night away. Twelve steps with her long muscular legs, one in front of the other, pausing to jut her hip out and cast a haughty stare. Turn and butt thrust. Reaching the end of the catwalk, she improvised a half-lean forward, bringing full focus to her bountiful cleavage, with a naughty smile and head tilt. Her shorts climbed significantly on the jutted walk and revealed a lot of fishnet encased butt cheek. Cameras flashed, and "ooh's and ah's", emanated from the usually bored spectators. The walk back was excruciating. Casi hoped people thought the tight grimace on her face was part of the act. As she passed through the curtains, she fell into Mary's waiting arms and cried out, not quite sure if she might vomit. The shoes were unlaced from her feet as Mary half-carried her to the nearest chair. Mary unzipped the shorts and helped her slide out before going to fetch water. Casi sank back to the chair with her head lowered into her trembling hands.

She responded to a tap on her shoulder and glanced into the ice-blue eyes of a Russian girl she recognized vaguely from past shows. "Take zis." She produced a large blue capsule. Casi shook her head and pushed the girl's hand away. "Da," the girl commanded, forcing it into Casi's palm with a firm nod.

Mary returned and touched Casi's forehead. "Honey, you're done, you can't continue. You gave it your best shot."

Casi thought of Kyle and how he had told her she wasn't ready, and the gaggle of girls sneering at her from the sidelines. She pictured the faces of the crowd gazing at her admiringly, loving her newfound curves and the sexiness she exuded. She put the pill in her mouth when Mary turned away and took a swig of water. She reasoned it would either work or kill her, but either way, if it made the pain stop, she would be thrilled.

Picking up on the positive reaction, a team of assistants readied her for the next walk. Her hair was teased higher; eyeliner darkened with severe brows. The next outfit consisted of a skin-colored, sparkly bodysuit, with a snakeskin scarf zig-zagging around her curves. Her breasts were secured with medical tape and two-sided adhesive to ensure no nipples would make an appearance. A G-string covered her front, but her backside left bare, only slightly obscured by the scarf. They yanked on thigh-high boots with neon acrylic heels. Casi was glad people dressed her because she wouldn't have been able to discern which end was up in this attire.

She was warm and cold at the same time, but she couldn't feel her legs. She stood, wondering if she had legs at all. She felt like a floating head and worried she may collapse, but oddly, her body knew what to do without her. She peered at the Russian girl,who gave her a pretty, knowing smile. Casi stepped out on the runway to the piqued interest of spectators anxiously perusing her new image.

Chin up, breasts out, swinging hips. Casi owned the stage like never before, stopping to make eye contact with photographers, causing one poor fellow to drop his notepad in a flurry of embarrassment. She smiled, she taunted, she teased, and they ate it up. She'd never felt so amazing before, and her priority when the show ended was to find the girl with the magic pills and become her new best friend. Each turn on the catwalk built her confidence until she was gliding on air. By the end of the night, she was the envy of all the girls. Mary was suspicious of her sudden recovery and quizzed her relentlessly until Casi admitted she took medication, lying it was prescribed by her doctor. Mary cautioned her about taking it easy and not to rely on the prescription to push herself past her comfort zone. She listened obediently and then went to find the Russian girl, whose name was Nadia. "You were a lifesaver tonight!" Casi chirped.

"Da, I see fire in eyes. I fix for you."

"Um, what are these?" Casi asked, not wanting to know if they were illegal or dangerous. She needed the euphoria to last, no matter what the cost.

"Not so much legal," Nadia said evasively.

"Can I get more?" she asked, afraid what the cost might be, especially since she was pushing her limits to pay off the bills.

"I bring for you. You do favor for me."

This was a road fraught with danger, but without hesitation, Casi said, "Yes, I will do it."

"Tomorrow, you meet me at the coffee on Rodeo," she said, mispronouncing the famous road.

"Coffee Bean?" Casi clarified.

"Da, noon," Nadia answered as she left.

❧

Kyle was waiting for her when she got to the apartment, having made a pasta dish, assuming she would be hungry. Casi greeted him excitedly and rattled on about the show, the outfits, how she was the star and had more likes on Instagram than any model at the moment. She realized she talked too fast, but was anxious to explain how incredible the evening had been.

"Are you on something?" he asked, scrutinizing her. She averted her eyes and undressed. He followed her in the bathroom as she shed her clothes. "What did you take?"

She stepped in the shower, not waiting for the water to heat. "Geez, chill out, Kyle. I took a pill. Ok?"

"What kind?" he pressed.

"My doctor prescribed it. Why are you on my case?"

"I'm concerned about you; talking a mile a minute and eyes glazed over. Your scar is red and inflamed and you're acting like you feel nothing," he said, glaring through the glass door.

She ignored him, singing to herself as she lathered her hair. Finally, he went away, and she looked down at the scar which was indeed agitated from the too-tight outfits and abrasive materials. She ran her finger over the red welt. It was numb. She shrugged. *What was wrong with not wanting to be in agony?*

She poked at her meal and avoided eye contact, feigning exhaustion. He cleaned the kitchen as she crawled into bed. She watched him loading the dishwasher and wiping the counters. She should be thrilled to come home to someone who cooked, but she hated how he penetrated her buzz. As he slid in beside her and pulled her close to him, kissing her neck, she prickled at the sensation of her skin crawling with bugs, and she felt she would suffocate from his proximity. "What's wrong?" he asked with concern as she flinched.

"Sorry, my hip hurts so much," she lied. He ran his hand over her, lovingly massaging the area, while she willed herself to drift off, cringing at his touch.

The next morning, she awoke in severe pain, hardly able to crawl out of bed. She made it to the bathroom and vomited. She ran the cold water and held a facecloth to her skin, trying to calm the burning sensation. Thankfully, Kyle left early for work. She Googled her symptoms and deduced she was dehydrated. She drank four glasses of water and ate a banana.

She got to Coffee Bean early and ordered a vanilla latte, sitting to face the door. After what seemed like hours, Nadia showed up, sleek in black skinny jeans and a tunic top, sunglasses, and bright red lipstick, her jet-black hair smooth and shiny. Casi hadn't bothered to put on makeup and felt out of place. Nadia bought a black coffee and dumped in five packets of sugar. Her mouth stretched to a beautiful smile, full of big white teeth. "How you feel?"

"Like crap," Casi admitted.

"Must drink much water," she insisted.

Casi considered this to be crucial information and would have appreciated knowing it the night before. Nadia handed her a Hello Kitty bag with a wink. Peering in, Casi noted a bundle of tablets and nodded. "What's the favor? Do I have to kill someone? Donate an organ? Have sex with your hideous brother?" Casi wasn't sure if any of those things would be an actual deal-breaker.

Nadia threw her head back and laughed, a deep, hearty sound

shaking her whole frame. "No! I'm artist. You have boyfriend put work in gallery."

Casi realized no one knew she ended her relationship with Alix. It appeared to be a fair trade, and she took the deal, not sure if she would be able to honor it. "He's in South Africa until the end of next month, but I'm sure it won't be a problem," she stretched the truth.

Nadia placed her hand on Casi's. "Take only one or half if can. Only when serious." It was obvious she should ask a lot more questions, but didn't really want the answers. At this point, ignorance was bliss.

By mid-day, Casi's phone rang off the hook. The show had been a roaring success, and she turned the mediocre designer into a fashion icon. Her 1960s sex-kitten portrayal was the highlight of the show, stated one headline. "Hello, full-figured fabulous, goodbye skinny Minnie," was the title of another. Casi wouldn't have thought of a size six as full-figured, but they loved it, and she could embrace being able to eat again. An urgent message from her agent indicated bookings were steadily increasing, including several lucrative lingerie and swimsuit shoots. She grasped the Hello Kitty bag in her shoulder tote and convinced herself she could handle it. Besides, she reasoned, Nadia said they aided extreme pain; she would monitor her pelvis and be cautious.

The editorials were a snap. Casi swallowed half a pill to take the edge off. She floated to the music, titillating the photographer with her scandalous poses, dancing erotically to the music. It freed her mind to dull the constant ache and the memory of being hit. She liked the warm fuzzy feeling, similar to a couple of cocktails in her veins. It was fun to experiment with her curvier body, bending to maximize her larger breasts with a sultry pout. Roy managed her makeup application as his personal responsibility. Her hip required work, and he reapplied concealer often as she rolled around on the set. Casi focused on the next level and standing out from the multitude of pretty girls waiting in the queue for an opportunity to surpass her. Days off were spent hiking the hills of Runyon Canyon, pushing herself to near exhaustion. She enrolled in kickboxing classes to fulfill her goal of maintaining fuller breasts but defining arms, abs, and legs. Blessed with long legs and solid muscle tone, it was a manageable task. She became the envy of the other models, unabashedly stripping down to don the skimpiest of swimsuits and blowing up Instagram. Although the camera and shallow-minded audience bought her ultra-poised act, Casi realized her dark secret was a ticking time bomb.

11

## CRASH AND BURN

Six weeks passed since her accident, and Casi noted Kyle's excitement as he planned a romantic trip to the coast. She reset the date for their getaway, sighting pain and discomfort still in her lower back. The truth was, the more she focused on being ultra-fit and managing her career, the less she wanted to be around him. In the beginning, she obsessed about making love to him. His rough hands on her body and the warmth of his mouth sent shivers down her spine. When he slept over, he gently caressed her, keeping himself in control. He confessed his concern of becoming too passionate, and unable to hold back which could harm her pelvis. She had laughed at first, but figured she should savor the sweet nature of their relationship before sex became the priority. The issue stemmed from her overwhelming desire for him and the contrast of residing in her alternate reality. The pills were numbing her emotionally, but they allowed her to push past her physical and psychological limits, making them addictive. Within three weeks, her supply dwindled to almost nothing, and she still had to make good on her commitment to Nadia.

She sensed Kyle was growing restless with her busy schedule and inability to make time for him, even when she was at home. When he produced tickets for a band, suggesting it would be an enjoyable way to spend an evening, she should have monitored her response better. "That's not up my alley to witness a bunch of old men jumping around on stage, convinced they're still sex symbols," she sneered.

"Tell me, Princess, what's your idea of fun? Want to go for a run? Or stare at your damn phone? It seems to be the most fascinating thing in the room!" he retorted.

Casi snapped, "Don't get pissy because you're not getting laid. I guess we don't all have such simplistic needs in life."

"Are you kidding me? You believe I'm hanging around here, cleaning up after you, making you dinner, and rubbing your feet, for the promise of sex?" He scoffed as he headed to the door, "You're truly the most narcissistic woman on the face of the earth. I've never had a problem finding women to sleep with. You initiated a relationship with me!"

She focused on her phone in an effort to further infuriate him, acting as if she could not care less he was leaving. She knew she should stop him. She should apologize, but something inside her wanted to destroy what they had and to punish herself for ever being happy in the first place. Her mother had been right; it would never have worked out. She popped the last pill in her mouth and washed it down with a glass of wine.

After he stormed out with a slam of the door, Casi realized he forgot his phone on the counter. She considered running after him, but instead watched him through the window to see him get in his truck with Ray Dawson. She stared at the phone for a minute, fully aware what she was about to do was wrong. Perhaps he had a password and she wouldn't be able to access it, she reasoned. She would be devastated without her phone, her lifeline, but Kyle rarely looked at his, using it primarily for business and to contact his brother. His call log confirmed this. Numerous calls to her, unanswered. A few to contractors and hardware stores. What caught her eye were the multitude to his brother, some at great length. It made sense since they had a business. She wondered if Kyle talked to Jake about her and asked him for advice. What would he say about her? She decided to scroll through his messages for clues.

The last text from Jake read, "Run, don't walk," which piqued her curiosity. Scrolling to the beginning of the feed, she saw a timeline of their relationship, interspersed with business details.

"When will cabinets arrive?" The day she had walked in the apartment, she recalled him setting the phone down. "The strangest thing happened to me, wait until I tell you about it!"

*Ha, the kiss!*

She finished her glass of wine, then grabbed the bottle and drank directly from it, sitting cross-legged on the couch, finding great interest in the forbidden treasure. She scrolled through more business jargon and supply orders.

*Boring, get back to talking about me.*

Then came the mother lode. A text about how sexy she was and how he would wait for her to go by the apartment, but she usually had her nose in her phone. "Should I try to talk to her?" Kyle asked.

Jake warned, "I would stay away. She is gorgeous in photos, but is probably a crazy bitch."

*Screw you, Jake.* She was glad Kyle hadn't listened to him. Although in retrospect, he didn't approach her, she came after him. *Maybe that's why he hesitated to take it farther?* A message about the roof. *Damn it, did he share everything?*

"I don't know what this girl wants. I'm considering staying longer and picking up work down here."

Jake's sage words, "Bang her and get it out of your system. Then come back and patch things up with Lauren."

*What a jerk! Who's Lauren?* She took another sip of wine.

Kyle explained Casi may be splitting up with her boyfriend and Jake responded, "If she's still living with him, they're not broken up, you're a distraction for her because she's bored."

"She's sweet, much more normal than you would suspect just looking at her," Kyle claimed.

Jake continued, "Definitely smoking hot, (they were obviously

Googling her modeling pictures). Live out your fantasy, but you're too good of a guy to fall for a scammer like her."

His brother began to piss her off. She chugged another swig of wine and kept reading.

"Casi was hit by a car, not sure if she's ok."

"Too bad you didn't bang her first."

"Asshole!" Casi screamed.

"Casi came home; she's pretty ragged," Kyle wrote.

"Gee thanks!" she swore.

"She's hotter naked, even with the bruises and scars."

"Are her tits real? Send a picture," Jake asked.

"Yes and no," Kyle said. He gave a few updates on her condition, and she guessed there had been more discussed over the phone. "I'm falling for this girl."

"Dude, you're in over your head, she's not the girl for you. You should meet Gail's friend, Mary Ann, if you don't want to reunite with Lauren. Not as beautiful as that chick, but totally normal. I'll attach a photo." Next came an image of an attractive woman, with medium brown hair and a pleasant smile. Not a head-turner, but Casi felt jealous of Jake's possible influence over his brother.

"She's alright, but I really like Casi, there's something special about her," came Kyle's sweet reply.

"Time to come back to reality, your dog misses you." There were a few more texts encouraging Kyle to come home. He had been gone almost three months, and it became apparent Jake was not happy.

Kyle confessed his suspicions of her drug use. "Everything was fantastic, but she may be doing drugs. She's coming home like a zombie and acting irritable. She lost interest in being intimate and pushes me away."

She understood why her words to Kyle had been extra hurtful as Jake replied, "Take it from me, who has the wife from hell. Do not get tied down. You're not even getting laid, why are you still there?"

"I'm contemplating walking away."

Now the last text made sense. "Run, don't walk."

Casi buzzed, having the whole dose of the pain pill mixed with the alcohol made her euphoric. She slumped back, Kyle's phone in her hand, furious with his stupid brother. Without considering the repercussions, she texted, "Hey, loser, your brother should learn to password protect his phone if you're going to text him derogatory (thank God for spell check) things about me. Why don't you stay out of our business, stop masturbating to my pictures, and go screw your hideous troll wife? He doesn't need your advice on dating, especially when there don't seem to be any decent women in your piss-ant hole of a town." She hit send before rereading it, wanting to hurt him for what she perceived as an attack.

She cranked the stereo, drained the last of the wine and walked toward the closet, swaying from the buzz. She ran her hand over the dresses, drowning in the silkiness of the fabric and roughness of sequins. Entranced by the sensation of the materials, she regretted letting Kyle leave, imagining how amazing his calloused hands would feel on her smooth, over-sensitized skin. Of course, he would have known she was medicated and questioned her to death. She realized that was her primary irritation; he made her accountable, and it annoyed the hell out of her. The accident played over and over in her head on a continuous loop. The sound of the engine, the crush of the gravel, the look of serious concern in Dylan's teary eyes. Before the accident, she had been on autopilot, floating through the days, accomplishing the tasks which were planned for her, attending events as requested, and dressing to please. Then came Kyle, and it was like holding a mirror up to her life, and she started to suffocate in the diminutive nature of her daily activities. She should be grateful for the second chance at life, a wake-up call to her true purpose, but she was more lost now than ever. Tears stung her eyes and she willed herself to stop over-thinking her life. Less than six months until she turned thirty. *Live it up while you can,* she challenged herself. She splashed water on her face and combed her hair, leaving it down. She applied heavy eyeliner, giving herself smoky eyes, and put a finishing touch of rose on her full lips. Chandelier earrings, black leather pants, made tighter with her new curves, and a plunging halter top over a black lace bra. She finished with six-inch suede mini-boots, and her favorite black leather jacket, with the red satin lining. She loved the zippers and chains, making her seem like a badass. She had a pleasing numbness caressing her body and wasn't going to waste it. A quick check on Instagram indicated the location of the party, and she sauntered out the door.

The nightclub had a line around the block filled with hopeful party-goers. She exited the Uber and bypassed the line with a nod to the bouncer who opened the ropes for her. It was obvious she was a model, and her presence meant more money for the club, as eager men wanted to buy her drinks. She walked to the top level and side-stepped the dancers on the floor. She spotted her crew of models in one of the private booths, seat-dancing to a popular tune. Nadia sat with the girls, super-sexy in a black net top over a barely-there silver miniskirt. The bottle service girls moved aside and handed her a glass of champagne from one of several $200 bottles purchased for the booth. She let the bubbles slide down her throat and enjoyed the vibration of the blasting music pulsating up from the hardwood floor. Casi stepped up on the seat like a pro and slid beside Nadia, who planted a red lipstick kiss on her cheek and gave her a knowing smile. For the next hour, she downed drinks and swayed with the music. Nadia pulled her toward the floor, and she obeyed, giving into the rhythm of the music as Nadia danced behind her, caressing her hips. She thought of Kyle and wondered if he was having a good time, wishing she hadn't been such a bitch. She let the music lead her into a sensual dance, making the men ogle them. The throng of the crowd and fog machine pumping an ethereal smoke into the room carried her to another dimension. The sharp bones of Nadia's frame pressed against her, and her heart started to beat rapidly. The air was too thick, and her throat constricted, choking her as blood surged through her veins like a levy let loose. She staggered forward. "I need air."

Nadia, unfazed, located a new girl to finish her pole dance. Casi tripped down the stairs, clinging to the railing in a desperate attempt to escape a fall. She made it to the bottom step before being forced to her knees by the pounding in her head. The bouncer ran over to her convulsing form and lifted her up in over-muscled arms, carrying her to a nook behind the stairwell. Models overdosing was not a good image for the club. He called 911, and the well-trained drivers used the back entrance, sirens off, to come and retrieve her. Somewhere, she had lost a boot. They transferred her to a gurney and lifted her into the back of the ambulance. The sterile white interior spun in circles while lights blinked like a strobe, pulsing in and out of view. Blurry faces peered at her, asking her questions she didn't comprehend. Her skin was clammy and on fire as her heart leaped from her chest. Then nothing. Silence, and a glowing bright star overhead indicated without a doubt, she was dead.

**12**

---

## CLUB GIRL

eath was not what she expected; noisy and cold. Her eyes fluttered open to see Kyle at her bedside, holding her hand. He looked defeated, his hair mussed, like he'd been running his hands through it. The fine lines around his eyes appeared deeper and more pronounced, changing his bright blue eyes to a weary aqua. Her hand felt small in his warm, firm grip. An intravenous line ran to her arm and her head pounded while her mouth seemed to have wall-to-wall carpet preventing her from swallowing.

"What the hell, Casi?" Kyle pleaded, appearing so sad it broke her heart. He had his phone in his other hand, which meant he had gone back to the apartment to find her gone. She wondered what Jake's response to her text had been, regretting sending it.

"You gave us quite a scare, young lady," the doctor announced without regard to Kyle. "You had heavy-duty painkillers in your system. Not a good combination with the amount of alcohol you consumed."

She averted her eyes from Kyle, who rubbed his face. "Someone at the club gave them to me; it was a onetime thing," she croaked, trying her best to sound convincing.

The doctor frowned. "The level of drugs in your blood work indicates you've been taking these for some time."

*Damn it, doctor know-it-all!*

"I didn't think you were taking the prescription anymore?" Kyle questioned, confirming his suspicions.

Before she could lie, the doctor annoyingly proceeded. "There are no prescriptions of this nature in your medical records. These are powerful medications used for trauma victims and should only be administered by a doctor. You don't realize how dangerous those chemicals were. I must report this."

"No! I only took them for my pain!" Casi cried.

She began to detest this doctor as he raised an eyebrow. "We took X-rays, and there's no indication of permanent damage. The fracture healed weeks ago, and with your significant muscle tone, you shouldn't be experiencing unbearable pain. Is there perhaps another reason you would need to take medications?"

*Wasn't he violating her rights by disclosing personal medical information? He must have assumed a relationship by the way Kyle took vigil beside her bed.*

Like a guardian angel, Mary appeared at the doorway and indicated the doctor should speak with her. Once they were alone, Casi had no alternative but to meet Kyle's glare.

"I'm sorry...." she started to say, but he shook his head.

"I can't do this, Casi. I care about you so much. For God's sake, I'm in love with you." He let the words sink in. "I can't sit here and watch you self-destruct. You're making one bad choice after another and pushing me farther away."

Tears sprung to her eyes, and she reached for him. He pulled his hand away. "Kyle! Don't leave me," she sobbed.

"I'm heading back to Washington. My brother has a lot of work and I'm wasting my time here," he said with disgust as he strode toward the door. He glanced back and his shoulders slumped. "It sickens me to discover Jake was right about you."

A sob caught in Casi's throat as she screamed for him. Kyle brushed between the doctor and Mary as they stood outside the room. The doctor peered at Casi, giving her the once over, shaking his head as he walked away. Apparently, Mary convinced him not to report the incident, against his better judgment. Mary came in the room and touched her cheek. "Oh, Baby Girl, what are we going to do with you?" Casi let the tears flow and hugged her as if her life depended on it. Mary rubbed her back, gently rocking her. She understood Casi just lost Kyle, and it was only the beginning of a rough road she would need to travel down to face her demons.

Casi returned home the next day, feeling like she'd been run over by a train. Every muscle hurt and her head pounded. She was glad the pills were gone, because the urge to get rid of this torment would have been overpowering. Nadia called to check up on her, or more likely to make sure she hadn't ratted her out. Although the club minimized the incident, word spread she had been taken away by ambulance. Casi decided to quash rumors and control the situation, (a technique she learned from Alix), and spin it to her advantage.

She posted a carefully posed selfie to Instagram, showing herself in a hospital gown, duck lips, wide eyes, (makeup cleaned up) and sexy bed head hair. "Don't forget to drink water after a heavy workout." It was believable since everyone saw how she exercised like a fiend. She was a well-seasoned club girl who could handle her liquor, and no one would question her claim. To ensure false stories weren't making the rounds, she arrived back in the club two nights later, svelte in a red mini-dress, grinding on the dance floor. Less ethereal without the drugs, but she balanced the booze to numb her enough to let loose. As predicted, photos of her looking gorgeous, scantily dressed, in a flash of lights, blew up Instagram and Facebook. The attention brought her more job offers, as everyone wanted to see a little more of Casi Roberts.

Casi hadn't talked to Kyle since he left, not sure what to say to redeem herself. She was angry he told her about being in love with her as he left. It felt like a punishment, a cruel way to torture her with what could have been. *Would it have made a difference if she had known?* She was aware of his deep feelings, the way he gazed at her, and touched her. She was jealous of how easily he could let himself love her, without games or pretense, intoxicatingly pure, happy love. *Maybe that was what scared her most of all.*

**13**

---

## BLACKBERRY FALLS

$\mathcal{K}$yle drove straight through to Blackberry Falls, determined not to show how broken he felt. He was furious Casi pushed him away and confused by her in general. From the first day she walked in the apartment where he worked, her beauty blew him away. When she kissed him, he thought he would explode. What kind of gorgeous woman walked up to a man and kissed him? Not a regular kiss, but mind-blowing and intimate. The way she teased and flirted drove him crazy. He had never experienced passion like that before, even with Lindsey, and certainly not with Lauren.

When Lauren had broken up with him on Valentine's Day, after he declined to propose, he needed to get away before he fell back in a relationship with her, predictable and reliable. Jake had lowered his head, watching Kyle pack up tools at the shop. "Why do you have to go far away? I'm sure you could find jobs in Oregon."

"I'm afraid if I don't do something drastic, I'll end up back with Lauren, again. It's time for me to move on. Take care of my house and Colt," he said, giving Jake a hug.

Kyle shook his head at the memory. It seemed like a lifetime ago, not just three months. Of course, he hadn't expected to meet Casi. Or to fall in love with her. He pulled in the parking lot of the bar and walked in, finding Jake seated on a stool. He put his hand on Jake's shoulder as he leaned over and took his drink with a smile.

"Hey." Jake's face lit up. "You're back!"

"Yup." Kyle downed the scotch in two sips.

Jake ordered two more drinks and turned to face him. "I'm glad you're home. Colt missed you."

Kyle whispered, "Turns out I was right about the drugs. She overdosed after drinking a bottle of wine mixed with heavy-duty pain killers."

"Is she dead?" Jake's eyes widened.

"No. She passed out at a club. I saw her at the hospital and told her I couldn't do it anymore." His voice cracked and he regarded his hands. "I can't believe I fell so hard for such a train-wreck of a girl."

"You've been cautious with your emotions since high school," Jake said. "She broke through your wall, but you'll get over her. You belong in this town, in your lake house, at work, and hanging out with me."

Kyle glanced at his phone, seeing a new post. Casi looking sexy in a red dress at a club. He turned the picture to Jake. "I guess she's out of the hospital and over me."

He shook his head, hating the girl who had broken his brother's heart. "Delete the stupid bitch."

Kyle slipped it back in his pocket. "I'm not ready."

"She's torturing you!"

"I'll get over her. Just not yet."

"Kyle! You're home," a pretty brunette exclaimed, coming to give him a hug.

"Hey, Lia." Kyle hugged her tighter than he had intended. Lia flirted with Jake as she ordered her drink and Kyle noted how familiar they seemed. "What's going on there?" he asked after she rejoined her friends.

"Nothing." Jake shrugged. "I haven't slept with her, but we've been fooling around while you were gone."

"You became a cheater when I'm not here to stop you?"

"You shouldn't have left me alone to make bad choices," Jake teased. "I've tried every which way to make it work with Gail. All she does is bitch and uses sex as a reward for good behavior."

"I understand, but cheating won't help. Did you turn my house into your love nest?" Kyle cringed.

"Only your couch. You should date Lia since I can't."

"No thanks," Kyle mumbled.

"Why not? Don't you think she's cute?"

"She's very pretty, but we've known her for a dozen years and I'm not interested in her that way." Kyle sighed. "Plus, I dated her sister for over three years."

Lia smiled at Kyle the next morning from her register as he entered the coffee shop.

"It's about time you got back," Gail remarked from a nearby table studded with uptight women in tennis skirts.

"Did you miss me?" Kyle strolled to her side.

Gail rolled her eyes as Jake eagerly came over with coffee. "Not as much as your brother did." She introduced Mary Ann, and he recognized her as the woman from the picture. He greeted her pleasantly, not wanting to be rude, but not interested in encouraging her. "Maybe my husband will spend more time at home now," she said, glaring at Lia behind the counter. "Your dog requires a lot of attention."

Kyle smiled, understanding the reference. "Perhaps you should work on giving him something to come home to, Gail."

She narrowed her eyes at Jake. "You need to be a better husband if you want to continue coming home."

"To the house I pay for?" Jake sneered.

Kyle noted Mary Ann's eyes perusing him and sighed, missing Casi with every fiber of his being. "Let's go, Jake. I'm sure Gail has her hands full running the town meeting."

As they left, Gail called out, "Good job on remembering Mother's Day. It was nice to spend it by myself."

"When was Mother's Day?" Jake questioned.

"Yesterday, you jerk," she replied.

"Isn't that something your kids should remember? Even though you act like my mother." Jake paled as he turned to Kyle.

"Damn it!" Kyle read his expression. "I'm sure Mom will be hurt and think I did it on purpose since I was pissed off."

"Why did you argue with her before you left? That's unusual coming from you," Jake asked as they got in the truck.

Kyle shrugged. "Mom claims I make you too much of a priority in my life. She said I'm overly self-sufficient and controlling. She was upset I didn't propose to Lauren."

After work, they drove to the small town they grew up in and walked in the farmhouse. Georgia chopped vegetables in the kitchen, preparing for dinner. Tears came to her eyes with surprise. Kyle hugged her. "I'm sorry I didn't call you for Mother's Day. I was driving back from LA."

"He forgot to remind me." Jake embraced her.

"It's only a day, I'm not upset. I assumed you were still out of town," she said, as her voice broke.

Their father frowned. "You should have called."

"Peter, it's fine. A visit is better than a call." Georgia turned away to hide her tears. "Can you stay for dinner?"

Kyle embraced her. "Let us take you out instead."

"Are you still angry with me?" Georgia whispered, broken hearted when Kyle left angrily after their fight and hadn't been in contact, not even answering the phone on his birthday.

"No. I went to LA for work." He kissed her cheek.

They settled around the table at the restaurant and Kyle told them about LA, trying to sound positive.

"How are the girls there?" Peter teased.

"Pretty fake, for the most part." Kyle fiddled with a napkin.

"It's a long time to be away from home," Peter pushed, seeing Kyle's reaction. "Did you meet anyone?"

Kyle glanced at Jake. "No one special."

Georgia watched Kyle fidget and push the food around on his plate. "Peter, stop grilling him. I'm sure he's happy to be home and back to his life."

Jake talked about the work at the shop and what the kids were doing in school, taking the focus off his brother. Kyle checked his phone to see another picture of Casi at a recent photo shoot, wearing sexy lingerie. Jake caught his eye and shook his head, wishing he would unfriend her and be done.

"Is everything ok?" Georgia put her hand on his.

"Yes, fine." Kyle slipped the phone in his pocket. "An email about supplies."

"Kyle, who's this woman you're not telling us about?" Peter narrowed his eyes. "You're moping around like a love-sick puppy."

"She's a girl I dated..." Kyle swallowed loudly.

"Who broke his heart." Jake sneered. "But, now he's home and that bitch can go to hell."

"Are you sure it's over?" Peter raised an eyebrow.

"Oh, I'm sure," Kyle sighed. "I guess I wasn't prepared for a city girl and how wacky they can be."

"Let's see a picture." Peter held out his hand.

Jake chuckled as Kyle's face blanched. "He has to find one where she's wearing clothes."

Kyle rolled his eyes. "She's a swimsuit model." He located a picture he had taken of her smiling at him in the roof garden.

"Wow, she's gorgeous!" Peter said.

"Oh my, she certainly is," Georgia agreed, quietly hating her for hurting Kyle.

"I take it by Jake's reaction, she ended it?" Peter asked.

"Pretty much." Kyle shrugged. "It's not like it would have worked out. I'm sure she'd never want to come to Washington and I hate LA."

"You'll find a nice woman closer to home," Georgia said.

"Her dad lives in Bellingham." Kyle wondered if he understood what a disaster his daughter was.

"You should give Lauren a call," Georgia suggested.

"Mom, that's over and I ruined a friendship by getting romantically involved with her in the first place." Kyle grabbed a piece of bread.

"I realize you weren't ready to commit, but she's a lovely girl. Give it time and things will work out." Georgia smiled.

"Time won't change anything," Kyle snapped. "Why can't you accept I don't want to get married and have kids?"

"I like to think of you having a partner in your life," Georgia sniffed, not wanting to rekindle the argument.

"Jake's my partner," Kyle challenged.

"Well, that makes you sound gay." Peter shivered.

Kyle chuckled as Jake look repulsed. "If I were gay, I wouldn't choose Jake as my lover."

"Is it because I'm fat?" Jake frowned at his significant middle protruding toward the table. "Perhaps Brian would be more to your liking?"

"Our accountant? He's not gay, is he?" Kyle asked.

"He sure dresses nicely." Jake winked.

Kyle shook his head. "Whatever. I like my life the way it is. Look at how happy Jake is."

Jake rolled his eyes. "What's not to love? The nagging? The whining? The constant bills?"

"You should think long and hard before having children, but a wife would be good for you." Peter wagged a finger.

"Yes, children will always disappoint you." Jake glared at his father and Peter shook his head.

8.

On the way back to Blackberry Falls, Kyle took the exit for Bellingham. "What are you doing?" Jake asked suspiciously.

"I'll buy you a beer." Kyle grinned.

"You're a moron."

"It's not like she talks to her dad." Kyle considered how disappointed Jack had been that he wasn't close to his daughter.

He located the restaurant, and they walked in the bar and surveyed the lively scene. People watched the game on the big screen TVs or sat laughing with friends. "Cool place," Jake said.

Kyle spotted Jack behind the bar with an attractive woman restocking glassware. "Damn, that must be his wife."

"Holy shit, she's a fox!" Jake scanned the honey-brown haired beauty with a curvaceous figure and silver-blue eyes. "She's Casi's mom? I guess she takes after her father."

"Step-mother. Her mother is a nutcase and not nearly as good-looking." Kyle turned to his brother. "She only inherited her perfect breasts from her mom."

Jack grinned when he recognized Kyle. "You're back in Washington!" He reached out to shake his hand.

Introductions were made and Jack poured them craft beers. Ava smiled at the brothers, having heard about Kyle. "You're home for good now?" she asked.

"Time to get back to work at the shop." Kyle exhaled and regarded his glass with remorse.

Jack sighed. "When did you get back?"

"Last night. We were visiting my parents in Elmvale and I figured I would check your place out." Kyle took a sip of beer.

Jack observed his sullen appearance and wondered what Casi had done to crush him. He leaned closer. "Sorry if I encouraged you to get together with Casi. I thought you two would be a good fit. I'm lying to myself to think I know that girl anymore." He wiped the bar and noted anger on Jake's face. "Not a fan of my daughter?"

"She treated my brother like shit," he scoffed.

"LA has changed her. She used to be sweet and charming. The prettiest girl in town." Jack sighed and poured another round. "You would have loved who she was back then."

"I'm in love with her now," Kyle mumbled into his beer.

Kyle adopted his regular routine, Coffee Junction in the morning with his brother before a long day at their wood shop fulfilling orders. Evenings were spent drinking scotch on the back porch, with his German short-haired dog, Colt, enjoying the lake.

"Gail wants to fix you up with her friend, Mary Ann. Remember, you met her at the coffee shop?" Jake said.

"I'm not interested in Gail's friends." Kyle cringed and Jake laughed at Kyle's disdain for his wife, mainly because of her constant rudeness, ordering him around and publicly chastising him. Uptight, in her tennis skirt, with pursed lips, in a compact frame, she was the town organizer. She sat on her throne with her 'ladies who lunch' group, bitching about their husbands and involving herself in every-one's business.

After days of not-so-subtle hints, Kyle agreed to a double bowling date, figuring his brother had been there for him through the whole Casi debacle and had ultimately been right. Kyle arrived late to the bowling alley, to the chagrin of Gail, who made a point of frowning at her watch. Mary Ann was attractive, slender with brown, shoulder-length hair. Similar to Lauren in coloring and stature, and worlds away from Casi. Her eager brown eyes perused Kyle, lingering over his lean frame and handsome face. He politely shook her hand before buying a pitcher of beer. Mary Ann sipped the brew with obvious distaste. Kyle pushed the image of Casi, laughing as she belted back a lager with sheer delight, out of his mind. Mary Ann proved to be a decent bowler and Kyle tried to appreciate her skill, even if he didn't admire her small-breasted, boyish figure.

Mary Ann and Gail excused themselves to use the restroom, and Jake sat beside Kyle. "What do you think?"

"She is similar to Lauren." Kyle rolled his eyes.

"She's pretty enough and it would be good for you to date her. She's nice and normal, nothing like that crack-pot, Casi," Jake assessed, making him laugh.

Mary Ann took her turn at the lane. Dressed in a light blue

sweater set and faded jeans, she smiled at Kyle. He nodded in return and looked down to the beep of his phone. A notification from Facebook, another Casi Roberts selfie, posted for the world to admire. Long, muscular legs, topped by a thin strip of material, revealing toned abs, and generous cleavage, barely contained in a midnight blue bra top. The hands of a man clasped her waist as they dirty danced. Casi's head was thrown back in ecstasy, haloed by a mane of streaked blonde waves. The caption read, "Rockin' my new do. Thanks, Dylan-love," with a hand-drawn heart.

He should have unfriended her weeks ago, tortured with every new post of her having fun, gorgeous and carefree. He wanted to not care about her anymore, to move on with a woman like Mary Ann, predictable and plain. Casi needed someone like Alix, moody and artistic. Kyle lied to himself that he would block Casi as soon as he got home, knowing full well he would go online and search for her latest modeling pictures to fantasize to. He noted Jake watching him with concern and turned the screen toward him. Jake's eyes widened at the photo. "Damn, could she be wearing less clothing? She's even sexier as a blonde."

"You're being incredibly rude!" came Gail's shrill voice.

Kyle realized he missed Mary Ann's strike. He poured another tall glass, downing it in seconds. Mary Ann strolled over, wounded at his disinterest in her game. He gave her a coy smile. "Do you want to get out of here?" Her face lit up, and Jake shook his head, realizing his brother's desperate attempt to get over Casi. Gail was pleased he had taken a sudden interest in her friend and then scolded Jake for pouring himself another beer.

Kyle opened the passenger door of his truck and Mary Ann looked ill at ease with the rugged interior, dog hair, and mud on the floor mats. She timidly moved wood samples from the bench seat as she slid in. Kyle gave her a smile as he hopped in the full-sized truck, indicating what his intentions were. He drove to the overlook by the lake and parked. The lights from the houses sparkled like stars through the trees as a delicate drizzle coated the windshield.

He hadn't been to the ridge with a woman since his early twenties when he had first moved to Blackberry Falls. Kyle had never lacked for girlfriends. Being handsome, athletic, and charismatic, he always had his choice. His biggest issue had been not taking it further than dating, finding everyone in a hurry to get married and start a family.

Mary Ann scooted closer and gave him a permissive smile. Kyle reasoned he hadn't been with a woman for weeks before the disaster with Casi, and she had left him more sexually frustrated. He pushed the memory of Casi's perfect, full breasts from his mind, and let his primal-self take over. He located a condom in the glove box and skillfully removed Mary Ann's clothing, sliding on top of her. As he thrust, he blocked her moans, picturing Casi in the outfit on Facebook, smiling at him and lifting her skirt ever so slightly to reveal lace panties.

## 14

# ROAD TRIP

Casi woke up lazily and stretched. Her head was woozy from the previous night's drinks. She was glad she switched to cranberry vodkas, able to pace herself better and not overdo it. Her clothes were strewn on the floor where she discarded them. She glanced at the naked man beside her. She invited him home, convincing herself she needed to be with someone intimately. Kyle held so much promise in the early stages, and his passion almost frightened her with its intensity. She often wondered if that's why she pushed him away, afraid he might break through the wall she built around her emotions should they ever make love. It would have been making love, not having sex. Kyle's emotions were raw and fearless. From the first time she kissed him, she could see it in his eyes. She had an unbridled desire to connect with him, to hold him so close there would be no definition between their bodies.

She shook off the feeling and slipped out of bed, not eager to wake the man. She pulled on a t-shirt, ironically one she stole from Kyle, cotton panties, and yoga pants. She would shower when the man left, not wanting to encourage him to consider this was more than a one-night stand. Thankfully he was a regular at the club who she had flirted with for some time, so their intimacy was predictable.

He awoke and gave her a sleepy smile. She informed him she had an appointment, and he needed to be on his way. He asked if he could take a shower. "Sorry, there's no time, I must hit the road. An Uber will be here in ten minutes."

He pulled his clothes over his well-defined body and moved toward the door. As he turned to utter the generic statement, "Thanks for last night," she shut him down with a nod.

She called Dylan and asked him to take her to breakfast. Although he was tired of hearing her whine about Kyle, she sweetened the deal with the promise of details from last night's hook-up. She would have to fabricate since she had fantasized about Kyle. He agreed to meet her at Denny's at ten, which gave her thirty minutes to get ready. She smelled the growing collection of shampoos in the shower; her new obsession. She realized a therapist would say she attempted to recreate the memory of the bath with Kyle, or maybe the steamy shower, but no fragrance of lavender or coconut could take away the pain in her heart. *Had Kyle seen the picture of her new hair?* She checked Facebook, and he hadn't 'liked' the photo. Even though 1452 people reacted to the picture, it irritated her he wasn't one of them. He'd been surprised by her blonde roots and suggested she return to her natural color. She had become tired of the brown, needing a change for her new image. Dylan readily agreed to bleach her hair back to a dirty blonde and add lemon highlights to brighten her face. He cut it to the top of her breasts, creating layers with long bangs, mostly to hide the scar on her temple, but not without reminding her she approached the age of Botox. Her agency loved the new look, which was good since she hadn't consulted with them beforehand, a definite violation of her contract. Her sexier image landed her higher dollar jobs and helped her to stand out in the sea of skinny brunettes. Casi gave her hair a quick blow dry and pulled on a long cotton dress with sandals.

Dylan was seated in a booth, having been there for twenty minutes, giving her a scolding glare as he eyed his watch. "Do you think this magically happens?" Casi said, gesturing toward herself.

"It doesn't seem like much happened over there this morning."

He frowned at her clean face and carefree attire. "I ordered you fried eggs, bacon, and toast, which I will eat because I don't want you getting fat." She laughed, glad she had him as a friend. The waitress poured a cup of coffee and Casi added cream, taking a sip from the steaming mug. "Details," he demanded. She described the club and what she wore, setting the stage. "Hello? I have Instagram; I saw your slutty outfit. Your hair looked fabulous!" She giggled and continued to talk about her lover, her mind again drifting to Kyle, and if he had seen the pictures. "Ok stop. It's Kyle, isn't it?" he questioned, catching her in a lie.

"Ugh. I can't believe he didn't comment on the picture! Did you think I looked hot?"

"Totally bangable. Maybe he's over you, moved on with some hometown hussy who bakes apple pies and blows him in the backseat of his car."

"He drives a truck; he doesn't have a backseat," Casi challenged, feeling surprisingly close to tears.

"Darling." Dylan grasped her hand. "You need to figure out what the hell you're doing. Stay here and make a life for yourself or move to some redneck village and marry your knight in shining armor. By the way, I heard of a loft for sale on Wilshire. You could afford it now that you're a hot commodity."

"I do need to make decisions in my life. Alix will be back next week, and I should be on my way to clearing out by then," she sighed, as she stabbed at her eggs.

Casi returned from breakfast with determination. She would be thirty in a little over three months, and she didn't want to end up the quintessential 'has been', or worse yet, 'almost was'. The first task was to clean the apartment and pack her belongings. Although she flirted with the thought of rekindling the spark she once had with Alix, she decided it to be a fruitless endeavor, buying her a few more years of hanging in the background as he radiated his talent.

She bought a used, red Volkswagen Beetle convertible and drove around the parking lots until Dylan was comfortable she hadn't completely forgotten how to drive. They took several trips down the coast, wearing their Ray Bans and singing at the top of their lungs. She adored the sun on her skin, the wind in her hair, and the freedom of having her own car for the first time in her life. She bought a bobble-head dog at the car wash and put it on her dashboard. She liked how it happily nodded its head as she rambled down the road, approving of her in his gentle way.

Casi drove to her mother's house to show her the new car. Sonya curled her lip with disappointment. "Darling, it's bourgeois. What about the BMW I told you about?"

"I couldn't afford it," Casi said. "I don't want payments. I paid cash for this one."

"I can see why." Sonya shook her head. "Why do you need a car in LA?"

"I might want to go somewhere else one day." She shrugged, annoyed she always had to defend her choices.

Alix returned from South Africa, looking incredible. Tanned and at peace with the world. A renewed connection blossomed between them, not romantic, but a deep kinship. He claimed her near death experience changed her and now she contemplated life on an alternate plane. She wasn't sure he was wrong. They spent the night smoking a joint and pondered the galaxies. She confirmed she had zero desire to have sex with him. He wasn't surprised, saying he recognized a spiritual bond between her and Kyle, which was why he gave him the key in hopes they would fulfill their destiny.

She showed him the scar on her hip, and he kissed it gently. "Babe, life is about the journey, not the destination. This is one stop on your trip."

Casi packed the last of her belongings and found the scrapbook. She thumbed through the photos, again feeling the pull of home. She knew what she needed to do. She made good on her promise to Nadia and packed a small suitcase. Alix told her to leave her things at his place, reminding her they weren't broken up, only traveling separate paths. Casi nodded and figured it was easier than getting a storage unit.

❧

The sun was out in full force on I-5, and she cranked the music and belted out the lyrics, feeling free and happy. She made it to Ashland, Oregon, and checked into a Holiday Inn. She called her father and informed him she would visit early the next week which meant three days with Kyle. It would either be horrible or incredible, depending on how he received her. She planned the trip to Bellingham as a plausible excuse to stop by Blackberry Falls, without the awkwardness of an extended stay. If things were uncomfortable, she would simply get back on the road.

The next morning, she showered, layering vanilla-coconut lotion and body spray. She chose lavender lace lingerie and slipped on a periwinkle sleeveless jersey dress. High heeled floral sandals completed the look. She brushed her hair back, smoothing scented wax through the ends to keep the waves in place. Light makeup highlighted her tan, recently obtained from driving around with the top down.

She got Kyle's address from a girl named Lia, who seemed to comment frequently on his Facebook pictures. Casi sent her a message saying she was a friend of his from LA and wanted to pay him a surprise visit. She readily provided the information, which Casi hoped meant she wasn't dating him. She scanned Facebook for signs he had moved on, but his relationship status remained blank, and she took it as permission to pick up where they left off.

Casi found the exit for Blackberry Falls relatively quickly, admiring the quaintness of the town with tree-lined streets. She got disoriented trying to find Maple Lane, making several illegal U-turns, until figuring out where to exit. She drove down the lane, and her stomach lurched. She tried to channel Alix's confidence in universal truths and let destiny take over. She rounded the bend and caught a glimpse of the lake, sparkling in the early evening sun. Kyle's back porch stood out, picture perfect, with bright Adirondack chairs and planter boxes featuring a colorful array of flowers. He looked severely sexy, sitting with his legs stretched out in front of him. She could see he was smoking a cigar and drinking what was probably scotch, with Colt beside him.

She parked on the side of his house. As she walked around the corner, Colt came trotting up, but Kyle's gaze remained on the lake, lost in thought. She petted the dog on the head, amused by the feel of his floppy ears, like strips of velvet. She stepped gingerly on the porch, unsure of what Kyle's reaction would be. She fluffed her hair and smoothed her dress, shaking with nerves. Colt nudged Kyle with his nose, breaking his concentration, and he glanced up in her direction, his face registering surprise. She smiled, trying to remember what she planned to say. She practiced a full apology for her behavior, explaining her state of mind and the pain she experienced. She forgot everything as he smiled back. She dropped her purse and gingerly walked over to him. He remained seated, long legs crossed at the ankle, with a look she couldn't interpret. "You look good. I like your hair."

Without another thought, Casi hitched up her dress and promptly removed her panties. He watched with growing interest and she tossed them to the table beside him. In a thankfully smooth gesture, she swung her leg over him to sit in his lap. She whispered in his ear, "How about that lap dance?"

## 15

## THE BROTHER

Kyle raised his eyebrows and started to speak, but she silenced him with a kiss. He returned her kiss hungrily, and she melted into him. She caressed his chest and he gazed in her eyes as he removed his shirt swiftly while she rubbed against the growing erection beneath her. He lowered his mouth to her neck, gently licking her collarbone as he unbuttoned her dress, revealing her lace covered breasts. Overcome with desire, Casi unzipped his jeans, positioning herself to take him fully. He didn't resist, and she gasped as he entered her, the passion he held back previously now released. He lifted his hips toward her, grasping her waist to make deep contact. As she rocked against him, he fondled her to bring her to orgasm, grinding against her to let himself reach a climax minutes later. Casi breathed into his neck, still reeling from the sensation. She pictured it for so long; the reality delivered almost instant satisfaction.

They remained intertwined and Kyle gazed at her lovingly. "How's your pelvis doing?" he whispered.

"What the fuck, Kyle!" A woman screamed.

Startled, Casi looked up to see a woman approaching from the side of the porch, and recognized her from Jake's text. She rebuttoned her dress and slid from Kyle's lap as he re-zipped his pants. It was undeniable what took place between them, and Kyle didn't hurry to defend himself. Casi stood awkwardly to the side as he slipped his t-shirt on, avoiding eye contact with the woman. Casi glanced at her lace panties discarded on the table, wishing she could retrieve them.

"I guess you forgot your brother's birthday dinner?"

Kyle exhaled while the woman glared at Casi, hate in her eyes. "This is Casi, a friend of mine from LA," he finally said.

"Oh, LA, that explains everything!" she shrieked.

"Casi, this is Mary Ann. We had dinner plans for my brother's birthday." Kyle stood slowly. "I'll call Jake and cancel." Mary Ann lunged forward and shoved her violently. Kyle rushed to her aid before she fell from the porch. "You need to leave," he instructed Mary Ann.

"You might have warned me you had a rabid girlfriend." Casi shivered as she regained her footing while Mary Ann stormed away in a flurry of curse words.

"Like you gave me time to say anything before you sexually assaulted me," Kyle said, with a twinkle in his eye.

The grating sound of a key scratching against metal indicated Mary Ann was livid. Casi winced at the thought of her red bug being violated viciously. Kyle sighed and called Jake, leaving a message saying he wouldn't make it to dinner. Casi followed him in the house and surveyed the spectacular, light-filled living room, bright with floor to ceiling windows facing the lake, and a huge fieldstone fireplace, complete with a hand-carved mantel. It had a brown leather sofa and matching recliner with two mission style chairs surrounding the fireplace. A giant flat screen TV completed the manly living area. The room gave way to a large pine dining table flowing into an open style, custom kitchen.

Kyle's phone rang and she could hear an animated male voice on the other end and assumed it was Jake. She heard laughter as he shook his head. "I'm not coming. I don't need the third degree by your bitch wife...No." He sighed. "Fine, but tell her to stay out of my business. We'll be there in fifteen minutes."

"We? As in me too?" Casi asked frantically, wanting no part of any scenario involving his brother.

"Jake wants to meet you. He's heard the whole story from his wife, who is Mary Ann's best friend."

"Wasn't it a bad idea to date the friend of someone you dislike so much?"

"We weren't serious, but I have bad judgment when it comes to women." He frowned at her.

She laughed and threw her arms around his neck. "We're not teenagers. I'm sorry if Mary Ann is hurt, but I had you first."

He pulled her tightly to his chest. "You are chaos, wrapped in pretty paper and will surely be the death of me."

They parked behind the steakhouse and walked hand in hand toward the restaurant. The place was packed, and Casi wished she changed into jeans, conspicuous in her body hugging dress. He led her toward a table in the bar, nodding to familiar faces on the way. She could feel eyes on her, which was not uncommon when she entered a room. They witnessed her holding hands with Kyle, probably wondering about the mystery woman. She grasped his hand tighter, partly to not get separated from him as he wound through the crowd, but the small-town vibe made her ill at ease. She recognized Jake from pictures on Facebook, the same piercing blue eyes as his brother. He had a huskier build, which she guessed he wasn't proud of, watching him adjust his t-shirt around his expansive middle. She assumed the pursed-lipped woman to be the bitch wife, well deserved of the title at first glance. A sullen teenager, named Olivia, grunted a greeting, while a young boy with a mop of curly hair was introduced as Reid.

Jake scanned her with a sly smile. "Oh my Casi, you do not disappoint. You're even hotter in person. Now I see what my little brother is in a twist about."

He gave her a hug, too aggressively, and Olivia said, "Gross, Dad," as Gail glared at her.

"I love the blonde hair," Jake whispered. "Very sexy."

She liked the reference to Kyle having been in a twist, thrilled he mentioned her. "Kind of short for a model, aren't you?" Gail sneered.

"I mainly do swimsuit and lingerie work," Casi stated.

"I can see why," Jake said with a wink.

"Mary Ann called me, Kyle. Nice going, asshole. Just couldn't keep it in your pants, could you!" Gail hissed.

"Drop it," Jake cautioned, and Kyle handed him an envelope containing a cute card about brothers being partners in crime, with a printout of reservations for a fishing trip.

"Great, exactly what he needs, more time away from his family," Gail snipped. Casi surveyed the kids engrossed in their phones and guessed they couldn't care less if their father went out of town.

The busboy filled their water, spilling it on the table as he peered at Casi's cleavage. Jake shook his head with an accusatory glare. When their table was ready, Jake slid into one side of the booth, pulling Casi beside him, proclaiming he wanted to sit beside the sexy supermodel. Kyle completed the trio, like bodyguards protecting her from the perils of scorned women. More alcohol was ordered and Casi gave in to the need to use the bathroom, whispering to Kyle, hoping she could slip out unnoticed. As she exited, Gail announced she would join her. Kyle positioned himself to block her. "She's okay on her own."

"I'll be fast," Casi called over her shoulder, then willed herself to go quickly before Gail broke through the human barricade. She returned with wet hands, unable to find paper towel, using her napkin instead. "It's all yours," she said brightly to Gail, who no longer needed to go.

The conversation was tense, animosity between the party-goers thick as molasses. Casi focused on her steak, which was well-marbled and juicy. "I thought models weren't allowed to eat," Olivia remarked, watching her plow through her meal.

Casi took a deep breath and forced a smile. "It's a charade." Kyle's slid his hand to her thigh in approval of her answer.

Gail continued to berate Jake throughout the dinner, and Casi wondered about her apparent misery. She kept herself in shape, and her clothes were carefully chosen and paired perfectly with jewelry. Her highlighted hair was overly coiffed, hardening her subtle prettiness. She understood why Gail would be angry about Mary Ann, but the permanent frown lines on her face indicated a woman who was often displeased. Kyle paid the bill, getting a thank you from his brother only. As they left the restaurant, Gail instructed Jake to get the Escalade, as it started to rain. Jake turned toward the parking lot, but Kyle put a hand on his shoulder. "It's Jake's birthday, and it's my duty as his brother to take him for drinks."

Gail stated, "He's had enough alcohol for the evening."

Kyle tightened his grip and grasped Casi by the hand. "You take the car, I'll drive him home when we're finished with our evening." He directed them up the street as Gail stared after them, mouth open in disbelief, getting soaked in the downpour.

The bar had pool tables and a dartboard, with a friendly atmosphere. A weight lifted off Casi's shoulders now that it was the three of them, although still unsure what to make of Jake. The brothers were greeted enthusiastically, not strangers to the establishment. Casi headed for the bathroom, over-explaining she had been too pressured to go entirely at the restaurant. The brothers laughed and found a pool table. Casi took her time, fixing her hair and makeup, before returning to join them. She discovered a cranberry vodka with a twist of lime waiting for her.

"I thought you might like that drink," a soft voice said.

She turned to sparkling golden brown eyes, smiling at her with a pleasant welcome. "Lia!" Casi hugged her tightly as if they were old friends reconnecting.

"You know each other?" Kyle asked, confused at the connection between the women.

"Facebook," they both laughed.

Casi noted Lia flirting with Jake and understood her eagerness to help her find Kyle. The brothers set up a game and Lia took Casi's hand, leading her to the bar to order more drinks. Jake whispered to Kyle, "Could be trouble," as Kyle nodded in agreement.

Casi danced to a song, keeping perfect rhythm as all eyes watched her. She leaned into Kyle, freely kissing him and cuddling against him. He put his arm around her waist, pulling her closer. The envy of every man in the room. "I love watching you dance," he said, entranced by how well she moved.

"I love you watching me." She kissed him passionately before returning to her drink at the bar.

Kyle came up behind her and rested his chin on her shoulder. "I'm glad you're here," he whispered. She leaned into him and sipped her drink contently.

"Your turn, brother," Jake called from the pool table, eyeing Casi, as Kyle let go of her begrudgingly.

"What do you think of her?" Kyle asked.

"She's gorgeous for sure, but she seems kind of wild."

"She's not a small-town girl and she's used to being in clubs in LA. She's having fun. A round of shots for my brother's birthday," Kyle called to the cocktail waitress.

One shot turned into two, and Casi's earlier nervousness washed away, and she turned it up a notch with her dancing. She ordered another drink, flirting shamelessly with the bartender who was being very attentive. Jake scoffed and Casi caught his glare. She narrowed her eyes. "What's your problem with me?"

"If only I could condense it to one issue," Jake answered rudely, the shots loosening his restraint.

"Come on guys, let's keep this friendly." Kyle tried to coax them, sensing tempers were about to flare.

"Your brother has a bug up his ass and is very liberal with his advice." Casi grabbed the drink from Jake's hand. "Tell me to my face what your issue is with me. That would be excellent coming from you, a man overly involved in his brother's life because he has a crap home life and would rather run to the bar then to spend time with his family." Kyle tried to intervene one more time. "No, Kyle." She put a hand on his chest as he attempted to take the drink from her. "I want to hear what he has to say. I'm a big girl, I can take it."

Jake turned to face her. "Where should I start? Should we begin with the way you flirt with every man in sight, including the busboy at the restaurant?"

"It's not my fault men find me attractive," she scoffed.

"You're gorgeous, a face and body beyond words. Like the constellation Cassiopeia." He smirked at Kyle, who rolled his eyes. "When I saw the pictures you posted on Facebook, I cautioned my brother to stay away from you. A good-time girl out for her next victim is what I said. Too bad I didn't write it in a text though, so when you were trolling through his phone, you could have seen it. What do I see? A spoiled little girl who bends men to her will by flashing her tits or tearing up when she doesn't get her way."

"Jake, stop," Lia pleaded.

"No, she said she can take it, and I'm going to give it to her. Kyle is way too good for you and you're trying to con him because you got bored in LA, or maybe you've slept with all the guys there and you needed a new one to sponge off," he said with disgust. "I wonder, Casi, are you still living with that boyfriend or are you taking care of yourself now?" When she didn't answer, he continued, "Just what I thought, you can't even quit your last sugar daddy before you reel in another sucker. I hope you can give him a good enough time in the sack to make it worth his while." He laughed when he saw the tears start. "You shouldn't have come here. Your kind belongs in LA."

Casi threw the drink in Jake's face and ran out the door, waiting until she got outside to break down.

"Thanks for the warm welcome," Kyle said sarcastically, as Jake wiped his face with a napkin.

Kyle rushed to Casi outside, as she stood crying beside the truck. "Forget him, he's drunk and miserable."

They drove home in silence and she wiped a tear. "I should leave in the morning. He's right, I shouldn't have come."

"I want you to stay with me; nothing else matters."

❦

She blocked Jake from her mind and came toward Kyle when they entered the bedroom. He was insatiable, wanting to please her in every way possible. Finally, she sank back on the bed, her body covered with a fine bead of sweat. He relaxed beside her, catching his breath. He propped himself up on one elbow and gazed at her. "I love you," he said honestly.

"I bet you say that to all the girls," she teased, uncomfortable with how easily he could express his emotions.

"I haven't said it to anyone since high school, and that turned out to be a crush." She took a deep breath and he put a finger to her lips. "I don't expect you to say it back. I needed you to understand how I feel."

"I have a broken gauge for love," she started.

"It's ok," he reiterated.

"My dad left when I was fourteen and it crushed me. I knew he loved me, but I saw the relationship between him and my mom grow into a horrible ball of hate. I vowed never to let anyone in who could hurt me like that. You met Alix. They can't get more emotionally distant. When I felt you falling for me, I did everything to push you away and make you leave me...and you did." Tears filled her eyes. "I'm unsure if I'm capable of loving you in the way you would want me to."

He held her close. "It killed me to leave you. I started to come back twice, but I knew if I didn't let you fall and get up by yourself, you would resent me in the end."

"I'm still not all the way up," she confessed tearfully.

"Then I'll wait patiently until you are."

Casi told him of her plans to visit her dad and return to her hometown to see childhood friends. "Turning thirty is messing with my mind. There's so much I should have accomplished by now." It felt good to talk about her feelings and not be judged or hurried.

Kyle gazed at her, running his finger along her bottom lip. "I met your dad in LA."

"You did?" she gasped.

"I asked him how you were doing when he brought you home." He paused. "I went to his restaurant with Jake."

"When?"

"When I got back from LA. He told me about his place and I stopped by after visiting my parents. Ava certainly is lovely. They seem happily married."

"Did you talk about me?" She began to cry, not wanting her father to be aware of the overdose.

"He had no idea we got together and I didn't mention anything that happened there. How long until you leave?" he asked, kissing her collarbone.

"Two days." She rolled over and opened the nightstand drawer to get a tissue. Instead, she found a stack of photos.

"Hey." Kyle reached for them to prevent her from viewing the contents, but she recognized the images of herself that Alix had taken in an instant.

"I saw you take a couple, but it seems like you have the entire set," she winced. "Is this your masturbating material?"

"No!" Kyle removed them from her hand.

"Tell me what you're doing with them." She slid up to sit and put her hand to his flushed cheek. "Kyle, the pictures are of me, I have a right to know."

"I originally took two because I liked how you appeared natural, like you weren't posing. I grabbed the remainder because I didn't want him to have them; to be able to see you nude when you weren't there anymore." He held the pictures tenderly, before handing them back to her.

"Alix used them for his paintings. He has this thing about capturing emotions and freezing them in time." She thumbed through the images, stopping at one when she first met Alix. A sexy curtain of her red hair draped over her bare breasts, a glimmer of anticipation of her lover. As Casi flipped through the photos, she felt an odd sense of traveling through the past. Her slight innocence at twenty-five gave way to a trimmer body and harder look. The sparkle in her eyes became more knowing. She came to one where she sat nude on the bed, shoulders slumped forward, tears streaming down her face, utterly crushed. The light from the window behind her emphasized the shadows of her thin frame.

"What emotion did he capture there?" Kyle probed.

"He cheated on me. For the first time. He was explaining how it wasn't a betrayal, but a cosmic instinct of attraction." She swallowed, remembering her devastation at not being enough for him. Kyle pulled her into the crook of his arm. She finished looking at the images, each one a testament of how Alix controlled her emotions, and how much she changed in five years. She thought of the box of pictures Alix kept by his desk, a photo essay of the women in his life, capturing them at their most intimate moments. She stacked them back in the drawer. "I like knowing they are here. Thank you for taking them." She turned her attention to the interior, intrigued at what other secret things he might have.

"Some things are personal." He playfully pulled her away from her search. Most of the contents were boring. A pen and paper, various outdoor magazines, the Kleenex from her original mission, the tears now dry. She laughed when she found condoms, pulling them out with a curious grin. "Now that you've brought it up..." He rolled his eyes in realization they had been having unprotected sex from the moment she arrived on his back porch.

"You don't have to worry, I'm a very careful girl." She smiled, but noted he wasn't satisfied with her brief answer. "I've been tested for every disease known to man as part of the medical workup they did on me in the hospital."

"Since then?" He shuddered to think Alix was back in LA.

"I haven't been with Alix since he returned. I've used condoms with anyone else." She averted her eyes. "How about you? You can't be satisfied groping my pictures. Also, from the devastation on Mary Ann's face, I can tell you slept with her."

Kyle shoved the condoms back in the drawer. "I've always used protection, except for the time a beautiful woman blindsided me on my porch." He continued to caress her hips, disturbed at how much weight she lost since he had left. Alix had control over her, wanting her to be as thin as possible, but he hoped the reaction she received for her curvier figure would be enough to encourage her to maintain it. "Should I be concerned about anything else? I don't like surprises."

"I'm on the pill. I have no desire to have an alien take over my body and then control my life for the next eighteen years." She peered at him to see his reaction. "Is my lack of maternal instinct a problem for you?"

"Not at all, I'm happy to be the only one having a claim to your exquisite body." He slid down to kiss her hip bones, making her moan with ecstasy while he demonstrated his point.

**16**

---

# REVISITING THE PAST

Jake leaned against his truck in the parking lot of Coffee Junction and shook his head when Kyle pulled up beside him in Casi's car. "Did you forget something at the bar the other night?"

Kyle opened the door for Casi. A broad smile expanded across his face. "I was supposed to drive you home." He shrugged. "You deserved to be abandoned."

Jake rolled his eyes and strolled to Casi. "I apologize for what I said. It was rude and your personal life is none of my business." He held up a tray of coffee. "Peace offering vanilla latte? I thought you might want to escape the lynching mob."

Casi glanced toward the coffee shop and noted a group of women staring her way. "Thank you." She read the regret in Jake's face. "I was drunk the other night too. Let's put it behind us and move on?"

Jake's lips curled into a humble smile. "You'll discover I'm not the easiest person to deal with when it comes to my brother."

"I understand you're very close." She hesitated. "Hey, I'm sorry about that stupid text I sent from LA. It was immature." She saw a flash of deep insecurity in his blue eyes. "I was drunk."

Jake's expression softened. "I'm sensing a theme."

Kyle chuckled. "You aren't an angel either."

"Far from it." Jake waved as he got in the truck.

"Get that taken care of in Bellingham and send me the bill." Kyle indicated the long scratch across the door.

Casi nodded and bit her bottom lip. "The second time I was in the hospital, did you pay the bill? When I was discharged, they said it was taken care of."

"You had enough to worry about." He gave her a final lingering kiss. "Text me when you get to Bellingham."

The weather was warm for June, and Casi enjoyed the rush of the breeze as she drove with the top down on I-5 to Bellingham. She realized she hadn't eaten the whole weekend, only pausing for coffee each morning. She giggled at the memory of spending two days in bed, getting to know each other intimately. No broken pelvis, no phones, no brother. It had been blissfully quiet and peaceful, wrapping themselves in blankets in the evening to watch the sunset from the dock. He showed her the constellation, Cassiopeia, and told her the legend of the beautiful queen. She suspected there might be more to the history given Jake's snide remark.

Casi took the first exit into Bellingham and headed north toward the lettered streets. She walked inside her father's restaurant and surveyed the few late morning customers. A heady aroma of bacon and hops from the adjoining brewery wafted through the air.

Ava added breakfast checks at the front counter, her perpetual smile lighting up her face. Her grin increased when Casi came into view. "You're glowing. I like your natural blonde, it's pretty on you." Ava hugged her tightly. "I'm thrilled you came to visit. We miss you." She smoothed a strand of hair from Casi's cheek. "It's been too long."

"Has it?" Casi shot back, instantly regretting her tone.

Ava inhaled sharply. "Can we move on, Casi? It's been over a dozen years."

Casi smiled as Jack came from the kitchen, beaming with happiness. She glanced back at Ava. "Sure, no problem."

Jack embraced her. "It's great to see you, Honey."

"Doesn't she look fabulous?" Ava gushed.

"She sure does." Jack shivered at the memory of her accident. "Come eat. I'll make you something special." He directed her to a table on the back deck.

Casi sat facing the water, letting the early morning sunshine on her face as she slipped into a peaceful trance. The sound of a chair scraping on the wood deck brought her back to reality. Jack set down a burger with Applewood smoked bacon, caramelized onions, gorgonzola cheese, and a balsamic reduction. Extra crispy fries with a pot of gravy completed the dish. "Exactly what I like." She felt like a kid again, rattling away to him while she indulged in his culinary creations. They talked easily, and he didn't press for details she didn't readily offer. She told him about her work and the breakthrough she made. She mentioned she would be moving out of Alix's, which he agreed was a good idea. She left out the nightclubs, the drugs, drinking, and occasional sex with strangers. She figured there were some things dads shouldn't know. "I stopped in Blackberry Falls to see Kyle." She waited for his reaction.

Jack smiled. "How'd it go?"

Casi blushed. "I surprised him."

"I'm glad you're happy, Sweetie." He touched a strand of her hair. "You look like your old self again."

After her huge meal, Casi was exhausted, and Jack gave her the key to the house. She parked in front of the restored 1912 bungalow with original fixtures and well-landscaped gardens featuring colorful flowers spilling from containers and hanging pots. It was a three-bedroom, white and green home with a lot of charm. The rooms were bright and airy, with big over-stuffed furniture in cheery patterns. Ava decorated the home with love, bringing in color and unique features. Casi wandered around, studying the framed photos that seemed to be the feature of the living room. Several of her modeling pictures were given center stage on the piano. Ava's nieces and nephews each had a special spot, and Casi smiled at the care Ava took to showcase each child through their many stages of life. She noticed an older photo of a laughing, pig-tailed little girl, with sheer joy exuding from her face. "That's me," she exclaimed, recognizing the girl with the shiny red tricycle. She continued her journey, highlighting the happy times of her childhood, and conceded Ava was the force behind it.

She carried her bag to the guest room and set it on the bed, adorned with a cheerful pink and lime green floral comforter. A vase of flowers from the garden was arranged by the bed. Another sweet touch to welcome her. She laughed when she saw an assortment of her favorite Canadian chocolates in a dish on the dresser. Nothing got past Ava. Casi stretched out on the queen-sized bed. She flipped through magazines on the side table, mostly house and garden editions, with articles on making the most of your home. Casi had a pang of sadness about her lack of domicile. "I'm basically homeless," she gasped with a shudder. She snuggled against the squishy pillows and drifted off to a wonderful scent-filled dream of pretty houses.

She woke a few hours later, groggy from a deep sleep. She peered at the clock and yawned while she calculated how much time she had to get ready. She swung her legs over the side of the bed and searched for her phone. It was surreal to think she hadn't checked it since arriving in Bellingham. She cringed as she riffled through her purse, realizing she had forgotten to text Kyle. It was nice someone cared should she be dead in a ditch, but she was not used to being accountable for her whereabouts. She found the phone and checked her messages. Two texts and one voice mail from Kyle expressing concern if she made it. Had she gotten lost? Was the car ok? *Did he think she was a moron?* She traveled all over the world by herself. True, she got lost often, and was rarely on time, but she eventually arrived with most of her luggage. She wasn't sure if she liked this 'checking in' thing. There was a reason she dated guys like Alix; he wouldn't have noticed she was gone. Kyle picked up on the second ring with deep concern in his voice. "I was worried. Did everything go ok?"

"Sorry. The trip was simple, no problems. I meant to text

you...then I smelled bacon." She giggled. "At least someone thought to feed me!"

He laughed, and they fell into an easy conversation. She told him she was getting ready to go back for the tasting menu, and she feared she would become quite plump while visiting. "More for me to love," he replied.

The tasting menu paired a flight of beer with small plates including lamb chops and a mint reduction and honey garlic chicken drumettes. The spicy beef kabob featuring a rich dark beer with chocolate notes came in first for her favorite. The flight had six selections, and the heat rose in her cheeks, indicating a slight buzz. She loved how proud her father was, telling everyone she was his daughter. He rarely mentioned her career as a model, as if the fact she was his daughter was amazing enough. Her mother always led with, "This is Casi, she's a very successful model," noting what ads she had been featured in.

Casi spent the weekend in the garden with Ava and Jack, talking about life and what her plans were. Ava urged her to finish her degree in a subtle yet insistent manner. In her early twenties, Mary had demanded she enrolled in night classes at the local college because she deemed it important to socialize with ordinary people. Casi enjoyed the curriculum, but partying was more appealing. She earned her AA degree, with extra credits toward a BA. Mary celebrated with cake and champagne. Her mother had been in Italy at the time, marrying Mario, ex-husband number three. She informed her father as an afterthought in a Christmas card. She rarely mentioned it since no one seemed interested in her brain.

Ava produced a folder with the courses highlighted she felt would be of interest to Casi. Ava's easy manner made Casi smile, understanding why she was a beloved aunt; steering her kin toward better choices and making life seem fun and doable. Casi agreed the online classes would be possible to fit with her schedule, although she wasn't clear how a degree would benefit her in the long run.

She raised an eyebrow at Ava's inquisitive smile. "Do I have something on my face?"

"I'm curious how things went with Kyle."

Casi giggled, forgetting Ava would have met him when he came to visit. "Good." The heat rose in her cheeks.

Ava grinned. "He certainly is handsome."

"He is." Casi bit her bottom lip. "I'm not sure if it was a good idea to visit him though."

Jack frowned and Ava nodded. "Long-distance relationships can be tough." She reached over and clasped Casi's hand. "Things have a way of working out. Give it time."

Bellingham was approximately seventeen miles from the Canadian border which made for an easy drive. As she headed north on I-5, she noticed a sign for Elmvale and took a detour. The town was tiny, framed by picturesque farms and a winding river. Shops and a diner lined the 'blink and you've missed it' main drag. She thought of Kyle growing up there, and it seemed odd to picture him amongst the farm folk. On a whim, she chose an independent coffee house and pulled in the parking lot of the woodsy establishment. She ordered a vanilla latte and sat at an outdoor table to enjoy the sunny day.

"Guess where I am?" She sang into her phone.

"Lost on I-5," Kyle replied.

*Geez, why did everyone question her navigational ability?* "Nope. I'm in Elmvale. I saw your face on a wanted poster. I understand why you left," she teased.

"It's entirely possible. Jake and I were quite the hell raisers in high school."

"Do you still associate with anyone here?" She glanced around at the average people.

"My parents, and most of the neighbors. A lot of people I went to school with still live there."

"You have parents?"

"Obviously. Georgia and Peter. They live on our farm on Apple Blossom Road."

"I should see where you were spawned," she challenged.

"Go ahead, I have nothing to hide."

"You've never mentioned them. I mean, you know all about my family, and even visited my dad's place."

"They're normal people, not much to say."

"It must be awesome to have normal people raise you."

Kyle chuckled at her interpretation. "Remember, I told you I'd been at dinner with them before I went to your dad's?"

"I guess I'm hung up on the fact you visited my father." She relaxed in her chair. "The weather is terrific here. I assumed it rained in Washington. I'm at a coffee shop called the Java Hut."

"My friend Nick owns it. Tell him I said hello."

They spoke for a few more minutes about the plans for the day while she finished her coffee and enjoyed the warmth of the sun on her face. She walked inside under the pretense of throwing away her cup. A quick check of name tags revealed Nick to be the tall, slender, and tired-looking fellow restocking the coffee beans. She walked over and struck up a conversation, mentioning Kyle as the inspiration for trying the coffee shop.

"Kyle's a great guy, I've known him since kindergarten!" He gave her an admiring once-over and nodded his approval. "Looks like he's doing pretty well for himself."

Unclear how her attractiveness level indicated Kyle's success in life, she simply smiled. "I'll tell him you said hello."

She finished her tour of the town, unintentionally passing Apple Blossom Road. She put the car in reverse and decided to explore. A red barn came into view, flanked by a white, two-story farmhouse. She sensed this must be Kyle's family home before noting the sign which read, 'Jensen.' She pulled to the side of the road and took a mental picture of the sunflowers and lush green grass spreading out from the farm. *What would it have been like to grow up here?* She could picture the two little boys, wrestling, and running free around the farm, without a care in the world. Rainy days would have been inside with a mom who made soup and grilled cheese sandwiches. Sunny days at the river, swimming, fishing, and throwing rocks. She felt a pang of jealousy for a childhood she never had.

Casi headed back toward the highway, glad she made the side trip. The crossing was swift mid week, and she answered the fundamental questions. A familiar feeling washed over her when she crossed the border. No matter how long she lived in the States, Canada would always be home. A sense of calm embraced her as she crossed to the soil, which breathed life into her. She smiled at the red and white flag, peacefully waving a welcome.

After a lengthy tour of her old neighborhood, she pulled into the Swiss Chalet parking lot. She reapplied her eyeliner and brushed bronzer on her cheeks. A swipe of pink lipstick brightened her face. Dylan did an excellent job on her hair, working with her natural waves, enhanced by the humidity. The layers framed her face like a golden mane, ensuring bangs covered her scar. Dark blue skinny jeans and a fuchsia pink halter top brought attention to her tanned shoulders and cleavage. She double-checked her reflection in the window as she approached. Over the years, her primary contact with her Canadian friends had been on Facebook. She crafted a somewhat false image of success in LA because she had a deep fear of failing and being labeled as the girl who could never make it in the industry. Her biggest concern after the accident was to be the tragic friend who could have succeeded had she used better judgment. She was late out of habit and because she didn't want to be the first one there, sitting awkwardly in a booth, waiting. She waved at the group, trying not to convey surprise at how much older they appeared.

Joey jumped up and hugged her and everyone took turns squeezing her and telling her how amazing she looked. She slid beside Joey, who swung his arm around her as if a dozen years had never gone by. Dawn was amused by Joey's flirting and poured her a beer. The years melted away as Casi chatted with her friends, picking at fries and chicken. She could hear the Canadian cadence in her voice return as she became more animated, and the beer flowed. When they left, she wanted to take a mental snapshot; so much a part of something, a member of a group. Not like the crews at the clubs, assembled of beautiful girls to lure men, but really belonging. Sharing common backgrounds and core values.

Dawn drove with Casi to the beach. They talked naturally, like they were teenagers again, laughing about their early years. Casi didn't share too much about her life, mostly mentioning she was 'seeing' someone. No, not an actor or an artist, just a regular guy. Kyle would fit right in, drinking and laughing with her friends. Her attraction to him was no surprise; he represented so much of what was precious in her youth.

"Do you ever hear from Katie?" Casi asked casually.

"Not since she moved to West Van, about eight years ago. Even though it's close, she kind of dropped out of the group."

"That's a shame."

Someone started a bonfire, and Casi took a seat beside one of the girls on a log. The rye was passed around, everyone taking a swig, like they were still in high school, coughing as the bitter liquid burned their throats. There were marshmallows, dares, and one naked guy jumping in the frigid water while everyone cheered him on. Casi laughed until her sides hurt, and Joey nudged her and suggested they go for a walk. She wrapped herself in a blanket and kicked off her shoes. With the bonfire as a sparkling side note, they reclined in the sand and Joey wrapped the blanket around them. He leaned forward and kissed her as they gazed at the stars. The kiss was not intimate, only an expression of a seasoned friendship. She laced her fingers through his and snuggled against his chest. They spoke honestly, all pretenses stripped away by the alcohol. He spoke of his pride in his children and watching them grow. His frustrations at work, and the mind-numbing routine of life in general. The passion was gone between him and Dawn, maybe it had never been there, but they had a comfortable rhythm and cared deeply for each other. They focused on the kids and their friends, and their general contentment as a family.

She told him about her world, her actual life. Explaining how she was terrified all the time, unsure what would come next. She talked about Kyle, how he awakened a fire in her she hadn't felt in a long time and how that surprised her. She noted how she balanced on the precipice of becoming the woman she should be and losing the girl she once was, and that scared her most of all.

Joey held her as she spoke, warm and accepting. He rolled to his side and gazed in her eyes. She studied the lines on his face, the worry that etched them, and the joy. She ran her fingers through his thinning hair and smiled. She had loved this boy. The hope rose in her that she was at least capable of the emotion. He leaned in for one more kiss, a final, gentle reminder of what had been. They slowly walked back to the bonfire. Someone produced a stereo and music blasted through the chilly night air. Dawn grabbed Casi's hand and dragged her toward the shore. They danced and sang, kicking the gentle lapping water under the moonlight, laughing as the sun began to rise.

Casi mentioned the intimacy with Joey, and Dawn howled with laughter. "Thank God! I swear he spends half his life on the computer scrolling through your modeling pictures, doing God knows what."

Casi clasped her hand tightly. "I'm completely lost. I'm unsure what I'm doing with my life and I might be in love with Kyle." The words swirled through her mind like a dam let loose.

"We're all confused. None of us have it figured out. You're one of us. You can drop letters from your name, but we know where you come from, and we've got your back." Dawn squeezed her hand. "You only fail if you never try."

# 17

# THE CONCERT

asi returned from Canada refreshed and ready to start working on a plan. Her friendships gave her strength and a sense of belonging she had been sorely lacking. She waited to call Kyle until she crossed the border to avoid additional charges on her phone bill. She liked the freedom, being able to blame her plan for not being able to connect 24/7. She stopped at a coffee shop on her way back to Bellingham, figuring she could sort out her emails and messages before she returned to Ava and Jack, who seemed to have a full schedule of activities planned for her.

There were twenty-five emails from Dylan; drama with Roy. A hair show award he won and how she abandoned him in his time of need. Several messages from her agency. Work was slow, but several possibilities were coming up. A warning about socializing and a request for current pics, ensuring she maintained her size. Casi took a quick selfie, sucking in her stomach and angling the camera to appear extra lean. She sent it to the agency. "Not fat." She got an immediate response of a thumbs up.

Several texts from Sonya scolding Casi for not informing her she went out of town. She listened to the first minute of the voice mail to find out how much money her mother needed and then made the transfer. Two messages from Kyle. He sounded annoyed or tired. He knew she would be out of the country, and she hoped he wasn't the needy type. She called him back and tried to sound cheery, launching into a quick recap of her trip.

"Sounds nice," he said, distracted.

"What's wrong? Your mood is weird." She covered the phone to muffle the annoyance in her voice.

"Nothing. Just stuff with work. Screwed up orders and supply issues. Jake and Gail fighting, the usual crap." He cleared his throat and changed the subject. "Do you want to go to a concert this Friday in Seattle? It's a cover band of Pink Floyd."

She rolled her eyes and considered claiming she had plans, but remembered how she'd blown him off the last time. She generally hated concerts, bothered by the crowds and noise. And Pink Floyd? Certainly not her kind of music. "Sure, sounds great," she lied, hoping her hesitation didn't indicate her complete disinterest.

Casi enjoyed time with Ava and Jack, doing their multitude of activities. They were a fun couple, attending festivals, making jam, and gardening. It was a new experience for her to be part of a family, wearing denim cut-offs, and going without makeup. She almost forgot about the concert and raced back to the house to get ready, hoping there wouldn't be too much traffic. She didn't know what to wear and had a limited wardrobe stashed in her car. She settled on skinny, low-rise, black jeans, with a studded belt, and high-heeled ankle boots. She threw on a red lace bra and topped it with a loose, graphic tank. She created a messy bun, leaving a few pieces trailing out at the front. She grabbed her leather jacket and applied black smoky eyes and mascara. She looked edgy, hard rock ready in her opinion. The traffic sucked, and she realized she should have considered Friday would be difficult. "Come on!" She pounded her steering wheel.

A text from Kyle buzzed. "Where are you?"

"Horrible traffic, sorry." She sent a smiley face.

She didn't have blue-tooth in her car, which was ideal. Hearing about how she should have planned better wouldn't get her there any faster. Dylan was relentless with his lectures on her untimeliness. She always countered with his many faults. She pulled into Kyle's driveway an hour late. Kyle, Jake, and Lia were standing by Lia's car, and Kyle looked pissed. She parked badly, disconnecting her phone from the charger.

"Sorry, terrible traffic," she called out, sliding into the backseat after giving Kyle a quick kiss hello.

"What the hell are you wearing?" Kyle frowned as he got in beside her and surveyed her outfit.

"Are you the fashion police?" She eyed his faded jeans and Pink Floyd t-shirt, surmising how sexy he looked.

"Is that an Alix Grey tank top?"

"Why yes, how fashion forward of you to notice." She hadn't considered how it might appear wearing a shirt featuring her ex-boyfriend's artwork. Lia started up a conversation, asking about her trip and trying to redirect the mood. A strange vibe hung between the brothers; Jake was uncharacteristically quiet, and Kyle seemed sullen. Casi regretted accepting the invitation and retreated to her phone, texting Dylan, giggling to herself at SnapChats he sent.

Parking proved to be a nightmare, and it didn't help Kyle's mood. The night was balmy, and she considered leaving her jacket in the car, but Kyle insisted she wear it over her tank top, indicating he didn't care for the visible red bra. He zipped it up and removed her hair tie, apparently not liking her messy bun. She slipped the band on her wrist. *I'll take one for the team,* was the look she gave Lia, who waited to read her reaction.

The stadium thundered with hard rock music and was crammed with fans. More than she predicted. Beer was ridiculously expensive, but both brothers brought flasks, and Lia had one tucked in her bra. She took sips from each, hoping the alcohol would enhance the general mood. She scanned her phone as the opening act started, checking another text.

"Enough of the damn phone!" Kyle removed it from her hand and shoved it in his pocket as she stood in disbelief.

By the time the opening act finished, she was dying of heat. She took off her jacket, cooler in the tank top. Kyle frowned at her and she yelled over the music. "It's too hot in here."

The cover band was good, and the alcohol gave her a decent buzz. She swayed to the music and enjoyed the rhythm. Suddenly, hands hoisted her to the stage as the crowd cheered. The guitarist serenaded her as the lead singer grasped her around the waist to dance with him. Not wanting to be a loser, she let herself go, swinging her hips and dancing chest to chest with the singer. The lights were bright and she couldn't see the faces in the audience but imagined Kyle was not thrilled about her dancing on stage like a stripper in her tight jeans and exposed bra. When the song ended, she returned to find Kyle's predictable glare. "It's all in fun. Lighten up." She shook her head and made a hand motion for needing water as she shoved through the crowd.

The bathroom seemed miles away and she bought a $5 water, downing it in seconds. She fixed her makeup while two teenage girls shared the mirror. "I love your shirt," one quipped.

"Thanks, it's an Alix Grey original," she said proudly.

As she exited the bathroom, she got turned around, not remembering which door she had come from. She pushed past the throng of people, walking through clouds of weed, and stepping on toes. The crowd went wild for a song featuring psychedelic lighting and an electric guitar solo. She decided to exit through the front doors and get her bearings. The air was refreshing, and she tried to clear her lungs of the thick smoke from inside. She remembered going to the right when they arrived and assumed she should head in that direction. She turned to re-enter the building and discovered the doors were locked. She paced back and forth, figuring someone would walk by and let her in. It turned cool and a light drizzle broke through the clouds. "Damn it." She kicked the door with the toe of her boot.

People hung out by the cars and she approached them to ask for an alternate way in. She reached for her phone to text Kyle she was locked outside. She recalled he took it and fumed all over again. The people were middle-aged stoners, reminiscing about the original Pink Floyd. They welcomed her to their circle, giving her an approving nod in her now wet top, plastered to her skin. One long-haired guy offered her the joint, but she shook her head, not wanting to add paranoia to her mounting bad mood. Another man offered his jacket, and she accepted, needing the warmth and feeling exposed. As the storm picked up, they huddled in a van, and she assumed she might be getting a contact high from the fumes. She enjoyed listening to them chat, stoned and not making any sense, but their passion and knowledge of heavy metal were enviable. After about an hour, she thought she heard her name and emerged to realize the rain had stopped. She yelled to the trio who appeared to be frantically searching for her. Kyle stopped in his tracks, and she realized climbing out of a van with stoners, wearing a denim jacket emblazoned with Led Zeppelin, might have something to do with the rage apparent in his face. She handed the jacket back and thanked them for helping her out. She walked toward Kyle as he stormed away. He turned back and tossed her leather jacket at her in disgust.

"Why are you being such an asshole? You took my phone away like I was a child! You violated my personal property." She raged after him through the parking lot.

He turned with her phone in his hand. *Please don't throw it*, her eyes begged. Jake and Lia stood on the sidelines, not sure if they should intervene. "You were acting like a child! A spoiled teenager," he barked, handing it back to her.

She snatched it from him. "Well, you're NOT my father."

Kyle scoffed as her eyes filled with tears. "Of course, here come the daddy issues. And the waterworks." Lia handed the keys to Jake and climbed in the backseat. Casi pulled her knees to her chest and cried silently with her head pressed against the window. Lia reached over and took her hand.

Casi planned to jump in her car the minute they returned, wanting to be as far away from Kyle as she could. The concert had been a mistake, and they should sleep it off and not escalate this evening into a fatal fight. Kyle surveyed her car as they parked. "I see you didn't have time to get the paint fixed."

"I've been busy," she barked.

Kyle opened the door for Lia as she got in the front seat. "This is private and not meant to be shared with your sister," he snapped, waiting until Lia nodded.

Jake backed the car out, anxious to retreat from the toxic environment. He glanced at Lia and exhaled. "Kyle's serious."

"I understand, Jake," Lia said, wondering if they thought she was dense. She already planned not to share anything with Lauren about Casi. Her sister would be devastated to find out Kyle fell in love with someone so fast.

"Thanks for a great evening!" Much to her chagrin, Casi dropped her keys, twice, before finding the car key.

"You're not driving, Casi. You've been drinking, and who knows what else," Kyle stated.

She could see he was poised to take away her keys if she resisted and she did feel buzzed, possibly even high. "Fine." To add emphasis, she threw them at him. "I guess you'll want those since you've appointed yourself the keeper of my possessions." To her further annoyance, he caught them. They walked in the house, and she kicked off her boots, sending them in different directions, pleased when one knocked over a picture on a shelf of Kyle holding a giant fish.

"Real mature, Casi," he said, fixing the photo.

"Why don't we discuss everything that's wrong with me! Wait, let's have Jake come back so he can join in the fun?"

She hadn't meant it as an invitation, but Kyle started in about how she couldn't commit to anything and acted like a lost child. Pissed off, Casi walked to the stereo and cranked it, dialing it to a station playing Flo Rida's, *'Ayer'*. She jumped up on the couch and proceeded to dance to the music, screaming the lyrics. She realized she reinforced his opinion of her acting like a teenager, but it was better than throwing things, which is what she wanted to do. She couldn't believe he could make her so angry. Her blood literally boiled. Kyle snapped off the stereo before Taylor Swift could belt out, '*Shake it off*', which seemed unfortunate. He continued his assessment. "You need to pull your shit together. It's like you're on a constant holiday, bouncing from one party to the next. For God's sake, you don't even seem bothered by the fact that you don't have a home. You're almost thirty years old, it's time to figure it out." His words stung with their truth.

"You've made me feel unwelcome here. I hate your man cave," she screamed.

"Don't worry, as soon as you're sober, you're free to leave." He stormed to the bedroom.

"Fuck you, Kyle. You're an asshole," was the best she could come up with. "I researched the legend of the stupid constellation, by the way. Thanks for saying I'm like a queen who is so vain, she would be willing to sacrifice her daughter to save herself."

"Seems like a suitable name to me." He threw bedding on the couch. She pulled the blanket over herself and patted a space for Colt, who watched their angry outburst. "No dogs on the couch," Kyle called out as he slammed the bedroom door. Colt crept up and snuggled into the crook of her legs, leaning his chin on her calves with a sigh. She petted his soft, floppy ears as she cried herself to sleep.

The next morning Casi awoke to see Kyle sitting at the dining table, coffee in hand, watching her sleep. Colt slunk from the couch and walked to his master, sitting at his feet, waiting to have his ears scratched. Casi emerged from the blanket, wearing only underwear and a tank top, having removed her jeans and bra during the night because they were suffocating her. She wrapped the quilt around her and sat on the chair across from Kyle. He poured her a cup of coffee and added cream. Her head pounded, and she was aware she had mascara smeared under her eyes and a severe case of bed-head. Kyle had showered and was handsome, but tired. "Casi, I have a lot on my plate," he spoke calmly. "Jake's marriage is crumbling, and it affects me and our business. Lumber prices are sky high because of the drought and there's a pine beetle outbreak to deal with." She hadn't considered the factors impacting Kyle's business; she assumed he went to work every day and made beautiful cabinets. He put his hand on hers as a peace offering. Hopeful the next words would be positive, she reeled when he said, "This is not a good time for us. I can't take on your baggage, on top of what I'm already dealing with." He quietly added, "You're not even emotionally mature enough to tell me you love me." His voice broke and her heart literally ached.

She wanted to sink in his arms and tell him he was being dramatic and everything would be alright, but she nodded as a fat tear slid down her cheek. She finished her coffee, allowing the scalding liquid to burn her throat, welcoming the pain. She pulled on her jeans and boots and stuffed her bra in the pocket of her jacket. She didn't care that she looked ragged; her heart just broke into a million pieces and she couldn't speak without crying. She walked to her car and Kyle handed her the keys. As she opened the door, he leaned in and touched her cheek with his thumb and kissed her gently on the forehead. Casi waited until she backed out of the driveway before cranking up her Meghan Trainor CD, letting the tears flow as she sang along.

# 18

# TEARS AND TRIUMPH

he traffic was light on the way to Bellingham, not giving Casi enough time to regain control of her fragile emotions. She parked haphazardly in the driveway and ran in the bungalow, past Jack and Ava. They eyed each other with raised eyebrows. "I missed the teenage years." Jack grinned and went back to reading his newspaper.

Ava put aside her cross stitching and went to the kitchen to put the kettle on. Several minutes later she knocked at Casi's door, not waiting to be invited in. She placed the teapot and cups on the nightstand and sat on the edge of the bed, beside the crying heap of her stepdaughter. She gently rubbed her back, waiting for the tears to subside. "Will it help to talk?"

Casi rolled over, a mess of mascara and snot. Ava wiped her face with a tissue as she wailed, "Kyle broke up with me."

Ava waited for another break in the storm while she poured the tea. Handing a cup to her, she asked, "Was it out of the blue, or did something happen?"

Casi swallowed her tea too fast, choking on the burning liquid as Ava steadied her cup. *It seemed Kyle was bothered by something ever since she got back.* "I'm not sure," she answered slowly, replaying the argument in her head, searching for clues. "We had a fight over stupid stuff, but then he went off on me about how irresponsible I am and how I have no direction in life. He called me homeless!"

"You have a home here for as long as you want."

Casi stared at her, wide-eyed. "The worst part is, it's all true! He read my mind and turned it around on me out of spite." She contemplated he had held a mirror up to her and she didn't like the reflection. He saw through her pretty exterior to find the ugly truth. She felt vulnerable and violated. Ava let her talk rapidly at times, then staring off into space. "I need to go back to LA," she admitted. Ava nodded in agreement and told her lunch would be ready soon and suggested she take a shower. Casi grasped her hand. "Thanks for talking to me. You always know how to help."

Ava smoothed the hair from her sodden cheek. "I've had my heart broken many times. I understand your pain."

The next few months were a flurry of activity. Casi enrolled in the classes Ava had suggested and balanced the courses between shoots and castings. She attended one Saturday class a month at the University and was pleased to find it challenging and relevant. She opted for the Business Management track, which she hoped would help her manage her career and provide future opportunities.

Her offer was accepted on a loft on Wilshire and she moved in her meager belongings. Inspired by Ava's beautifully decorated home, she talked Dylan into going to flea markets with her on the weekends after brunch.

She bought a queen-sized bed and spent a fortune on 1500 thread count sheets. She adorned it with big puffy pillows, with no purpose, other than to be pretty. She had one chair, a find from the flea market, which almost killed them as they tried to carry it up the stairs, stopping every other stair in a fit of laughter. A pretty pine desk in the corner was a treasure from the antique store on Vine. She set it up to do her schoolwork, putting it at an angle to the window, wanting to watch the world bustling around a few floors below while she sat perched in her sanctuary. She added an antique pine hutch to feature her tea cups, liking how it added charm to the room. Her bathroom exploded with a beach motif, including candles and shells. It smelled like coconuts and reminded her of being on vacation.

From time to time, she thought of Kyle. They were still friends on Facebook, and she would occasionally chat to Lia, but never about the fight. She kept it light, with only basic information about her life. Kyle posted pictures of the fishing trip he took with his brother. Tanned and shirtless, he held a giant salmon. It seemed he spent a lot of time hunting, sharing pictures of himself in camo with dead ducks and a huge deer, his gorgeous blue eyes smiling at the camera. She wondered if he got back with Mary Ann but pushed it from her mind, not wanting to think of him kissing anyone as passionately as he kissed her. It was distressing Sonya had been right; he lived a small-town life which suited him, with no place for a crazy city girl like her.

October came and her mother organized a thirtieth birthday party at her luxurious home in Beverly Hills, a perk of her most recent marriage. The partygoers gathered around the pool, highlighted by fairy lights and candles. Sonya hired a top-notch caterer who provided a shrimp fountain and an ice carving. The champagne flowed and Casi was spectacular in a plum, beaded top, high-low cocktail dress, which clung to her curves as if it was painted on. Everyone raved at how great she looked with her cascade of blonde hair flowing over one shoulder. Although the party was spectacular, she wished she could have celebrated with Kyle.

Dylan brought a young handsome date and cuddled with him by the palm trees. Alix gave her a giant canvas, titled 'Casi's vision', featuring a swirl of colors in a feminine form, with floating objects emitting from what appeared to be the head. Her mother gave her sparkling diamond earrings, pointing out how expensive they were. Ava and Jack attended and brought a hand-carved ancient ivory totem, representing her roots in Canada, connecting with her life in California.

It didn't surprise her not to hear from Kyle. They hadn't spoken since the fight, and it was unclear why he didn't unfriend her on Facebook. She often thought about how defeated he appeared as she got in her car, not angry anymore, just broken. She received over 1500 messages on Facebook, so he had to notice her birthday. She felt slighted by him, not sure if it was an oversight or intentional. She couldn't understand how he could go from loving her to cruel in record time. She didn't bother Lia with questions. She liked her as a friend and understood it wouldn't be fair to make her the go-between.

Casi focused on her career, sculpting her body with intense workouts and careful eating. She kept her partying to a minimum, going to the clubs only a few times a month. She enjoyed the freedom of the dance floor, and the vibe from the party helping her lose herself in the music. Her favorite place to dance became the loft, sliding on the hardwood floor, and jumping on the bed in her underwear. She realized after a month, the apartment adjacent housed a man with a telescope which prompted her to purchase curtains.

She spent most of her free time with Dylan. She briefly dated a guy named Alejandro from her Saturday class, picking him out because he seemed like someone she would never fall in love with. Handsome, twenty-four, and fit from soccer. He had been good in bed but lacked the passion she needed to stop dreaming about Kyle. After a few months, she ended it to avoid the three-month mark of perceived commitment. He took it well enough, not interested in her as a person, but made it known he would miss having sex with her.

Casi was surprised when her friendship with Alix grew. He proved to be a remarkably good listener and helped guide her emotionally. He treated her tenderly, and she realized he was someone who would be in her life forever. She kept the relationship as a friendship, deciding she liked him better as a friend than a lover.

The career focus paid off, and she was busier than ever after Christmas, which she celebrated with Dylan trying to cook a turkey and failing. She flew to Aruba for a swimsuit shoot the next day. She found out a month later she had been chosen for the cover, featuring her in a coral pink, crocheted bikini, with minimal coverage. She knelt in the white sand, legs spread, as she leaned forward, cleavage on full display. She had been thinking of Kyle, imagining he watched her, anticipating making love. It was no surprise the photographer said the photo oozed sexuality, and the editor chose it for how men would relate to the sultry pose. They didn't realize she pulled her wet hair to the side and pushed her hip out to maximize the exposure of her scars. She hadn't let Roy put any cover-up on and insisted on minimal makeup. She wanted to make a statement about how women were portrayed, which Dylan laughed at because of her sexy pose. The scar on her hip snaked down in a jagged pattern; reddened from the amount of swimming and rolling around in the sand, making it more visible. She loved the photo, considering it to be the truest depiction of her. It made her feel strong to see herself exposed in such a way, and the scars were part of her now. The female editor loved the concept, and titled the picture, 'Raw and Sexy'. Casi framed the cover and put it up in her loft as a reminder to herself to stay strong and focused.

She spent half of January at Fashion Week in New York, and although it excited her how her career took off, the travel became exhausting. They had a party for her at one of the clubs when the magazine hit the stands in February and everyone wanted a signed copy. She had a great time dancing and partying and didn't want to go back to her loft alone. She perused her options at the club but wasn't in the mood for a random hook-up, so she texted Alejandro, who readily agreed to meet her at his place. She requested Pit Bull's album while they had sex, not wanting to be distracted by his tiny shared apartment, decorated like a college dorm.

# 19

# COVER GIRL

Casi drove home early Sunday morning, satisfied, yet lonely. After she showered, she checked Facebook for photos from the party. Some were generic party shots, but many featured her dancing clad in leather pants and a sequined halter top. She wished Kyle would comment. Even a negative post would prove he still thought about her. Surely the magazine had to be out at stores in Blackberry Falls, and it would be impossible for him not to notice she was on the cover.

She opened a message from Lia. "Fantastic cover! OMG, so proud of you :) Kyle hasn't said anything, but I'm sure he's seen it. I'm worried about him. He had Colt put down after Christmas. He was fourteen and his liver failed. Super hard for Kyle."

"Oh, no!" Casi clasped her hand to her mouth as tears sprung to her eyes. "Colt was such a great dog!"

"Jake's going to counseling, fat lot of good that will do! He's pissing me off, hot one minute and cold the next. I'm exhausted by his games. I should have my head examined, getting involved with a married man. Maybe I'll take a page from your book and sleep with the new bartender, so cute! Kyle's like a zombie since you left. I haven't seen him laugh since summer...when you were here. Sorry the concert sucked, he was being an ass. It was something between him and Jake. BTW, he's not dating anyone, especially Mary Ann! I heard he had a thing with a rep from the lumber company, but she lives in Seattle. Did I mention how scandalous you look on that cover!"

Casi considered that Lia had known Kyle and Jake for at least a dozen years. She wouldn't have mentioned personal things about Kyle if she wasn't concerned about him. She checked her calendar for the coming week, assignments due for school, but no class on Saturday since finals started the week after. Her agency was holding off on bookings, letting the popularity of the cover raise her day-rate. Mary had a lot to do with it, managing her career from the sideline, ensuring she capitalized on her success. On a whim, she clicked on flights to Seattle. She could fly standby if she left in the next hour, which would put her into Seattle around two. She booked the ticket and threw together a small carry on. She could finish doing her hair and makeup on the plane, assuming it would be raining in Washington, and she would have to touch it up before she saw Kyle. Before she could convince herself she was insane, blindsiding him yet again, she drove to the airport. Things had been left unsettled, and it was the last piece of her life that was not in place. She needed clarification, even if she didn't like what she heard.

After an uneventful flight, she picked up a rental car and headed out in the gray weather. She didn't like driving in rain and was glad when she turned off the freeway to the small town. She wasn't sure where Kyle would be on a Sunday afternoon, and had only messaged Lia an emoji smiley face, not knowing at the time she would jump on a flight like a maniac. As she drove the main street, she noted Kyle's truck parked in front of the family-owned grocery store, Roth's.

She parked a few spaces away and checked her face in the mirror. The weather was mostly overcast and drizzly rather than rainy, which helped her hair. She wore a soft blue cashmere sweater, with dark jeans and knee-high, spike-heeled boots. She hoped she didn't slip, realizing rain boots would have been a better choice. She grabbed a basket as she entered, making sure to wipe her feet well on the carpet. Halfway through the store, she found him in the liquor aisle, where an attractive woman chatted him up while he made his selection, Jack Daniels. The woman tried hard, flirting and making her single status obvious. Casi hung back, pretending to check out vodkas while she kept an eye on him.

"Can I help you find something?" the man stocking the shelves eagerly asked her.

Kyle said goodbye to the woman and pushed his cart to the next aisle. Casi shook her head and moved on, intent on spying. She told herself it was for his sake. If he seemed fine, she wouldn't intervene and fly home. She trailed behind him through the produce aisle and meat section, where he shook hands with the butcher and discussed sports. He added a few more items to his cart, not seeming to be in a hurry. Several women checked him out as he passed by. He nodded back, but made no effort to flirt. He pushed his cart to the express lane. She noticed her magazine on the end-cap of the check stand and held back to see if he responded to it. *Had he bought a copy yet?* She discarded her empty basket on top of a stack of toilet paper and moved closer. He picked up a woodworking journal and thumbed through it while he waited his turn. *Are you kidding me?* The woman in front of him made room on the conveyor belt. He smiled and thanked her as he unloaded a case of craft beer, Jack Daniels, a chicken, and an assortment of colorful vegetables. The woman made comments about his groceries, striking up a conversation. He answered, encouraging the flirting as he put the journal back.

"No dessert?" the woman asked suggestively.

"I have ice cream at home," he said with a wink.

Casi pushed past the mother with twins, who had more than fifteen items, whispering she needed to reach the gum. The mother glared at her, not moving the grocery-laden stroller. Casi slipped in, making sure to run her hand over Kyle's backside while she reached toward the candy rack. He glanced over his shoulder, not sure what to make of the advance, seeing only the woman with toddlers. Casi grinned and pressed herself toward the rack behind him out of sight and tossed a copy of her magazine with his groceries. He greeted the cashier as she began scanning. "Hi Jeannie, how's it going?"

"Good Kyle, same old routine, you know how it is." She glanced at Casi as she caressed his hip unseen, making Kyle flinch. He discovered the magazine and picked it up in confusion.

Casi breathed in a low, sexy voice, "Wow, a dirty magazine and a bottle of Jack. Someone is having a party for one!"

Kyle turned in shock toward the voice. "Casi! It was you messing with me all along?" His eyes glistened with happiness and he embraced her tenderly.

The cashier finished ringing up and tried to get Kyle's attention to pay, aware he had become completely focused on the beautiful girl. "Kyle? Hon, $54.93," she asked for the third time. He opened his wallet but couldn't concentrate on the transaction. The cashier smiled and pulled out three twenties, then handed him the change. "Hon, don't forget your groceries," she reminded him. Kyle moved his cart out of the way of the impatient mother while the cashier gave up trying to explain it was an express lane and started ringing up the pile.

"What are you doing here?" Kyle put his money back in his wallet, not sure what to do with the coins.

"I thought I'd swing by on my way to see my dad." Casi glanced at her phone in the pretense of acting casual.

"Do you have time for a drink or something?" Kyle fidgeted with the zipper on his jacket.

"No, sorry, it's only a quick hello, and then I have to hit the road." She bit her bottom lip to prevent a giggle from escaping.

"Well, it was good to see you." Kyle's expression changed to disappointment and his shoulders slumped.

Casi's heart ached for the pain in his demeanor. She threw her arms around him. "That was a joke. I came to see you because I heard about Colt from Lia."

Kyle breathed heavily against the crook of her neck. "You run circles around me, you crazy girl. I have dinner on at the house if you want to come over."

"That would be convenient since I came to see you." She waited for him to grasp the concept.

Kyle shook his head. "Of course. I'm still in shock from seeing you. It's not what I expected on a Sunday afternoon." They walked outside and he glanced over her attire. "Didn't you bring a jacket?" Without waiting for an answer, he unzipped his and settled it around her shoulders. He slid the hood over her hair and kissed her on the cheek. "Do you remember how to get to the house?" He chuckled when she nodded and pointed in the wrong direction. "Follow me."

She rushed in the house after him and immediately shed her clothing. "Damn that rain is really coming down!"

His jaw dropped and he immediately redirected his gaze away from her skimpy lingerie. "I can put your clothes in the dryer. Did you bring something to change in to?"

"I have a bag in the car." She picked up her sweater from the floor. "This is cashmere. You can put it on a towel on top of the dryer."

Kyle took her clothing and went to change. He returned with a flannel shirt and handed it to her. "Put this on for now." He poured two glasses of whiskey and set them on the table before putting away his groceries.

Casi slid up on the counter, parting her legs to place one on either side of him. She held the magazine in front of her. "What's your opinion?"

"You're beautiful. That's incredible, you got the cover."

"Do you notice anything?" She moved it closer.

"Do you think I didn't buy it the second it came out?" He averted his eyes from the cover.

"Look closer."

"You can see your scars. Your choice?"

"Yup, the new me." She turned on one hip as she pulled down the side of her panties.

Kyle jumped away and turned his back to her while he rubbed his temple. "This isn't a good idea."

"I'm trying to show you something."

He glanced over his shoulder and noted the script under her scar, *Life is about the Journey - March 16th*

"The date of your accident." He nodded. "I like the meaning and I'm glad you've embraced the scar."

She unbuttoned her shirt and reclined while she ran a hand over her taut stomach. "Would you like to see it up close?"

"Nope, I can read it from here." He pulled the flannel over her exposed lace covered breasts. "Food is prepared here."

She frowned and stood, grasping his arm when he moved away. "What's going on?"

"I'm not sure why you're here."

"To make sure you're alright," she reiterated.

"It's a long way to come for a hookup." He refilled his glass and took a long sip.

"Is that what you consider me?"

"I'm not sure what else you would need from a redneck work-man," he said accusingly.

"Why do you sound like my mother?" She narrowed her eyes and bolted for his computer, clicking on the icon for Facebook, suspecting he wouldn't have logged out.

"Casi stop!" He froze, surprised by her agility and perception. She glared at him as he approached and he considered his options for physically removing her or unplugging the computer, aware she didn't respect his private messages.

Casi clicked on his inbox. "When did you become friends with my mother?"

"She added me this summer."

"You may not be tech savvy but you grasp the concept you don't have to accept every friend request?" She put her hand on her hip and stomped her foot.

"Yes, but I was curious what she had to say." He crossed his arms over his chest. "That message is private."

"It concerns me." She read it in a dramatic voice. "Darling, Kyle. You're a very sweet man and kind to Casi while she recuperated from the terrible accident. I'm concerned you're in over your head and you don't understand you're a distraction as her career is taking off." Tears welled in Casi's eyes as she read the words, dated the week of the concert. That's why he'd been in a bad mood. "I'm sure you have a perfectly average life in your small town and I wish you well, but Casi's father has informed me she came to visit you, and it's a huge mistake. She's rather lost, and a meaningless affair with a workman is only keeping her from staying focused. She's better suited for a well-bred man who can provide for her in a more appropriate manner. It's best if she doesn't lower herself to your lifestyle, which will create misery in the end. You're very handsome and I can see what drew Casi to you, but don't be naïve and believe this is more than a fling for her. She has several excellent propositions lined up, and it's time for her to return and fulfill her obligations."

"Why didn't you tell me?" She deleted the message and blocked her mother after reporting her for inappropriate posts.

"Every word of it was true, and you proved it!"

"You started the fight at the concert!"

"I was in a bad mood after reading the message. You showed up an hour late, in a sleazy outfit, plastered with your ex-boyfriend's artwork. You were blatantly mocking me!"

"No I wasn't! I figured that's what people wore to concerts. How was I supposed to know..."

"That us backwoods folk aren't savvy enough to mix with you city girls?" He glared at her unspoken words.

"You're creating issues that don't exist." Casi turned away. "I don't feel that way."

"Casi, what do you want?" Kyle stepped closer. "Am I a random hookup for you?"

She drew him toward her and kissed him passionately. He lifted her in his arms and carried her to the living room. Without a word, he tossed a blanket by the fireplace and guided her to the floor while he pulled off his clothing and joined her. She writhed beneath him as he explored her, electrified by his unbridled desire. His hands caressed her smooth skin as he entered her, and she moaned, bringing her hips to greet him. He thrust so intensely she bit his shoulder to ground herself. The sensation rose up her spine as she threw her head back in ecstasy, and he shuddered on top of her. He rested his head against her neck and breathed heavily before sliding beside her and wrapping her in his arms. "I guess you'll be leaving now that you got what you came for."

"You've met my mother and understand the relationship we have. Why are you taking her words to heart?" She gazed in his eyes and noted the doubt. "I love you. What does it matter what anyone else thinks?"

"It's too late, I don't love you anymore. I've moved on." He caressed her back and sighed.

"I'm sorry, I don't accept that. I wasn't ready before, and I needed to accomplish too many things." She rose up on one elbow and ran a finger over his bottom lip. "I bought a loft and decorated it like a real home with a plant and everything. It was part of my transformation to prove we are destined to be together. Stop fighting it."

"I don't believe in destiny. And I sure as hell don't have faith in love." He ran a hand through his hair and exhaled. "We can't be together. It'll never work. My life is much simpler without you." He squeezed his eyes shut. "You did it again!"

"Rekindled your love?"

"Forced me to have sex without protection."

"The passion was mutual. The condoms were an oversight." She grinned. "Besides, you're the only one I ride bareback." She fell back and laughed hysterically as he shuddered at the imagery. Kyle jumped up and strolled to the bedroom. "Where are you going?"

He returned with a small wrapped package and placed it between her breasts. "Happy thirtieth birthday."

"You remembered?"

"How could I forget? You were so afraid of entering a new decade." He gazed at her lovingly. "But your career took off and you're doing great. You didn't need me at all."

"I did and I do." She sat and unwrapped the package to reveal a pendant with an intricate filigree of yellow gold, placed over purple jade, depicting the tree of life. "It's beautiful!"

"I bought it a while ago, but it never seemed like the right time to give it to you. I thought about coming to LA, but I didn't want to pressure you." He fastened the clasp and arranged the pendant between her cleavage. "Do you believe this could actually work between us?"

She smiled. "We won't know if we don't try."

The fire crackled and Casi snuggled deeper into Kyle's arms, waking to the sound of Jake's voice. "Oh great, I see trouble is back in town. When did you get here?" He grabbed a beer from the fridge and surveyed them sprawled on a blanket. "Cool scar, I couldn't quite make out what the tattoo said on the cover." He glanced between her and the magazine.

"Back off, Jake." Casi tugged the blanket around her.

"Unusual choice for script. I'm touched you wanted my name on your ass, though," Jake chuckled.

Kyle grabbed the magazine from his brother. "Get her bag from the car while we shower."

"Why prolong the misery? She'll run away when she's done with you." Jake narrowed his eyes at Casi.

She wagged a finger in his face. "He left me both times. I'm the one who keeps trying to fix things."

"Very true." Kyle directed her toward the bathroom and flipped his brother off. "Get her bag."

Jake tossed Casi's suitcase on the bed and ladled stew in bowls. He sliced bread and set it on a plate glancing up when they returned. "How long are you in town?"

Kyle cocked his head. "I just realized you flew this time."

Casi shrugged. "I got a standby ticket without a return." She smirked at the concern on Jake's face. "I should head back in a week because part of my road to success includes finishing my degree and I have finals."

"Getting that GED finally?" Jake scoffed.

"Business Management." Casi shoved past him to locate cutlery in the kitchen drawers.

"On your left." Jake eyed her. "Don't get comfortable."

Casi turned with her hand on her hip. "Why are you here instead of with your family?"

"My brother has been depressed since he lost his dog. I'm helping him cope." Jake grabbed a bottle of wine and glasses.

"You can take the rest of the week off," Casi asserted.

Kyle chuckled. "There's room for both of you here. We have a busy schedule coming up, including a party to celebrate the tenth anniversary of our business. It would be nice to have you attend that with me."

"I won't book my return flight until we decide on the right time." Casi smiled. "Maybe you could come back with me for a while and pick up more work in LA?"

Kyle grasped her hand. "Let's take it one day at a time."

**20**

---

# TOAST OF THE TOWN

Casi made use of the day to work on her school assignments while Kyle was at the wood shop. She sent a quick text to Dylan, realizing she had blown off their Sunday brunch. He was shocked she flew to Washington on a whim and couldn't believe she didn't consult him beforehand. He informed her he would never forgive her for ditching him for 'that man'. Several texts later, she switched her phone to silent and concentrated on her assignment. She slipped on the reading glasses Dylan had gotten her as a joke gift for her birthday, but found quite necessary to read for longer periods of time. Kyle said she could use his computer, knowing she already discovered the message from her mother and assumed he didn't have anything else to hide. Later in the day she tried not to snoop as she scanned the internet for research materials, but the recent search history caught her eye when she saw her name. She clicked on the link and it pulled up images of her in the sexiest of poses, including the recent cover shot in the tiny bikini. "You pervert," she laughed as she imagined him perusing the photos lustfully. It excited her to know he thought of her sexually when he was alone. She often pretended he watched her as she posed, teasing the camera with a sultry pout, spreading her legs, and arching her back, his blue eyes following her every move.

"Hey, it's the sexy schoolgirl." Kyle grinned from the doorway as he set down several grocery bags.

She yanked off the glasses in embarrassment and pushed him away when he came up behind her and kissed her neck, running his hand over the top of her breast. "I'm working on my assignments." She quickly minimized the search history.

"Ah, you're no fun." He kissed her cheek and went back to the kitchen to unload the groceries.

Casi clicked the history closed and watched him humming to himself as he organized the fridge. *No fun, huh*? She slipped into the bedroom and located several items, realizing she had never dressed sexy for him. She posed by the desk and placed the glasses back on. They made everything over two feet away blurry, but she wanted to complete the sultry look. She switched on the radio, still on her pop station, and the perfect 'Brittany Spears' song came on. "Can you help me with my homework since you're so smart?"

He laughed at her sarcasm, shaking his head as he turned around. "Sure, little Miss college girl." He stopped dead in his tracks when he saw her dressed in thigh-high stockings, with a skirt so short it skimmed over her panties. The waistband was rolled down to reveal her belly button, with a white shirt tied below her breasts, barely contained in a black lace bra.

She pulled her hair into a high ponytail, and she stood twirling the ends. "You got your degree at the UW, maybe you could teach me a thing or two?"

"I'm sure I can give you an education." He set his beer on the table. The outfit had its intended effect as he came behind her, bringing his hands to untie the blouse. His breath was warm on her neck, and she found the role-playing erotic. He surprised her by bending her over the desk and lifting her skirt, giving her a playful slap on the backside as he tossed her panties to the side. Her textbook was open inches from her face, and she tried not to read the page on International

Import Taxes as he thrust against her. He pushed the books to the ground, and she cringed as her phone, still on its charger, followed. It was exciting to see Kyle step away from his cautious nature. He turned her around and lifted her assertively on the desk, bringing her legs around his waist, as he continued to make love to her. She closed her eyes to the blurriness of the room as the desk rocked under her.

"Ah, the naughty schoolgirl fantasy?" Jake chuckled as Casi screamed and tugged her shirt to cover her breasts.

"Damn it, have you heard of knocking?" Kyle chastised.

Jake picked up a textbook. "I remember this class. But I don't recall girls dressing as seductive as you, Casi. I've seen your almost naked photos. Now I'll have additional currency for my spank bank." She reached down and threw a binder at his head, missing as he ducked in anticipation.

"Why are you here again? You know she's in town." Kyle glared at his brother as Casi rushed to the bedroom.

Jake narrowed his eyes. "Sure, I can't get enough of her company." He surveyed the groceries on the counter. "At what point did she lure you away from your task?"

Kyle frowned. "I got sidetracked."

"Apparently." Jake walked to the fridge and grabbed a beer. "I would encourage you to finish but your buddies will be here in a few minutes and they're expecting food, not a stripper."

"Stop criticizing her," Kyle hissed as he tidied the desk.

Casi pulled on leggings and a sweatshirt, then cringed, remembering her lace panties were somewhere in the living room. She came out to discover Kyle had reorganized her books, placing her phone on top, unharmed.

Casi wrapped herself in Kyle's arms as he stirred a pot, and he kissed the top of her head. She peeked over his arm to witness Jake's glare. "What?" she snapped.

"I'm trying to figure out your angle." Jake filled a bowl with chips and set it on the table.

"Don't waste your time analyzing our relationship. Don't you have your own things to work on at marriage counseling?" Casi gave him a satisfied grin.

Jake's nostrils flared, and he eyed Kyle. "I didn't tell her. You may want to consider who you give that information to."

Jake rolled his eyes. "Lia." He took a swig of beer. "The good news is I'm learning how to deal with difficult women. I'm sure that'll be helpful if you're planning on sticking around."

Kyle pulled Casi closer and told her about the six guys who would be coming, one being the butcher she had seen at the store. He explained he was always the host because he had the best TV, and usually no women around. Casi took this to mean she should not be the annoying girlfriend. Around five o'clock, several men came in and helped themselves to drinks and took a seat facing the TV. They indulged in snacks as they yipped and cheered for their team.

*Oh, my God, could this be more boring?*

The friends gave her a quick nod but were more interested in the game as they kicked back, drinking and eating. She flipped through a magazine as she sat at the table. It was a Wild Turkey edition, which thrilled her as much as the game. She wanted to grab her iPad, but when she tried previously, they booed and yelled, claiming she blocked a big play. "A Jake is an immature turkey, isn't that fitting?" she proclaimed, pleased with her find.

Jake belched loudly in reply and held an empty beer bottle up. "Make yourself useful, Casi. Get me a drink." She grabbed a bottle from the fridge and shook it violently before handing it to him. She made a dash for her iPad as he opened the beer to an explosion of foam. "Bite me, Casi."

"Watch the sofa." Kyle frowned and shoved his brother. Casi handed Kyle a beer with a sweet smile and squeezed between them, ensuring she gave Jake a kick with her boot as she slid in. Jake elbowed her and Kyle pulled her on his lap. "I swear you two are like children." She sat back against him, triumphant with her win. She twirled her hair in sections until he moved her elbow from in front of his face. She played Candy Crush on her iPad as Jake tried to knock the computer out of her hand. After thirty minutes, Kyle whispered in her ear, "Can you stop wiggling around, I feel like I'm getting a lap dance."

"Gross." Jake hit his brother on the arm.

The game ended and everyone went home, to her delight. She achieved twelve new levels in Candy Crush, and her vision blurred. Jake helped clean up, taking the trash outside, and Kyle followed him with the recycling. "Thanks for putting up with her. You anticipate coming over here to get away from Gail, and now suddenly this woman you don't like is here."

"It doesn't matter," Jake said. "I didn't like Lauren either."

"It matters to me. Please give her a chance?"

"I'm not going to stop coming over unannounced, so you may want to start having sex in the bedroom. It sure is an unexpected activity in this house." Jake chuckled.

"It certainly is," Kyle agreed.

The next morning, Casi accompanied Kyle to Coffee Junction before he left for Seattle. "I see the tramp is back in town," Gail announced to the women at her table, who nodded obediently.

"Let it go," Mary Ann stated.

"Maybe you can let that arrogant jerk treat you like a convenient place to put his dick while he waits for her, but I have enough trouble dealing with my stupid husband." Gail eyed Casi in skinny low-rise jeans and a sweater which fit her svelte body like a glove. "Someone needs to show her she doesn't belong here."

"She's very friendly with Lia," said one timid woman, who redirected her gaze to the floor.

Gail watched Casi laughing at the counter with Lia, making plans for Happy Hour. "She is. You think Lia would have more loyalty to her sister."

One woman bravely stated, "I imagine Lia prefers her since she's not bothered by the attention Lia gives your husband."

"Exactly!" Gail spat.

Kyle took Casi to the wood shop, and she admired the old stone building, converted from a dairy, beautifully restored and bestowed with hanging flower baskets. A young woman sat at the desk as they came in and handed Kyle messages with a slight blush. Kyle muttered, "Thanks, Amy," lost in the notes. Jake took the liberty of introducing Casi to the receptionist as Kyle's girlfriend. A brief look of defeat passed through the girl's eyes, as she took in the gorgeous woman standing before her.

Casi followed Kyle to the office he shared with Jake. She surveyed the framed degrees and certificates on the wall. There were several pictures of softball teams they sponsored and a photo of them accepting an award of excellence from the Chamber of Commerce. "Impressive," she said.

Kyle's desk was well organized and functional, whereas Jake's desk seemed to be in disarray, giving her the impression Kyle took on most of the business responsibilities. She thought it odd he was the younger of the two, but seemed more responsible. Kyle led her to the workroom to show her around. A small showroom displayed sample woods and styles, but since their work was custom, it was limited to wood choices and stains. A lot of lumber was stacked to one side and several large pieces of machinery, workbenches, and a hand tool area spread through the building. He pointed to a yellow line on the floor and told her when the machinery was running, she could not cross it. She laughed and then realized he was serious. She slid on a workbench and turned up music on her phone, distracting them as they measured a frame. Kyle came over and kissed her. "You've had the tour, now hit the road." She wrapped her legs around him and swung her wrists over his shoulders, giving him a sultry pout.

"Um, Mr. Jensen..." Amy hesitated at the edge of the worktable. "You have a phone call."

"Thanks, Amy. I'll be right there." He unwound Casi's legs from his hips. "You need to leave or I'll never get work done."

Lia met Casi at Happy hour, which seemed well attended by the locals. She smiled at a handsome bartender and nodded to Lia. "Is that the guy?"

"Yes, isn't he cute?"

"Darling. Did you sleep with him?" Casi watched him stocking glasses while he flexed his muscles.

"No, he's not my type," Lia sighed.

"But Jake is?"

"He's very handsome." Lia wrung her hands. "I don't mind his extra weight. I like a burly man."

"He seems grumpy all the time. Why doesn't he divorce Gail? I don't see the value in that marriage." Casi sipped her cocktail and perused the appetizer menu.

"It's mostly because of the business, they've worked hard to make it successful. Gail always threatened to destroy it if Jake steps out of line. The event tomorrow night is a big deal for them. They moved to this town and built their business from scratch, and they're both well-liked in the community. Which is why Jake is worried about you making Kyle look like a fool. People here are not like they are in a big city, everyone is in everyone else's business."

"They're in each other's business in LA." Casi grinned and signaled for another round. "Why do you put up with him? You're amazing, beautiful, and funny, and you like to drink."

"I kind of have a bad history with men. I get attached and hope they like me, but then they never stick around. My sister says it's because I'm a doormat." She glanced away. "Jake is different, maybe because we're not having sex. We've known each other a long time and I'm comfortable around him. He doesn't pressure me, although I wish we could take it further."

"Is he hesitant because he's married?"

"He doesn't want to let his kids down and make them grow up in a split family. I respect that because I grew up without a dad and it was tough. When he first moved here, he was in good shape, but over the years he's gained weight and he's self-conscious about it. That's why he's comfortable around me." She frowned at her voluptuous figure.

"You're gorgeous, Lia. You're perfect the way you are." Casi grasped her hand. "Let Jake work on his own issues."

The bartender continued to pour extra strong drinks. When he noticed them swaying, he said, "I'll give you a ride. My shift just ended."

They toppled into his truck and he dropped off Lia, and then pulled into Kyle's driveway. She thanked him, intending to give him a kiss on the cheek, but he turned his head and kissed her full on the lips, leaning in for more. She put a hand to his chest. "I'm drunk. You're darling, but I have a boyfriend." She turned to find the handle, and the door flew open. Jake unceremoniously yanked her from the truck with a few choice words for the driver. She pulled her arm away, rubbing it from his firm grip, staggering as she walked. "It's no big deal. I was with your girlfriend at happy hour," she slurred.

"You don't stop, Casi. It's always party time for you." He directed her in the house and slammed the door.

She switched on the stereo and started dancing, her head spinning from the alcohol. "The problem is you hate your wife and can't make it with your girlfriend. I guess it drives you crazy when you see me with your brother, it gets you all hot and bothered." She pulled off her shirt and rubbed against him, smoothing her hands across his chest. "I bet you fantasize about me when you're whacking off." She kissed his neck and slid her hand slowly over his stomach with a giggle. "Why don't you let me give you an education? I heard you need lessons."

"What the hell, Jake?" Kyle bellowed.

"It's not me you have to worry about." Jake successfully untangled Casi and shoved her away.

"Get out!" Kyle commanded.

"I'm going to barf." Casi rushed to the bathroom.

"Good luck with that," Jake scoffed as he exited swiftly and jumped in his truck, peeling out of the driveway.

Kyle snapped off the stereo and went to check on Casi in the bathroom. She sat beside the toilet, legs askew, hair mussed, with mascara smudged under her watery eyes. She looked pitiful, but to his annoyance, still beautiful. "You make it hard to love you." He filled a glass with water and handed it to her.

"I wanted to teach him a lesson for being such a jerk to me all the time. He grabbed me and hurt my arm," she sobbed, trying to see if he'd left a mark to prove her claim.

"You were going to have sex with him as punishment?" He handed her aspirin. "Do you want our relationship to fail?"

She drank the water with shaky hands. "I only teased him, and then I planned to walk away and make him feel like an idiot." She inhaled and closed her eyes to steady the spinning room.

"I think you're both idiots." He stormed out and sprawled on the bed, trying to assess what he had seen. It did look like Jake fought to push her away. Casi was gorgeous, but even Jake, with all his faults, wouldn't hurt him, especially after everything Kyle had been through with her. He understood she was an insatiable flirt, not fully realizing the effect she had on men. With a sigh, he got up and went into the bathroom. She was crumpled on the tile, crying. He lifted her up in his arms. "Why am I always picking you up off bathroom floors?" He put her on the bed and slipped off her jeans before pulling the covers up.

"Kyle?" She reached out for him.

"Go to sleep." He bent and gave her a kiss on the cheek, still damp with tears. "Happy Valentine's Day," he whispered. He watched her for a few minutes, her breathing soft and even, and wished he didn't love her so much. He had forgotten it was Valentine's Day. Lauren sent him a heartfelt message on Facebook, asking if they could try to make it work again. It had been a year since their break up, and she wanted desperately to get back together. She wished him a happy Valentine's Day, and he realized he had a girlfriend he should be getting flowers for. He walked to the kitchen and took the bouquet of roses he purchased from a roadside stand and put it in water. He sat at his computer and sent Lauren a message simply saying, "Happy Valentine's Day. I hope you're doing well."

**21**

## HEADACHES AND HEARTBREAK

The next day, Kyle walked in Coffee Junction alone. Jake sat with the gossip circle to irritate his wife, but also to keep a safe distance from his brother. He ordered his coffee from Lia, who asked about Casi. "She's pretty hung over, she'll be spending most of the day in bed. She planned to hike around the lake. I'm not sure if she'll be up to it later this afternoon, but I gave her the map for the trail," he replied.

"Sorry we got so drunk. I think the new bartender poured the drinks extra strong," she said innocently.

"It's not your fault, she's a grownup. She's the one paying for it today." He approached his brother, who flinched as he put a hand on his shoulder.

"Why do you put up with it?" Gail snipped. "It's bad enough she makes a fool out of you, but now she tries to go after my husband?"

"Why do you tell her these things? She always twists it to suit her agenda." Kyle narrowed his eyes at Jake.

"You made a mistake breaking up with Lauren," Gail snapped. "You're so desperate to make it work with this woman, who doesn't belong here, that you can't even see how stupid she makes you look."

Kyle stormed out, tired of being under attack. Jake walked swiftly after him and got in the truck. "I'm sorry."

"You seem to be sorry about a lot lately, Jake."

"You know how Gail is, she hears bits of information and needles me until I get tired of hearing her voice. I explode and tell her everything to get her off my back." Jake slumped in his seat.

"I'm sick of your shit with Gail. I'll sell the damn business if that's what it takes to get rid of her. Let me be happy with Casi."

"I saw her kissing the bartender. He gave her a ride home." Jake turned to glare at him.

"I don't care about him. I'm sure he took advantage of her being drunk off her ass, which he aided in. It doesn't bother me she's a flirt and has no boundaries with kissing," Kyle sighed.

"Then why are you upset she molested me?"

"Would you have slept with her?" Kyle asked quietly.

"What?"

Kyle turned and faced his brother. "Would you have slept with her if I hadn't come home, taken her up on her advances? She's gorgeous, I'm sure you couldn't resist."

Jake stared him straight in the eye. "No, Kyle. She's beautiful, but she's your girlfriend. I wouldn't cross that line."

"I need to be able to trust my brother." Kyle rubbed his temple. "This time."

"You can trust me. That's in the past, and I'd never do it again. I understand how much Casi means to you. Besides, she had no intention of sleeping with me. It was a game to try to get me worked up. She seems to find it amusing I don't like her touching me. She always pokes at me."

Kyle noted Jake's sullen manner. "What else happened?"

Jake shrugged. "She said she heard I needed practice and laughed when she ran her hand over my stomach. I know what she thought. It wasn't a sexy scenario you walked in on. She tortured me. Why am I always the target of these evil women who want to hurt me?"

"I'm sure it amused her to see you get upset. It's a game you both excel at."

"Whatever, she won. I'm out of the game."

Kyle realized he would have to tell Casi to stop teasing Jake, knowing she didn't understand the deep wounds he had from his childhood. "When Gail told you she was pregnant, you stepped up and did the right thing. You've taken care of your family for sixteen years. It's time to end it and move on. You need to find someone you can love and who makes you happy."

Jake shook his head. "I'm not capable of loving anyone outside of our family." Kyle squeezed his hand, sympathetic to his difficulty sharing emotions.

Casi woke up with a throbbing headache. Kyle left a coke, two aspirins, and a map of the trail. She regretted drinking so much, but she hated hurting Kyle even more. Some details were still fuzzy, but the parts she did remember were embarrassing. She didn't know why she had a need to antagonize Jake. He was pissed when he saw the bartender kiss her and grabbed her so aggressively; he scared her. She wanted to regain control, and that was the only way she knew she could easily dominate a man. She noted even though she danced half-naked and rubbed against him, he didn't have an erection. She drank the coke slowly, hoping it would calm her queasy stomach. She slipped her phone in her pocket and set out for the lake. It was seven miles around with significant hills. She gauged she could do it in about two hours, leaving her an hour to shower and get ready. She set her phone on Pandora and put in her earbuds. A decent day for February, in the mid-50s, with puffy clouds in the blue sky. The trail was indeed challenging, and her legs burned by the halfway point. She stopped to take a sip of water and check the time.

"Excuse me, do you have the time?" asked a fellow hiker.

Although she just checked, she glanced down again, out of habit. In an instant, she fell to her knees. Her phone flew from her hand and a dirty boot stomped on it, smashing it to pieces. Another man crept behind and pushed her down, pinning her arms to her side, as she madly tried to kick him. "Get her feet, Jimmy."

"She's feisty," he replied, as she sought to twist free. He smelled of beer and body odor. He pulled her shirt up, exposing her bra. "Nice tits," he laughed, pinching the bra wire against her skin as he tried to undo it.

The smaller one clawed at her leggings, and she managed to kick him in the face, flipping herself over to her stomach and getting a face full of dirt. "That's how you want it, huh? Cool tattoo," he admired as he slid his hand over her scar. Casi located a rock, swinging wildly at the man above her. It barely made contact, but knocked him off balance enough for her to free herself from his hold. She lunged for the trees. "She ain't goin' nowhere." He grabbed her foot, and she pulled out of her shoe, scrambling toward the bushes, rolling as she hit the hill. She heard them racing behind her in a heated frenzy. Void of options, she dove in the lake and swam as far from the shore as she could. She plunged deeper, slowing her breathing and willing herself not to give in to the fear of the icy water. She swam halfway, then tapered toward the shore, as the sky began to darken. She hoped the men gave up, unable to see her in the dim light. She clung to a nearby dock, teeth chattering, as she tried to get her bearings. She climbed out of the frigid water, having lost her second shoe. She sat for a brief duration before resigning herself to a long freezing walk home.

Kyle stood at the bar, martini in hand. He ordered a Moscow Mule for Casi, over an hour ago, and it sat on the bar untouched. His jaw clenched as he tried to keep his temper in check, calling her phone a fifth time.

"She'll be here, Buddy. She's terrible with time." Jake slapped him on the shoulder.

Gail looped her arm possessively through Jake's and stared down Lia. "No Casi?" she asked, stirring the pot.

"Not yet," Kyle snapped, turning his back to her.

"Well, that's a shame, it's such a big night for you boys. The whole town is here, except for the new bartender. I wonder where that handsome young man is?"

Jake pulled away from Gail, giving her a dirty scowl, angry at her attempt to antagonize Kyle. "She wouldn't." Jake tried to calm the anger he could see rising in his brother.

"I guess you should have invited Lauren, she would have made it on time," Gail said as she walked off.

Well wishes and congratulations were said, and the cake was cut. Kyle seethed silently at Casi's absence. After two martinis, he quit drinking, knowing it fueled his temper.

"I'm heading out," Jake said, as Kyle sat alone at the bar, not welcoming any attention.

"I'm calling it a night." Kyle shoved the martini he had been nursing beside the untouched Moscow Mule.

He walked in the house and noticed the lights on in the bedroom, and he could hear the shower running. He surveyed the clothes on the bed, topped with the jade pendant. He knocked at the bathroom door. "You cannot possibly be this horrible with time!" There was no answer. "I waited for you, for four God damned hours!"

"Go away."

He tried the knob and found it locked. He went to the kitchen and returned with a paring knife and a screwdriver. Several twists later, the lock sprung open, and he witnessed Casi sitting on the floor of the shower, hugging her knees and crying. She had deep scratches and bruising on her arms. His rage boiled over. He knelt and pulled her to his chest. The water was icy cold and she shivered with chattering teeth and blue lips. He wrapped her in towels and held her close, rubbing her back. The crying stopped and she stared off into space. He carried her to the living room and started a fire and yanked blankets from the sofa to cocoon her. He put a pair of his wool hunting socks on to her frozen feet. Changing out of his damp clothes, he snuggled beside her, rocking her gently. He was afraid to hear what happened, sickened by the appearance of an attack. A lump rose in his throat, as he put his cheek to hers and whispered, "Are you ok?"

Tears flowed again. "Two men attacked me on the trail."

"Do you need to go to the hospital? I'll call the police."

"No, no," she pleaded. She took a deep breath and told him what happened, in a rush of tears, hiccuping through the part where she swam across the lake.

"You jumped in the lake? That's half frozen!"

"They destroyed my phone." She cried as his rang.

"Is Casi ok?" Jake asked hesitantly.

Kyle stated flatly, "No, what do you know about it?"

"Gail may have been involved. Some guys are talking crap." Jake hesitated.

"Where are you?"

"The bar," Jake sighed, estimating it would get rough.

"Stay there and don't let them leave," Kyle demanded.

He arrived in minutes and stormed over to Jake, waiting outside. Kyle raised a fist. "How were you involved?"

Jake backed up. "I knew nothing. I would never hurt her."

Kyle recognized the men as soon as he entered. Two drifters who hung around town, causing trouble. He strode over to the man with the beard, and before he could snap, "What the hell do you want?" Kyle punched him square in the jaw.

Jake hit the younger man, keeping pace with his brother in intensity and brutality. The men got in a few licks of their own, protesting, "We didn't touch her."

"Some lady gave us a hundred bucks to scare her, and make her leave town," the bearded one claimed.

The seasoned bartender stood behind the counter, meticulously polishing glasses. After a significant amount of time passed, he set the last glass down. "It's time you boys call it a night." He judged the revenge the brothers came for had been exacted. Kyle dealt one final kick to the man's ribs as he writhed in agony. He wiped the blood from his lip, and grabbed Jake's arm, pulling him off his victim. He nodded to the bartender, and they walked out as quietly as they walked in.

Kyle pulled Casi in his arms as she slept by the fire. She rolled closer to him, seeking the warmth he offered. Throughout the night, she tossed and turned, crying out and shivering. Each time, he soothed her, whispering in her ear, and rubbing her back. When she awoke the next morning, the embers glowed in the fireplace and the sun shone across Kyle's bruised face. He was on his back, one arm behind his head, a dark welt on his ribs, and a gash on his lip. He stared at the ceiling, deep in thought. Remorse crept in his eyes. Casi traced the script beneath the scar on his rib cage as he spoke. "When I was a kid, I was surrounded by love and happiness. Growing up in my small town made me fearless. Jake and I would fight like normal brothers, but I was never afraid. Once, when I was fourteen, I was dancing in my dad's shop. Everyone laughed and cheered me on. Some kids from school teased me as they passed by. Jake took off and beat the crap out of them. My dad and his business partner, Earl, didn't stop him; they were angry the kids made me self-conscious. Kids learned fast they better not mess with me unless they wanted to go against Jake."

"He always looked out for you? It seems like you're the more responsible brother," Casi said.

Kyle smiled. "I'm better with money and business things, but he took good care of me when we were growing up. The summer I graduated high school, everyone hung out at the river, ready for our lives to change as we headed in different directions. Jake had been at college for two years. My best friend, Grady, had big plans to travel the world, claiming he couldn't get out of Elmvale fast enough. His family was poor and life had been tough, but he was determined to make it, and convinced me to go with him. We bought backpacks and created an itinerary to go to Europe and see the sights. He wrote that in my yearbook." He ran a finger over the words, *Dare to Dream, Hope, Trust, Seek, and most of all, Love.*

"We had a blow-out party on the last day of summer. We were invincible, speeding around in our boats and having fun." He paused for a long moment and she feared where this might go, remembering him mentioning the scars from a boating accident. "I woke up in the hospital, my mother crying beside me, and my dad convinced I wouldn't make it. Jake was a wreck, and told me about the accident and how four kids died, and Grady was one of them."

"No!" she cried, unprepared for the fatal ending.

"After I got out of the hospital, I was a zombie. I couldn't process losing my best friend and the tragedy of the accident. I went to college with Jake. I got the tattoo as a reminder life is unpredictable, and you can never take it for granted. It is a tribute to Grady, and all he would never accomplish." A tear slid down her cheek for poor Grady, and a teenaged Kyle, so distraught. "Jake went with me and I cried in his arms while he reassured me everything would be okay. Even the tattoo artist cried because he had done Grady's, only months before."

"What was his?"

"A dragon, he sketched himself. It was incredible." He ran his hand over his scar. "Jake wouldn't let me give up, and eventually, I started focusing on my classes. I vowed to be responsible and make good choices. I've kept my head down, dedicated myself to the business, built this house, and tried to be the son my parents were happy not to bury that day."

"I'm sure your family is proud of you. You're an amazing person." She laced her fingers through his.

"When Jake found out Gail was pregnant, it overwhelmed him. It was my turn to help him stay focused on finishing college and get a job. I chose this town and promised him we would have a successful business here after I graduated if he trusted me to make it work. Everything I have done since then is to honor that commitment.

"I'm sorry I missed the party to celebrate."

He cleared his throat. "I love you Casi, but..."

"Please don't break up with me!" she pleaded, sensing the next words out of his mouth.

He brushed the hair from her face. "I'm angry you were attacked. You should feel safe, and I should have protected you."

"I'm ok. I'm devastated about my phone, but I should have been more aware when I was hiking," she sighed. "I've been mugged before."

"The attack was planned. Gail paid some guys to scare you, and to try to make you leave."

She looked at him with concern. "Was Jake part of it?"

"Absolutely not! He would never hurt you. And I need to make sure you don't hurt him."

"What do you mean?"

"I need you to dial back the teasing. You believe it's funny, but he's more sensitive than you realize. He's made a million mistakes and can be an ass, but that's stuff between us. I don't need you pointing out his faults and making him unwelcome. He's my brother, and he's going to be part of our lives."

"Our lives? So, we're still together?"

"Of course, you nut! Why did you doubt that?"

"I got confused with your incredibly long story. You said I love you, but. That's usually the start of a break up." Her eyes filled with tears. "That's how you ended it the last two times."

He hugged her to his chest. "I'm sorry I've scarred you. I promised to make this work, and I've accepted all your faults."

"My faults?"

"Your complete lack of timeliness and inability to stop kissing other men."

"I can't help the time thing, it is innate. Kissing is how I express myself but I only kiss you passionately," she clarified.

He ran a thumb over her bottom lip. "I can accept that. I'm not a jealous person, but honesty is important to me."

"I won't lie to you and you can trust me to be committed to our relationship," she confirmed.

# 22

# TAKING FLIGHT

The aroma of French roast coffee wafted through the bedroom, mingling with the steam from the shower in a fragrant mist. "Jake's here." Kyle grinned at Casi as he toweled off.

"He comes in and makes himself at home?"

"You'll need to get used to it." He gave her a kiss before he walked to the kitchen.

"Why don't you have any food?" Jake stared in the fridge.

"I've been preoccupied and haven't made it to the store," Kyle teased. "Casi made a chicken the other night."

"She cooked?"

"She took cooking classes at the community center with her former doorman. It needed more seasoning, but she was excited about making a meal." Kyle pulled out the chicken and placed it on the counter beside a loaf of bread. "Why were you at the bar last night? You left before me."

"I left because Gail promised me sex. Mary Ann warned her she should be nicer because other women might want me. I guess she's jealous of Lia's affection."

"That surprised her?" Kyle scoffed.

"She figured she should make an effort. It started out alright.

Then she asked me a million questions about Lia right in the middle, and I got pissed off and confessed I've been fooling around." Jake put together a sandwich.

"She sure pushes your buttons and gets you to talk."

"She should work for the CIA," Jake agreed. "She shoved me off and told me to go to hell."

"Does she want a divorce?"

"I hoped we were headed there. I'm unsure why she has random conversations while we have sex. She needs to stick to the task. It's only a few minutes." Jake grinned.

Kyle chuckled. "Dirty talk is always good."

"Sure, I'd go for that. I don't want to hear about the kids needing braces, or all the ways I've failed her over the years."

"Try covering her mouth."

"I tried. It pissed her off. I was tired of her bitching so I went back to the bar, and that's when I heard those guys bragging about the hundred bucks they made."

"They told you it was Gail?" Kyle frowned at a smear of mayonnaise on the counter and handed Jake a paper towel.

"They were talking about the uptight bitch who runs the town. I made the leap myself and started asking questions." Jake leaned closer. "They mentioned Casi's tattoo."

"Assholes!" Kyle swore. "Did you go home last night?"

"Nope, I went to Lia's. I didn't want to be seen sneaking out this morning, so I left when it was still dark and slept in my truck until I saw you guys were up." Jake stopped when he noticed Casi coming out of the bedroom.

"Go dry your hair, it's cold out," Kyle instructed. He waited until they heard the whir of the blow dryer. "You shouldn't have slept with Lia until after you were divorced."

"I realize that. I need to put it in motion. I'm not sure where to start." Jake rubbed his arm in distress.

"I'm going to LA with Casi." Kyle surveyed his reaction.

Jake grasped the counter and exhaled. "For how long?"

"I'm not sure." Kyle squeezed his shoulder. "I need to be with her, even if it's for a week. I'm not ready to say goodbye."

"I understand." Jake nodded. "I can't handle it anymore, we have to sell the business." He looked toward the bedroom and whispered, "The panic attacks have become really bad. I'm sorry I'm letting you down, but I'm headed toward another breakdown."

"You're fine," Kyle said tenderly. "I'll help you get through this. Everything is in your control, ok?"

Casi returned and wrapped herself in Kyle's arms as he leaned against the counter. He kissed her hair, loving the softness and aroma of grapefruit, the warmth of it against his bare chest. "Where did the flowers come from?" Casi raised an eyebrow when she noticed the colorful display.

"Those are yours for Valentine's Day," Kyle said.

"When was Valentine's Day?" Casi paled.

"The day you were trying to make out with Jake."

"No!" Casi covered her face and Jake laughed.

"Yup, you missed out. I had a whole romantic evening planned." Kyle noted the tears welling in her eyes. "Actually, I forgot too. The flowers were an afterthought on my way home."

"They're beautiful." Casi turned to give him a kiss.

Jake reached out and smoothed his thumb over her jaw. "Is that bruise from yesterday?" Casi shrugged, and Kyle pulled up her sleeve to show him the scratches. "God damn it! You said she wasn't hurt. They claimed they were paid to scare her." He paced the kitchen and breathed heavily. "I'm done with Gail. She can take it all and I'll live in a damn trailer."

Casi grabbed his arm. "Why don't you come with us to LA? My mom's attorney has represented her through three divorces and she's always done alright. You could get an idea of what to expect and how to protect the business. My mom owes me a huge favor for meddling, so the consultation would be free."

Kyle nodded. "It's a great idea. We'll make a plan today after we get coffee."

§

Kyle put his arm protectively around Casi as they entered Coffee Junction. She leaned close to Lia when they approached her register. "We're heading to LA, want to come?"

"I'd love to, but how do I get off work without notice?" Lia whispered back. Casi relayed a plan, and Lia smiled, explaining to her manager she needed time off to attend a funeral in Seattle.

Jake grinned at Kyle. "I guess I have a date."

"Where the hell were you?" Gail's shrill voice radiated.

"As far away from you as I could get." Jake held a middle finger up without turning around.

Mary Ann noted the bruises on the brothers and her jaw dropped. "What happened? Did you guys get in a fight?"

"We're fine." Kyle smiled at her. "The other guys probably aren't feeling great this morning."

"We're going to LA for work," Jake stated.

"No, you're not," Gail answered, aware the other women at the table were watching for her reaction.

"I need some distance from you." Jake walked away before she could answer and held the door for Casi.

"Gail, what did you do?" Mary Ann grabbed her hand. "Casi has bruises on her face!"

Gail bit her lip as she regarded her hands. "My plan might have backfired."

§

"First, let's get tickets, and then I'll call my mother and arrange an appointment with the lawyer." Casi sat at Kyle's desk.

"I usually research the best prices before I book." Kyle observed her speed and navigation of the sites and handed her his credit card. "You seem to have a handle on it."

"I need your phone since mine got smashed to smithereens, never to be seen again." Casi wiped a fake tear.

"Did you delete your text messages?" Jake interjected.

"It's not my fault you guys are imbeciles with technology and are under the impression your conversations are private."

Kyle kissed the top of her head as he gave her his phone. "I'll buy you a new one in LA."

"I can take care of it." She smiled at him.

"I would like to do it," Kyle insisted.

Casi tried to recall her mother's phone number, searching for the sequence in her mind.

"Hello?" Sonya hesitated.

"Hey, Mom, it's me."

"Me who?"

"Mother, you have one child, how confusing can this be?"

"I don't recognize the number. Where are you calling from?" Sonya said with suspicion.

"My phone broke, so I'm using Kyle's; the redneck workman from the small town of Blackberry Falls." Casi waited for her mother to interpret her tone.

"Darling you're so dramatic." Sonya sighed. "Why are you in Washington? It rains there."

"Fewer wildfires, so that's awesome." Casi rapped her nails on the desk. "I didn't call to discuss the weather."

"Did you drop your phone again? I keep telling you to buy one of those heavy-duty cases. You need to take better care of things, Casi. You're always on that damn thing and you should consider your career and the fact they need to reach you. What if you had a job? Do they know Kyle's number? When did you become so dependent on a man..."

"Stop!" Casi interrupted. "Set up an appointment with your lawyer to meet with Kyle's brother to discuss a divorce."

"He's very expensive."

"You can cover it and I won't tell Dad you meddled in my relationship with Kyle. He adores him." Casi smiled with satisfaction.

"Jesus Christ!" Sonya swore. "Do you have any Vicodin? My back has been acting up."

"I'll bring you some when we come for the appointment."

They checked in at the airline counter and the agent explained he had three seats together, but someone would have to sit in another location. They regarded each other to see who the odd man would be. Casi voted Jake.

"Actually, I was hoping to work on proposals to make use of our time on the flight." Kyle locked eyes with Jake to convey his understanding and noted the relief in his face.

The agent grinned at Casi. "I could upgrade you to first class, I have an opening. No charge."

Casi leaned over the counter in a pretense of trying to see the screen, batting her eyelashes. "How thoughtful."

"She's shameless," Jake said in disbelief.

"Name?" he asked, not taking his eyes off her cleavage.

"Lia," she purred, figuring she should get the elite experience for her first flight, even if it was only a couple of hours. She took the boarding passes and waited until they were around the corner to hand them out.

"You're my idol!" Lia clasped the ticket to her chest.

Jake settled in the aisle and Kyle took the window seat, sandwiching Casi in the middle. Lia excitedly sat in her first class accommodation, feeling like a celebrity. After they were in the air, Kyle asked Casi for a pen, eyeing her giant purse, convinced there would be one in the generous contents. "We should create an itinerary to maximize our time." Casi smiled at his organized nature, and hoisted her purse to her lap, searching in despair. She upended it on Jake's unsuspecting lap, irritated she couldn't find the pen. She used him as a table while she sorted through receipts and trash and Jake wriggled beneath her touch, muttering obscenities. She threw unnecessary paper and trash in an air sickness bag.

They watched in awe as she placed tampons, a brush, three lipsticks, and a compact mirror back in the tangerine leather bag.

"Hey!" Jake grabbed a trio of condoms and slipped them in his pocket. He gave his brother a wink, as Kyle shook his head, wondering how long those had been there, and for whom they were intended. A nude colored thong and matching strapless bra were the next shocking items for the brothers, unaware they were a staple for a model to have on hand. She put back the gum, Tic Tacs, and another lipstick before picking up a wine opener.

"How did you get through security?" Kyle cocked his head figuring they were more interested in giving her the pat-down. More trash piled into the barf bag along with a half-eaten muffin. "Hand me that." Kyle reached for an energy bar.

After tossing Ray Bans in the purse, Jake was left with a lapful of coins and crumbs, which Casi tried to retrieve. "Watch the merchandise." Jake brushed the crumbs off and collected the coins as payment for the use of his lap. Casi found her iPod and put in her earbuds, forgetting what she originally searched for. She seat-danced to a song only she could hear, as she handed the surprised flight attendant the full air sickness bag.

"Do you still need a pen?" A man across the aisle handed it to Jake. "I would have given it to you earlier, but I was curious to see what else she had. It's like a clown car, it just kept coming!" They laughed as Casi, now lost in her music, tuned them out.

Mid-flight, Casi announced she needed to use the restroom, amongst protests she could wait an hour. "Whose idea was it to get coffee at the airport?" She wagged a finger at Jake.

"Crawl over." Jake flipped the page of his magazine.

She scooted across, facing him, and tripped on his foot, which resulted in a knee to his groin. Jake shoved her off, sending her headlong into the lap of the man who lent them the pen. "Jake!" Casi yelled, trying to untangle herself.

"Who gets out of a seat like that?" Jake winced at his injury and turned to Kyle. "She's too comfortable touching me. She's like a damn monkey, always poking at me."

# 23

## LAWYERS AND LOFTS

Kyle smiled in response to seeing the scratches on Casi's car had been fixed when they arrived in LA. She pulled up to the pay booth and realized she threw out the parking receipt with the trash from her handbag. "Why didn't you leave it in the car?" Kyle sighed and handed her cash to cover the maximum rate. Casi explained to the cashier how she threw out the receipt by mistake, blinking tears from her big hazel eyes. He charged her for a day pass and they were on their way.

They arrived at her mother's house in Beverly Hills and Sonya welcomed them with warm hugs, planting a lingering kiss on Kyle's lips. He grinned at Casi with twinkling blue eyes. "Your mother expresses herself the same way you do."

"This is your brother? Very handsome." Casi made the motions of throwing up while Sonya gave him a wet kiss.

"I like your mom," Jake whispered.

The attorney, Stan Levitz, was a well-dressed older man, who sat quietly and listened to Jake's story while Kyle filled in the financial details. Kyle was handsome in jeans and a flannel shirt, and Casi fantasized about the wild sex they would have when they got back to the loft. Lost in thought, she watched his long fingers stroking his iced tea, wiping the condensation from the glass. "What do you think?" Sonya repeated.

"Sorry, I wasn't paying attention," Casi admitted.

"I've never seen you so gaga over a man. It's distressing," Sonya said. "Maybe I'll have a go at the brother."

"No!" Casi glanced at Lia, thankful she hadn't heard.

"I'm considering remodeling the kitchen, getting rid of this pedestrian ambiance for something more custom." Sonya waved her hand to the expansive cabinets. "Don't you agree, Sweetie?"

"Whatever you want." Her much-older husband, Burt, replied as he gathered his golf clubs and shuffled to the Porsche.

"Fantastic idea." Casi noted dollar signs and a cover story for their trip. "I hope Kyle's work will be up to your standards."

"Darling, let it go. I never questioned his talent. I only want the best for you." She motioned to her own magnificent home.

"I don't require someone to buy me stuff. I can take care of myself. It amazes me you liked Alix so much, a guy who is all show and owns nothing. If you want to compare men, Kyle is more manly for providing for himself and building his own house. And so much better in bed!"

Sonya threw her head back and laughed. "Diamonds don't mean a thing if a man can't take care of you in the bedroom!"

The lawyer explained how the process could be lengthy and tedious. Since the brothers owned the business jointly, the priority would be protecting Kyle's interests. Jake would lose the house, but Kyle assured him the large home was too extravagant for his budget. The lawyer emphasized they shouldn't mention the divorce until they had the business protected. He advised them to be cautious and not rush to file since it would work in their favor if Gail initiated the divorce. Jake said he put in sixteen years, so six months would be a cake-walk. The lawyer surveyed Lia and spoke in a hushed tone. "You'll want to be discreet with your girlfriend since it's something your wife can use."

"Gail doesn't know Lia's here," Jake offered.

"Lia has a way of repeating things innocently, without realizing she's divulging information," Kyle noted.

Jake jutted his chin at Casi. "Do we trust her?"

Kyle nodded. "Yes, she's trustworthy."

On the way home, Casi showed them the tourist sites and took them shopping. She insisted Kyle buy new pants for a club opening he didn't want to go to. "I went to the Pink Floyd thing," she countered, realizing it might not be the best example. He settled on black jeans, with a periwinkle silk shirt he claimed was too slippery to be practical. She reminded him he wouldn't be chopping wood in it, and he would thank her later when he didn't feel like a hillbilly in the club. "What size are you, Jake?"

He froze and glanced at the tags on the shirts. "They wouldn't have anything to fit me here."

Kyle tried to redirect Casi's attention while Jake fidgeted, but she reached past him to the rack and grasped a few items. "LA stores mark sizes differently to make people feel good. Try these."

Kyle glanced at her selection and nodded. He hung them in the fitting room and whispered, "If it doesn't fit, you can say you don't like it. I'm sorry I didn't suggest you bring a dress shirt. I was unaware we would be going to a nightclub."

Jake barely had the buttons fastened before Casi entered the change room and assessed the attire. "Perfect." She smoothed the hem around his hips. "You can leave this type of shirt untucked." He glanced at his image and she leaned closer. "A directional pattern like this is flattering because it brings the focus to your eyes."

"It suits you," Kyle confirmed.

Casi chose a pewter mini dress, held together in the mid-section with large silver hoops. Kyle suggested it couldn't possibly be enough material for a dress and pointed out she owned enough belts. She winked at him as she added a pair of black lace panties to her pile.

Kyle carried their bags up to the loft and set them by the large mirrored closet, dividing the bathroom from the sleeping area. Casi waved around the room as its tiny size made a tour unnecessary. Kyle noticed the giant painting behind her desk and recognized the work instantly. "A present for my birthday. It's called Casi's vision," she informed him.

Kyle grinned at the swirls of color and objects floating around what appeared to be a head. "I imagine that's a true depiction of what it looks like inside your brain."

Lia used the restroom while Jake poked around in Casi's fridge, taking the only beer. "You're out of beer."

Kyle investigated the remnants of the plant on the window sill and laughed as he touched it, and the last leaf fell to the floor. "I forgot to have Dylan water it," she wailed.

"This place is darling." Lia admired the room. "You should get a kitten, it would make it even cozier."

"Imagine what she would do to a cat if she can't even keep a plant alive," Kyle mused. Casi stripped off her leggings and sweater, standing in her underwear as she contemplated the contents of her closet. Jake rolled his eyes at Kyle, not used to seeing a woman so comfortable with her state of undress. "Sooner or later you'll see her fully naked. She isn't shy."

"Let's hope its sooner," Jake joked.

Kyle frowned at the makeshift kitchen with melamine cabinets. "This is a great place but lacks a proper kitchen."

"I'm sure she can order takeout just fine." Jake winked.

Casi turned up the radio and continued to stare in her closet. Kyle came up behind her and peered in. "That's a lot of shoes." He gasped at dozens of shoes haphazardly stacked on cheap racks.

"They need a better living situation. It's like they're in foster care, waiting for their forever home," she sighed, eyeing the precarious heap. Kyle caught Jake's eye and shook his head, knowing she didn't mean to be insensitive. "Lia, do you want to get changed before we go for coffee? Jake can get your bag?"

"I'm good." Lia considered Casi's perfect figure and smoothed her sweater to cover her hips.

Kyle pulled off his flannel shirt and t-shirt, handing them to Casi, who happily made room in the closet. He sorted through his bag. "It sure is a lot warmer here."

"Casi, what does your tattoo say?" Jake squinted at the framed cover shot on the wall. Casi pulled the edge of her underwear down and Jake laughed. "Why did you put Kyle's birthday on your ass?"

"It's the day I got hit by the car." She indicated the scar.

Kyle smiled at her. "It's also my birthday. I planned to ask you to dinner when you got back from Malibu."

"Really? I would have said yes."

An upbeat dance tune came on, and Casi turned up the radio as she jumped up on the bed with expertise to dance it out. Jake watched her in awe and Kyle laughed, "Jesus, wait until you see her at the club. I'm sure she'll blow your mind."

There was a knock on the door, and Jake answered it to find a handsome Argentinian, holding a leather jacket. He opened the door wider and turned down the radio, announcing Alejandro's arrival. Casi's cheeks burned as Alejandro relayed in his soft, lilting accent, "You left your jacket at my place Sunday morning when you left. I tried calling you, but it goes to voicemail."

Jake grinned. "She left it when she slept over this past Saturday night?" Naïve Alejandro explained he and Casi dated, giving too many details on how she came over after the club. She covered her face, realizing how it appeared.

Kyle extended his hand and took her jacket. "Hi, I'm Kyle. As of Sunday afternoon, I'm Casi's boyfriend. Thanks for dropping this off." He closed the door as Alejandro walked away in confusion.

"I wondered about the red light outside your door, but now I realize why it's there! How old is that kid?" Jake teased.

Casi rushed toward the bathroom and Kyle pulled her toward him. "All that matters is what happened after you came to Blackberry Falls." He cringed. "He wore a condom, right?" Casi nodded as a tear slid down her cheek.

"I'm curious. Did junior drop you off at the airport when you were done with him? I guess that gave you two hours to rest up before hopping back in the sack?" Jake questioned.

"Did you want to discuss why you're here with Lia, while your unsuspecting wife is at home?" Kyle challenged.

"Nope, I'm good." Jake strolled to the window.

Casi splashed water on her face and applied simple makeup, trying to dispel the redness of her cheeks. Kyle hugged her. "I knew you weren't a virgin when I met you. We were apart when you slept with him. I wasn't a saint either."

She studied him in the mirror. "I didn't lie about being in love with you, Kyle. You're the only man I want to be with."

"I know." He nuzzled her neck. "You have been for a while. You were too afraid to admit it."

Casi snuggled against him. "Since you picked me up from the bathroom floor when I fell after my accident." She pulled on jeans over her boy shorts and slipped on a graphic t-shirt. She added high-heeled, brown boots and put a pair of sunglasses on her head. "Let's hit it." She stopped when she noticed a package on the counter and squealed with delight. Dylan replaced her phone, sympathetic to her loss. He'd imported her contacts and downloaded her apps. He made the wallpaper a selfie of himself in a thong, ultra-sexy and stretched out across her bed with a red rose. He'd left it with a bow and a Valentine's Day card, on top of a box of chocolates.

"Dylan remembered Valentine's Day," Jake joked.

"Too bad he couldn't water your plant while he was here." Kyle rolled his eyes.

Casi kissed the screen and slid it in her purse. She caught Jake's confused expression. "I want it to know it's loved." She tore open the box of chocolates, popping one in her mouth before offering the contents. She grabbed a few more as they headed out the door, making Kyle laugh.

The brothers waited in line to get hot dogs from Pinkies while Lia pressed for details about Alejandro. Casi declined the hotdog they brought, saying she'd eaten at her mother's, which Kyle knew wasn't true. They walked to Coffee Bean, and she ordered a black iced coffee. She walked to a table, still intent on her phone, and Kyle changed her order. Casi sat with her legs crossed, sunglasses on, lost in social media. Kyle set down a blueberry muffin and an iced vanilla latte.

She pushed the muffin away and took a sip of her coffee, looking up in surprise. Kyle put his hand over the screen and whispered, "Sweetheart, you need to eat something. You've only had a few chocolates all day." She smiled at him, liking being called sweetheart. She'd been somebody's babe for way too long. She tore off a piece of the muffin and popped it in her mouth, washing it down with a sip of the latte. Kyle arranged his chair to sit with one leg on either side of her as she leaned against him. Normally he wasn't in the habit of public displays of affection, but he was drawn to protect the fragility she emanated, standing guard while she radiated her pure light. Jake watched them, the way he sat with her and how he touched her protectively. He had never seen Kyle so in love with a woman and realized why his brother had been devastated after they broke up. Casi really was the love of his life.

"He sure is different with her than Lauren," Lia whispered.

"Yes, he is," Jake agreed. "Head over heels in love."

"It's sweet," Lia sighed.

Jake put an arm around her in an effort to be affectionate. "Have you said anything to Lauren?"

"She went ape shit over Mary Ann, I assumed she didn't need to hear Kyle is dating someone else." Lia sighed.

A lot of people recognized Casi, chatting her up as they passed by. A hopeful man asked if she would be at the club, not bothered that she sat in the arms of another man. She nodded, not giving him much attention before he moved on. She raised her phone to show Kyle something on the screen. "What the heck is SnapChat?" Kyle asked, unclear why she received videos of Dylan eating a sandwich.

"Carbs will make you fat, Darling." Dylan snatched her mostly untouched muffin. Casi didn't glance up as he leaned in to kiss her, and Kyle moved back, trying to avoid being too close to the scene and the scent of patchouli. "Hello Kyle," he said stiffly.

"Hello, Dylan. Thanks for getting Casi a new phone. She was lost without it," Kyle mumbled.

"You must be the brother." Dylan glanced at Jake.

Jake assessed the well-coiffed man in skinny jeans, loafers, and a designer t-shirt. "I am."

"Hmm. Not as handsome, and nowhere near as fit. More on the husky side." Dylan curled his lip. "Who's this vision of loveliness?" He ran his fingers through Lia's silky dark hair.

Lia blushed as she introduced herself. Dylan demolished Casi's blueberry muffin, then stole her half-drunk coffee, not worried she'd spent the last half an hour chewing on the straw. Kyle winced at the familiarity between the two, and the lost hope of even getting a latte in her. He worried she was anxious about something, maybe seeing Alix? She was too comfortable with the club setting to be concerned about judgment from other girls. He swallowed at the thought it might involve him; *was she worried he would embarrass her? A small-town hick in a world of metro-sexual Demi-gods.* He decided it was something more personal, discreetly scanning her texting over her shoulder. Alix, of course. He could feel the jealousy inside him ignite. He didn't understand why Alix had this hold over her. Casi opened a new tab and confirmed the top people would be at the club before putting her cell down. She leaned in and gave Dylan a kiss goodbye, snatching her coffee back and taking a sip before Kyle could ask if she wanted a new straw. He found it disturbing the way they shared drinks without concern for germs. It gave him an unintentional intimacy with Dylan, by proxy. He took the drink from Casi, tossing it in the trash as they left.

## 24

# NIGHTLIFE

Casi took an exorbitant amount of time primping, layering lotions and body sprays, and using countless products to get her hair just right. Kyle flipped through the limited channels on TV, considering it would not be wise to ask if she would be ready soon. It took him twenty minutes to shower, shave and dress, then another ten to fight Casi off with hair gel and spray. She managed to get a few swipes in, accenting the natural wave in his hair. He considered it unmanly to smell like ginger and vanilla, and have stiff hair, but gave in to make her happy.

She came out of the bathroom after what seemed like hours. She looked like she stepped straight out of the pages of a fashion magazine. Rhinestone studded stilettos led to mile-long, toned legs, shimmering with body lotion. He had been right about the dress, barely covering her hips, before giving way to smooth abs, visible under the silver hoops, attempting to connect the four inches of material stretched across her breasts, in what appeared to be a bra. Her cleavage was outstanding and majorly exhibited. Her blonde streaked hair cascaded around a perfectly made-up face, featuring huge hazel eyes with long dark lashes. She wore the pendant he gave her, and he swallowed any negative comments. "You look lovely." *Worth the wait.*

The car service was a black Mercedes with gray leather interior. Casi crossed her legs as she scanned her phone, and Kyle put his hand on her thigh in an attempt to prevent Jake from peering up her dress. As Casi sent a text, Kyle wondered where she planned to keep the phone at the club, making note the Barbie-sized dress did not come with pockets. He considered if he became the keeper, it might become lost. "Why are you smiling?"

"I'm thrilled to be going to the club." Kyle beamed.

The car dropped them in front of the nightclub where a long line wound around the corner. Kyle groaned, hating the whole scene. Casi exited the car with practiced grace, never revealing what she wore beneath her skimpy skirt. She laced her fingers through Kyle's and took the lead, past the line, and up to the front rope. Lia scrambled to keep pace, aware she would never get in on her own. The no-neck bouncer opened the rope and let them pass with a nod, closing it back after Jake. Casi sauntered up the steep stairwell with ease and crossed the dance floor to private seating. A U-shaped leather sofa defined the area. Models lounged, glued to their phones, the blue light casting an unnerving creepiness to their emaciated faces. A bar dominated the center of the lounge, serviced by scantily clad women in a bustier and hot pants. As Casi entered, space materialized and champagne was distributed. Kyle felt uncomfortable in the setting, and he chugged the champagne without realizing it.

"Easy there, Cowboy, we have a long night ahead of us." Casi nudged him.

"I might get lost on my way back from the bathroom and go hang out with stoners in the parking lot." Kyle grinned.

"Fair enough," Casi giggled.

Casi checked in on Facebook and set her phone on the coffee table as she greeted models with a kiss. "Don't even think about it," she warned, sensing Kyle might swipe her phone.

Kyle scooted beside Jake and Lia, willing the night to be over. Casi chatted to the models about upcoming jobs and gossip. Alix's latest girlfriend, a beautiful, doe-eyed girl named Sterling, seemed more interested in her phone and biting her nails than being with Alix.

Casi noted she was messaging a lanky surfer and figured Sterling would soon be off to find happiness with him. The bottle girl brought a tray of champagne and Casi took another, then turned to Kyle. "Wouldn't you prefer a martini?" He reached for his wallet, and she stopped him and shook her head. "Jake?"

"What?" He cringed.

"Would you also like a martini?" Casi giggled.

"Oh, sure." Jake blushed.

She whispered to the bottle girl as she placed the drink orders. The server came back with the cocktails, giving extra attention to Jake, leaning forward while she stood between his knees. He acted severely uncomfortable with the attention, trying not to stare at the girl's cleavage, inches from his face.

Kyle poked Casi in the ribs. "You're naughty!"

Casi stepped up on the couch between the brothers, continuing to the back ledge where a few models were dancing. The girls parted, letting her take the lead. The song was sexy, and she danced erotically, making the most of her dress to accentuate the curves of her body, leaning into the other girls as they became part of her chorus line. They watched her perform from below, admiring her technique and skill on the foot-wide stage. When she shimmied along the ledge, they had an unintentional view up her skirt.

"Jesus!" Jake averted his eyes. Lia laughed, noting the vantage point made the view of Casi seem sexier than she'd intended. Kyle was mesmerized by her swaying hips, and oblivious to anyone else.

Alix held up a hand to assist her from the stage. "Hey, Babe, did the car work out?" He planted a passionate kiss on her lips and gave her a squeeze as he nodded to Kyle before he left.

"We're just friends." Casi assured Kyle.

Kyle pulled back from her. "Don't kiss me with those lizard lips." She threw her head back and laughed. Without missing a beat, she turned to the bottle girl and kissed her sensually, to which the girl responded willingly. Jake's mouth dropped, and Lia went wide-eyed as they watched the scene.

Jake whispered to Kyle, "Erotic!"

Casi turned back to Kyle, slipped up her skirt, and sat across his lap. "No more lizard lips." He sat speechless as she molded her mouth to his and ran her tongue across his bottom lip, giving him a gentle bite, before kissing him deeply until he moaned. She tasted of champagne and strawberry lipstick. He had to admit, maybe all the kissing she did made her highly skilled. She lap-danced to the next song, moving rhythmically on him. Although he had been to strip clubs before, he had never been this aroused. The room faded away, and he only saw Casi, feeling her move against the fabric of his jeans, translating the music with every gyration. He slipped his hands under her skirt, caressing her smooth skin and feeling the silkiness of her underwear. He forgot about everyone else, willing to take it as far as she let him, having lost any restraint. Lia pulled Jake to her, redirecting his attention away from Casi, letting Kyle have his fantasy.

"Good to see you kids getting along. You have a spiritual connection." Kyle felt the brush of leather as Alix sat beside him.

Casi turned her head. "Did the club owners arrive?"

"Just got here," Alix confirmed, taking her by the hand. "You don't mind if I borrow her for a minute, do you?"

Kyle slid his jacket over his lap as she climbed off and Jake chuckled. "That girl is insane."

Casi laughed with the owners, flirting and charismatic. Kyle noted the models taking selfies, undoubtedly posting them to Facebook and Instagram, telling everyone they were at the club. But only Casi experienced the party.

The eager man who talked to Casi at Coffee Bean came up and put his hands on her hips, dirty dancing behind her. Lost in the music, she danced along. Kyle stood and Jake tried to restrain him, but he pushed him away. "It's cool." He walked to Casi and smiled as he took her hand in his and gave her a twirl, wrapping her back in his arms. "Would you like to dance with me?"

"Always," she replied.

They danced for a few more songs before returning to the sofa, hand in hand. "I haven't seen you dance like that since you were fourteen," Jake teased.

Casi squeezed in beside them, crossing her leg toward Kyle, and running her foot up his pant leg. They sat with their fingers laced together, talking and caressing each other. She glanced at Jake, feeling him shiver. "Are you ok?"

"I'm fine." He rubbed his arm, not convincing her as his breathing appeared labored.

She whispered, "Besides Kyle, you're the best-looking guy in this place."

"There are a lot of people here, that's not my comfort zone," he whispered back, in a rare episode of sharing, adjusting his shirt, and wishing he was as lean as his brother.

"They're only concerned with themselves." She pointed to girls on their phones and the men desperate for their attention.

She squeezed his hand. "Can you stay here with me for a minute?" he whispered, clutching her hand tighter.

"I am happy to." She slid closer to him and laced her fingers through his, making conversation about the different people in the club. "When I first modeled on the catwalk, I was terrified I would do something embarrassing."

"I'm sure it was difficult." Jake strained to breathe.

"To get over it, I thought about shoes." He raised an eyebrow, and she smiled. "Suede with snakeskin, or pimento leather pumps with silver accents. Thinking about shoes calmed my mind. They are fun and fabulous and perhaps the only thing I don't find stressful."

Jake relaxed against her shoulder. "Tell me more."

She rattled on about her favorite styles and colors, expanding to boots, as he nodded. "Better?"

"I didn't know it was humanly possible to have such a passion for shoes. It's like Kyle's fascination with documentaries, but for useless stuff." Jake chuckled.

She kissed him on the cheek. "Use my technique, it helps." She pulled Lia with her to join a group of girls on the dance floor.

"Are you alright?" Kyle asked. "We can leave if you need to get some air, maybe go for a walk?"

"I'm fine now. She talked me down from the ledge."

Kyle put his hand against Jake's, knowing the connection helped ground him. "Fascinating conversation on shoes."

"Surprisingly helpful," Jake said, relaxing against the sofa.

They took a cab to an all-night diner at Casi's suggestion. Kyle noted that whatever made her anxious before the club, subsided. It bothered him the way Alix touched her, an implied ownership and intimate knowledge of her body. He wasn't jealous of their past relationship, but concerned about the emotional hold Alix seemed to have over her.

They all ordered waffles with bacon, slathering them with butter and maple syrup. Casi took a bite and syrup dripped down her chest. She threw her head back and laughed as Kyle didn't miss a beat to lick it off. "You guys are too much," Jake declared, as Lia gazed at them wistfully. Jake held his phone under the table, sending a text with a sigh.

Casi looped her arm through Kyle's as they walked in the chilly air. He put his jacket around her while he shivered in his thin, silky shirt. The street was lively with couples and groups of people returning home from clubs and parties. They heard the zip of skateboards behind them, but before they could move out of the way, a sickening thwack erupted and Jake was hit full force by something in one of the skateboarder's hands. He fell to the ground, grabbing his twisted arm as a bone protruded. Casi staggered on her stilettos to the bushes and promptly threw up. Time stopped as Kyle considered going to her aid, running after the skateboarders, or assisting his brother. He knelt beside Jake, writhing in pain, and dialed 911. Casi slid down the wall and slumped on the sidewalk, shaking her head. Lia crawled to Jake and held his head in her lap. Kyle was put on hold, and after fifteen minutes of people stepping over them on the sidewalk, he called a taxi instead.

25

_______

# SAND AND SURF

Exhaustion overcame Casi and Kyle when they returned to the loft, and they threw themselves in the shower to wash off the blood and vomit before crawling in bed. Kyle fell asleep in an instant, but Casi felt refreshed and worried if she closed her eyes she might miss her meeting in three hours. She watched him sleeping, having pushed her multitude of pillows to the floor as he stretched out across her bed. He was beautiful, taut defined muscles, and a lean build. His tattoos were enough to be sexy, an accent to a well-built body. She considered waking him and getting him aroused, but she would wait. Weary from being the responsible one all the time, he deserved to sleep. She would rock his body in a few hours, she thought with a smile.

She opened Facebook and perused the posts from the evening. Although she rarely took selfies at the club, there were always dozens of pictures with her in them. It was fun to see it from someone else's perspective, a bystander to her social life. She had been tagged in photos, a lot of her dancing. She scanned the ones of her with Kyle. *How did they appear as a couple?* It seemed odd she had been Alix's girlfriend a year ago, and now she made out with someone else, as he sat beside her. She accepted a while ago Alix would be an important part of her life and her career. She had been drawn to his power, his confidence, and his image. When Alix led her over to the owners, he told her they shared a cosmic connection, but Kyle was her soulmate. He wasn't jealous of their relationship and had been one of the people urging her to get back with Kyle after the fight. He said they brought out the best in each other. She wished he stopped there, and not continued by saying, hopefully, he would inspire her to be on time since it was a fatal flaw. Her nervousness about going to sleep was due to her meeting being with Alix, and she didn't want to blow it, aware there was a lot riding on it.

She scrolled through the photos, unabashedly thrilled with her choice of outfit, and how it accentuated her body. She had been tagged in a picture where she sat on Kyle's lap, his hands up her skirt, her back arching as he kissed her neck. Extremely erotic, and it made her happy it was him kissing her. The comments were mostly positive, "Hot. Sexy couple. Who is the heartthrob with his hands up Casi's skirt?" She realized only Dylan knew anything about him, as most of their romance had been in Washington. A couple of guys made sexual references, wishing they were the one under her. One girl wrote, "Slut", but Casi didn't care. She never let negative comments bother her. She felt they reflected on the person posting more than the one being called the name.

She came to a picture that stood out from the others. She sat beside Kyle, their fingers laced together. He looked at her with such love in his eyes as she gazed at him adoringly. Even though her dress was skimpy, the way she positioned herself against him unknowingly portrayed a tender moment between two people deeply in love. She made it her profile picture, then changed her relationship status. "Casi Roberts is in a relationship with Kyle Jensen." She giggled as she added hearts like a schoolgirl.

She decided to get ready for the meeting. She hadn't told Kyle about it. After last night's events, she was too exhausted to explain all the details. Alix told her the owners of the nightclub were interested in investing in a new company which sold surfboards, accessories, swimsuits, and wetsuits. He had been very animated about opportunities for her to become involved. He explained she needed to be sensational at the club, and he would introduce her to the owners. When Alix kissed her, he whispered how amazing she looked, praising her on knocking it out of the park. It thrilled her to have pleased him, feeling like she failed him so many times in the past with her aimlessness, missed installations, and general lack of commitment to her career.

Alix requested she showcase her looks again for the meeting, which was more challenging in a daytime setting. She chose a knit wrap dress in a light cream that would hug her curves, accent her cleavage, and bring attention to her legs. She paired it with brown knee-high boots, wanting to appear more professional than stripper. She left her hair down and applied simple make up.

She leaned down and gave Kyle a kiss, saying she would be back in a bit. "Where are you going?" he asked sleepily.

"I have a meeting," she whispered.

"Casting on a Sunday?"

"Yup." She decided not to explain as he yawned.

She caught a cab and arrived at Coffee Bean, three minutes early. The owners of the club were investors who liked to help small businesses get ahead. Alix met them at one of his installments, mentioning his friend Johan's company. Johan was from South Africa and wanted to build a business based out of LA. They were interested in Casi as the model to represent the brand, having been impressed with her cover. Johan especially liked the rawness of the photo, the lack of retouching, and how her scars were visible. He insinuated he would like to see her scars up close and personal. She engaged, flirting with the investors and letting Johan put his hand on her knee. The deal Alix proposed would give her ten percent of the company, which could prove to be lucrative. After the meeting, she shook hands with the investors, turning her cheek, as Johan leaned in for a kiss.

Casi met with Stan Levitz at a small café, to go over the contract. She started to feel the effects of no sleep, too much caffeine, and a lack of food, having thrown up her only meal after Jake's attack. She gave him the papers from the investors and he agreed it seemed like a good deal. He asked her to have Kyle set aside time to go over his partnership agreement to evaluate the business. "Since Jake will be out for a while, it'll be a good time to assess the current value, before the high-dollar custom work comes in."

"How did you know Jake got hurt?" She cocked her head.

"Kyle told me." He engrossed himself in the menu.

"When?" She knew Kyle had been sleeping when she left, and it sounded like the business paperwork was drawn up.

"Honey, it's not important." He patted her hand.

The image of Jake's arm, the skateboarders, and Kyle's wavering statement to the police flashed through her mind. "It was a setup!" People stared at the commotion.

"Please calm down," he said in a hushed tone.

"Did Kyle know?"

"Not all the details."

She walked back to the loft, needing time to unwind, piecing together what she knew. Kyle spoke to the attorney at length at her mother's house. Jake, as usual, didn't pay attention and wandered around, leaving Kyle and Stan in deep conversation. She thought it had been good for Kyle to speak to someone about the business, someone who would understand the burden on him. Whose idea had it been? Surely, Kyle could not have known thugs would come and smash his brother's arm? She saw the beauty of the plan. Jake had been instructed not to talk about divorce, to let Gail file papers. He specialized in pissing her off and he prepared himself to lose the house, car, and most of his savings. If he became injured, especially his right arm, he would be unable to perform his duties. Kyle handled the business side and finishing work. Jake was responsible for building frames and pre-work, which Kyle could do or hire an apprentice. With Jake injured, it would make sense to buy him out, reducing his net worth.

"Oh Kyle, what did you do?" she sobbed.

She realized she was a hypocrite, flirting and flaunting herself to land a business deal, yet shocked Kyle would resort to dirty pool to get ahead. She wrestled with how she would bring it up, under-standing it was none of her business and she had only been asked to relay a message.

She opened the door and saw Kyle had showered and sat on the bed reading a hunting magazine. He was handsome, shirtless in jeans, hair still wet. He smiled. "You must be exhausted. Did you sleep at all or just go to your casting?"

"I didn't sleep, and I wasn't at a casting," she snapped.

He seemed confused. "I thought that's what you said when you left this morning."

"I lied because I didn't want to tell you I met Alix for coffee." He raised an eyebrow and waited for details. His lack of reaction was not what she wanted. "It wasn't only Alix. There were investors there, and a guy from South Africa, who kept putting his hand on my leg. I haven't determined if I should sleep with him..." she practically yelled. "You know how it is, anything for business, even selling out your brother!" She threw her boot at him for emphasis, in case he didn't get the reference.

He ducked and slid off the bed. "Casi, why are you yelling and throwing boots? I don't understand why you keep shoving Alix in my face, and who's this jerk from South Africa? Am I not giving you enough attention?" He hugged her, and she knew her exhaustion turned her into a two-year-old having a tantrum.

"Why Kyle?" She broke into tears.

"Why what? Casi, I'm not following what's going on." He led her to the bed, removing her second boot, as she told him what Stan said and how she connected the dots. Kyle laughed and sank back on the bed, his hands behind his head. Casi regarded him tearfully as he confessed. "It was Jake's idea. His master plan to stick it to Gail." He chuckled. "He got the idea when the lawyer explained we needed to place a value on the business. He relayed it while we were waiting for the hot dogs. I told him he was insane, but he insisted it was the only way to protect what we built. We'll give Gail a fair share, but we can't let her ruin the business out of spite. I saw him talking to those skater kids by the hotdog stand. He gave them $200 and said he would text them an address."

Casi recalled Jake texting when they were at the diner, being uncharacteristically quiet. "That's a terrible plan! I can't believe you scared me like that; making me barf on the sidewalk. And you lied."

"I didn't realize it would be so brutal. He got his money's worth. It wasn't intended as a lie, I only eliminated the facts. Speaking of half-truths, tell me about this non-casting, you little liar." He pulled her to his chest.

"Oh, I altered the truth about that," she mocked. He chuckled, and she put a hand to the side of his face. "It's a business opportunity to get a percentage of Alix's friend's company. Those were the investors I met last night at the club."

"With Alix."

"And Johan and the investors. I would get ten percent, plus my pay as the model for the campaign."

"Did Alix like your dress?" he asked, undoing the belt.

"He said I was beautiful."

"Did the South African put his hand all the way up your leg?" He pulled the dress open and rolled on top of her.

"Only to my thigh."

"Did you want him to?" He hovered above her, inches from her face.

"No." She kissed him softly.

"Next time you can tell him to keep his paws to himself. Inform the vultures you belong to a man who loves you deeply and knows how to take care of your intimate needs." He demonstrated what he meant, as she arched her back and tore at the sheets, writhing in ecstasy. He made his way to her breasts, kissing her so passionately, she knew it would leave a mark. His need to impress upon her he was the only man she would ever want became clear. He thrust into her and she watched the muscles in this arm twitch, clawing at his back to bring him closer and deeper inside. She wrapped her legs around his waist and raised her hips to greet him as he breathed heavily against her neck, sending a vibration down her spine. She relaxed, and he gathered her in his arms, holding her while she slept.

She awoke a few hours later, somewhat refreshed and hungry. She walked in the bathroom. "Do you want to call your partner in crime and see what he wants to do for dinner? There's a good sushi restaurant close to their hotel." She peered in the mirror and gasped, not expecting the marks trailing from behind her ear to her collarbone. "What the heck?"

"I should ask you the same thing." He turned to show her deep scratches on his back.

"You're not the model," she laughed, not realizing the intensity of their lovemaking at the time.

They met Jake and Lia at the sushi restaurant. Jake played the role of the victim perfectly, needing assistance to do everything. Casi saw how it would drive Gail insane, making her seem worse when she abandoned her disabled husband.

"I know someone who can get you phenomenal painkillers, you'll be floating on air," Casi said as Jake winced in pain.

"Don't go there." Kyle poked her in the ribs. "She knows."

Jake looked disappointed. "You said you wouldn't tell her."

"I didn't. She figured it out from something the lawyer said. She's a smart college girl." Kyle tickled her.

"Excuse me?" Casi frowned. "Why am I the only one not in on the plan? You people are evil little connivers."

"I only found out back at the motel," Lia claimed.

"Is it because I walk on a higher moral ground than you all, perhaps?" Casi assessed.

"Hardly." Jake shook his head and Kyle snickered.

"I didn't want to ruin your night at the club. I couldn't tell you at the hospital. And then I fell asleep. You left early for your ménage à trois," Kyle explained.

"I didn't tell you because I didn't want you to blab and spoil it." Jake popped a piece of sushi in his mouth.

Casi stuck her chop stick in his cast, making him yelp with pain. "I'm excellent at keeping secrets."

"Like your new Facebook status?" Jake rolled his eyes.

"What did you write?" Kyle quickly pulled up the app on his phone. It thrilled him to see her post and photo, having witnessed her linked with Alix long after they broke up, and then a lack of status, indicating he didn't rate. "I accept your relationship request," he said with a kiss.

26
_______

# SHARKS

Kyle set his duffle bag on the bed, gathering his belongings in preparation for the trip back to Washington. As he put clothes in, Casi took them out, partially to tease him, and because she was sorry he would be leaving and wanted to prolong the visit. "Stop it." He chuckled and eased a shirt from her hand.

"You can leave a few things here, in case I miss you."

"You've stolen most of my t-shirts." He pointed to the one she wore emblazoned with a salmon. "I'll be back next month to start the job at your mom's place."

"Good, then you can leave clothes here." She crawled to him, clad only in the t-shirt and white cotton underwear. He thought it undeniably sexy how she mostly wore cotton bikini panties rather than thongs. He loved how comfortable she was with her body, and the practical underwear only highlighted the promise of what it concealed. She flopped on her back and smiled, t-shirt pulled up to reveal the bottom of her breasts as she ran her hand over her stomach, trailing her fingers up the leg of his jeans.

A knock at the door halted her progression as a voice sang out, "I've got coffee and pastries, Darling."

"Coffee!" She somersaulted off the bed.

Kyle shook his head, observing she was like the ball in a pinball machine, flitting about and changing course on a whim. "Put some clothes on!" He watched her scamper to the door.

"It's only Dylan." She swung the door open.

"He's still here." Dylan frowned at two coffees.

"Yes, he doesn't leave until the morning. I have a meeting, so I'll leave you to your gossip." Kyle grinned and took a sip from one of the coffees before handing it to Casi.

"Hey!" She giggled and sat at her bistro table, long legs swinging. She opened the pastry bag with glee to find a chocolate croissant. Kyle kissed her on the temple, then took a bite from her pastry as she pushed him away.

As he left, he overheard Dylan say, "Tell me about those love bites all over your neck, you vixen!" Kyle shuddered at the thought of her recounting any of their lovemaking and hurried out before he could hear more.

❧

It had been hard to leave Casi this time. Kyle saw the tears in her eyes as he kissed her goodbye at the airport while she tried to act casual, talking a mile a minute about the things they would do when he came back to see her. "This is the first time you're leaving me, with the promise of coming back," she noted.

He grasped her chin in his hand and made direct eye contact. "We're together, Casi, and distance isn't going to change that." He saw her wipe her eyes discreetly as he walked toward the security checkpoint.

His relationship with Lauren had been simple. They evolved from a friendship to a romantic relationship, without passion. They enjoyed doing things together, and he looked forward to planning activities, as they had many shared interests. She didn't demand a lot of his time, being busy in her career, and he was satisfied, even if the sex was lackluster. When she started to push for more, he saw his world imploding and seized the first opportunity to end it. Casi was different. The damn girl had gotten under his skin. The feeling of her beside him in bed, her constant sunny demeanor, easy laugh, and insatiable desire for sex had him spinning.

Jake drew Casi to the side, pretending to hug her goodbye. "Please don't sleep with any other men," he pleaded.

Casi's jaw dropped. "Why are you saying that?"

"You don't understand everything about him. It would crush him if you betrayed him. He loves you, and he doesn't fall in love easily." Jake squeezed her hand.

She ran her hand over the scars on his arm. "I believe there's a lot I don't know." She hugged him and was pleased when he hugged her back without reservation.

"Maybe in time, I'll let you in," Jake said with a smile.

Casi returned to her loft and cried in her pillow, chastising herself for falling apart over a man. She tried to find the motivation to work on her class assignments, but failed miserably and went out for coffee instead. Her mind constantly drifted to what Kyle was doing. He would be home by now. Had he noticed she stole another t-shirt, a pair of socks, and his razor? She put the razor by the sink in the bathroom, imagining him standing in front of the mirror shaving his handsome face, wrapped only in a towel. She put the socks in the drawer with her own, a masculine statement, making her socks feel not quite so alone. She wore the t-shirt to bed, hugging it to her to ease the loneliness. She surveyed the loft which seemed empty, despite its small size. Kyle said she needed custom-made, reclaimed pine cabinets in her kitchen to compliment the brick. He envisioned a bar style counter, maybe incorporating a rustic steel beam. She laughed, saying she only used the kitchen to store her takeout menus and wine, and then they made love against the faux granite counter.

She went on Facebook to play Candy Crush and distract herself. Kyle accepted her relationship request, making it official. She could see he was online and on a whim, sent him a picture of herself topless. He messaged her back, saying it made it more difficult for him to be away from her. It was unusual to be pining away, counting the days until he would return.

&

"Who's Casey Roberts?" Lauren demanded as she scrolled through Facebook and spoke to her sister on the phone.

"Casi is a woman Kyle is seeing." Lia corrected the pronunciation as she prepared to be interrogated.

Lauren tried to access Casi's profile, but it was restricted. She could see the profile picture and was distraught at the loving way Kyle gazed into the beautiful girl's face. "Is it serious?"

"They only just got together," Lia lied.

Lauren noted Casi's location. "She's from LA?"

"Yes, she lives there." Lia held her breath.

"He met her when he went there last year for work! That's why he barely responds to my messages. I hate him!"

"It's been a year since you broke up, maybe it's time to move on?" Lia waited for the breakdown to follow.

"You don't know what it's like to love someone!" Lauren sobbed in the phone. "This isn't something I can get over. He is the man I am destined to marry and have a family with."

"Well, maybe in time that will happen." Lia shook her head suspecting Kyle never felt the same way about her sister.

&

Jake played his injury to the max, increasing the brutality of the attack each time he told the story at the bar, as people bought him sympathy drinks. Gail was predictably cranky with his whining and constant demands. His kids were interested for a brief period upon his return, seeing their father as the victim of a vicious attack by thugs on the mean streets of LA. His constant presence in the house wore thin, and everyone wondered when he might be ready to go back to work. Kyle continued to run the business, using the wood shortage as an excuse to limit orders on paper. On the sly, he wrote up quotes for custom work in LA, delaying start dates until after a buyout of the business.

After a few weeks, Gail stormed in Kyle's office demanding paperwork on their finances. He happily complied, including Jake's medical bills and expenses for the LA trip.

"I don't understand why you both had to go there!" She narrowed her eyes. "Does he have to hold your hand while you screw your girlfriend? God knows he wouldn't be able to give you any pointers in the bedroom." Kyle assessed her skinny legs topped by a tennis skirt, boxy figure with small breasts, and pinched face, and wondered how she changed so much since college. He remembered how she used to be petite and attractive, but the years hardened her, and the permanent scowl masked a once pretty face. "Are you listening to me?" she asked, while he pictured her as a chicken in a skirt. "Wipe that smirk off your face. We have bills to pay, and I have a loser on my couch, eating potato chips, watching TV, and scratching himself!"

*A couch and TV he paid for,* he wanted to say. "What do you want me to do?" he asked, sitting back in this chair. "All we have is this building and our profits from the custom orders, which are slow. It's not my fault if Jake spends every penny he makes; I'm not his keeper."

"Sell the damn business!" She shoved his neatly stacked papers to the floor as she whirled out.

"No problem." He bent to pick up his paperwork, annoyed it was in disarray, but thrilled she took the bait.

She stopped at the door and turned as a tear ran down her cheek. "I tried, Kyle. Things have been bad the last few years, but I was there in the beginning and I made a lot of sacrifices."

"I realize you did." Kyle sighed. "You two don't work anymore. Let him live his life and you go live yours."

"He won't like being alone. I still care about him, and I've always protected his secrets. And yours."

"I appreciate that, Gail. You'll both be happier and you'll get a fair share of the business so you can move forward."

He phoned the lawyer and went online to book his ticket to LA. He called his parents to inform them he would be out of town for his birthday and give them an update on Jake. "You're spending a lot of time in LA?" Georgia noted sweetly.

Kyle couldn't tell her about the work he had lined up. "Mom, there's a woman there I'm going to visit."

Georgia sounded hopeful. "The one you met last year?"

"We've been off and on..." he hesitated. "I'm in love with her, and we're trying to make it work with a long-distance relationship. I'll bring her to meet you when she comes here."

"I am so happy for you!" Georgia exclaimed, realizing Kyle never told her he loved any woman before, not even Lauren.

He packed his duffle bag and threw in a few extra items he would leave at Casi's, aware of his missing razor and socks, and her thievery of his t-shirts. He liked that his things were keeping her company while he was far away. He wondered if she used his razor to shave her legs, imagining the blade making its way up her silky skin as she lathered up in the shower. His pulse quickened at the thought, and he was anxious to get on the plane.

Casi heard from Alix that the Sand and Surf deal went through and finalized the details with her lawyer. It excited her to be involved in something of such magnitude. She applied what she learned in her college classes to force herself to understand the language of the contracts, ensuring her best interests were being considered.

Mary had been pleased when she shared the details of the deal. "That fellow has been good for you, Casi," Mary said. It was true, Kyle pushed her to be the best version of herself; one she didn't know existed before him.

Casi was nervous to tell him the first shoot would be the day of his birthday. She pleaded with Alix to change it, even by one day, but he insisted everything was booked. In a cosmic coincidence, the location was Malibu, a year to the date of her accident. She prayed this wasn't a precursor to an ugly outcome.

They rushed back to the loft after she picked Kyle up from the airport, eager to rekindle the flame after almost a month. They made love desperately, with the raw passion of lovers in tune with each other's desires.

Afterward, Kyle sat in her chair and watched her dance while she ate ice cream. "I talked to my mother about you."

"Oh?" She twirled to face him.

"I told her I was in love with you." He swiped the bowl from her hand and took a bite.

She slipped on his lap, reclaiming her spoon. "Moms make me nervous, I feel like they're judging me."

"My parents will adore you." Kyle smiled.

Casi walked to the kitchen to put her empty bowl in the sink. She caught Kyle's concerned look and washed it properly. She shrugged. "Remember the Sand and Surf deal?"

"Yes," he said slowly.

"They booked the first shoot. In Malibu."

"That's great!"

"It's on your birthday, and I can't change it." She put the bowl away, glancing over her shoulder for his reaction.

"I understand you have to work." He held out a hand and drew her on his lap. "Malibu, huh? That's random. It'll be a year to the day of your accident."

"This time I have reservations at a steakhouse for your birthday. And you'll get lucky." She snuggled against him.

"I bet I would have last year, too." He winked.

"True," she giggled.

"Will Alix be at the shoot?"

"Yes."

"And that pervert Johan?"

"Most likely." She assumed he would since he handpicked her as the model and would want to be involved.

"Maybe I should come and protect you from sharks and speeding cars." He hugged her tightly.

She wondered if the sharks were Alix and Johan. "You can come and watch me strut my stuff." She was curious what he would think, seeing the technical side. He had seen the finished photos but had no idea what it took to get the perfect shot.

Johan greeted her with a kiss before she could turn and say, "This is my boyfriend, Kyle, and he came to watch the shoot." He visibly sized up Kyle, shaking his hand cautiously. He remarked to Alix that he might be a distraction for Casi. Alix insisted he would make her even sexier as she taunted him while she posed.

Kyle settled in the sand, trying to keep out of the way while she worked. The prep work was tedious, and he didn't understand why it took so long to get ready. She was perfect already. He watched them wet her hair, putting on a mountain of product to make it tousled with waves. Spray, crimp, and twist. Her body was oiled and bronzed, the makeup kept to a minimum. A sultry smudge of eyeliner and waterproof mascara, then layers of lip gloss, and bronzed cheeks to appear as if she stepped out of the surf. She removed her robe and stood with her back to him, wearing only tiny bikini bottoms. He watched Johan salivating and wanted to punch him. Oblivious to the attention, Casi patiently got tugged into a bright pink, shorty wetsuit. They left it unzipped, arranging her cleavage. *That's not practical. Why would anyone not zip up a wetsuit if they were surfing? It defeats the purpose,* Kyle thought.

Alix stood nearby; surf shorts slung so low on his hips. Kyle could clearly read the script across his pelvic bones, *Redemption.*

Kyle wondered how he kept his shorts on considering Alix was a real surfer who traveled the world in search of the perfect wave. Casi came over to Alix as he held a surfboard. She had prepared Kyle, she would be posing with him as he was the male model for the shoot. Kyle surveyed his tattoos, wondering what the inspiration behind them had been, figuring how personal his own were. He shook his head when he read the one on Alix's left shoulder blade, *Life is about the Journey.*

Casi focused on where to stand and what the lighting director said to her. Kyle was glad she wasn't distracted by him and tried not to make a scene when he realized Johan, clad in equally low slung surfer shorts, and a ridiculous number of tattoos, joined the shoot. It made sense, as it was his company, the brainchild spawned from his love of surfing.

The trio posed with Casi in the middle, legs spread, back arched, standing in the surf. A few shots from the back, making sure to lift the wetsuit up enough to expose her tanned cheeks. Kyle focused on Casi and how great she looked and fantasized the two surfers were about to be eaten by sharks. She was helped up on a surfboard, almost exposing her breasts as she tried to balance. Although extremely comfortable in the water, she never surfed and struggled to stay upright. After several attempts and a face-plant which left a red mark on her chin, they determined she should remain seated as if she paddled in. She did better at that, swinging her legs open wide and putting her hands in front of her, leaning forward to make the most of her cleavage. The stylist waded out to fix her makeup and re-position her hair. The photographer snapped away while Casi bobbed on the surfboard as the waves intensified, leery of something slowly swimming past her bare foot.

After several hours, and eight versions of wetsuits and twelve bikinis, Kyle could see she was shivering and assumed she must be starving, only having a banana and coffee for breakfast. He resisted the urge to wrap her in a towel and bring her a sandwich, keeping his promise not to interfere. He was glad he picked up snacks, and kicked back in the sand, eating a deli sandwich and potato chips, washed down with a coke. *Woodworking is much more interesting,* he thought, growing bored with yet another fluff and primp of the model. The shoot finished and everyone hovered around the laptop attached to the digital camera to see the proofs. They seemed pleased with the quality of pictures to launch the campaign. Casi slipped on black leggings and a long sweatshirt, pulling her Uggs on her freezing feet. She hugged everyone goodbye and tromped up the beach.

"I hope that wasn't too boring," she said.

"Not at all how they portray it on the Playboy channel." Kyle chuckled and pulled her to his chest, feeling the chill of her skin against his cheek.

"Can we put the heat on in the car?" she chattered.

He was glad he hadn't been the jealous boyfriend, and he saw firsthand that no matter how little clothing she wore, the Casi on a shoot was not the same woman he ravaged at home. He smiled, thinking he knew her so intimately. He witnessed the lust in her eyes as she made love to him, only trusting him to take her to that level of passion.

❧

At dinner, Kyle took her hand. "I need to ask you something, and it's important you don't lie to me."

She laughed. "I haven't slept with Alix since you and I have been back together."

"That's good. But that's not what I wanted to ask you. I need to know the meaning of your tattoo and why Alix has the same one on his shoulder."

"Oh, that! When Alix came back from Africa, you had left, and I was very lost. I felt bad about my scar and my circumstances. We were hanging out, talking about the meaning of life." She didn't mention the pot they were smoking at the time. "He said life is about the journey, not the destination, and I focused too much on where I should be, rather than living for today. He took me to his local place, and I got the script with the date. The accident changed the course of my life and I wanted a permanent reminder, other than the scar. He chose to have the same phrase as a statement of our time together since I am part of his journey in life."

He nodded, aware Alix still loved Casi and could understand why

218

he would want to share something with her. "Thank you for being honest." He squeezed her hand.

"We both have past lives. You share a lot with your brother that I'll never be a part of. That's what makes us great together; former relationships have influenced us."

"You're right, and I do love the woman you are."

"You never mention anyone you've dated. You seem like someone women would be throwing themselves at. How come you never got married or were not in a serious relationship?"

"The longest one was a little over three years. I've never had a desire to be married, and I'm not interested in having children. That usually turns women off after a few years. Plus, you are the only one I have ever fallen in love with."

**27**

---

## PAPERWEIGHT

The buyout papers were drawn up, based on the present value of the business. The building had been assessed and future earnings were factored. Casi was impressed at the value of the business, especially considering they were low-balling it. They had to be careful not to raise suspicion since Gail would consult an attorney. Casi was surprised Kyle shared his financial information with her, talking openly about what he had in his retirement portfolio, how his house was paid for, and what he brought home monthly. He had a good financial head on his shoulders, while Jake had a wife who didn't work, two kids who would be going to college in a few years, and a large mortgage and car payment, leaving him financially strapped. She thought it was funny how different the brothers were. She liked how Kyle's choices afforded him the ability to live a comfortable life.

Jake and Gail signed the buyout papers the morning he had his cast removed. The attorney handed Jake the check, and he refused to look at it, glaring at the wall behind Kyle's head.

"It'll be ok," Kyle whispered.

Gail took the check smugly, assuming she created financial hardship for Kyle and became the sole receiver of Jake's half. She had been eager to make the deal and hadn't factored in Jake not having an income. She saw the dollar signs and jumped on it.

When they returned home, Jake went to the kitchen and poured himself a scotch, as Gail shook her head. "It's a little early in the day to start drinking!"

"Do you have any idea how hard that was for me to do today?" Jake glared at her.

She shrugged. "Don't worry, Kyle's still your brother. You just don't have a business with him anymore." Jake threw his glass against the cabinet and put his head in his hands. "Clean that up!"

Jake texted Kyle. "Can you meet me at the bar?"

"When?"

"Now." He swept up the glass and wiped the counter, then headed out without informing Gail.

He was seated at the bar when Kyle came in, having ordered two drinks in anticipation. "It's only on paper, Jake. You still have half of the business and the building."

"Gail will spend the money in no time, and I'll never be able to buy back in." He turned with tears in his eyes, factoring in the reality of the situation. "Everything I've worked for, that we built together, is gone. We'll get divorced now, and I'll have nothing to my name."

Kyle put his arm around his brother's shoulders. "Everything will work out. Let it go and be done with it."

"All I ever wanted was the business; it's the only thing I am proud of. When you were at college, you kept telling me to be patient. Now it's gone."

"The wood shop is thriving. This is a financial arrangement to protect your assets. You have to trust me, ok?"

"You're the only one I trust." Jake swirled his drink.

"Do you remember when you started working?"

"At fifteen, and I loved it. I had money, and I accomplished something every day," Jake recalled.

"I begged Dad to allow me to get a job too, and he wouldn't let me because I was too young," Kyle stated.

Jake smiled at the memory. "You made flyers for the Jensen brothers' business, doing yard work and handyman stuff."

"Although I misspelled business, Mom thought it was cute, so she didn't tell me." Kyle rolled his eyes.

"You put a lot of work into those flyers," Jake chuckled.

"I did it because you squandered your money on pot, condoms, and dirty magazines," Kyle reminded him. "You wanted a truck, but weren't able to save enough."

Jake scowled at him. "So, you're reminding me I was a loser, even at fifteen? I guess I haven't improved my situation."

"No! I'm pointing out that together we could accomplish our goals. I helped you save for the truck and then we got more work because you had a driver's license."

"I took you to a lot of cool places," Jake added.

"You've always been a great big brother." Kyle whispered, "Everything is still half yours. We built it together and we'll always be partners."

Gail filed for divorce the next day, wanting to ensure the majority of the money would be coming her way. Jake was still not cleared for work, required to attend physical therapy before the doctor would release him. As requested, Jake delivered the divorce papers to Kyle at the shop. He surveyed the work going on. "This is killing me to not be here; I'm completely lost."

"Remember, you can't come by for a while." Kyle mentioned as they got in the truck. "No Lia either."

The attorney drew up the paperwork, giving Gail everything she asked for, except alimony. They offered her the full sum from the buyout, plus half of Jake's retirement. Jake would pay child support and keep the children on his medical plan, but Gail would need to get her own health insurance within three months. She would also get the house and the car. Gail signed the paperwork a week later, happily taking off her ring and throwing it at Jake.

He shook his head as he retrieved it from the floor. "I remember how you pressured me to buy this. I wasn't even out of college and you had me locked down. I hope it was worth it."

She shrugged. "I'm unclear if any of it was worth it, Jake. I only know I couldn't take it anymore."

Gail walked in the coffee shop and sauntered up to Lia's register. She held up her left hand. "There you go. He's all yours. No more sneaking around, you can have him." Lia blinked in surprise, not having talked to Jake for weeks. Gail joined her friends and announced, "After sixteen years, I'm single again."

"What are you going to do now?" Mary Ann asked.

Gail bit her lip as her heart dropped and tears sprung to her eyes. "I really don't know."

❧

Jake packed his clothes and belongings while Gail stood at the end of the bed and watched him. "You don't mind if I take my clothes, do you?" he asked sarcastically. She shook her head and wiped a tear, turning her face in embarrassment.

Olivia stared at him with tears running down her face. "Why do you have to leave, Dad?"

"We talked to you about how this would work. You and Reid will live with Mom, but you can come and visit me anytime you want," Jake said softly.

"I don't want you to move out," Olivia cried.

"It will be hard in the beginning, but we'll all be happier if Mom and I aren't living together." Jake zipped his suitcase.

"Where will you live?" Reid asked.

"I'll stay with Kyle for a while, and then an apartment." Jake shivered at the idea of living alone. "There will be room for you guys to come and stay with me."

Jake walked to his truck with his bags and Gail put her hand on his chest. "What happened to us?" she asked.

"We were only ever together for the kids."

"But we had good times, too."

"Not enough." He turned back and took her hand. "This was inevitable; neither of us should be shocked." Gail nodded as he threw his bags in the truck and waved goodbye.

❧

"When do I start feeling like my life's not a total disaster?" Jake asked, walking in Kyle's house with a duffel bag.

Kyle glanced at him from where he sat on the sofa. "Grab a drink and come watch the game."

Jake sat beside him. "When can I come back to work?"

"Tomorrow." Kyle beamed.

"Really?"

Kyle nodded. "The money has been transferred to Gail's account and I've set up automatic transfers for the child support. You no longer have a mortgage or car payment."

"I didn't consider that. So, I might be ahead financially every month?" Jake calculated the numbers.

"Considerably. We'll put part of your salary toward buying back into the business and start rebuilding your retirement account. Casi's not coming until at least June, and there's no rush to get an apartment. Your truck is paid for and you're debt free."

"I'll be a full partner again once I pay you back?"

"You're a full partner now." Kyle put his hand on Jake's. "Have you talked to Mom and Dad?"

"I'm not looking forward to telling them I failed at one more thing," Jake mumbled.

"It's not a failure to end a bad relationship. You need to tell them before they hear about it from the kids."

❧

Georgia came out to the porch, drying her hands. "Did you come for dinner?" she asked eagerly.

"Sure, dinner sounds great," Kyle answered.

Jake got a beer from the fridge, handing one to Kyle as they headed to the living room. Peter glanced at Georgia and raised his eyebrows, aware they were about to hear some news. Peter poured Georgia a glass of wine and fixed a scotch in preparation. "How's everything at work?" Peter asked, noticing a darkness appear on Jake's face as he leaned back on the sofa.

Kyle nudged his brother. "Jake wants to tell you something."

Jake shook his head and stared at the wall. "Gail and I are getting divorced. I'm staying with Kyle for now and I'll get an apartment this summer. I sold my half of the business to pay her off," he said, choking up on the last part.

Peter grinned, and Georgia exclaimed, "That's wonderful!"

"You're happy?" Jake gasped.

"That woman has been making you miserable for years. You've taken care of your kids and given them a good start." Peter strode over and squeezed Jake's shoulder.

"Did you hear the part about selling the business? Everything I've worked for all my life? I have nothing now, no home, and half my retirement is gone." Jake met his father's eyes.

"I'm sure Kyle has worked out a way for you to buy back in over the years. You're young enough to save more money for retirement; you'll be fine," Peter stated.

Kyle told them about the plan he put together and how Jake no longer had any debt. "The house was too big anyway," Georgia agreed. "How are the children taking it?"

"Reid seems ok, and Olivia's upset," Jake said.

"It was no good for them to be in an unhappy home. You'll have better relationships with them on their own," Peter said.

"I thought you'd be upset and tell me I was a failure."

"We've never felt that, Jake. You had a tough choice in college, and you did the right thing. You've taken care of your family and built a business with your brother. We've been very proud of how you've led your life," Peter concluded.

**28**

## KITTENS AND CLOSETS

Casi stuffed most of her wardrobe in her car and gave the loft a final perusal. She gave up on the plant after it dropped its last leaf. It remained a stick for a while before she started to feel like it watched her, accusing and blaming her for its demise. She chucked it and put up a pretty picture of the flowers in Ava's garden instead. She offered Dylan the use of her loft since it was close to his salon. He claimed it wasn't much of a consolation prize when she got to spend the summer at a lake house. She told him it would be for one month and he said, "Who stays in LA for the summer?"

Kyle met her at the car and gave her a kiss. He was barefoot with shorts and a t-shirt, and she was anxious to slip into something cooler herself. He peered in the car. "Moving in?"

She laughed. "I couldn't figure out what to bring, it seemed easier to throw it all in."

"Wow, that doesn't make you look homeless at all." The joke was funny this time because it wasn't true. The drive had been sticky and hot. She feared getting baked with the top down, and her air conditioner ran on overdrive, chugging to keep up with the sunny weather. She wriggled out of her jeans, regretting the clothing choice for the trip, unable to tolerate the feeling of damp material against her legs any longer. "Damn, can't you wait until we get inside?" Kyle admired her lavender underwear with the lace insets.

"I'm too overheated to even consider sex." She gazed at the lake with longing.

He grabbed her hand, sensing she was about to jump in the water. "Ok, but I want to show you something first." He led her toward the front door and stood behind her with his hands over her eyes and nudged her forward. Her hip struck a bar stool with a thud. "Oops, sorry." He shoved it aside.

In a few more steps, the edge of a table caught her shin and magazines flew to the floor. "I'm starting to have trust issues," she said, fearing what body part she might lose next.

They reached what she determined must be the bedroom, and he removed his hands. He faced her to the wall toward the bathroom, and she wondered if he had sexy lingerie waiting. Thankfully, the house was cooler than outside, putting her more in the mood. She walked through the entrance of the bathroom and did a double-take. The room was twice the size, with a shower built for two, and a huge soaker tub under the window, over-looking the lake. The vanity contained a deep sink in a long counter, featuring a generous selection of lotions, powders, and sprays, arranged in a basket. Fluffy towels hung from hooks by the shower. Kyle grinned. "I went to a store in the mall and asked them to put together a bunch of that stuff you like." Before she could say anything, he took her hand again and led her to the bedroom which had at least six feet added, with a large bay window. "Look." He pointed to the bed. "Big pillows with absolutely no purpose in life." She laughed at his depiction of what she valued. "And this will come in handy." He opened the closet doors to reveal an enormous walk-in closet.

"Oh, my God!" she shrieked, stepping in and surveying the expansive interior. His clothes were arranged on one side. He put a few of the things she left on what appeared to be her section. "My red suede pumps!"

"Yep, no more foster care, they have a forever home."

"It's fantastic. Did you do this yourself?" she asked.

"Jake helped me. I wanted you to feel welcome; there's space for both of us." He embraced her. "No more man cave."

"I may never want to leave," she teased.

"That would be fine with me."

Something soft touched her arm, and she spotted a tiny kitten with big blue eyes staring up at her from his hands. It mewed, and she cuddled it to her chest. "How darling! Can I name her Jezebel?"

"That's a terrible name, but she's yours and you can call her what you want. I'll simply oversee her care to make sure you don't forget to feed or water her." He petted the kitten's head.

"I love her!" Casi kissed her fat belly. "I've never had a pet. I always wondered what it would be like." She launched into a convoluted story on her history of wanting a pet and her mother's insistence of not allowing it, even when she was living in LA and paying the bills. She digressed to a discussion on Sonya's incessant desire to quash her dreams and put her down.

"Can you focus for a moment? I've been down on my knee for five minutes." Kyle fidgeted on the hard floor.

"Did you trip? I thought you were tying your shoe." She tickled the ball of fluff and giggled when she purred.

"I have bare feet." He removed the kitten from her hands while he untied a pink ribbon from its neck and held up a diamond and emerald band. "Casi, I'm trying to ask you to marry me, and you're not making it easy."

"What? Why?" She stumbled back.

"Oh, Jesus." He leaned back on his heels. He reconsidered why he imagined a romantic proposal. It had all gone so much better in his head.

Casi sat cross-legged in front of him. "I'm confused, Kyle. Do you think I am the white picket fence, soccer mom type?"

"I prefer puppies to kids. I love you, Casi, and we can create our own version of happily ever after. I rushed things, and maybe I misread what we had." He gave her a weak smile and placed the ring on a shelf.

Casi put her hand on his. "You surprised me. I never thought of myself as someone's wife."

"I understand." He glanced away.

She smiled at him, so handsome and hurt by her hesitation. She reached out and touched his face. "You've never mentioned marriage before. I didn't believe you wanted that in your future either."

"I am happy with my life, but I met you and I wanted more." He shrugged and regarded his hands.

"Can I see the ring?"

"Will it make a difference how you answer?"

She held the platinum band with a large center diamond flanked by emeralds and smaller diamonds. "It's not very traditional. What made you pick this one?"

"I thought the emeralds were the color of your eyes, and the diamonds are superb quality." He shrugged. "I felt it suited you and complimented your unique style."

"Marriage, Kyle? How would that even work for us?"

"If you don't like it..." He tried to take it back from her. "I can return it. We don't need to get married. I honestly don't know what I was thinking."

"Oh, I love the design! It's the most beautiful one I've ever seen. I can tell you put a lot of effort into picking it out." She raised an eyebrow. "And money."

"It's not cheap." He chuckled and slid it on her finger. "You can keep it. I bought it for you. It doesn't have to be for an engagement. You can wear it on the other hand if you prefer."

She pulled her t-shirt off and reclined on the floor in front of him as she uncrossed her legs and put them over his. She held her hand up and admired the ring, then glanced at Kyle and laughed. He was distracted by the shirt she flung on the floor. "You're dying to put it on a shelf, aren't you?"

"Yes, I am," he admitted. He ran his hand over her stomach and Jezebel pounced on top, making Casi giggle.

"What would life be like? How would it differ from what we have now?" She wiggled her fingers for Jezebel to paw at.

Kyle reached over and pulled the straps of her bra down and unclipped it. He placed it on a shelf. "See? There's lots of room for your things. I can't imagine marriage would be any different." He bit his cheek. "I guess I like the idea of the commitment to each other."

"Because you don't trust me?"

"I do trust you." He slipped her underwear off and tossed it in the hamper.

Casi laughed. "You have a place for everything!"

"I'm very organized," he said with a smile.

"Maybe that's why you like the institution?"

"True." He leaned forward to kiss her.

"What did Jake say when you told him?"

"I'm insane and you're not the marrying type. It would be only a matter of time before this small town made you claustrophobic."

She put her arms around his neck and pulled him toward her. Jezebel grabbed her hair, pouncing against them as they kissed. Kyle laughed and grasped the kitten by the scruff of the neck and put her inside the laundry hamper. "Kyle! Are you putting her on a time out?" Casi giggled.

"I would like to make love to my girlfriend, uninterrupted."

"Girlfriend? I thought I'm your fiancé now?"

"You declined my proposal." He frowned in confusion.

"I asked why you wanted to get married."

"I love you, and want to spend the rest of my life with you as my partner," he clarified.

"You're the only man I'll ever love and my heart belongs to you always and forever."

"Wait. Are you saying yes?" His eyes widened.

"Yes. I would be thrilled to marry you," she said sincerely.

"You will run circles around me."

They made love on the closet floor while Jezebel mewed from the laundry basket until she fell asleep. They swam and tanned on the dock for the rest of the afternoon. Jezebel fell in the lake when she lost her balance chasing a bug, and Kyle jumped in swiftly to rescue her, as Casi screamed. They dried her with a towel, and she curled up in the crook of his arm to nap. He barbecued steaks while Casi made a salad, and they discussed how marriage would work, dividing their time between LA and Washington. They agreed it was a pretty good arrangement, and with his pending jobs in LA in the fall, they would be together a lot of the time. She suggested she stay the whole summer since the campaign for the Sand and Surf line wouldn't start up again until late August.

"When did you want to do it?" she asked.

"We can wait a year if it'll make you more comfortable."

"This is going to be a busy year," she sighed.

"We can wait longer, there's no rush," he offered.

"What if we didn't?"

"If we didn't get married?" His face registered disappointment. "I told you I'm happy to be with you. I don't need to have a piece of paper."

Casi laughed. "I meant if we didn't wait. Maybe we could have a simple ceremony in the fall, with our families."

He raised an eyebrow. "You do want to get married? And you want to do it sooner rather than later?"

"You're going to have to try harder to keep up."

"Jeez, you're telling me." He shook his head. "I'll get married any day, and anywhere you want."

"I'm not the kind of girl who's dreamed about my wedding since I was a kid. I've done a ton of fashion work modeling wedding dresses. The whole puffy, white dress and dove thing is not me." She couldn't imagine herself getting excited about bridesmaid attire, party favors, and planning where people would sit. "I don't see the value of spending a bunch of money on a one-day affair and a dress I only wear once."

"Cool with me." He nodded with relief. He remembered Jake's elaborate wedding. He should have known then Gail would be a nightmare. He also considered how Lauren planned a ceremony before they were even engaged.

"Let's do a destination wedding! We can pick an amazing beach and just show up!" Casi clapped with excitement. "My mom did one for her fourth wedding, and it was amazing."

"I'm unclear what that is, but it sounds perfect. I'm in!" It seemed like a good start to agree on what the actual wedding should be. "Want to go to the bar and celebrate our very mature decisions in life?"

Kyle pulled Casi in his arms outside the bar. "You're absolutely sure about this wedding, right? I'm serious about you keeping the ring and even Jezebel. Although, she'll have to live with me so I can take care of her. I don't want you to feel pressured. It won't end our relationship if you change your mind."

"Why are you asking me this? I said yes." Casi frowned.

"I don't want to look like a fool if you run out on me at the last minute," he confessed.

"I am absolutely sure." She gave him a confirming kiss.

They entered the building hand in hand. Casi wore a short jean skirt with a crocheted top over a bustier, and red high-heeled sandals. Jake sat at the bar, in his usual spot, watching the game. Casi was shocked to see Gail sitting with Mary Ann and a few friends, sharing a pitcher of Margaritas.

Kyle surprised Casi by grasping her around the waist and lifting her to sit on the bar. "I'd like to buy a round to toast the soon to be Mrs. Jensen," he announced proudly.

Casi whispered, "It'll still be Roberts professionally."

Kyle nodded, and they kissed to loud cheers from the crowd. Jake rushed to his side and put an arm around his shoulder, beaming at the news. "I'm glad you accepted." Jake eyed Casi with relief.

"I almost didn't, considering you would be a part of the package." She noted the pain dance across his sapphire eyes and she threw her arms around his neck. "I'm teasing!"

Jake exhaled and hugged her. "I'm going to have to get used to your twisted sense of humor, you Crazy Monkey."

"Do you think we'll ever get along?" she asked.

"I guess it'll depend on how you treat Kyle," he declared.

Mary Ann tried not to appear stunned, but the tears threatened to come. She turned to Gail. "Wow, did you ever expect to hear Kyle announce that?"

Gail shook her head. "Hell, no. I thought he was a confirmed bachelor, especially after what happened with Lauren." She put her hand on Mary Ann's. "Are you ok?"

Mary Ann gave her a meek smile. "I'm alright. I guess part of me always hoped Casi would get bored and go back to LA."

"Congratulations!" Lia gave Casi a hug and surveyed the ring. "Wow, gorgeous! It's so unique. I love the emeralds." She swallowed her jealousy. "Are you moving here full-time?"

Casi explained how they would divide their time for the first couple of years. She poked Jake in the chest. "You'll have to take care of your brother when I'm not around."

"Even though you'll be married, I get to spend time with Kyle, and you aren't going to bitch and moan about it? It sounds like the perfect relationship to me." Jake gave her a high-five.

"Congratulations." Gail smiled as she walked over.

"No snide remarks?" Kyle asked.

"I've had a bit of a wake-up call since Jake and I split up. I am happy for you two," she confirmed.

"I'll walk you out." Jake helped Gail with her jacket.

Casi strolled to the jukebox, and Lia put her hand on Kyle's arm. "Well, that's a surprise. You've been with her six months and you've changed your stance suddenly?"

Kyle sighed, "I never loved Lauren. We were good together for a while, but I was serious about not wanting to get married. I met Casi over a year ago. We may have only been dating a few months, but I've been in love with her since I first kissed her."

"Is Casi aware of your relationship with Lauren?"

"What's to know? We dated."

"You dated my sister for over three years, and she assumed you guys were getting married!" Lia narrowed her eyes. "She told the whole town you were proposing on Valentine's Day! You devastated her when you backed out."

"We just started to talk about marriage, and I was blindsided by her reaction when we went out to dinner," he lied.

"Come on, Kyle! The two of you and your constant planning for the future? Surely you knew she expected a proposal after three years! Even your mother thought so," Lia shot back.

"How do you know what my mother thought?"

"Lauren still talks to your mom." Lia shrugged. "Your mother told her she was sorry you hadn't proposed and hoped you would come around, eventually."

"Does Lauren know about Casi?" Kyle cringed.

"She saw the relationship status on Facebook and freaked out. I'm sure she'll hear about the proposal and be crushed."

"Tell her so she doesn't find out from your mother."

"You should do it, Kyle!" Lia snapped. "You were friends for a long time, you owe her that."

Kyle winced. "We've barely talked in over a year. I would love to be friends with her again, but I'm not sure if we can go back. I regret I ever took it farther and messed up what we had in the first place."

Jake walked Gail to her car. "I appreciate you congratulating Kyle on his engagement. I was frantic Casi would say no and crush him." He shrugged. "I'm not sure how she will fit in around here."

"I don't like your brother, but he's crazy for Casi and she seems to be making him less of a robot. I'm genuinely happy for them." She leaned forward and kissed him on the cheek. "I was a terrible wife, but maybe down the line we can be friends again."

"Our marriage wasn't all bad. I'm glad we have the kids." Jake pulled her to his chest. "We were so damn young, we never got a chance to find out who we were supposed to be as adults."

"I don't think you've hugged me since college, it's nice." Gail rested her head against him. "We wasted too much time yelling at each other and being miserable."

"I should have been more affectionate," he sighed.

"I pushed you away," she admitted. "Don't hurry to settle down again. You don't like being alone, but you deserve to get out there and have fun." She ran her hand over his chest. "It was cruel to chastise you about your weight. I did it to hurt you. You're a very handsome man."

"If I knew you could be kind, I would have divorced you years ago." Jake grinned. "You're a lot prettier when you smile."

"Mary Ann told me I am an evil bitch and no one will ever want me if I don't change, so I'm trying," she admitted.

"I like you better this way. You remind me of a girl I knew in college." Jake grinned as he walked back to the bar.

Lia approached him. "What did Gail want?"

"She gave me the schedule for the kids. We're trying to be more civilized, to make it better for our children."

"What's going on with us?" she questioned.

"Lia," Jake sighed. "Do we have to define a relationship? My divorce isn't even final."

"I didn't ask for a commitment. You've kept me at arm's length, even though you moved to an apartment weeks ago."

"One week ago," Jake corrected. "I like you, but I'm not ready to get into a relationship right away." He glanced at the women congratulating Casi and understood her jealousy. "Do you want to come to my place tonight?"

Lia smiled, understanding what he suggested. "Sure."

Mary Ann ordered another drink at the bar and Kyle came up behind her. "Congratulations, Casi's great," she said.

"Thank you." Kyle put a hand on her arm. "You never let me apologize properly for what happened on the porch last year."

"Jesus, Kyle!" She blushed. "I shouldn't have pushed her or scratched her car. I was ridiculous."

"You had every reason to be upset." He put an arm around her shoulders. "It was unplanned. I never meant to hurt you."

"At first, I was pissed, then embarrassed by my behavior. You're a great guy. After you broke up with Lauren, I felt lucky to get to date you. I would have loved to have something more with you."

He smiled at her tenderly. "I'm sorry for how I handled everything. You deserved better. The problem was, I'd already fallen in love with Casi in LA, and as much as I tried to get past it, the minute I saw her again, she was all that mattered."

"Was I fooling myself that you liked me?" She bit her lip and glanced away.

"I did like you. I wasn't using you," he said truthfully.

"I realize how much you love Casi, and she's amazing. I'm happy for you. Although, I will say I'm surprised."

"Me too!" He chuckled. "She's everything I ever wanted and more, and it suddenly seemed right." He hugged her, and whispered, "Jake's single now."

"He's the kind of trouble I don't need," she laughed. "Even though it didn't work out with us, I'm glad I got to know you better." She winked. "The sex was amazing!"

After another drink, Mary Ann walked over to Casi. "Congratulations." She extended her hand.

Casi threw her arms around her. "Thank you."

"Kyle adores you and I'm glad you said yes." Mary Ann admired the ring. "Stunning, it suits you perfectly."

"Mary Ann, I appreciate how much class you've shown. If I didn't love Kyle so much, I would have backed off and let you have him because you deserve someone incredible."

"Thank you." Mary Ann resigned herself to the fact she liked her, despite her best efforts to hate the beautiful woman.

"Jake's single." Casi nudged her.

"So I keep hearing," Mary Ann laughed.

Congratulatory shots made the rounds and Casi hit the dance floor. By the third song, every woman in the bar danced with her and the engagement party became an unplanned, roaring success.

## 29

## APPLE BLOSSOM ROAD

Casi blinked at Jake, frozen in place as she stood topless in the bedroom. Kyle rushed in the room and chuckled. "I guess I'm too late to warn you Casi was changing to go swimming?"

"Jesus, Jake, you look like you've never seen a woman topless before." Casi giggled and casually strolled to the bed to retrieve her bikini top.

"It's so much better than I expected," Jake confessed.

Casi shrugged. "Get used to it. I'm not shy, and I'll be living here." She shivered at the possibility of relocating to a small town.

Kyle smacked his brother on the back as she walked out. "I guess you can stop asking me to take a picture, huh?"

Jake turned with a giant grin and summarized his experience. "Incredible!"

"Are you coming swimming?"

He shrugged, insecure around Casi. He surveyed Kyle, ultra-fit, with his swimsuit low on his hips. "I don't know..."

"Why not?"

"I need to start getting back in shape."

"Then come swimming!" Kyle shoved him.

Jake changed to his swimsuit and walked down the dock with his t-shirt on, planning on jumping in the lake unnoticed while Casi swam. It surprised him to see she was such a good swimmer, not timid at all in the water. He pulled off his shirt, and she climbed on the dock with a smile. "Hold on a second."

"I'm aware of how fat I am," Jake sighed.

"Don't be ridiculous; I wanted to check out your tattoos." She touched the one on his upper right arm cascading over his shoulder and chest, a mosaic of the symbols of the Pacific Northwest. "Very cool." She raised her eyebrow at the cobra poised to strike on his left arm. "What's the snake for?"

"I'll tell you about it when I get to know you better."

Casi ran a finger over the script on his upper right rib, *However long the night, the dawn will break*

"Nope. Are you done checking me out?" Jake pulled away from her with a scowl.

"You're not fat and you shouldn't be shy around me." Casi gave him a quick hug before diving back in the lake.

❧

"Who do you look more like, your mom or dad? Obviously I take after my dad for the most part." She regarded her chest. "And only my breasts came from my mom." Casi folded Capri pants to add to her suitcase for the visit to Elmvale.

"Thank God you didn't get her wacky personality." Kyle chuckled. He hesitated at his dresser and contemplated his response. "Actually, I was adopted so I don't resemble either parent."

"What? Jake's not your real brother?" Casi's jaw dropped. "You have the same eyeballs! How's that possible?"

"He's my real brother." Kyle grinned. "We were in foster care when we were little, and my parents adopted both of us."

"Like my shoes!" She clasped a hand over her mouth. "I'm so sorry, I didn't mean to be rude when I said that at the loft."

"It's ok, it was funny," Kyle assured her.

"What happened to your real parents?"

"These are my real parents you'll meet," he declared. "I was two and Jake was almost five, so I don't remember anything. Our birth mother was young and couldn't raise us when our father died." He regarded his suitcase, evaluating how much he wanted to tell her. "Jake went through a phase in high school, wanting to find her and dragged me with him to Seattle."

"What was it like meeting her?" Casi asked in disbelief.

"Weird. She was spaced out on drugs, scratching, and distracted. She kept forgetting our names and had no recollection of giving us up. She said our dad was a musician who overdosed."

"Do you keep in touch with her?"

"She hit us up for money, and I was out of there. Jake told me he tried to find her again, years later. After he had kids he had an urge to reconnect. He found out she died, I would guess of drugs," he finished, unfazed by the story.

"That's tragic. Do you wish you'd gotten to know her better?" She blushed at the recollection of his devastation when she overdosed and felt ashamed.

"It is what it is. I had no connection to her. My memories are with my parents. I never needed to find her in the first place."

They approached the exit for Seattle and Kyle pulled the truck over. "Are we here?" Casi asked glanced up from her phone.

"We're only in Seattle, but that's the point."

"What point?" She scrunched up her face in confusion. He smiled and put his hand on hers. Casi giggled and peered out the window. "Are you serious? On the side of the road?"

"What are you talking about?" His eyes widened when she undid her seatbelt. "Casi! I'm not suggesting sex!"

"How am I supposed to know what the protocol is in small towns?" She shrugged.

Kyle shook his head. "I wanted to say it would be nice if we could have a conversation on the drive, and perhaps you could look out the window and appreciate this beautiful state."

"I've been this way before. Remember I came last year?"

"Did you pay attention, or were you on your phone?"

Casi rolled her eyes, realizing none of the landscape seemed familiar. "Let me finish my text." She giggled and held it toward him, sending it before he could stop her. "Dylan, I have to get off the phone because Kyle is requesting a blowjob on the side of the road and I need to concentrate."

"Great, one more reason for Dylan to hate me." Kyle glanced at her as he pulled back on the road. "You were ready to comply, weren't you?"

Casi winked. "You'll never know for sure."

Lia waited a few days before phoning her sister. She wanted to inform her mother first in preparation for Lauren's distraught call. Lauren lived in Seattle, so Lia hoped she hadn't heard. "Hi, Mom," Lia said, coming in her mother's kitchen.

"Not working today?" Fran peered up from her paper.

"I'm on my way, but I wanted to stop and see you."

Fran lowered her glasses and sighed. "What pickle have you gotten yourself in now? I've told you a hundred times to search for a better job. You don't push yourself hard enough."

Lia ignored the criticism. "It's not about me. I'm not sure if you heard... Kyle's engaged."

Fran glared at her. "Kyle Jensen is getting married?"

"Yes. I just found out," Lia lied. "I guess I should call Lauren before she hears it from someone else?"

Fran laughed harshly. "Isn't that perfect! He tells your sister he has no interest in marriage, and then a year later he's engaged? Who's the woman?"

"She's from LA. He met her when he was working there last year." Lia helped herself to a cookie from the jar.

"Last year? When he went to LA a week after he dumped your sister? What a conniving bastard!" Fran hissed. "You don't need sweets, Lia. It'll only add to your waistline."

Lia left her mother's house and called her sister, hoping to catch her after work, anticipating she would be upset. "What's up?" Lauren yawned.

"I wanted to talk to you before I went to work."

"I just got home. I had the early morning shift."

"Kyle's getting married," Lia blurted.

After a long silence, Lauren said, "Are you serious? It's not Mary Ann, is it? Lindsey's married, even though she always tries to get back together with him."

Lia could hear she was crying. "It's the woman he's been dating from LA. They announced it the other night at the bar. Everyone was surprised, only Jake knew."

"Fucking motherfucker," Lauren screamed. "He lied about not wanting to get married. He didn't want to marry me!"

"I guess," Lia said quietly.

"Did you ask him?" Lauren yelled. "I'm aware you're still friends with him and his stupid brother."

"He said he never wanted to, but then he met Casi and everything changed," she repeated.

"What does she do for a living?"

Lia hesitated. "She's a swimsuit model."

"I fucking hate him!"

Lia wasn't sure what else to say. "He said he would like to be friends with you again," she offered.

"That's one hell of a consolation prize. Are you still seeing Jake?" Lauren fumed.

"Kind of. He got divorced." Lia frowned. "He doesn't want to get tied down, so we're keeping it casual."

"Men always tell you that, Lia! Stop being a doormat. What does he think of this woman Kyle's marrying?"

"He doesn't like her, but you get how that goes."

"Why are you wasting your time with him? Both of those brothers are assholes!" Lauren concluded.

Casi wondered if Kyle was excited to tell his parents about the engagement as she watched him with one hand on the wheel, tapping along to the music. She pictured him as a teenager, skinny and tough, raising hell. "What?" He smiled at her.

"I was thinking of you in high school and wondering how much you might have changed," she giggled.

"Maybe I'll take you there and show you around."

"Hold on!" Casi grabbed his arm. "What have you told your parents about me?"

He pulled to the side of the road, realizing he should have talked to her before they left. "When I came back from LA last year, I came to visit them and Jake was with me."

"Oh, no." Casi massaged her temple.

"Don't worry, they don't know why I left LA."

"What did Jake say?"

"He may have called you a few names." Casi rolled her eyes, imagining the jabs. "I told my mom I loved you, and she said she looked forward to meeting you," Kyle concluded.

They drove up the long driveway, and she had butterflies in her stomach. A tall, slender man, with wavy gray hair working in the garden, waved when they pulled in. A pleasantly plump woman with an apron on stood on the porch, eager with anticipation. Kyle parked and got out of the truck, coming around to open the door for Casi. She stepped out slowly, regretting her outfit. She should have remembered she was coming to farm country, not spending the day in LA. It had been warm when they left and she dressed in tiny white shorts and a leopard bra top, with a loose fitting black tank. She wished Kyle suggested she dress more demurely. Kyle shook hands with his father and introduced her. Peter shook her hand heartily and gave her a genuine smile, making her like him immediately. They walked up the stairs to the wraparound porch. Georgia stepped forward and gave her son a hug, then turned to Casi, taking her in her arms, and welcoming her. Kyle sat on the porch swing and directed Casi to sit beside him, putting his arm around her.

"I didn't expect you to be blonde," Georgia commented.

"I'm naturally blonde. I dyed it for modeling, and it was a lot longer," Casi said nervously as she hid her ring with her other hand, not wanting to spoil the surprise.

"I like it." Peter winked.

"I do too." Kyle smiled at her.

They drank lemonade and talked about business at the wood shop and the renovation of the house. Kyle obviously spoke about her a lot to his parents as his mother kept looking at her and smiling. Peter sat in the Adirondack chair, nodding and praising Kyle for his hard work. Georgia hung on every word, her pride and love abundantly apparent.

"Has Jake settled into his apartment?" Georgia asked.

"Yes, he's fine. The kids have been able to visit a lot." Kyle exaggerated and noted the relief in his mother's face.

"And work?" Georgia glanced at Casi.

Kyle chuckled. "Casi knows everything. It was her idea to take Jake to LA to meet with a lawyer and get advice."

"My mom has been married five times and has used the same attorney in three divorces." Casi pulled at a thread on her shorts. "I thought it would be good for Jake to talk to someone with a lot of experience."

"My goodness! Five times." Peter raised his eyebrows.

"I've never been married," she blurted. "My dad lives in Bellingham and he's been with my stepmother for years." Kyle laughed at her attempt to sound more stable than her mother. They asked about her work, hearing she was a model, but interested in knowing more about it. She told them about the Sand and Surf contract, and then mentioned she finished her Bachelor's Degree, so they would assume she was fairly bright.

Georgia stood and invited them in for lunch. Kyle put a hand on her arm and smiled. "Actually, we wanted to tell you something first. Casi and I are getting married. We're planning to do it this fall since we both have busy work schedules and we don't see any point in waiting." Casi was glad he left out her hesitation and distraction leading up to saying yes. Kyle noted his mother's glance at Casi's mid-section. "She's not pregnant."

"Kyle!" Georgia blushed.

"We're very much in love and want to start our lives together." Kyle kissed Casi's cheek.

Peter gave Kyle a hearty handshake. "Terrific news, Son!"

Georgia cried as she hugged them, repeating, "This is so wonderful. I'm thrilled."

During a lunch of cold cuts, freshly baked bread, and pie, they talked about their plans; a destination wedding on a beach...somewhere. Casi hoped his mother wouldn't be disappointed with their choice. "That's smart. Couples spend too much money on these things. Remember Jake's wedding? Such an extravagance! Too many people, and Gail bossing everyone around. You're better off doing what pleases you and focusing on your future together. I can't wait to tell everyone at church on Sunday. They'll be so pleased when they see you, Kyle, and meet your beautiful fiancé." She touched Casi's cheek tenderly.

"Church?" Casi's eyes widened. "I'm not sure if I packed anything appropriate to wear." She figured she had already failed with the meeting the parents attire.

"I'm sure you'll look lovely in anything you wear. You're so pretty," Georgia praised.

"I'll help you figure out something." Kyle swept his eyes over her outfit, not realizing before what she had on.

"That's sweet, you're going to be such a wonderful husband," Georgia gushed. The phone rang, and she went to answer while they cleaned up from lunch. She kept her eye on them as she pulled the receiver around the corner. "Hello, Dear." She waited for Lauren to speak through her tears. "Yes, we heard. Kyle brought her home to meet us."

Kyle carried their bags upstairs and put Casi's suitcase down in a room decorated with floral wallpaper and twin beds, sporting home-made quilts. "There you go." He grinned.

"Where are you going?" She frowned at the beds.

"To my room." He strolled across the hall.

"Are you kidding me?" She rushed after him and surveyed his teenage room, containing trophies, books, and mementos. "Why can't we sleep together? We're over thirty and engaged."

"Nope." He sprawled on his twin bed with a grin.

"We can push the beds together in the other room." Casi stomped her foot in despair.

He shrugged. "Totally wouldn't work. This is an old house, with no privacy."

"Are we Mormons now, sleeping separately, and going to church?" She shivered at the disturbing turn of events.

"I guess you should have taken me up on my offer of roadside sex." He gave her a wink.

"Jeez, if I'd known about this sleeping arrangement, I would have!"

## 30

# HOMETOWN

Casi searched through her suitcase, not prepared for life in the country. She slipped on pale blue, low-rise cargo pants, a white, v- neck crop top, and pulled on white Converse. "Better?" She asked. Kyle answered with a kiss, then informed his parents he was taking Casi around town.

"I'm making pot roast for dinner, Honey. One of your favorites," Georgia called out happily.

Casi could hear her chopping ingredients in the kitchen. "I'm going to get fat visiting here," she whispered.

"I'll give you a workout later." Kyle patted her on the backside. She pictured the twin bed and knew that was a lie.

Kyle pointed out landmarks and hangouts as he drove. She loved seeing him in this town, so comfortable in his surroundings. They stopped by the high school and strolled the halls, checking out the trophy cases and old senior photos. He had shown her his yearbooks in his room, and the inscription by his best friend, Grady, wincing at the memory of his tragic death. It was fun to see this handsome, grown man standing in the halls where a lanky teen experienced his formative years. He pointed out pictures of Jake, involved in various sports, always the star player. He showed her his trophy, with a photo of himself in a baseball uniform, a big grin on his young face. She broke into a rendition of 'Hey Mickey', as if she were a giddy cheerleader, twisting her hips and doing high kicks. A teacher shushed her, and she turned to see a group of teenagers in class, wide-eyed. Kyle grabbed her hand, and they ran down the hall laughing.

The bell rang, and the teens spilled out. It was the last day of school and they were excited to celebrate. She was jostled by backpacks, separated from Kyle by a sea of hormones, when a scrawny boy handed her a flyer with eager anticipation. "Wanna come to a party tonight? It's gonna be off the hook!"

"I'll think about it." Casi gave him a wink and accepted the flyer with a smile while the boy and his friends checked out her backside. Kyle tried to throw away the invitation, but she stuffed it in her pocket and ran toward the field, with Kyle in hot pursuit. He tackled her on the 5-yard line, rolling with her in the grass. He put his arm under her neck, as they admired the blue sky and puffy clouds, and shared stories about their high school years.

After dinner, they chatted with his parents on the porch, while Kyle and his father enjoyed a scotch. Casi told them an edited version of the proposal and Georgia smiled, intrigued to hear about Kyle's romantic side. Peter slapped his knee. "That's where the calico kitten went. I thought the fox got her."

"I noticed her last time I was here and knew Casi would love her." Kyle smiled. "Remember Jake with the kittens when he was a kid?"

Peter grinned. "Sneaking them up to his room to cuddle."

"Jake doesn't seem like someone who would be interested in small fuzzy animals," Casi challenged.

"That's why he hid them. He didn't want anyone to see his soft side." Kyle blanched, realizing he accidentally shared his brother's secret.

Casi helped Georgia bring the glasses in the kitchen while Kyle answered a call from Jake. Casi hesitated at the counter, slowly wiping the same spot with a dish towel. Georgia nodded to Peter, indicating he should head upstairs to bed. "I was nervous to meet you. I'm sure you heard all kinds of terrible things about me from Jake." Casi stared at the floor.

Georgia laughed. "He's very protective of his brother, as I'm sure you've realized."

"I really do love Kyle," Casi asserted.

"To be truthful, I assumed I wouldn't like you. I was angry Kyle had been hurt, and I wasn't sure what kind of woman you were. When I saw you with him, I knew you were genuinely in love." Casi nodded, glad she could see the depth of her feelings. "I've always been concerned he's too involved in his brother's life, fixing his mistakes. Kyle is self-sufficient and regimented, and I wondered if he would ever find a woman who would understand their relationship. You're perfect for him, and I'm thrilled to have you as my daughter-in-law. Both Peter and I adore you." She hugged Casi tightly.

Casi enjoyed the warm embrace. "I'm sorry I dressed inappropriately. I didn't expect Washington to be so warm, and I wasn't thinking about how I looked."

"Don't worry about those things. You have a darling figure; wear whatever you want. We'll never judge you."

"Should I be worried about Jake?"

"You'll have to accept he's a big part of Kyle's life and be patient with him. It takes him a long time to warm up to people, and he's not comfortable being touched," Georgia warned, seeing how gregarious Casi was.

"I've noticed." Casi giggled.

It was still early when Casi went upstairs, and she wasn't eager to turn in alone for the evening. Kyle sprawled on his bed, talking on his phone to Jake about an order. Casi came in wearing black skinny jeans, with combat boots, a printed tank, and a black leather jacket. She had smoky eyes and had straightened her hair. "I gotta go, I think Casi joined a biker gang." Kyle grinned. She held up the flyer to the party, crinkled from being stuffed in her pocket. "Hell, no!"

"Come on, take me to the party," she pleaded.

"I'm not hanging out with a bunch of teenagers."

She straddled him on the bed. "You will if you want me to go to church on Sunday," she said with a sultry kiss.

❧

They arrived at the party in the skate park by the river, twenty minutes later. Techno music blasted through the evening air. A few kids rode skateboards, but most lounged around on their phones, smoking pot and drinking. "You came!" The boy from the high school exclaimed, surveying Casi's edgy attire approvingly while he handed her a drink in a red solo cup.

"Don't drink that," Kyle whispered.

"Dude, want a beer?" the kid asked.

"Sure." Kyle glanced at the keg and wondered if it was illegal to drink with under-aged kids. He poured himself and Casi a beer, insisting she toss the unknown cocktail. A few girls were dancing, and Casi went to join them.

"Damn, she's slammin'!" stated a boy who appeared to be about fourteen, while Kyle cringed.

After dancing and a couple of drinks, Casi searched for Kyle, suddenly afraid to be alone with teenagers who were getting increasingly drunk. She spotted him with relief at one of the ramps, riding a skateboard with remarkable talent, doing a flip with the board. The teenagers were impressed and asked for pointers. "You've got skills!" Casi joined the group and a boy handed them a joint. "No, thanks." Casi waved it away. "We're on our way to a Rave," she informed him, wanting to sound cool, rather than old.

"Where's the Rave?" a girl asked enthusiastically.

"Uptown," Casi said over her shoulder, leaving the kid to wonder where uptown could be. She thanked the boy who invited her, then leaned in and gave him a kiss, to a chorus of whoops from his buddies, who slapped him on the back. Kyle looked at her questioningly as they walked to his truck. "I figured I would give the kid something to dream about."

"You have a thing for teenage boys now?" Kyle asked.

"A boy couldn't handle me. I need a man to rock my world." Casi gave him a playful shove. He knew that was true and smiled at the star-struck teenager who would never forget the kiss he got from the prettiest girl at the party. As they drove away, Casi regarded the crowd immersed in their phones and taking random drugs to avoid feeling anything. "We're so much cooler than them!"

Kyle nodded. "I wouldn't want to be a teenager in today's world. They don't seem to do anything, except stare at their phones." He laughed and poked her in the ribs.

Casi rolled her eyes. "I do other stuff, too."

On Sunday, Casi pulled clothes from her bag while Kyle reclined on the bed and shook his head. She held up a floral miniskirt and paired it with a bright pink halter top. "Did you bring a sweater?" Kyle imagined her cleavage on full display.

"I only have my leather jacket." She sighed and sorted through her bag, finding a denim one near the bottom. She got a thumbs up from Kyle, who watched with a grin as she took off her robe and dressed. She twirled, giving him a peek of her panties. He reached over and adjusted the skirt at the waistband to make it longer.

They climbed in the backseat of his parents older Buick. Peter eased his foot off and on the gas pedal, making the car sway back and forth. They had eaten a breakfast of pancakes and sausages, and Casi feared it might reappear if they didn't get to the church soon. She put down her window and tried to breathe in the cool morning air. Thankfully the church was not far, and she climbed out, shaky-kneed, in record time. Kyle took her hand as they walked up the steps of the quaint white country church. She hoped it would not be the kind of service where you had to know when to kneel, pray, and cross yourself. The sermon was simple, and Casi was energized by the cheery message.

"How freaked out are you?" Kyle laced his fingers through hers as they walked down the church steps after the service.

"Not at all, it was lovely," Casi said, enjoying the community and welcoming congregation.

They were invited to a picnic by the river which they could thankfully walk to. It seemed as if the entire town came to celebrate the glorious day. Casi recognized the boy from the party, now smartly dressed in Dockers and a white polo shirt. He blushed deeply when she said hello, getting nudged by his friends. Georgia excitedly told ladies from the church about the engagement, and they turned to Kyle approvingly, whispering to Casi how she landed a good one. They gushed over the ring, then asked if there would be babies soon? Such a pretty girl. Surely she and Kyle would have darling children. She smiled stiffly and shrugged, not wanting to explain her lack of mothering instinct.

Casi turned to get another plate of food, and Georgia walked beside her. "Kyle mentioned he shared with you how we adopted them. They've been the joy of my life, everything I could have asked for." Casi sensed she noticed her hesitation at the question and would deliver the talk on the joys of motherhood. "Think long and hard before you have children, if at all. They should be a blessing, not something you feel pressured to have. Kyle has never been the paternal type, and I don't sense a burning urge in you either. You're young, and maybe that will change, but Peter and I love you and only want what's best for you and Kyle."

Casi turned and hugged her in appreciation for the unconditional acceptance. "Thank you."

Georgia gave Peter a lemonade and sat beside him on a blanket spread out on the grass. "What do you think of our soon to be daughter-in-law?" he asked.

"She's perfect for Kyle." Georgia beamed.

"I do too. I haven't seen him this relaxed and happy since before the boating accident. She seems to bring out the playful side in him." Peter watched Kyle tickling Casi's nose with a blade of grass as they sprawled on the lawn.

"It's heartwarming to see the boy in him again."

"She sure is pretty," Peter observed. "I wonder how Jake will handle this. I'm sure he never thought Kyle would get married, and he's used to having his brother to himself."

Georgia smiled. "I predict Jake will have his jealous periods. Kyle chose a woman who will understand his relationship with his brother, maybe without even knowing it."

While they relaxed after the meal, kids played games, chasing each other, and throwing a Frisbee. Several children waded in the river and splashed the ones on shore. It was refreshing to see people of all ages, having fun with their families and enjoying being outside. Not a cell phone in sight. Casi realized she left her own phone on the charger in her bedroom. For the first time, she had no desire to text anyone, not even Dylan.

**31**

---

# DOUBT

eter scanned Casi as she helped herself to a glass of lemonade. "Would you like some?" She held up the pitcher.

He shook his head. "Do you want to see the animals?"

"Sure." She downed the lemonade and set the glass by the sink and followed him outside. He led her to the chicken coop, telling her about the different varieties. "Oh my God! Look at the hair on that one!" Casi clapped her hands and giggled. Peter laughed and reached in, handing her eggs. "Yuck! They're still warm." She crinkled her nose. Peter nodded and opened the gate to the goats. "I don't have to hold anything from them, do I?" She raised an eyebrow.

"No." Peter whistled and several baby goats came running to him, chased by dogs to keep them in line. He petted the dogs and gave them a treat from his pocket.

"Do they run loose?" she asked.

"The dogs protect the property. The baby goats slip through the paddock so they ensure they don't wander off." He silently counted them and nodded.

Casi approached cats lounging outside the barn. "What are their names?" The orange one hissed and flicked its tail when she tried to pet it. "Is this Jezebel's mother?"

"They don't have names. They're here to eat rats. That one is male and most likely fathered your kitten. He's knocked up most of the females around here." Peter shrugged and Casi secretly named them Bubba and Gumbo.

Peter strolled to the barn and Casi followed. "This's so cool!" She surveyed sheep and pigs, and he directed her to a small hutch and opened the door. He took the eggs and placed a tiny bunny in one hand. "She's so cute!" She blanched. "You aren't going to eat her, are you?"

"The rabbits are for fun, and that one is a boy."

"What about the other animals?" Casi's eyes widened.

He shrugged. "It's a farm."

"Peter!" She recalled the lamb they had for dinner the night before and regretted enjoying it so much.

"Where do you think meat comes from?"

Casi hugged the bunny and frowned at him. "I prefer not to see my dinner walking around first."

"Should I show you the vegetable garden, or will that traumatize you?" He took the rabbit and put it in the hutch, then gave her back the eggs. They walked to the garden, and she stopped in her tracks.

"What the heck is that?"

"Alpaca," he chuckled. "Georgia makes yarn for knitting."

She observed the large vegetable garden. "This seems like a lot of work."

"It is, but it's a good way to live. What is it you like about living in LA?" He cocked his head.

Casi grinned. "I don't have to grow or slaughter my food."

"True. You realize Kyle will never leave Washington?"

"This is your plan? Find out my real motives for marrying your son?" She pouted and surveyed the eggs.

"I adore you, but I'm concerned this might not work."

Casi turned her head as tears sprung to her eyes. "I'm not the right woman for Kyle?"

Peter grasped her elbow, assuming they were being watched from the kitchen window. He led her to a rose garden and asked her to sit on a bench. "You're beautiful and sweet, and surprisingly funny. Kyle has created an admirable life for himself. He has an amazing house on a lake and he built his business from sweat and hard labor. He's a wonderful brother and son. I'd love to see you add to his life." He squeezed her hand. "But, I won't allow you to take away from it."

"Do you suspect I'm a gold digger?" She narrowed her eyes. "I've had many opportunities to marry for money and I'm not interested in a man's bank account." She cringed at the statement, making her sound like she dated excessively.

"I'm not sure what your life in LA is like and how that'll work with Kyle being in Washington." Casi relayed their plan of living between the two states. "Do you believe that will work?" Peter brushed hair from her cheek.

"It has to," she cried. "I love him so much."

"You love the man, but do you love his life?"

"You sound like my mother." She wiped a tear angrily, almost dropping an egg. "She says Kyle is small town, and I'm fooling myself that I would be happy long term. She doesn't even know we're engaged."

"Kyle is small town." He shrugged. "He's hardworking and honest. He puts his family first and takes care of his home. He's part of his community and loves the outdoors."

"You don't think I'll fit in?"

"It's important to enter into marriage with your eyes wide open. Don't expect to change him." He took her chin in his hand. "And don't lie to him about your life."

Her mouth dropped. "Are you suggesting I would cheat?"

"I would expect you to have the same values he does and make your relationship a priority." He held his hand out and directed her back to the house.

Kyle narrowed his eyes when they entered, and he noticed Casi had been crying as she handed the eggs to Georgia. "What did you say to her?"

"I wanted to get to know her better," Peter said.

"Are you ok?" Kyle embraced her protectively.

"I'm fine, we had a good talk. I saw crazy baby goats and held a tiny bunny. Plus, there's a weird thing called an Alpaca!" She kissed him and went upstairs to change.

Kyle glared at Peter. "Did you tell her not to marry me?"

"I was curious to see what her expectations were and how she pictures a marriage working living between two states."

"That's our problem," he charged.

"You've always made excellent decisions in your life and contemplated the impact on everyone around you. I see you throwing caution to the wind, and I wonder if you have considered all that marriage entails. Be prepared when things get tough and remember how much you love her. She'll be part of this family, and we'll always be there for both of you."

"Why do you assume things will get difficult?"

"There are always challenges! Do you think it was easy for us when we found out we couldn't have kids? Then we took on you two? That certainly tested us. Jake was a handful as a youngster and it escalated in his teens. We love him dearly, but we couldn't have handled it if we weren't terrific partners."

"Neither of us wants children," Kyle stated.

"That'll make it easier. Do you honestly see her being happy living in Blackberry Falls?"

"I will move to LA if I have to." Kyle set his jaw.

"You knew things weren't right with Lauren, and you were smart not to commit to her, even though you had a lot of pressure. You'll be a good husband and you couldn't have found a prettier wife." Peter winked.

Casi tried to learn the recipes Georgia skillfully prepared. Her adult education classes only gave her the basics, and she could see she had a lot to learn. She liked watching Georgia prepare the food. The thought put into each step, always yielding an excellent result. Georgia gave her a cookbook which belonged to her mother, with a worn cover and pages threatening to leap out. Favorite recipes had been marked with a red pen, with comments like 'delicious with cinnamon', or 'great for a cocktail party'. She hugged the book, tickled she had been considered important enough in the family to receive the cherished heirloom.

When they retired for the evening, Kyle kissed her goodnight in the hallway between their bedrooms. "We can be super quiet," she pleaded.

He grinned and eyed her figure. "Not possible."

She slunk back to her room and slumped on the bed. She wished she could have slept in Kyle's room, so she could snoop through his teenage stuff during the night. She was tempted to check out Jake's room, but knew she would be mortified if she was caught. She was in awe of the pictures everywhere in the house, featuring the boys through every stage of life. Missing teeth, black eyes, and goofy smiles stared out from artfully arranged pictures on every wall and surface. She was jealous of his childhood room, waiting for him whenever he needed to reconnect with his past or take a step away from the complexities of adulthood. She wondered if he came here last summer after the fight, and how much he might have shared with his parents. She fidgeted in frustration. She wasn't tired, and she kept wondering what Kyle was doing. Was he sleeping? Talking to his brother on the phone? She listened to the quietly creaking house and checked for text messages. She called Dylan earlier to tell him about the engagement, and he replied, "I despise you! How could you abandon me for that man?" Then he told her how happy he was, and started making plans for her wedding hair, saying, "It will rock Kyle's world."

Casi decided to call her mother. "Did I wake you?"

"No, no, I was doing... something," Sonya said, with slurred speech, making Casi roll her eyes.

"I'm in a town called Elmvale, meeting Kyle's parents."

"Why?"

"Because he asked me to marry him." Casi bit her lip.

"Oh, my God! You didn't say yes, did you?"

"Yes, Mother, I did," Casi snapped.

"Why, Casi? You're not seriously considering moving to that tiny town, are you? What will you do? Cook and clean and get fat while you have a bunch of redneck children running around? I don't see you in that life," Sonya chastised.

"I don't see myself in that life either!"

"I don't understand why you'd want to get tied down."

"Why did you want to do it five times?"

"Don't be hateful," Sonya said sternly. "I put aside my career to manage yours. Who would support me? Your father? Oh, that's right, he abandoned us!"

"Mom, I'm not discussing this with you." Casi felt the heat rise in her cheeks. "I'm marrying Kyle!"

"I guess there's always a first marriage. I hope you scored a large ring. That always comes in handy to pawn when times are tough." She laughed bitterly. "What's your plan for this event? Doves and a myriad of bridesmaids?"

"No!" Casi hissed, figuring Sonya pictured a hick ceremony. "I want a destination wedding. I have no time or interest in planning it. Maybe you should do it since you have so much experience. I like the one you had in the Caribbean."

"A destination wedding sounds wonderful," Sonya hummed. "I would be happy to put together something like that. How many people are you inviting?"

Casi did a quick count. "Maybe about twelve. Kyle's family and mine, plus Dylan and Mary, of course."

"Of course, we couldn't forget Mary. You'd be lost without your precious mentor. I hope she approved. She monitors your every move," Sonya snipped.

"Mom, plan the details, please. We want to do it in October." Casi regarded her hands and noticed dirt under her nails as her mind drifted to the baby goats and if she should sneak out and play with them.

"Obviously, your beloved father will walk you down the aisle. He always steps in for the glory when I've done all the hard work. I imagine Ava will have the perfect outfit and glare at me with those deceitful wolf eyes of hers."

"Why do you always say that? Ava is beautiful. Leave her alone." Casi exhaled.

"Silver-blue eyes are disturbing. She looks like an alien. You should consider that if you plan on spawning with a man who has blue eyes. Mixed with your hazel, it could be freakish."

Casi scrunched her face at the odd comment. "I'll keep that in mind."

"Are Kyle's parents country bumpkins?" Sonya pried.

"They're lovely people, but it's the strangest thing." She paused for dramatic effect. "Georgia cooks every meal from scratch, and she has been married to Peter for almost forty years! Can you imagine?"

"You're a horrible daughter," Sonya snapped.

"Goodbye, Mother. Plan a wonderful wedding for me."

She decided to call Mary, wanting her to know about the wedding before she heard about it from Sonya. "Hello, Sweetie," Mary answered happily, in sharp contrast to her mother.

"Kyle asked me to marry him," Casi blurted out.

"I hope you said yes! He's perfect for you."

"You're the only one who's pleased for me." Casi started to cry as she told her what everyone else said.

Mary laughed. "Don't worry. Your mother doesn't know you at all. I can see why Kyle's parents are concerned, but you and Kyle are good together; you make each other stronger. Have you told Ava? I'm sure she will be thrilled. She and your father love Kyle and were very happy you got back together."

"I'd like to tell them in person." Casi imagined the warm hug Ava would give her and genuine interest she would show in the marriage. "Do you think I'll be a good wife?"

"You'll be an excellent wife. As soon as you figure out your needs don't always come first."

"Mary!" she exclaimed, accepting the truth.

She told her about the sleeping arrangements at the farmhouse. Mary laughed, "Don't they have a barn?"

"I thought about it, but I'm concerned there may be spiders in there," Casi lamented.

After she hung up, Casi regarded her phone with increasing boredom and got an idea. She stripped to her bra and panties and reclined on the bed, taking a photo. She double-checked she was indeed sending it to Kyle, having learned from mistakes in the past. She waited. *Maybe he was sleeping and hadn't heard his phone?* She sank back on the pillows with a sigh, then heard a beep on her phone. "Wanna go for a ride?"

He didn't have to ask twice and she pulled on shorts with a t-shirt. She was in the hall in minutes where she literally ran into him waiting by the stairs. They sneaked out of the house, giggling like two teenagers. He drove to the river where the full moon was lighting up the sky. They rolled down their windows and let the balmy summer night breeze in. He put his arm around her shoulders and kissed her, sliding her down on the bench seat. It brought back memories of her high school boyfriend, Joey, and the times they slipped away to make out in his pickup truck. Kyle leaned up on one elbow and ran his fingers through his hair like he was distracted. "What's wrong?" she asked, sensing a hesitation in him.

"I was thinking about Mary Ann," Kyle said absentmindedly, remembering the last time he'd had sex in his truck, only fantasizing at the time it was Casi.

"Kyle!" She scooted away from him, tears in her eyes. *Was he sorry he'd brought her here? Lamenting he wasn't marrying a woman like Mary Ann, pleasant and low-key. Someone he wouldn't worry about having the proper outfit for church?*

He chuckled. "No, not like that. Well, actually...forget it." He smacked her on the knee. "Come on," he called as he jumped out of the truck.

He walked toward the river and shed his clothing without a hint of shyness. She watched him wade in the river, the moonlight highlighting his taut body. She rushed after him and pulled off her clothes, throwing them on top of his. The chilly water made her shiver, but it was refreshing in the warm night air. She swam to where he stood near a cluster of large rocks on the far side of the river. He leaned against the boulders and waited, watching as she emerged from the waist deep water. He held one hand out to help her across the current. He kissed her and pressed her against the large, smooth rock. She relaxed on the rough surface, still warm from the hot day, and dug her feet into the sandy bottom of the river. He kissed her neck, trailing toward her breasts. The warmth of the stone, in contrast to the cold water rushing by her thighs as he pressed against her, was erotic. She moaned as he lifted her leg around his waist, making good on his promise to give her a workout.

The next morning as they prepared to leave, Kyle's phone rang. He paled when he saw Lauren's name on the screen. Georgia saw him panic and corralled Casi. "Honey, there was something I wanted to show you before you left," she said, leading her down the back stairs.

Kyle took a deep breath. "Hi, Lauren." He sat on his bed and held the phone away while she called him every name in the book. When she broke down in tears, he put the phone back to his ear. "I'm sorry this hurt you."

"Sorry? How the hell did you think it wouldn't hurt me? Did you run out and find the first woman you could to prove how you weren't going to be forced into a marriage with me?" She turned his words against him from the night they broke up.

"I never planned on getting married," he reiterated. "I met her, and then everything changed."

"When did you meet her?"

"I only asked her to marry me a week ago."

"That's not what I asked!"

"Fine. I met her the week I went to LA."

"After more than three years with me, not to mention the ten years of friendship before that, and the shit I put up with while you were off and on again with Lindsey... you met another woman a week later, and fell in love?"

He rubbed his temple. "Yup, pretty much."

"You're a God damn bastard, Kyle. I fucking hate you!"

"Well, that sounds a lot like the night we broke up." He shrugged as she hung up without saying goodbye.

Casi was unclear why Georgia needed to show her the canning room, but thought it was nice she seemed to like her.

"How did it go?" Georgia whispered as she hugged Kyle.

"She set a new world record for curse words in one conversation," he whispered, giving her a kiss as they left.

Georgia laughed, expecting the call as the phone rang. Peter came in and watched her, listening as she kept repeating, "I understand, Darling. It shocked us, too."

"Tell her to move on. Kyle certainly has," Peter said.

32
______

# FETISH

The line for the border the next day was light, and Kyle breezed through with his enhanced driver's license and her passport in hand. Casi hadn't realized he did a lot of business in British Columbia, sourcing materials. He explained the ease of having a Washington license, allowing him to use it for travel to Canada and Mexico. She gave him a kiss, understanding he was enticing her to move there.

They arrived at the Swiss Chalet right on time, greeted by her friends, who were eagerly awaiting an introduction to her fiancé. "We have a lot of great restaurants around town, we're not hicks," Dawn teased, giving her a hug. Casi loved the fries and the predictability of the surroundings and enjoyed hanging out with friends, drinking and laughing, without regard for annoyed patrons, who planned a lovely evening out at a trendy place. "This is Kyle?" Dawn asked, surprising him when she leaned in and planted a wet, lingering kiss, while Casi threw her head back and laughed at the private joke.

"Your friends are friendly." Kyle smiled and shook Joey's hand as they shared a long, visual moment of who knew Casi best, stare-down.

The beer flowed, and the group took turns telling embarrassing

Casi stories. Kyle hadn't known about her name originally being Cassidy and thought Casi suited her better. They busted up with laughter about the time she and Dawn had been caught skinny dipping by the local police who made the girls write a letter of apology to the senior center who had been on a bird watching tour at the time of discovery. "Remember when?" became the theme of the evening, and Kyle enjoyed hearing the antics she pulled in high school, skipping class, and her infamous dance parties. He was pleased to learn the woman he loved was the same fun-loving person, instead of an awkward geeky girl, with bullying issues.

Casi surveyed the group. "We've chosen to do a destination wedding. Will you guys be hurt if we only have our families?" She bit her lip.

"Ah, but we invited you to ours and it was killer!" Joey whispered in her ear making her blush. He put his arm around her shoulders and gave her a squeeze. "Seriously, run away to tie the knot. That damn thing cost our parents a fortune, and we should've used it to buy a house instead."

"Totally! It took us years to save for the dump we live in." Dawn nodded. "We were in our early twenties and still in party mode. A lovely celebration sounds ideal. We can do a girls thing when you get back and see the pictures."

"Thanks for understanding." Casi smiled at Kyle. "I am excited to be married to the love of my life. I'm not jazzed about planning and all the hoopla."

Dawn grasped her hand. "You have your priorities straight. Enjoy the day with your handsome prince."

They moved the party to the beach, and Kyle admired the driftwood logs around the fire pit as they wrapped themselves in a blanket. The rye was passed around, and this time, Kyle and Casi moved down the beach to make love under the stars.

"Your friends are awesome." Kyle cuddled with her later in the evening on the pullout in Dawn's and Joey's basement. He cocked his head. "Is it strange for you that Joey married Dawn? You dated him in high school, right?"

"Yes, he was my first lover," she teased, shoving him playfully. "We had been friends for years before that. We were a close-knit group and after I left, he and Dawn began dating. I was thrilled when they decided to get married. They had similar goals for their future and it honestly seemed natural they ended up together." Casi shrugged. "Joey's a great guy and I'm happy he has a good life." She snuggled in his arms and considered how she had enjoyed watching Kyle interact with her friends, talking about hockey and music, even inviting Joey to a concert in Seattle later in the summer since they shared the same taste in music.

Dawn told her the next day how much everyone liked Kyle and how perfect he was for her. "I'm glad you chose him. Not one of those metrosexual androids you seem to date in LA. They never seemed to fit with our fun girl."

They breezed through to Bellingham, in time for dinner at Jack's restaurant. Jack and Ava were waiting for them on the front deck, arm in arm. Jack stepped down and shook Kyle's hand, explaining Sonya called with news of the engagement, and they were brimming with excitement. "She was upset at the prospect of me walking you down the aisle. She feels it's grossly unfair." Jack surveyed Casi's reaction to her mother's rant.

"She gets to plan everything. The only thing I'm insisting is you walking me down the aisle. Too bad if it upsets her. It would be incredibly weird for it to be her." Casi stomped her foot in annoyance, already anticipating her mother's meddling.

Kyle noted Jack's confusion on how to best handle the situation and sensed he was hesitant to criticize her mother. "I understand in a traditional engagement I should have asked your permission for your daughter's hand." Kyle grasped Casi's hand. "I assessed she was more of a modern woman who would prefer making the decision herself."

Jack smiled with relief as he understood what Kyle was suggesting. "So perhaps instead of walking her down the aisle to give her away, I should escort her to her destination."

"Of which she is freely choosing." Kyle nodded.

"Well put. I accept your invitation to guide me." Casi threw her head back and laughed. "We know I'm bad with directions and it could be a confusing trip."

"I'll get you there safely." Jack kissed her on the cheek.

Casi walked alongside Ava to the brewery. "Mom claims I'm making a mistake, and even Kyle's dad voiced concerns."

"Take it from me, if you love him, nothing will stop you from making it work." Ava glanced at Jack. Casi nodded, realizing Ava had been through a lot to make her partnership work, including a bitter ex-wife, and shamefully, a spiteful, teenage stepdaughter.

Casi hugged Ava. "Thank you for always supporting me. I realize I've been a pain in the ass since I was a teen." She pulled back and regarded Ava's familiar silver eyes. "How long have I known you? I feel like you've been in my life forever."

"A long time, Sweetie." She smoothed Casi's hair back. "You've always been my little girl and I've dreamed of the day you would find your true love. I'm ecstatic you chose Kyle."

Casi relaxed in her embrace. "Now that I'll be in Washington, perhaps we can spend more time together?"

"I would be happy to get you acclimatized."

They took a tour of the brewery, which interested Kyle immensely. He chatted in depth to a pair of brothers who were working on a new craft brew. The older brother, Robert, attended the University of Washington, and Casi could see they had an instant kinship. Riley wore a Call of Duty t-shirt over his slender build, and expressed an interest in woodworking, making Kyle aware of his availability for an apprenticeship once the work at the brewery slowed down for the season. Kyle eagerly took his information, estimating he would be a good fit for their growing business.

Jack and Ava set up a booth at the brew-fest the next day and Jake arrived with his children. Reid cut his curly mop of hair and appeared more grown up. Olivia sported a nose ring and neon pink highlights. Ava smiled at the rebellious daughter, expecting she would give her father a difficult time. Jake removed a beer from Olivia's hand and shook his head. "Not for a few more years."

"This place sucks," Olivia sulked.

"They have a teen section by the waterfront." Ava pointed to the lively area set up with arcade games and food. She noted Olivia's glance at a lanky boy and figured that fueled her enthusiasm to join the group with her brother.

"Thanks." Jake sighed. "Not much interests her these days. I'm new to the single scene and unsure how Gail manages to entertain them. It was easier when they were small."

"Teenaged girls can be a handful." Jack chuckled and handed Jake a cider. "You're going to have a new sister-in-law."

"Yup, I'm stuck with her." Jake shrugged.

"She'll grow on you." Jack topped up his glass.

"If Kyle's happy, I'll put up with her."

Jack whispered to Ava, "He's starting to like her."

"There might be more to him than the angry bad boy image." Ava regarded Jake, greeting Casi with a hug before turning to give his brother a lengthy handshake.

Kyle stopped at a display on fermentation and spoke in depth to the brewer. Casi fidgeted beside him,, touching the vials and dishes while Kyle gently moved her hands away and gave his brother a pained look. Jake chuckled and grasped her arm. "We'll meet you at the end of the row."

"Thanks." Kyle kissed Casi on the cheek.

"What did you think of the parents?" Jake asked.

"Your dad gave me a lecture on the reality of marriage, and your mom tried to teach me how to cook." Casi took his cider, helping herself to a generous sip.

"Did they tell you I'm their favorite son?"

"They said you were a juvenile delinquent."

"I wouldn't be surprised."

"I heard you had a kitten fetish when you were a kid." Casi noted the anger and darkness appear in Jake's eyes and regretted her comment. "They actually said you liked to hold them. I made up the fetish part," she tried to backtrack. When she noticed him shut down, she led him to Jack. "Dad, tell Jake something embarrassing about me from my childhood."

Jack shrugged. "Well, one time you cut your own hair and your mom was so mad she made you go to school, even though you looked like a hillbilly."

Jake smiled, but Casi dug deeper. "Did I do anything which might be considered strange?"

"You thought your toys were real and would have long conversations with them, even arguments. That was a little disturbing." Jack raised an eyebrow.

"Whatever happened to Jamie?" Casi asked as Jack paled.

Ava put her hand on his and smiled. "Your teddy bear?"

Jack regained his composure. "I'm not sure. We can search through boxes in the attic and check if he's there."

"That would be fun to see him again," Casi said.

"It would." Jack hugged Ava closer and exhaled.

Jake strolled with Casi, smiling at her inability to listen to the preparation of the products and only interested in samples. "When I was younger, I was very attached to Kyle."

"Because of foster care?" she probed.

He shook his head. "Kyle tells you too much, but yes. My parents were fine with us being close because I felt better with him by my side. My dad warned me kids at school might find the touching odd."

"Can you define touching?" She glanced at him sideways.

"Hugging, not freaky perverted shit. I had a hard time at school because it was difficult for me to be away from Kyle. My parents would bring him to drop me off and pick me up each day. I would tell Kyle everything I learned and he would listen intently. That's why he's ridiculously smart. Two years later, he started kindergarten."

"Kyle's three years younger than you."

"Did you miss the part where I said school was hard for me? I started late and Kyle started early."

"Sorry, go on."

"Kyle had been there a few weeks, and everyone loved him. One day he saw me on the playground and ran over to share what he learned. He hugged me, and kids laughed and called us names."

She could see the memory hurt him. "So, you were traumatized?"

"No, I punched him in the face, called him a cry baby, and laughed with the other kids."

"Jake!" Casi's hand flew to her mouth.

"They called my dad, and he was furious. He took me to the barn and gave me the belt, but I wouldn't cry."

"I'm sure that was hard for your father. He seems sweet, not like a strict dad who's mean."

"My mom was livid. She told him you couldn't hit a broken child. It only made them shatter into more pieces. I went up to my room and cried. Kyle came in and hugged me and told me he was sorry." He grinned.

"He's a good brother."

"He's an amazing brother. My dad heard us talking and realized I'd reacted to being teased. He felt like shit and apologized for hitting me."

"Did you forgive him?"

"Sure, I was wrong, and I hated how I hurt Kyle. It was his first black eye," Jake chuckled. "My dad took us out for ice cream, and then we made up a secret brothers' handshake instead of hugging in public."

"The thing you guys do?" Casi tried to replicate the moves.

Jake grasped her hands to halt the action. "Yup and don't try to learn it. It's only for brothers."

"Is that when you started cuddling kittens?"

He rolled his eyes. "The kittens were soft and enjoyed being held. I also liked the rabbits, if you have to know everything, Miss. snoopy pants."

"I got to hold the bunnies, they were super soft." Casi hugged him. "Thanks for sharing, it makes me like you more."

"Don't get used to it. Gail never knew I was adopted and neither do my kids," he cautioned.

"I'll keep it to myself," Casi promised. "Jezebel! We forgot her at the house." Her eyes widened with fear.

"Nice to remember you have a kitten who should be cared for. Excellent parenting. I fear the day you have children." He noted a darkness appear in her expression. "It's a good thing Kyle arranged for me to watch her."

"Did you try to cuddle my kitty?" Casi joked.

"Do you realize how dirty that sounds?" Jake asked, making her blush as she replayed the comment in her head.

# 33

# LADIES WHO LUNCH

On their way back to Blackberry Falls, Casi sighed. "Do you believe our marriage will work?"

"Are you having doubts?" He grasped her hand.

"I'm not, but everyone except Mary and Ava said I'm being foolish. Even your dad."

"All that matters is what we think. My parents loved you. My dad felt it was necessary for you to understand how important this is to me." Kyle gestured to the landscape.

"I promise I'll give it a chance." She gave him a kiss. "I have the campaign this year in LA, but after that maybe we can work out something where I spend more time here."

"I like that idea." He grinned. "I don't expect you to become a small-town housewife and raise redneck children."

"Did you overhear my conversation with my mother?"

"Parts of it. You were yelling. I warned you the farmhouse doesn't have any soundproofing." He chuckled.

"She agreed to plan the wedding. She said everyone needed a first marriage." Casi poked him.

"Does that make me your first husband?"

"First and only. I'm sincere about marrying you and I understand what that entails." Casi surveyed the fields brimming with flowers and produce.

"I'm anxious to spend time with you doing ordinary things like going for walks and getting coffee." Kyle beamed.

"Two of my favorite things!"

"Let's stop on our way." Kyle squeezed her hand.

They stopped at Coffee Junction to get iced coffee. As they waited in line, a baby wailed while the mother tried to deal with a toddler who pitched a fit. The intensity of the screams sent chills down Casi's spine, and she shivered unintentionally, watching the poor disheveled mother tending to her children. Kyle embraced her and whispered, "I thought we could get a puppy to complete our family." She smiled in agreement as the child's screeching hit an all-time high.

A few weeks later, they had a fat puppy from a breeder in Oregon. Another German shorthair, with brown and white spots. Casi had been asked to leave the training to Kyle since it was important for the dog to understand his commands while hunting. Often Kyle would slip in bed at night to find her cuddling the puppy and growing kitten, trying to hide them under the covers. "You're spoiling them," he said affectionately, relocating them to their beds, figuring they would make their way up momentarily, but hoping he could make love to her uninterrupted.

Kyle tried several names, still missing his buddy, Colt. Casi laughed as the dog jumped and spun in circles. "Good boy, Dingo." She clapped and encouraged him.

"Please don't call him that. He'll think it's his name."

"Call him what?" Casi asked with a sly smile.

"Dingo." Kyle cringed as the puppy came running to him. "Damn it." He raised an eyebrow at Casi. "You did that on purpose, you little sneak."

"It's a darling name, isn't it Jezebel?" She cuddled the cat, who purred her approval.

"Thank God we are not having children." Kyle shook his head and gave the dog a biscuit.

Kyle yawned and checked the clock, wrapping Casi in his arms. He had gotten used to sleeping with her beside him and was not looking forward to her returning to LA in another month. He felt disconnected from her when she was away, as if she had her life, and he had his. He hoped some of her partying at the clubs would not continue now they were engaged. Before they had gotten back together, he hated seeing the photos of her dancing intimately with men. His only recourse was to never publicly 'Like' her pictures, his secret form of punishment. He loved her new profile picture of them, gazing adoringly at one another. He wasn't a fan of Facebook, but when the relationship request came, he felt like a little boy who had gotten the note back, with 'yes' checked in the box asking if she liked him.

Casi smiled over her shoulder. "Morning sex, how fun."

He chuckled. "You need to wake up earlier for that."

She put a pillow over the clock and rolled on top of him. "I can feel you're interested."

"I have no control over that." He tried to move her aside.

Casi eased herself on him, bringing his hands to her breasts. "I have no control over myself either."

"That's different." He exhaled and gave in to her advances.

Kyle heard the front door. "Damn it." He yanked the pillow from the clock. "Make coffee," he called to Jake. He rolled on top of her. "Let's finish this," he whispered, thrusting harder and putting a hand over her mouth. She giggled like a teenager trying to hide from her parents while she had sex with her boyfriend. He climaxed, and she gave up on having an orgasm, distracted by the sounds of Jake making coffee. Kyle grinned. "I'll have to take care of you tonight." He gave her a kiss and got up to shower.

She wrapped herself in the blanket as Jake came in the bedroom. He scowled at her. "Kyle's never late." He set a cup of coffee on the bedside table.

"Thanks." She scooted upright.

Jake surveyed her. "What do you do all day?"

"Not much. Go hiking or hang out at the lake." She shrugged. "I'm used to working. I'm not sure what to do with all this time off."

He furrowed his brow. "Are you tanning topless?"

"Maybe." She gave him a wink.

"Kyle has neighbors."

"Yes, I've met them." She giggled and he shook his head and turned toward the bathroom. Casi jumped up and threw on under-wear and a t-shirt, pushing past him. She slid on the vanity as he informed his brother of her nudity. "Tattletale." She poked Jake with her toe.

Kyle smiled as he shaved. "My neighbors have teenage boys, Casi. I imagine they would find great interest in you."

"Luke, Jordan, and Tanner. They offered to do the yard work," she informed him.

"I do my own gardening," he replied.

She put her arms around Jake as he stood in front of her. He tried to push her back, but she wrapped her legs around his hips. "Stop it, Monkey Face!" He attempted to unwind her.

Kyle noted Jake was uncomfortable with the attention, and put his hand between them. "Why don't you get ready, and we'll take you to coffee?" Casi jumped off the counter in a flash, rushing to get dressed.

"We're already late." Jake seethed.

"I'm redirecting her away from you," Kyle whispered.

Casi came back in minutes, wearing a short pink dress and sandals. She pushed in beside Kyle to brush her teeth as he paused mid-shave. She stepped back to fix her hair and put on face cream while Kyle finished.

"You're even prettier without makeup. It's not normal." Jake observed, scrutinizing her face closely.

She laughed, and Kyle grabbed her before she could hug Jake again. "Put your coffee cup in the kitchen," he directed.

*

They arrived at Coffee Junction and Kyle laughed. "Oh look, all your girlfriends are here," nodding to Lia at the register, and Gail and Mary Ann sitting at a table nearby. Jake shoved him and went to the group after giving a nod to Lia.

"Why's Jake being strange?" Lia asked Kyle as he ordered.

"He's no more strange than normal," he said in all seriousness, not comprehending what she meant. "Casi's coming in." He glanced toward the door, wondering how it could take her longer to get there when she left before them.

"What's the gossip today?" Jake asked Gail as he took a seat beside her.

"Is that what you believe we do all day?" she asked.

"Yes, I do." Jake chuckled.

Casi rushed in and explained how she turned right instead of left and then got confused. "It is only three miles, Casi," Kyle said, unsure how she could be so directionally challenged.

Jake called her over to the table. "Why don't you ladies tell Casi the fascinating things there are to do around town. She thinks the only excitement is tanning topless and driving the neighbor boys wild." Casi plunked on his lap and put her arm around his neck. "Gail, please inform her how I don't like being touched. She's annoying with her constant need for affection." Gail smiled, enjoying his discomfort.

Kyle set Casi's coffee down and placed a blueberry muffin beside it. "If you're done terrorizing my brother, we need to get to work. We're late." He laughed as she took her coffee and leaned back against Jake.

"I hate your wife." Jake sighed and picked her up in his arms to stand up. He placed her back in the chair and messed her hair. "My brother has never been late a day in his life until you came along."

Kyle gave her a kiss and smiled back at her as his brother pulled him toward the door.

"How did you make Kyle late?" Gail asked.

"Morning sex." Casi shrugged.

"I'm surprised he went for it. Was it on his schedule?"

"He tried to resist, but I covered the clock."

"Hey, Casi." Lia approached the table.

"Hi, Lia." Casi scooted her chair over and Gail indicated a free space, not as an invitation, but not a rejection either. "What does everyone do all day?" Casi inquired.

Mary Ann laughed. "I have a job, but I work partially from home. I meet Gail for coffee a few times a week."

"What's your job?" Casi asked.

"I'm a sales rep for a jam and spice company. I fill orders for the local stores and do promotions at trade shows."

"Really?" Casi considered it sounded a lot like the job the woman from Seattle had. "That seems interesting."

"I like it." Mary Ann grinned when she made the connection. "I'm aware of the sales rep Kyle dated in Seattle. I guess neither of us could compete with the swimsuit model." Casi threw her head back and laughed at Mary Ann's wit.

"I don't work," Gail sighed.

"You have a college degree, right?" Casi asked.

"Yes. I was a psychology major, with a minor in early childhood education. I met Jake in a biology class." She rolled her eyes. "Kyle took the same level classes because he is severely intelligent and encouraged Jake to finish on time. I made the comment about scheduling because Kyle was obnoxious with his rigorous organization. Even now, he makes coffee at home to drink while he gets ready and then stops for a vanilla latte. Predictable and scheduled."

Casi smiled. "What was Kyle like in college?"

"A pain in the ass, just like he is now. Jake was fun back then, and extremely handsome. He had a wild side and was up for anything, parties and outdoor adventures. Kyle also participated, but he was more regimented, never missing classes and making sure Jake turned in assignments. I realize I don't seem like I could let loose, but we were both different. I saw the control Kyle had over his brother, and it drove me nuts. To be honest, I never loved Jake, but I'd set my sights on him, and I wasn't going to let anyone get in my way, especially Kyle."

"The accidental pregnancy?" Casi suggested.

Gail shrugged. "All I ever wanted was to be a mother. When the kids were small, it was the best time of my life. I knew what to expect, and I took on the mother role perfectly. Georgia was wonderful, giving me advice and making me feel I had a purpose."

"How did your family feel about you getting married so soon after college?" Casi pressed.

Gail shrugged and Casi noted the deep sadness. "My father passed away months after the wedding so I'm pleased he was there. My mother lives near San Francisco with my brother's family. He's a tech guy and his wife is an ad executive. My mother cares for their children while they work. They say I threw my life away because I was a stay-at-home mom." She smiled at Casi. "What about you guys? Kyle's always been anti-kid."

"Although it's very unpopular, I don't see myself as a mother. It doesn't interest me." Casi sipped her coffee.

"You're perfect for Kyle. My one reservation about him dating Mary Ann was she wanted kids," Gail remarked.

"Probably too late now. I'm thirty-six," Mary Ann noted.

"You still have lots of options," Casi said. "You could have one on your own, or even adopt when the time is right."

"True. The thing is, the longer I've waited, the less I want them," she confessed. "Babies seem like too much work."

"There's nothing about it that appeals to me. Diapers, crying, whining, and neediness." Casi shuddered. "Not to mention the financial impact and how they destroy your body."

Gail laughed. "You have to do it when you're young and naïve. You can't over-think it or no one would have them."

"I like your kids. That's the age I enjoy them," Casi said.

"You can have them. I don't understand them anymore. I don't know where my babies went. Someone stole them in the night and replaced them with sulky teens." Gail turned to Lia. "How about you? Are you interested in having kids?"

Lia blushed. "I'd like a daughter."

"If you're planning on doing it with Jake, be warned, he's broke. I would be surprised if he wants more children. He spent the last sixteen years raising ours." She noticed Lia fidgeting with her sleeve. "I'm aware you're dating Jake, it doesn't bother me."

"Jake doesn't want to be tied down," Lia mumbled.

"It makes sense. He only married me because I got pregnant, and the last few years were rough."

"When's the big day?" Mary Ann asked.

"October. We're doing a destination wedding because I don't have any interest in planning it," Casi joked.

"Sounds ideal," Mary Ann said wistfully.

"You don't want a big wedding with lots of bridesmaids? Perfectly choreographed from the book you've been assembling all your life?" Gail teased. Lia looked away, annoyed she was making fun of Lauren.

"God no, that would be my nightmare! I've given the job to my mother. I'll show up and enjoy the party," Casi laughed.

Gail checked her watch. "We're headed to the lavender festival in Sequim. Do you want to come?"

"Sure, why not?" Casi climbed in the backseat and sent Kyle a text while they drove. "I'm going to the lavender festival with the ladies who lunch in a weird named place. My nightmare has come true; I'm officially a hick."

Kyle replied. "Take time to admire the landscape. It's a beautiful drive. The Hood Canal is phenomenal."

Casi texted Dylan. "It's the middle of the day and I'm not wearing makeup. I'm going to a lavender festival, with women from the coffee shop. Small town?"

Dylan replied, "You need to get back to LA before you get a perm and start wearing mom jeans."

She giggled and tucked away her phone, gasping at the sensational scenery around her. "Wow, this is an incredible view!"

They walked around the festival, and Casi found lotions and honey she liked, buying some of each. They discovered an area serving wine, and after a few drinks, they started sharing. Gail put her hand on Casi's. "Last winter, when I paid those creeps to scare you at the lake, that's all they were supposed to do. I wanted you to think this town was full of rednecks and losers, so you'd go back to LA. I'm sorry they tried to take if further, that was never my intent."

"It did scare me, but actually it brought us closer. Kyle was angry about what happened. That's why Jake went with us to LA."

"And Lia went too," Gail said with a smile.

"You knew?"

"Your friend Lia is sweet but naïve. She let it slip how brutal Jake's injury was. She didn't realize she revealed she was in LA, having an affair with my husband."

Casi shrugged. "I guess we're even."

"I guess we are." Gail agreed.

"Did you ever cheat on Jake?"

Gail hesitated. "Two years ago. Our marriage was over. I'd done everything to push him away, but he was so loyal! I'd lost interest in having sex with him because it always turned into a fight. My tennis instructor was very attentive."

"You actually play tennis?" Casi's eyes widened.

"Of course," Gail laughed. "It was a brief affair. I almost told Jake, hoping it would make him leave me. I didn't want to be the one to end it."

"Why didn't you tell him?"

"I saw him kissing Lia one night as they left the bar. I got insanely jealous!" Gail smiled. "Kyle was in LA, which is why Jake spent too much time with Lia. He was miserable without his stupid brother. When Kyle came back, he was unhappy. We fixed him up with Mary Ann and everything was better for a while. We all hung out together, and Jake stopped seeing Lia."

"Is that why you hated me?" Casi questioned.

"We were happier before you came," Gail confirmed.

"It wouldn't have lasted," Mary Ann interjected. "I liked Kyle. He had everything going for him; handsome, intelligent, a gorgeous house on the lake. We had interesting conversations, fun dates, and he's great in bed."

"What's wrong with all that?" Casi asked.

"Kyle made it clear from the beginning he had no interest in marriage or kids. He said he had a plan for his life, and he was happy to date, but I should never expect more."

Gail rolled her eyes. "Kyle's running narrative to all the women he's dated over the years."

"I respected how he was upfront. I was married in my twenties and it was disastrous. I'm not in a hurry to commit again, and I knew he didn't have feelings for me." She regarded Casi. "The worst part about seeing you guys together on the porch was the way he gazed at you. That was the first thing I noticed. The love in his eyes as he held you. That's why I shoved you, I hated you for being the one he fell in love with. After you went back to LA, and he was broken up about it, I tried to get back together with him. I hoped you'd damaged him enough that he would be happy to be with me."

"Oh, Mary Ann," Casi said. "I'm sorry."

Mary Ann grinned. "When I saw the cover you did, I flipped out! Everywhere I went, I was bombarded by your gorgeous face and voluptuous body."

"Jake bought the first copy." Gail giggled. "He told everyone Kyle had slept with you as if it made him cool by proxy."

Casi laughed, "Jake's demented."

Gail grasped her hand. "I've known Jake for twenty years, married for sixteen. I see you reaching him in a way I never could. He's starting to let you in, and I'm sure one day you'll discover all those secrets he's never wanted to share with me."

"Jake's constantly irritated by me and that's why I mess with him. I never had siblings. I didn't realize how much I missed out on not having someone to torment."

"He didn't like you because you hurt Kyle," Gail clarified. "Now that you're marrying his brother, he'll grow to love you. That's stings because he's only ever loved Kyle." She shifted in her seat and took a sip of wine. "When Jake was fit, he had much more confidence and a raw passion that was super sexy. Over the years, he became less passionate, and less interested. I blame myself. After the kids, I didn't want him to touch me. Everything hurt, and my body rearranged itself without my consent. He would beg me to get it on, and it seemed like every time I gave in, one of the kids needed something. It became rushed and more like a chore. Married sex, especially as a parent, is hard. With my tennis instructor, it was just sex. No bills, no kids, no damn brother. If I were to be intimate with Jake now, I would slow down and enjoy being with him. We went from dating in college to married with a baby. We never had a life as a couple. I thought things would be better if we were divorced, but I didn't realize how much I needed him to be my partner when it came to raising the kids."

## 34

# SUMMER'S END

Casi struggled to catch her breath as she entered the wood shop, grasping the work table. "Did you run here?" Kyle scanned her colorful spandex shorts and running bra.

"This is a little farther than I anticipated," she panted.

Kyle grinned. "It's about eight miles."

"You can make me a yummy dinner to renew my energy level." She gave him a wink. "In case I'm in the mood later."

"We'll go to the store on the way home. I assume you want a ride?" He gave her a kiss. "I don't want you to waste any more energy on anything I'm not also enjoying."

Casi noted the disappointment on Jake's face as he contemplated another evening alone. "Why don't you come and have dinner with us?"

Kyle nodded. "We can watch a movie."

"Sure, I'll come. I'm tired of the bar." Jake chuckled.

Jake shook his head as they entered the grocery store, watching Casi walk ahead of them in her workout attire. "I can't believe you let her go out in public like that."

"Let her? Do you think I have any control over that woman?" Kyle balked. "Check out the women in here wearing tights, she looks a hundred times better than they do."

Jake grinned. "They're called leggings, but you're right, she is way hotter."

Kyle raised an eyebrow. "How do you know what they're called? Gail wouldn't have been caught dead in something so revealing."

"My daughter informed me after I told her she looked like a whore wearing them," Jake cringed.

"Jesus, Jake!" Kyle shoved him.

"I suck as a father. I don't understand her. She goes out of her way to shock me and gets pissed off when I react."

"Yet another reason I don't want kids. First, they're exhausting with all the time required to care for them and the constant crying. Then they're cute for about five years, until they get annoying as hell again," Kyle explained.

"I won't argue with you." Jake shivered. "I have two more years with this one and then I'm done. Thank God, Reid is easier, except I don't grasp his new fascination with religion."

"Olivia will be eighteen, but there's still college. I don't believe the angst will end for many more years," Kyle noted.

"I'll pay for college, but she's on her own to pay for alcohol, drugs, and tattoos." Jake whistled and added chips and dip to the cart.

"She's doing drugs?"

"Yup. Gail found pot in her room and she got a butterfly on her ankle. It goes great with the dyed hair and a nose ring."

"You have a wild one on your hands." Kyle turned toward the meat aisle, losing track of Casi.

"I'm sure Mom and Dad consider it karma," Jake sighed.

Casi stopped at the movie rental kiosk and waved them over. "Let's rent a movie rather than watching what's on TV?"

"We can pick one from home. Kyle has all the channels and they offer on demand rentals," Jake scoffed.

"Why pay three times as much?" Casi cocked her head. "You don't know how to use the kiosk, do you?" Jake turned away, and she noticed a look between him and Kyle. "Why don't you get what we need for dinner, and I'll show your brother how to rent a movie?" She pulled Jake toward her as Kyle slowly strolled down the produce aisle unsure about leaving his brother in a possibly tense situation. She pointed to the highlighted section that said, 'rent movies' and read it aloud.

"I can read. I'm not stupid," Jake growled.

"I can too, but I wouldn't walk in your wood shop and be able to use those machines in there," she said gently.

He nodded, realizing she wasn't trying to make fun of him. "Ok, walk me through this." He stood behind her as she showed him the different options, how to view the new releases, and read the descriptions, scrolling through the titles. He surprised her when he put his arms around her, resting his chin on her shoulder, while he read the synopsis. "Let's get this one." He pointed to a violent war movie.

"Too bloody. Can we compromise on something with a plot at least?"

"No romance, I hate those sappy ones." He nodded to a spy thriller, and she added it to the cart. Casi indicated the checkout and asked him for his email address and credit card. "I don't like giving that information."

She explained it would make it easier for him to rent movies in the future. He handed her his card, and she completed the transaction and gave him the movie. "See? Easy." She smiled at Kyle hovering to the side with the groceries, realizing he had been watching them.

"It's simple when you do it." Jake surveyed the machine.

"I guess it's good I'm marrying your brother. I can help you navigate technology." Casi poked him.

Jake's phone beeped, and he was confused why he'd gotten an email from the kiosk. Casi took his phone and explained it confirmed his rental and sent him a promo code. "Maybe you should put your phone number in there, in case I have questions," he suggested. She added her number, reorganized his apps, and changed his ringtone with lightning speed. She giggled when she added a picture of a monkey as his screen saver.

"She seems to have a knack for technology," Kyle commented.

"Yet, she can't figure out how to make coffee," Jake joked.

Casi rolled her eyes. "We all have things we excel at and other things can be challenging."

Summer drifted to an end and Casi lazed on the dock, enjoying the last carefree days, considering fall would be busy with the campaign firing up, and the wedding. She smiled at the thought of being a married woman. She never pictured herself as a wife and wondered what other changes might be in store for her.

Kyle reclined beside her and gestured to the calm lake. "Could you get used to living here?"

She shrugged. "It's beautiful, but I'm not sure if I'm ready to give up LA yet."

"Want to go for a drive?" They got in his truck and she texted for the next twenty minutes. Kyle took her phone and put it in the glove box as she stared at him in horror. "You can text Dylan anytime, I want you to pay attention to where we are." He redirected her attention to the landscape. "You're anxious to get back, but please give Washington a chance."

"That's fair." She realized she hadn't been anywhere except the lake. Kyle pointed out farms, telling her which one produced what as he waved to the farmers. They stopped and bought a box of vegetables from one of the roadside stands. "What does your family farm produce?" Casi asked.

He chuckled. "It's a hobby farm." He elaborated when he realized that didn't clarify anything. "It used to be an apple orchard. My father grew up there and after their parents died, they divided up the acreage, since it wasn't profitable as a business anymore. My dad kept the ten acres with the house. His brother has fifteen acres on the other side of the river, and his sister sold the remaining twenty acres because she prefers to travel most of the time."

"Then how did your dad make a living?"

"He's a plumber. He had a shop with his best friend, Earl. They retired a few years ago. We aren't wealthy people, Casi, but we live a good life and plan well for our futures. I've been upfront about all my finances," he said sincerely.

She smiled at him. "I respect the way you live your life. I need a partner, not a sugar daddy."

"We'll do well together. You'll have a home and security. You'll never have to worry if the bills are paid."

He parked in a nearby field and gathered buckets, handing one to her as he took her hand. "What are we doing?" She surveyed the large field spotted with bright green bushes.

"Picking blueberries."

They walked through the field and he showed her how to tell which ones were the best to pick and made her taste some. "These are excellent." She popped a few more in her mouth, making a face when she got a sour one.

Kyle laughed. "That one was still green. Fat and blue is what you desire. Now fill your pail."

Casi regarded the bucket with dismay. She considered her phone, locked away in the truck, feeling lost without it. She watched Kyle happily picking while he chatted to other families. She shook her head and glanced around, realizing his point. Perpetually focused on her phone, she was unaware of her surroundings. She had been in Washington for two months, and other than enjoying the lake, she made no effort to do anything except complain about missing LA. She searched the vast blue sky and listened to the birds, able to breathe deeper as a sense of calm washed over her. She smiled at Kyle and bent down to start picking. After they were done, they drove around the town and he showed her shops and places she hadn't seen. They stopped for dinner at a roadside cafe and listened to a local band, then strolled the streets, hand in hand, stopping to chat to friends.

Jake came over the next morning and made them blueberry pancakes, setting them on the table on the back porch overlooking the lake.

"Do you like Washington better now?" Kyle asked, hoping she had a better sense of where they lived.

Jake scoffed, "How could you not love it here? It's the best place in the whole world."

Casi giggled. "That's what the Californians say about California! They claim everyone wants to live there."

"We encourage that because we don't want them here." Jake smirked. "We have trees, the ocean, lakes, rivers, fishing, hunting, stars, wildlife." He held up his fingers and kept counting. "Down to earth people, great summers, and radical rain storms. Plus, Kyle and I live here. What do you love about LA?"

"Dylan and my work are there." Casi scrunched her face and considered what else she liked. "It's sunny a lot."

"Smog, traffic, too many people, noisy, expensive, too hot, no water, no greenery," Jake stated.

"That's true." Casi gazed at the lake. "Don't you find it too quiet out here, and too much rain?"

Kyle laughed, "If you need noise and action, you can be in Seattle in twenty minutes. Here we have the lake. The sky is incredibly blue and full of stars at night. The rain doesn't bother me. I work inside and when I'm home, I love watching a storm over the lake. Who cares if I get wet walking to my truck when I get to live in paradise?"

Casi realized how rarely she went outdoors in LA. "Maybe I'll get used to it in time, but remember my work is there."

"You'll fall in love with Washington. Besides, you're getting old, and will need to find a different line of work," Jake teased.

❧

Kyle made dinner while Jake turned on the TV to watch the game. Casi strolled to Jake and smiled. "Now that you're single, it's time for an education."

Jake pressed back against the sofa as she leaned toward him. Kyle stood in the kitchen, watching her intently. She giggled and reached in Jake's pocket and pulled out his phone, then sat beside him, making him put his arm around her so he could see the screen. "Let's start with the camera. Kyle got you this phone specifically so you could take pictures at the shop if he needed more information."

"Yes," Jake sighed.

"How's it working for you?" Casi winked at Kyle, who had lamented his brother couldn't figure out how to send photos.

"Not well."

"You can take a photo like this. Or tap here and you can take a selfie." She snapped a picture of them sitting together. She demonstrated how to crop and edit the photos, even adding hand-drawn hearts.

"I won't be sending Kyle pictures with hearts."

Casi explained how to add text and the easiest way to send the picture. Kyle looked at his phone as the message appeared, smiling at the picture with hearts. "We love you, Kyle."

"Good job," Kyle praised.

"Now you take one." Casi handed the phone to Jake.

He took a picture of Dingo, cropping it to his nostrils. He sent it to Kyle in a text. "Dinner smells good."

Kyle chuckled. "You've created a monster. I anticipate getting a lot of funny texts from Jake."

"How did you send the picture of Mary Ann to Kyle in LA?" Casi narrowed her eyes and regarded Jake.

"Gail did it," Jake admitted.

"You're a very fast learner," Casi complimented. "Now we'll speed you up on texting."

"Shouldn't I learn one thing at a time?"

"You'll be fine." She pulled his other arm around her.

"You're trying to get me to hug you," Jake surmised.

"I'm making sure you stay focused." She turned the phone sideways. "It's easier to type like this."

"I didn't realize it turned like that." Jake's eyes widened. She showed him how to use the predictive text and suggested using his thumbs to type. "This is so much faster!"

"Training wheels are off, send a real text. Not to Kyle."

"He's the only one I contact."

"Text Olivia," she challenged.

"I have no idea what to say."

"Ask if she wants to go shopping. I'm sure she needs school clothes," Casi suggested.

"She won't want to go with me."

"Ask her." Casi felt him tense and snuggled against him.

Jake asked if Olivia wanted to go to the mall and got an immediate response. "Is this a jk? You never text me," with a questioning emoji face. He peered at Casi, who explained jk was joke and then showed him how to use emoji.

"Casi's teaching me to use my phone. I thought it might be fun to go together, but I can give you money to shop with your friends." Jake's breathing became labored and Casi noted the stress rising as he waited for her answer.

"Uber-cool you're learning! I added you on Facebook. Can she teach you how to message? I want to go to the mall with you. It would be cool." She included a heart and a smiling emoji.

Jake smiled at Casi. "Thank you."

Casi nodded and accepted Olivia's Facebook request. "The best way to know what your kids are doing is to relate to them in their own environment."

"Is that how Kyle deals with you?" Jake's eyes crinkled with amusement. "You understand teenage girls pretty well."

"Remember, I was one." Casi elbowed him. "My dad was super important to me." She squeezed her eyes shut and Jake stroked her arm. "Until I pushed him away and we barely spoke for years." She swallowed. "When my parents divorced, I felt he abandoned me. He started a new life and left me behind with my mother."

"I guess you have some good advice for me." Jake embraced her and gave her a kiss on the cheek.

She grasped his hand. "Why are you still wearing your wedding band? It's time to get yourself back on the market!"

"I wanted to remove it, but it was stuck. I forgot about it because I'm used to it after all these years."

"Come on." She led him to the kitchen. She filled a glass with ice water and immersed his finger. "I'll show you the trick models use when they can't get the rings off after a shoot."

Kyle came over and stood beside him. "You've had that ring on a long time. Are you ready to take it off?"

"It's time." Jake nodded.

Casi took his finger from the water and massaged coconut oil around the band. "Ok." She slid it off with ease. "No longer taken." She read the emotion on his face and decided she should let him be alone with his brother. "I'm going to take a shower before we eat."

"Are you ok?" Kyle probed.

"It's different." Jake shrugged. "I took mine off, and in less than two months you'll be putting one on."

"It's strange to think I'll be a husband."

"You chose a good woman. You'll be incredibly happy with her. You were smart to wait for the right girl."

## 35

# DOMESTIC GODDESS

Kyle watched Casi stroll up to the house in her pink floral bikini. Her face lit up when she noticed him and she rushed to greet him. "Did you already shower?" She stepped back and surveyed his freshly shaven face and crisp shirt.

"Apparently, I'm going out with the guys tonight." He embraced her and felt the warmth radiating from her skin. "You're getting super tanned. People will think you were on vacation."

"Who knew Washington had sunshine?" She snuggled against him. "Where are you headed to? A work thing?"

"Jake said to be ready at 6:00. Maybe Lia wants to hang out?" He smoothed her hair from her face and gave her a kiss.

"I can entertain myself." She cranked the stereo and jumped up on the coffee table to dance.

"Are you sure? You've been alone all day and I feel bad taking off for the evening." He held his arms out to catch her as she leaped forward with abandon.

She hugged him. "Have fun with your brother. I'll be fine."

Jake arrived at 6:00, perpetually on time like his brother. They headed out of town and Kyle sighed, "We're going to a strip club, aren't we?"

Jake chuckled. "Not my idea. It's about the guys getting away from their wives and your impending nuptials are the best reason to have a guy's night at the Evil Eye."

Kyle had been there a few times. The girls were pretty enough, but his interest in other women had waned. He planned to make it a fun night for his friends and act like he was having a good time. He ordered a martini and watched the women parade on stage, working the pole with enthusiasm. He appeared eager as they strutted, but he pictured Casi in her cotton panties, sexier than the revealing G-strings. His friends bought him a lap dance, which paled in comparison to the one Casi gave him, but he made a show of putting bills in her thong. By one in the morning, he was happy to leave and thanked everyone for a great time.

Casi sat on a stool in the kitchen, staring at a cake on the counter. "I see you had an exciting evening?" Kyle commented.

"I made you a cake! It has whiskey in it!"

"Let me jump in the shower, I reek of cigarette smoke." He threw his clothes in the washer to avoid permeating the house. He took a quick shower, washing his hair twice to get the aroma out. He came back and noticed Casi set out two plates. He could hear the washer running. "Aren't you the domestic goddess?" He grinned and cut a slice of the fantastic chocolate cake.

"It has a caramel whiskey glaze." She wiggled her shoulders as she took a bite. Kyle was pleased to see her excited about the cake, which was delicious, to his surprise. "I can understand why people have kids, there's not much to do all day when you don't work." She stabbed at her cake and he took a second piece, hungry from only having alcohol and a few onion rings. "I've been thinking..."

Kyle couldn't swallow, suspecting the next words were about having children. Everyone warned him about a woman's biological clock and how even though she claimed she didn't want kids, the minute she had a ring on her finger, everything would change. He thought they were on the same page, but as he watched her cuddling Jezebel, he became concerned. He wondered if he should spit out the cake to avoid choking and attempted to appear calm as she continued.

"The next few years will be pretty busy with the Sand and Surf line as we build it up. I'll have a few years most likely before they will want a younger version. And..." she paused, and he could feel the cake lodged in his throat. "I'm considering taking some marketing and merchandising classes to add to my business degree, and then maybe see what other opportunities come along." She directed her gaze to him to garner his reaction. "Why do you look like you're going to throw up?" Kyle coughed, hoping the cake would slide down. "Don't you think it's a good idea? The classes are online, and even though there's a time commitment, I can do them here or in LA." She watched as he swallowed and wiped his brow. "Oh, my God! You thought I wanted a baby!"

"Something like that," he said meekly. He went to the sink and poured a glass of water.

"Hilarious! Don't worry, the only baby I'm interested in is getting this idea underway," she giggled.

"Thank God." He kissed her on the forehead. "That's the best idea you've ever had. I'm proud of you for accomplishing so much and continuing your education. Your cake is fantastic by the way, even though I almost choked on it because of your big announcement."

"Ray Dawson sent me the recipe." She took out the plastic wrap to cover the cake.

"That's hysterical you didn't even know his name all the years you lived in that apartment. and now he's your cooking buddy." Kyle shook his head.

She shrugged. "I wasn't interested in other people before. Now that I know him better, I enjoy his enthusiasm. He was a big hit at our adult education culinary classes. Everyone wanted to be his partner because he's very talented." She swept her hair behind her shoulder in mock vanity. "But he chose me."

"He was smart. Please thank him for the delicious cake recipe and tell him I'm anxious to try more."

"Where did they take you tonight?" Casi frowned at the cake. "Should I put it in the fridge or leave it on the counter?"

"Counter is better for cake." Kyle reached under the plastic and pinched off another bite. "We went to a strip club!"

"Wow, racy stuff. Did you get a lap dance?" She shimmied her hips with a twinkle in her eye.

"Yes, but yours are much better." He grabbed her and lifted her up in his arms to carry her to bed.

They worked all afternoon on Casi's car, wanting to make sure it was safe for the road. When they came inside to watch the game, Casi sat beside Jake, putting her feet in his lap with a smile. He rolled his eyes, then leaned forward and put his beer on the coffee table and started rubbing her feet, making her moan. "Why have you denied me your skills?"

"Why do you think I waited until the last night? I have to pry you off me constantly. You would've been insatiable."

Kyle laughed and told them to come to the table as he brought over platters laden with food. Casi hugged Jake. "Incredible massage, thank you."

Jake pushed her feet off his lap. "Don't get used to it, Monkey." He washed his hands and pulled out a chair. "Dinner smells amazing. What did you make?"

"Chicken Milanese with polenta and roasted vegetables."

"Did your mom teach you guys how to cook?" Casi asked.

"Yes, she did. I've always taken more of an interest than Jake because I worked in a restaurant in college. I enjoy the science behind it." Kyle poked his brother in the middle. "Jake likes eating."

Jake nodded. "That's the best part! I like barbecuing and cooking game, I don't do all the fancy stuff he does. But then, I've never been to cooking classes, like he and La..." Jake coughed, realizing he shouldn't elaborate on Lauren being a chef. "Gail did all the cooking. She didn't like me in the kitchen."

"Were you happy when you were first married?" Casi set the bread on the table.

"Why are you asking?" he grumbled.

"Answer the question." Casi reached for the butter.

Jake shrugged. "I wasn't happy to have a family and responsibilities straight out of college. After Reid, I got used to the routine, and I liked it. I went to work every day, and Gail took care of the kids. I came home to a clean house with dinner on the table and the laundry done. I enjoyed the predictability."

"Gail said it was the best time of her life when the kids were small. She stated the same reasons." Casi beamed.

"It's nice she didn't hate me the entire time." Jake exhaled and passed her the polenta.

"She never hated you. Her bitterness stemmed from feeling lost as the kids got older and she could see everyone else moving on with their lives." She noted the relief on Jake's face.

"Did Gail say she didn't hate me either?" Kyle asked.

"She dislikes you," Casi giggled. "Mainly because she feels you are too disciplined. She liked it when you lived with them and believed you were all working together for a common goal."

"We were. That's why we were fair with the divorce settlement. She deserved a share of the business." Kyle set his fork down. "You're spending a lot of time with her."

"You told me to discover more of Washington. Gail has a lot of time on her hands and has taken me around to shops and antique fairs. She's actually super nice. Mary Ann drove me around Seattle. Wow, what a cool city!" Casi paused mid-bite. "Have you heard of a town named Leavenworth that's not a prison? It's darling! I felt like I was in Europe."

"It's a beautiful place." Kyle smiled at her enthusiasm and spooned polenta on her plate. "We should take the train there around Christmastime. The decorations are amazing."

"Did you go with your parents?" Casi sipped her wine.

"Sure, and I've been with friends." He glanced at his chicken and wondered if he should mention Lauren. "Anyway, I'm happy you're getting to know Mary Ann better, she's an interesting person and is the perfect guide for this area." He noted her wry smile. "What am I missing? We're over the porch thing, right?"

"Totally! Gail needs you to help her manage the money. She's afraid to ask you, but she's worried she's making too many mistakes and is unsure how to invest it properly. She doesn't trust anyone but you to advise her. She says you're incredibly good with numbers and make sound decisions."

Kyle shook his head. "Tell her to come see me at the shop. I'll set up a plan for her, and Brian can do her accounting."

Kyle led Casi to the bedroom, making love to her most of the night. They collapsed in exhaustion, breathing heavily, and holding hands. "You realize I won't see you again until the wedding?" A sob escaped as she exhaled.

"I know." Kyle rolled toward her and ran a hand over her stomach as he gazed at her. "I'll miss you."

"What are you most looking forward to about being married?" Casi touched his cheek.

"That we'll be together forever, no matter what happens," Kyle said without hesitation.

"It may not be easy living apart a lot of the time."

"It won't be. That's the part I'll hate the most." He put his forehead to hers and sighed. "I understand you need to go back for the campaign and when you came here this summer, you had no idea we would be engaged. Promise me if things aren't going well, or you decide you don't want to be there anymore, you'll let me know."

"And you'll come get me?" Casi brushed her lips against his and memorized the moment to replay when she felt lonely.

"In a heartbeat." Kyle pulled her in his arms and caressed her back, holding her until she fell asleep.

Casi's mother had given them several fabulous locations for the destination wedding. They decided on Hawaii, to Sonya's dismay, calling it generic. They factored in the direct access for everyone, and no one had been there, so it would be romantic and tropical. Casi had spent a week on a yacht in her early twenties sailing around the islands, but when they were scheduled to dock in Maui, a tropical storm blew in. They retreated for a safer harbor, watching Maui pass by in a sway of palm trees. It had been dubbed the 'almost Maui trip'. It seemed like the perfect location for them to celebrate with their families. Her father insisted on paying for the wedding and picked up the tab for the flights and resort. One of the things Casi anticipated, in addition to the lack of effort needed on her part, was being able to spend a week with everyone rather than only getting one day.

The morning she left to drive back to LA, they stopped by Coffee Junction. Kyle pulled a chair over to Gail's table. "Good morning, Kyle." Gail smiled and Mary Ann greeted them while Jake brought coffees and pastries. Kyle put his arm around Casi and she leaned closer, wiping tears as she sipped her coffee. "Heading back to LA?" Gail asked. Casi nodded and Kyle handed her a scone.

"We're going to Hawaii for the wedding," Jake announced.

"How exciting!" Mary Ann said.

Gail watched Jake looking at Lia helping customers at the register. "Are you taking Lia as your date?"

"I'm considering it." He exhaled and raised an eyebrow.

"It's a good idea." Gail nodded, understanding he was seeking validation. "Unless you want to take me."

Jake chuckled and eyed his watch as Kyle tenderly wiped Casi's tears. "We need to get to work." Kyle brushed the crumbs from Casi's shirt, suggesting she use the bathroom before she got on the road. He put his elbows on the table and leaned his face in his hands with a sigh. "You'll see her in a few weeks. You'll have an amazing time in Hawaii and then guess what?" Jake smacked him on the back. "You'll be married and have her in your life forever. And ever."

Kyle gave him a half-hearted smile. "Six weeks seems like forever. I don't know if I can do it." He rubbed his chest.

"We have a ton of work to keep us busy." Jake stood when Casi returned and pulled her into an embrace. "Don't do anything to make me hate you, Monkey Face."

She giggled and hugged him tightly. "I promise I won't. You better take good care of him for me. He's my world."

Jake nodded. "I've kept him safe for thirty-five years."

Kyle stood, throwing away their trash before he grasped Casi's hand. "I'll see you guys soon." She waved, unsure when she would actually be back. They walked out to her car, and she leaned against the door while Kyle pressed into her, wrapping his arms around her.

"I'm going to miss you like crazy." he breathed in the crook of her neck.

"Next time we see each other we'll be getting married."

"I hate saying goodbye to you." His eyes filled with sorrow.

She nodded, unable to speak as the tears rolled down her cheeks. She considered telling Alix to forget the campaign and not return to LA. But it wasn't a possibility. Not yet, anyway.

**36**

---

# ISLAND ESCAPE

On the flight to Hawaii, Casi contemplated the irony of feeling like she was going on vacation with her best friend rather than committing herself to a major life decision. Perhaps it was because everything had been planned for her, or maybe she was oblivious to the magnitude of what she was about to do? She smiled at Dylan in the seat beside her and her heart leapt with the notion she would be reunited with Kyle in one more day.

Casi checked in at the resort and was anxiously approached by Sonya. "Mom, give me a break. We landed about two seconds ago!" Casi narrowed her eyes as Dylan rushed away with a lame excuse of needing to find a bathroom. She listened to her mother's list of rants then agreed to meet her for a cocktail at the pool once she was settled.

"Don't keep me waiting." Sonya put her hand on her hip. "Your father hasn't opened a tab yet, and it's grossly unfair to expect me to pay."

Casi rolled her eyes and waved goodbye. She let the peaceful beauty of the location ease her into vacation mode and focused on her excitement of being with Kyle. She hung her wedding dress in the closet, trying to avoid more wrinkles than necessary. It was far from traditional, but she believed it suited the occasion with style and sophistication. She kept it in the garment bag, saving it as a surprise. She put away her clothing, consisting of swimsuits, lingerie, sundresses, and shorts. Another terrific part of the destination wedding, unpack and you were done, wedding and honeymoon in one.

She slipped on a sundress and sandals and went to the pool. Sonya ordered her a Mai Tai and appeared to be on her third. "Where's Burt?" Casi glanced around the patio. "Did he go to play golf?"

Sonya shrugged. "He couldn't get away from work."

"Are things not going well with number five?"

"Let's focus on your wedding, Darling." Sonya sipped her cocktail and fiddled with the large solitaire on her finger.

Casi regarded her mother with a familiar sadness for her inability to stay in a relationship more than a few years. The reality of her future brought trepidation for how it might impact her own life. She swallowed and decided it could be an argument for another day. "This is a perfect location. Thanks for all your hard work. I'm excited about the wedding."

"It won't last," Sonya snipped.

"Why do you keep saying that?"

"Darling, I'm not trying to be unkind. Kyle's sweet and extremely handsome. He's ordinary, and you'll get bored as your career takes off."

"I'm over thirty, Mom. My career has gone as far as it will go in the modeling world." Casi downed her drink.

"You never know what opportunities will present themselves in the future." Sonya gave her a sly smile.

"Please stay out of my career. And my relationship."

The next day they relaxed by the pool, waiting for everyone to arrive while Dylan fussed around Casi, making sure she didn't end up with tan lines or raccoon eyes. After the fourth time of him tucking in her straps, she threw her bikini top to the side and put a hat over her face, much to the delight of the lifeguard. She was tipsy by the time Kyle arrived and tried to lure him to bed while he attempted to unpack. He told her there would be no sex until they were married, and she claimed he was an extortionist. They went back to the pool and ordered drinks while they enjoyed a swim. Jake pulled a lounge chair over to his parents and ensured they had cocktails. "This is great to have everyone together for a vacation, huh?"

"It's lovely." Georgia smiled at his calm demeanor. "You're looking fit. Are you happier about things?"

"I've been spending a lot more time at the lake." Jake raised an eyebrow after regarding his trim physique. "I may have lost a few pounds."

"A few?" Peter chuckled. "At least forty. Didn't you notice your clothes hanging off?"

Jake shrugged. "Kyle orders shirts for work and I put on what fits. I'm convinced he is discrete to avoid another meltdown, like when I realized I wore a 3x. I went to the mall with Olivia and she made me buy new pants because she inferred I had no style."

Peter nodded. "You look great. I'm happy to see you in better shape. I was concerned about your health."

"I know, Dad." Jake relaxed in his chair.

Georgia smiled. "Lia seems nice."

"Who's Lia?" Peter asked.

"Peter!" Georgia shook her head. "The woman Jake invited to the wedding. You met her an hour ago." She pointed to her sitting under an umbrella beside the pool. "She's Lauren's sister."

"I'll bet you remembered Casi an hour later," Jake teased.

"True. Casi leaves quite an impression." Peter chuckled and turned to where Casi reclined on a towel with Kyle stretched out beside her, propped up on one elbow. He put drops of water in her belly button, making her laugh as she playfully pushed his hand away.

"She's been good for him. Kyle is comfortable around her." Georgia smiled at their banter.

"She has," Jake agreed. "I like her more now that I've gotten to know her. It's awesome how happy she makes Kyle."

"Are things serious with Lia? I don't recall you mentioning her." Georgia considered Lauren's rant about Jake's apparent disinterest and wavering attention to her sister.

"I like her. I'm still finding it strange not being married. I was used to my routine with Gail and the kids. Even though I was miserable most of the time, I knew what to expect," he said.

Georgia reached over and put her hand on Jake's, wanting to cry when he held her hand tightly. "Give it time, Sweetheart."

"Don't rush into anything," Peter cautioned. He noticed Jake holding his mother's hand. "You're a wonderful father and you've made those kids a priority."

Jake smiled. "Thanks, Dad. I have my hands full with Olivia. I'm glad the child-rearing years are almost behind me. It'll be cool to be an adult with no responsibilities."

Peter nodded. "You never got a chance to be independent. It will be good for you to enjoy yourself for a while."

Casi jumped in the pool, staying underneath the water for a long time as she swam laps. Jack laughed as he walked over to Georgia and Peter, bringing them cocktails. "That girl has always been part fish," he said, watching her resurface. Ava followed him, svelte in a one-piece, with a sarong tied around her hips. Jake stood, giving Ava an appreciative nod, and brought them chairs to join his parents.

"Did you want a drink?" Jake strolled to Lia and kissed her.

"No, I'm fine." She adjusted her wrap.

"Do you want to go down to the beach?"

"I don't feel like it." Lia glanced at Casi in a floral bikini.

"We could go for a walk. The gardens here are incredible."

"Jake, I want to sit and relax. Do I have to be constantly doing something on this vacation? I'm already overwhelmed by Kyle's insane list of activities for the week." Lia pouted.

"You don't have to do everything on it. He wanted to ensure

people had a good time." Jake rubbed his temple in frustration. Kyle rushed toward them and wrestled Jake into the pool. Lia sighed, thinking about the scolding she had gotten from her sister and mother because she was going to Hawaii to celebrate Kyle's wedding. They warned her Jake was using her and reminded her how she always let men walk all over her. She shook her head, determined to prove them wrong. She would make Jake commit, one way or another.

Sonya put an arm around Casi's waist. "Are you going to introduce me to your in-laws? Hicks make me nervous."

"Mother! Are you high?" Casi frowned at her glazed eyes.

"You are so dramatic!" Sonya averted her eyes. "A pain pill for my back hardly constitutes being high."

Casi introduced Sonya to Georgia and Peter while Ava nodded hello. Jack stepped forward to give her a hug and complimented her on the great job she did picking the location. Sonya smoothed a hand over her generous cleavage on display in a pretense of acting demure. "I wanted it to be convenient for everyone. Casi's used to much more extravagance; we'll have to see how this small-town life agrees with her." She moved a piece of hair from Casi's face. She scanned her figure and sighed. "As soon as this wedding is over my darling daughter, you'll need to get back down to your modeling weight. You inherited those hips from your father's side, I'm afraid." She patted Casi's hip. "I wish you hadn't gotten that tattoo, it's so tacky!" She turned her nose up and adjusted Casi's bikini bottoms to cover it fully.

Jack's jaw clenched when tears sprung to Casi's eyes and Ava put her hand on his arm, suspecting he was on the verge of lashing out. "Luckily, she also inherited those gorgeous long legs and tiny waist. A perfect hourglass figure! I have a tattoo that I've never regretted." Ava pursed her lips and Sonya narrowed her eyes while tension filled the air.

Kyle jumped from the pool and wrapped himself around Casi, kissing her on the neck. "How déclassé Casi, you wouldn't behave that way in LA." Sonya scowled at them.

"Mom, please stop," Casi whispered.

Jack stood and grasped Sonya by the arm, redirecting her to the bar. "Let me get you a drink."

Casi wished she could stop the tears from falling as everyone waited for her reaction. "Don't let her get to you," Kyle whispered. "This is our life; we'll live it the way we choose." She pulled away from him and jumped in the pool.

Ava gave Georgia a meek smile. "Sonya has that effect on her." She glanced at her stepdaughter swimming laps. "Moving to Washington will be a positive step. She needs the stability." She twisted her hands together. "I've missed having her close."

Georgia reached over and patted her hand. "We adore Casi and look forward to getting to know you and Jack better."

Jack watched Sonya sipping her drink and shook his head. "Where's Burt?"

"In LA."

"Headed for your fifth divorce?" Jack asked, aware of how agitated she got when her marriages were coming to an end.

She downed a vodka tonic. "Why am I the bad guy for wanting what's best for my child? The daughter I practically raised by myself. You show up for the highlights and upstage me."

He sighed, tired of the argument. "Can we please make this week about Casi and Kyle? They're amazing together, even if you can't see it. He makes her happy, and she loves him."

"What's she going to do in Washington? Serve coffee like the dull girl Jake brought?"

"She'll need to transition in her career. She needs to find her own way. Stop pushing her and making her feel bad."

"Transition? Her beauty will fade and he will leave her. What will she have then?"

"Kyle loves her. He sees more than just a beautiful woman," Jack scoffed.

"Banking on love never works." She glared at him. "I hope she's smart enough not to get pregnant or she'll find out how hard it is when he loves the child more than her."

Jack exhaled. "Casi wasn't our only problem." She waved him away with disinterest and ordered another drink.

Jake sat at the end of the pool waiting for Casi to resurface. When she came up for air, he asked, "Want the story on my snake tattoo?" She grinned and tread water. "When I was seventeen I'd been in a lot of fights. I was angry and had some trouble at school. I'd gotten the nickname, 'Jake the Snake'."

"Because you were slimy?" she teased.

He frowned. "Snakes aren't slimy. It is because I would strike without warning. Anything and everything pissed me off. I went to a place in Seattle and lied about my age." He turned to show her the complete image.

"It's very cool. Did your mom freak out?"

"Absolutely! She had a heart attack when I took Kyle two years later to get the salmon." Jake grinned.

"When he was only sixteen?" Casi gasped.

"Yup, it made him appear tough." He reflected on his intent to remind kids Kyle had an older brother they should be afraid of if they messed with him.

"What inspired you to get the other ones?"

"You only get one for today. You seemed like you needed cheering up." He splashed her with a wave of water.

"I hate how bad my mom makes me feel. I believe I'm happy, but then I second guess my choices."

"You heard our birth mother was a drug addict, right?"

Casi's eyes went wide. "Do you think my mom is using, again? She said she's only taking prescriptions."

"She's on something." Jake shrugged.

"What should I do?"

"Live your life and let her live hers." He jumped in the water. "Marrying Kyle is the best decision you'll ever make. He'll always be there for you. And you get me in the deal, too."

**37**

---

# NUPTIALS

The day of the wedding, Casi awoke in Kyle's arms to a glorious sunny day. He held true to his word about no sex before marriage and pushed her in the shower, alone. The downside of an evening wedding was she felt lost all day waiting for the main event. In the afternoon, she strolled the beach with Kyle, holding hands as the water lapped at their feet. He kissed her and sent her to get ready, and that's when it happened.

It started as she watched Kyle walk away to meet Jake and Lia for a drink, and the enormity of the commitment hit her. She sank to the flower-filled stairs, shaking and crying.

"Well thank goodness," she heard her mother say.

"It's about time; we were beginning to wonder if you were human." Ava rushed to her side.

Georgia's bubbly laugh filled the air. "A wedding day wouldn't be right if you weren't on the verge of bolting."

The three women laughed as they helped her up, explaining they had been watching her all day for a sign of a breakdown and were becoming suspicious she was medicated.

"It happens to everyone," Ava said.

"It happened to me all five times," Sonya agreed.

"What if I don't love him enough?" Casi wailed.

"You do." Georgia soothed. "It'll only grow from there."

"What if I'm making a huge mistake?"

"You can undo it," Sonya advised.

"You are perfect for each other." Ava frowned at Sonya.

"I might not be ready for the changes marriage brings. Can't we just live together?" Casi questioned.

"Every day you wake up, you're making a change from yesterday, and that's a good thing." Mary's calm voice filtered through the chatter of reassurances. Casi exhaled and flung herself into her mentor's arms as the other women stepped aside with reverence to let Mary take charge.

Dylan pushed in the circle carrying a glass of champagne. "Well, look who is finally having her breakdown." He held the flute above Casi's head. "Only two drinks before the ceremony. Sip slowly." She nodded, and he handed her the glass.

Casi relaxed in a bubble bath, while Ava ironed her dress, Georgia painted her nails, and Sonya had several glasses of champagne of her own. Mary turned on the stereo, aware Casi always perked up with music. She pulled a stool beside the tub and took Casi's hand. "My Little Peanut, you've been through so much over the years, enough for a lifetime for some. Believe Kyle was put on this earth to be your partner and to help you navigate. Together, you will build a beautiful life and always have each other to lean on. Now put on your party dress and let's go get your man."

Ava held the door open and giggled with the women as they headed out to their own rooms. She rolled her eyes when Sonya poured another glass of champagne. "Sonya, we need to go. Dylan is here to do Casi's hair."

"What's the hurry? Her precious daddy will take over so why shouldn't I enjoy the party?" Sonya motioned around the room with her glass, spilling champagne, which set her off in a fit of giggles.

Ava and Mary locked eyes and shared a private moment before Mary grasped Georgia's arm. "I'm anxious to get to know you better. Kyle is a wonderful man. I'm thankful for him being in Casi's life."

Georgia glanced back at the scene and assessed Ava had it under control.

Ava nodded to Dylan, and he redirected Casi to the desk to begin his masterpiece; curling, braiding, and twisting. Ava extracted the glass from Sonya's hand and escorted her out in an unusual show of force. "Jack has one child. Let him enjoy tonight without your theatrics. We've been more than patient with your bullshit and breakdowns. I've stayed out of Casi's life as I promised, but she's a grown woman now and you must stop derailing her every time something good happens. Kyle is amazing, and she's truly happy." She stepped closer with fire in her eyes. "What kind of pathetic mother are you that you would interfere with your daughter's happiness?"

Sonya yanked her arm back. "I'm the only mother she has! That's one thing you can't take away from me."

Jack came around the corner and eyed the two women engaged in a heated argument. "Is everything alright?"

Ava plastered a smile on her face. "Casi is finishing getting ready. With Dylan's help, she'll be right on time."

Jack nodded and slipped an arm around her waist. "Sonya, do you need help to locate your room?" He watched her stagger in the wrong direction.

"I'm going to the bar. I don't need help from you conniving bastards." She held a middle finger up and stomped away.

Jack sighed and gazed at Ava. "She can't even keep it together for one day. Is Casi alright?"

"She's fine." Ava sank into his arms and regulated her breathing. "Mary will help us keep a leash on Sonya."

"It must be nice to see your old friend again."

Ava exhaled. "It is. I've missed her. She's been a tremendous help throughout the years."

"I'm thankful we have her monitoring Casi." Sorrow danced across Jack's face. "I was paranoid about the elements affecting my daughter in LA, but perhaps I should've been more concerned with her mother's influence."

Casi and Dylan talked casually, and she began to get excited about the impending nuptials. Dylan narrowed his eyes. "I'm only going to say this once because I prefer when you're miserable and unhappy, or drunk." He grinned. "Kyle is amazing. You couldn't have found someone better for your twisted little self, or who loves you more. You may not see it, but he worships the ground you walk on. I've been your best friend for nine years, and this is the smartest choice you've ever made!" He yanked her hair to minimize her happiness from his appraisal. "Alright Princess, rise." He helped her slide on her dress and did a final primp. "The stage beckons, Darling. I shall meet you on the other side." He gave her a kiss and nodded to Jack as he left. "Your lovely daughter awaits. Perfectly on time thanks to me."

Jack took a step back when he saw her. Tears sprung to his eyes at the vision of his daughter. "You look beautiful, Sweetie." He gave her a kiss on the cheek and held out his elbow for her to grasp as they followed the stone walkway leading to the ceremony site. He stopped at the edge of the garden to wait for the cue.

Casi turned to him. "I'm nervous."

"I am too. Imagine seeing my baby girl all grown up and taking the hand of a man to be her husband. It means you're a woman now." He gazed at her with love.

"I've been a woman for a while now, Dad," Casi giggled. "What if I'm a terrible wife?"

"Just be his partner. There are no rules," Jack advised.

She grasped his arm tighter as the melody of a ukulele started. They heard a Hawaiian singer begin, 'Somewhere over the rainbow'. They stepped out from the grove as everyone stood. Casi's nervousness melted away when she saw Kyle at the altar between the palm trees with the sun beginning to set. He was incredibly handsome in navy slacks with a white embroidered silk shirt. Jake stood by his side, smiling at her with brotherly love, proud she would join their family. On her side, Dylan was fabulous in tan slacks and a printed shirt. She hadn't wanted bridesmaids, only the people standing up for her who were always in her life. She studied each face as she floated down the aisle, pleased she kept it small.

These were the people who loved her, the ones she needed on her team.

Kyle watched Casi walk through the grove, and her beauty took his breath away. He knew she would not wear a traditional gown, only slightly concerned what she might come up with. He wanted her to have the wedding as she chose, letting her figure out what she needed to be comfortable with the union. A vision in cream lace over lavender silk with a beaded halter-style top. Shorter in the front, above her knees, and tapering in the back, almost reaching the ground. As always, she dressed perfectly for her body type, elegant with a hint of what would be revealed to him later. When she grasped his hand, a shock vibrated throughout his body, and his heart pounded in his chest. *This is the woman I waited for all my life without even knowing it.*

The Hawaiian minister started the ceremony. The words were simple, about love and honor. Casi tearfully gazed into Kyle's eyes, as he whispered, "With you by my side, I'll dare to dream, hope, trust, seek, and most of all, love." They exchanged simple bands and everyone clapped as the minister placed leis around their necks and pronounced them man and wife. They strolled to the beach and gathered around a large rectangular table surrounded by lanterns and adorned with flowers. A simple Hawaiian fare of grilled ahi, Huli-Huli chicken, Kalua pig, plantains, and rice overflowed from beautifully garnished platters. Mai Tais were the preferred drink for most of the guests. The conversation, riddled with laughter, continued well after the meal finished.

Kyle stood and raised his glass in a toast. "I'll always have to share Casi with the world, especially on the dance floor. Thank you for sharing her with me. She is without a doubt the best thing in my life." He leaned down and gave Casi a lingering kiss.

Casi had chosen a Meghan Trainor song, her only request for the wedding. Kyle twirled Casi out on the dance floor to, *'Love you like I'm gonna lose you'*. When John Legend began the chorus, everyone wiped away a tear and held their partner closer. After several more songs, Jack took Casi's hand and pulled her to the center of the floor, smoothly leading her in a classic dance number that transitioned to a pop routine. Casi cocked her head and fell in step beside him while the familiarity of the moment washed over her. "Where do you think you got your talent from, kid? Don't you remember who invented the dance party?" Jack chuckled and Casi let herself be whisked away with the music, bringing a chorus of applause as the choreography intensified.

Jealousy enveloped Sonya, recalling the father-daughter routines, and she turned to Kyle. "She always was a Daddy's girl. I hope you can compete."

Kyle scowled. "He's her father, there is no competition." He nudged Jake and whispered, "Does she look high to you?"

"High as a damn kite." Jake shook his head.

Everyone took a turn dancing with Casi, who seemed to have endless energy. She reached out to Jake. "Come on, brother-in-law, don't you want to dance with me?"

"Since we're going the non-traditional route, why don't we drop the in-law part." Jake swept her in his arms.

Jack stood beside Kyle in the sand and watched from the sidelines. "How long did it take Casi to say yes after you proposed?"

"She freaked out, but she warmed up to the idea." Kyle grinned with amusement in his sapphire eyes.

Jack chuckled. "She's not traditional, but she loves you deeply. My advice is to be patient as she figures things out in the next few years and let the love grow from there."

Kyle nodded. "I'll always take care of her."

"I know you will. It's good you have a brother to help reel her back in at times." Jack smacked Kyle on the back.

"How worried should I be about Sonya?"

"About her influence on Casi? Or the drugs?"

"Both," Kyle sighed.

"Sonya has a pretty firm hold on her so I would encourage you to persuade Casi to move to Washington permanently. LA's no good for her," Jack advised. "Sonya is an addict of varying degrees. Casi is aware but prefers not to acknowledge it. She doesn't share Sonya's nature."

Dylan pushed through the dancers to take Casi's hand. "Ok, you guys have had her long enough." She winked at him as the racy song began, and Dylan mirrored an immaculately timed dirty dance routine with precision and skill.

Jake turned to Kyle and chuckled. "Why do I suspect they do this on a regular basis?"

Kyle grinned. "Most likely in their underwear at the loft."

Jake scanned the area for Lia and found her sitting to the side. "Do you want to dance?" She smiled and took his hand. "Are you having fun?"

"It's a lovely wedding," Lia said. "Casi looks gorgeous."

"So do you." Jake held her close.

Georgia danced with Peter and hummed with satisfaction. "I love our new daughter-in-law."

"Me too. I'm glad we got rid of the other one."

Georgia giggled. "Peter, you're bad!"

"That woman made Jake miserable." Peter shrugged.

"Gail was good for him in the beginning. He needed stability. I'm glad he's finding his own way now." Georgia relaxed in his embrace. "We did a good job raising our boys."

"You can finally rest now that Kyle has found a perfect partner to live his life with." Peter gave her a squeeze.

They danced in the warm night air, and guests of the resort and neighboring hotels came to watch the party. Casi beckoned them to join in, and they overflowed to the beach as they danced the night away.

A glow of sunrise edged toward the horizon while Kyle and Casi strolled barefoot to their room, fingers laced together. Dylan pushed between them and grabbed Casi's hand and pulled her in the bungalow, instructing Kyle to wait outside. "I have one last wedding present for my princess." He directed her to the chair. "Ok Baby, don't get used to this, it's a onetime deal." He undid the braids, twists, and clips while she smiled. He fluffed her hair, releasing it in soft waves and helped her out of the dress and hung it in the closet while she changed to a sexy cream lace negligee. Dylan nodded approvingly as she reclined against the pillows, and he arranged her hair one last time. He strode outside and slapped Kyle on the backside. "Go get her, Tiger."

Kyle shook his head and realized he would never quite understand Dylan's uniquely close relationship with Casi but knew it was part of the package of loving her. His heart skipped a beat when he saw her looking more exquisite than ever. Moonlight reflected off her cascade of golden waves, bathing her in an ethereal light and accenting every soft curve of her body. She gazed at him with love as he embraced her and she sighed, "This has been the best night of my life; I don't want it to end."

Kyle kissed her passionately and held her in his arms. "Don't worry, our story is just beginning."


Always and Forever

# WHISKEY CAKE

**Serves 12**

1 cup whiskey

2 cups granulated sugar

8 ounces salted butter

¾ cup cocoa powder

2 cups all-purpose flour

1 ½ teaspoon baking soda

½ teaspoon kosher salt

2 large eggs

¾ cup sour cream

1 teaspoon pure vanilla extract

4 tablespoons salted butter

¼ cup dark brown sugar

¼ cup whiskey

½ cup powdered sugar, sifted

1. Preheat oven to 350 degrees. Grease and cocoa powder a Bundt pan.

2. In a medium saucepan, bring the whiskey, sugar and butter to a boil. Remove from heat and whisk in the cocoa powder until smooth. Set aside.

3. Combine the flour, baking soda, and salt in a medium bowl. In another bowl, whisk the eggs, sour cream, and vanilla. Add the whiskey mixture to the egg mixture and stir well. Add the flour and whisk until combined. Pour batter into prepared pan, and bake for 35 minutes. Cool for 10 minutes and unmold.

4. In a medium saucepan, bring the butter, brown sugar, and whiskey to a boil. Remove from heat and whisk in the powdered sugar until smooth. Drizzle over warm cake and slice into 12 pieces.

## THE CATWALK SERIES CONTINUES
## WITH HOPE

**Happily ever after comes at a steep price as past relationships and betrayal threaten to destroy a marriage.**

Newlywed Casi Roberts struggles to find balance between her career as a model, a failing business deal, and living between the quaint town of Blackberry Falls and the chaos in Los Angeles. Kyle Jensen questions his choice to follow his heart when everything he values is threatened and his new wife becomes a stranger.

Devastation, jealousy, and lies, force Casi and Kyle to focus on what they cherish and believe in each other. They soon learn true bonds cannot be broken while loyalty runs deep. Through faith and sacrifice, Casi learns who she can trust and who she should fear. She navigates a new path, discovering the truest meaning of love and what is worth fighting for.

Family and friends suffer disturbing circumstances and devastating events, forcing them to make difficult choices. When secrets from the past begin to surface, lies unravel and relationships are shattered. Hope prevails when they learn to face their fears and open their hearts to the power of love.

**The second novel in the Catwalk Series continues an epic journey of love, intrigue, and triumph, revealing deeper stories within the captivating saga.**

HOPE- HOPE IS THE LIGHT WHEN DARKNESS DESCENDS

Canadian-born author, Suzy Quenneville-Orpin, has always had a vivid imagination and a keen desire to write. Suzy views the world through her own narrative, weaving in the fascinating challenges, triumphs, and lifestyles of the people she meets. An unapologetic daydreamer, Suzy's early experiences in Toronto and Woodland Beach, Ontario provided the perfect upbringing to fuel her creativity and discover the wonder of the roads less traveled. A move to the west coast brought new opportunities and in particular a love for the Pacific Northwest.

Follow Suzy to discover more about the CATWALK SERIES
    www.sqorpin.com
    www.facebook.com/sqorpin
    www.twitter.com/authorsqorpin
    www.instagram.cm/sqorpin
    sqorpin@yahoo.com
    www.amazon.com/author/sqorpin